# VOW OR NEVER

## DANIELLE DEXTER

AF374379

This is a work of fiction. Names, characters, places, and incidents either are the product of the author's imagination or are used fictitiously. Any resemblance to actual persons, living or dead, events, or locales is entirely coincidental.

Copyright © 2026 by Danielle Dexter

All rights reserved. Published in the United States by Cupid's Arrow Press. No part of this book may be reproduced or used in any manner without the written permission of the copyright owner, except for the use of quotations in a book review.

First Edition 2026

*Cover design by CAP Graphics*

**Paperback ISBN:** 979-8-9918831-6-0

Also by Danielle Dexter

STUPID LOVE
ELASTIC HEARTS
WHAT MELTS THE HEART
THE STONEFLOWER REVOLUTION
THE 12 EXES OF CHRISTMAS

# Vow or Never

Danielle Dexter

Cupids Arrow
PRESS

TO ALL THE WRONG ENDINGS THAT
LED US TO THE RIGHT ONE.

# Part

# ONE

# Chapter One
## Three Beans & A Plot Twist

*Everly*

His suit looks as if it had been painted on him—thanks to its deliciously tailored fit. I desperately wanted to remove that painting and lick the canvas underneath.

*God, I hope he has a big paintbrush.*

He was leaning against the bar as if he'd been sculpted to stand there: sleeves rolled up, broad shoulders, a loosened tie that said: "responsible adult by day, problem night." His hair looks annoyingly untouchable and tousled to perfection. Even his jawline was sharper than my mother's critique of my life's choices. (Trust me, she would have a field day with the one I was considering right now.)

*Ugh, is that a tattoo peeking out of his sleeve?*

*Yep. I'm a goner.*

But this was not the night I had originally planned. In fact, I had planned a completely different night altogether. As in: I had a date. So, part of me wondered whether this intense attraction I felt for this stranger had anything to do with it.

I chose this bar for its atmosphere. The Last Chapter leaned aggressively into its literary theme—and I love it. The exterior signage was written in gold script, suggesting literary prestige, while the interior featured exposed brick, warm lighting, and enough literary-themed cocktails to spark anyone's creativity. It was one of my favorite spots in the city (besides a few indie bookstores). Not to mention, it was a coffee shop by day and a bar by night, so you could spend an entire day here and never feel like you overstayed your welcome.

Every table was hand-painted with covers of literary classics, while giant dictionary pages shaded the overhead lights. The menus were written on library cards. Even the bartenders wore suspenders and quoted from famous novels to people who didn't ask. It was the perfect place to read and drink without a second glance. That is why I decided to stay.

As I mentioned, I didn't plan to come here alone, but I was unfortunately ghosted. I was DNF'd before my date even got past my cover (my online dating picture, that is). What's worse, he couldn't even bother to send me a simple "Sorry, something came up" text or one to let me know that his poor grandma is sick and there is no one else nearby to bring her soup. Instead, I got nothing. Rude.

So, I had two choices: go home and binge-watch some reality shows on Netflix, or stay for a drink (or two) since the bar was also known for making some of the best martinis in town. The espresso martini, or the "Java & Juliet," is my all-time favorite, so I ordered one and decided to spend the evening enjoying my drink and the next unsolicited romance manuscript from an unknown author, devouring both the drink and pages full of forbidden love, angst, and enough spice to make me think I was drinking straight hot sauce.

Maybe it was the mix of alcohol and bad-boy MCs that sparked my interest in this hot stranger. Trust me, I've read enough romance novels to know this could work in my favor. Then again, I've read plenty of thrillers, too. So maybe not.

Either way, it seems like I have a good chance of being tied up.

*Nope.* I shake my head. There's absolutely no way this is going to go from me eye-fucking him to actually fucking him.

Then, he looks over at me.

When our eyes meet, he smiles—slow, warm, and confident. It's the kind of smile that says he knows exactly what kind of effect he has on women and isn't sorry about it in the least. I swear, if this guy ends up being single, I might die of shock. Because if I were his girlfriend, I would put handcuffs and a ring on him so fast.

*Nope. I shake my head again. I seriously need to stop reading so many romance novels. Maybe I should try reading other genres.*

In the spirit of being ghosted with nothing to lose, I offer a tipsy smile in return as The Last Chapter hums with low conversations and the clink of glasses, while the bartender tries to impress a group of giggling women by reciting quotes from *Wuthering Heights*. As the sun continues to set, the bar's warm, amber lighting seems to wrap us all in an inspirational glow as I keep sipping my martini, pondering which genre my night might fall into: romance or thriller.

At exactly 9:00 pm, my best friend, Morgan, FaceTime's me for our preplanned bail-me-out-of-this-horrible-date call, in case my online dating match turned out to be a total disaster and I needed a fake emergency to bail.

"Everly!" she shrieks into the phone. "I fell! Come quickly!" I peer into the screen and see her lying dramatically on the floor in her bedroom.

I laugh. "Have you fallen and can't get up?"

"You need to come right now," she continues, somehow forgetting she is on camera as she leans over to grab her wine glass from her bedside table.

"And cut!" I exclaim. "Show's over. He stood me up."

"What? Are you serious?" She pulls herself off the floor. "And you're still there?"

"Well, since I'm already here, I decided to stay for a drink and catch up on work," I reply.

"I guess the alternative is you at home watching *Love isn't Blind* in your pjs or some other reality crap like that."

I laugh. "You mean, *Love is Blind?*"

"But *is* it?" She tilts her head toward the phone.

"According to my view right now, it's not," I whisper. "There's a really hot guy here…"

"Show me," she says as I tilt the screen toward the hot stranger. Her eyes widen as if she were trying to swallow him whole. "Hot seems too lukewarm for this guy," she continues. "I would say he is too hot for humanity—the kind of guy who could ruin you in the best way."

"Which probably means he's a huge asshole," I say as I turn my phone back.

But just as I'm about to take the last sip of my martini, a voice suddenly whispers in my ear. "Who's a huge asshole?" I look up from my phone to see the hot stranger I've been ogling all night, standing right beside me.

"Um," I hesitate. "No one."

"Are you sure?" A crooked smile commandeers his face. "I figured that if I was going to be on camera, I at least deserved to make a better debut than the one you gave me." He points at my phone.

"Uh…" the word vibrates off my lips, with nowhere to go. "I have to go, Morgan," I say quickly before ending the call.

"May I sit here?" He motions toward the empty seat in front of me.

"Uh…"

"So, what are you drinking?" he asks, shifting the topic since I apparently can't contribute any words. I watch as he lifts my empty glass to his nose, which is slightly crooked at the bridge, as if life had thrown a punch, but he swung back harder. "Let me guess, the Java & Juliet? I bet you didn't know that this is one of the only bars within a few block radius that knows exactly how to serve an espresso martini right."

"Is that so?" I look at him. "And what exactly is the *right* way?"

"The three beans," he says, pointing to the espresso beans at the bottom of my now-empty martini glass. "They say it's bad luck to have an espresso martini without the three beans." He smiles.

Up close, his features are much more striking. His face is full of sharp angles combined with a dangerous charm. He possesses a shadow of stubble along his jaw and a mouth that looks like it's no stranger to saying reckless things and perhaps, *doing* reckless things, too.

"You don't say? Well, I could use all the luck I can get." I smile in response.

"I think that can be arranged." He swallows the last of his bourbon, then signals the bartender for another round.

With fresh drinks in front of us, he raises his glass to make a toast, only to stop suddenly. "What is that unamused expression all over that pretty little face of yours?"

"Who says I'm not amused?" I smirk.

"Your face," he says, which renders a laugh from me.

"Am I interrupting your sexy reading time? Let me guess… Are you reading about forbidden love? No?" He looks at me for confirmation. "How about a sports romance? I hear it's a hot genre right now. Are you into hockey players? Bad boys?"

The way the word "bad" left his lips was like a flicker of a match, catching me on fire.

"It's none of your business," I say, peering at him as I tuck the manuscript back into my bag. "Do you like to read?"

"I love to read," he says before taking another sip of his bourbon.

*Damn. He's hot. And he's a reader? Could this be a trope? Hot boy reader? If so, I definitely need to expand into this market.*

"What's your name, by the way?" I ask.

"Reese." He smiles, revealing a set of dazzling white teeth. "And yours?"

"Everly," I answer.

"Well, happily EVERLY after," he chuckles.

However, I don't laugh. I freeze. *Did he just say that? No one has ever...*

But then his laughter continues, and I have no choice but to shift my focus back to him.

*God, he has a good laugh. Low. Warm. It's the kind of laugh that can fog a woman's decision-making skills.*

"Was my joke too cheesy?"

"Just a little," I tease.

"Well, I do have a way with words," he winks.

"Next, you'll be telling me you're a writer," I say with a chuckle, catching a bemused look in his eyes. Given my profession, I have a knack for spotting writers in the wild. "Wait. Are you a writer?"

"I guess you could say that." He shrugs, setting his glass on the wooden table, which is decorated with the cover of *Beauty and the Beast*. "But the real question is whether you want to get back to what you're reading or enjoy some company?"

"No. You can stay." I smile. "I could use some pleasant human interaction."

"Perfect," he says, a devilish grin spreading across his face. "I excel at being pleasant."

"Arrogant."

"Accurate," he replies, as if studying me. "So, tell me, Everly, why are you here alone?"

"I like the atmosphere," I say.

"Is that so?" He leans back in his seat, crossing his arms.

"Fine," I admit. "I was stood up. My date never showed."

"Well, his loss is my gain," he says as that crooked smile of his reappears on his face.

This man looks like trouble wrapped in a well-tailored suit. I stare into his warm brown eyes, noticing how expressive and mischievous they are. He wasn't polished or corporate. He didn't give off that starving, pained-artist look. He was effortlessly attractive, yet seemingly dangerous in the best way. He was the kind of leading man you read about and swoon over.

Still, there was something in the way he watched me across the table that suggested he was also the quiet and observant type. His gaze was steady, focused, and intent. He made me feel as if I were sitting inches from a flame, at risk of being burned. I couldn't help but sweat.

"So, what kind of writer are you?" I finally ask my guard, lowering as he orders us another round.

"The best kind." He smirks, and my stomach does flips like it's auditioning for the Olympics. It's as if he knows exactly how to tease me without overstepping. He's verbally edging me, and I can feel myself getting hotter.

After the last sip of my third espresso martini reaches my tongue and slides down my throat, we somehow move on to shots.

"Nothing with amaretto," I say.

"How come?" he asks.

"Nut allergy," I snort, laughing at how nerdy it sounds, which makes Reese laugh even harder.

So, we end up settling on a shot called "The Plot Twist," which is served with a candied citrus zest curl.

"Be careful with this one," the bartender says as he serves our shots. "This shot has definitely lived up to its name."

And the bartender was right. After a couple of shots, Reese and I start laughing uncontrollably. We laugh so hard we can barely stay in our seats at the bar. And then…

He kisses me.

He smells like sandalwood and ambition. *Ugh, this man is definitely trouble.* I could feel. Taste it. *Delicious* trouble.

And yet, I immediately wanted another sample. Fuck that, I wanted to devour this man. And in the history of Everly Hart's love life, this wasn't normal for me.

His initial kiss was quick, as if he was testing the waters. Once I gave him the go-ahead, it grew into a slower, deeper kiss, showing that he was eager to explore how far he could push the boundaries. I could tell he was protectively keen and deeply attuned to my emotions, moving in sync with them to make sure I wouldn't get turned off or throw a flag on the play (there's the sport's romance reference for you).

Soon, his mouth starts to trace the curve of my neck. I exhale as if I had been holding my breath all night.

*Ugh, this wasn't like me!*

I was a responsible adult. I asked questions. I dated with intention. I Googled people. But tonight? I did none of that. Not even a quick social media check in the bathroom. Nothing. Tonight, I'm the woman letting a hot stranger at a bar press his lips to mine while Death Cab for Cutie hums softly in the background. This evening was what romance novels were made of. And I couldn't help wondering whether this supposed writer hasn't crafted a few of his own.

Eventually, we stumble into a narrow hallway leading to the restrooms. He presses me gently against the wall, his forehead touching mine, his breath warm as he brushes a stray lock of hair from my cheek.

"Tell me to stop," he murmurs against my skin.

I can't. I won't.

Instead, I ask, "What's your name again?" I tug his shirt, pulling him closer as I feel the intoxicating effects of both the drinks and him. I just have no idea which one is getting me drunk faster.

His lips part again for just a moment. "Reese," he finally says. "And you're Everly."

*God, the way he says my name…and remembered it.*

A beat passes before he looks at me as if I'm trouble wrapped in temptation. "Should I ask where this is going?" he asks.

I grin. "You really don't need to."

His answering smile is devastatingly hot.

"Last chance to back out," I whisper as I run a hand through his hair, loving the way he exhales at my touch.

"Are you kidding me? There's no way I'm backing out." He smirks. "If it's all right with you, I'd like to take you home."

"What about your friends?" I ask, referring to the guys he was here with.

"They will be fine. They were just some people I met at a wedding." He kisses me again.

"OK. Your place or mine?" I ask.

"Whichever one is closest." He kisses me once more.

# Chapter Two
## Safe Words



The cab ride to my apartment blurs with the rush of the cold night air, while our hands stay laced together as we steal kisses between streetlights. By the time we reach my apartment door, my pulse is a live wire. Each touch electrifies with the current pulsating through my veins. The only sounds I hear is the soft thud of the door closing behind us as I laugh against his lips. He lifts me into the air as my legs wrap around him. He whispers my name like a promise (one I hope he'll keep.)

As the heat between us continues to rise, our hands lock once more. Reese kisses me as if every second counts. I kiss him, knowing that they do.

The city's glow filters through the windows of my small New York City apartment, casting soft beams of light across the space. My navy-blue sofa with mismatched throw pillows, the overflowing bookshelves lining one wall, and a plant I've been meaning to water are suddenly illuminated. For the first time, I don't care what he thinks of my place. None of those trivial matters seems to matter. I feel free.

Reese's mouth skims along my jawline as if he already knows exactly where I'm most sensitive. My breath catches—half gasp, half laugh—because, go figure, the hottest man I've ever been with would know exactly what to do without being told. It's as if he has already memorized a map of me.

"This is a terrible idea," I whisper, a thought I shouldn't have said out loud.

"Mm," Reese murmurs against my skin. "If it's so terrible, why does it feel so good?"

His hands glide to my hips. They feel firm and confident, yet he still checks my reaction every step of the way, hoping that with each satisfying inch, I might just grant him a climactic mile. However, I am in no rush to reach the finish line. I want to take my time. And by the look in his eyes, I can tell he does, too.

He presses me against my bedroom wall, making everything feel as if I'm caught between reality and a very hot dream.

"Tell me to stop if you want me to," he says again, his voice low and rough. "But I beg that you don't."

The truth is, I should tell him to stop. One-night stands aren't my thing. They never were, and they never will be (again). Yet here I am, about to have what I anticipate will be the best sex of my life, and I'm considering ending it for moral reasons. But you want to know what I think about morals? Fuck morals. I was stood up. It's been a year of horrible dates. And I can't remember the last time I felt this much chemistry with someone. So why shouldn't I let my hair down and have a little fun?

Since my knowledge of one-night stands comes from the books I've read, I realize I still need to protect myself in more ways than one. As a serial romantic, I can't allow myself to fall for someone I barely know. I don't care that I can now identify his body in a lineup by how his bare chest feels because there is a good chance I'll probably never see him again.

"We need rules," I say, pulling at his tie.

"Like a safe word?" he kisses the back of my neck.

"Wait," I lock eyes with him. "Do we need one?"

"We might," he winks.

"Well, I was thinking that since this is just a one-time thing, we should keep things as casual as possible," I begin, trying to catch my breath while sounding in control. But I was far from in control. In fact, I was enjoying being dominated by him.

"I was thinking no last names, no exchanging of numbers, or even having any expectations. We keep this completely—"

"Casual?" he looks at me as if his eyes hold a secret he isn't revealing.

"Exactly," I affirm

"Even though I now know exactly where you live?" he says, kissing me again.

"One minor inconvenience," I reply.

He nods as if taking it all in. "And the safe word?"

I tug him by the waistband and whisper, "You pick."

His laugh is wicked yet delightful as it ghosts against my mouth. Then he lifts my shirt over my head slowly, reverently, and my body reacts before my brain can even catch up. The blood rushes below my waistline, creating an anticipation that tightens everything inside me.

*I want him. I want him. I WANT him.*

Reese's fingertips trace my waist, then glide up my spine, sending a shiver through me. "Are you still OK?" he asks. I swear no man should ever sound this gentle. Or this tempting. Men like him need a warning label.

"Ask me again in an hour," I say, breathy.

He chuckles sinfully, and I melt. "I will take that as a yes," he says.

Then his hand unbuttons my jeans as his fingers slip beneath the fabric of my panties. I inhale sharply. My pulse jumps like a jackhammer. My common sense has gone out for a smoke break and hasn't returned.

*Paging Everly Hart. Are you there?"*

He kisses me as I moan into his mouth.

Before I even have a chance to register what's happening, his kisses grow intense and all-consuming. They make it seem as if he's been waiting all night just to taste me. His mouth is warm and hungry, tinged with bourbon. My saliva moistens as his hands explore my body as if they need no guidance. I clutch his shirt as if it's the only steady thing in my life.

He carries me to my bed as my restraint begins to fade. Instead of fighting it, I surrender to it, to him, to the impatient way he rips off my clothes, and I nearly tear off his. This behavior is so unlike me. I have never been this uninhibited with anyone before. And I don't even know his last name.

It makes it more exciting that way.

My fingers explore the lines of his shoulders, the dip of his collarbone, and the way they trace along the tattoo sleeves on his arms as if telling a story. Heat sparks between us like static. For the first time in my life, I feel empowered.

As we move together with increasing urgency, our kisses deepen. Hot, sweaty flesh presses against hot, sweaty flesh as our voices moan with need. His breath hitches when I pull him closer, just as mine does when he slips inside.

It was then that I no longer cared about being stood up. I no longer cared that one-night stands were so out of character for me. This was exactly what I never knew I needed.

There will be no exchanging of last names or phone numbers, and no worries about having high or low expectations for what this should or shouldn't be. We can lose ourselves without regret or concern for how we might feel come morning. I am living in the moment. It's all I care about. That's it. Nothing more. Nothing less.

And as the night unfolds in a wave of heat, breath, and whispered moans that were careful at first but quickly gave way to reckless abandon, the only things that seem to exist between us are the rise and fall of two bodies that need no help finding a rhythm. We move in sync. We know what each other wants—needs—without exchanging a word. Everything comes naturally. It's unfairly too perfect for this to last only one night. Still, I have to keep reminding myself that it's probably all he wants. I refuse to romanticize my way into another heartbreak.

Not to mention, these are my rules. MY rules. And I refuse to break them just so he can break me.

Much later, tangled in sheets and feeling the press of Reese's arm around my waist, we end up talking. We talk for hours, getting to know each other in the only way people can do late at night.

When we finally drift off to sleep, I just hope I didn't reveal too much. Even though I said for us to have zero expectations, he met every single one and more.

# Chapter Three
## It's Better this Way



For a moment, I almost forget where I am. I open my eyes, discovering a room that doesn't seem familiar. It smells faintly of vanilla and freshly cleaned laundry, unlike my apartment, which normally smells like whiskey and cedarwood musk.

Soft morning light filters through the half-closed curtains, casting gold across the unfamiliar walls. Pictures line the dresser near the foot of the bed. Books are scattered throughout the room, as if there's not enough space to keep them all, so they've become pieces of furniture themselves. And that's when I feel it: a warmth pressing against my side.

I turn my head to see Everly asleep beside me. Her hair spills across her pillow in gentle waves. One arm is tucked under her cheek. Her breaths are slow and steady. She looks peaceful. Angelic. Beautiful. Words I have never used in the same sentence before. She sleeps in a way that makes it seem as if she has let her guard down, which she rarely allows.

I'm honestly unsure what to do, so I remain perfectly still, afraid to disturb her.

I can't remember the last time I woke up next to someone and thought about staying. Usually, by now, I'm gathering my clothes and making a quick exit. But this? This feels different.

Peaceful.

Dangerous.

My gaze drifts over her face instinctively. It's almost automatic. It feels as if I'm trying to memorize the gentle curve of her mouth, the crease between her brows, as if she carries thoughts even while sleeping. Worse still, I want to know what those thoughts are. When I met her, I knew she was the kind of woman who second-guesses herself too often. I can't understand why that is. She is smart, beautiful, and capable of conquering the world if only she found the courage.

A strand of blonde hair falls onto her cheek, which I catch myself before tucking it back behind her ear.

*What am I doing? This is not me.*

I'm not a romantic. I don't romanticize. I catastrophize. I don't fall in love or, for that matter, believe in it.

I force myself to lower my hand to resist the temptation as the memory of last night flashes back in fragments.

*Ugh, her laugh. And how she laughs with her whole face, not just her mouth. It's infectious.*

And the way she challenged me? Usually, girls would give in to my every whim and flirt politely. But Everly? She didn't. She didn't fall for my usual tricks. It was as if she brought a few of her own and flipped the switch.

Our banter was fantastic. She was sarcastic, funny, honest, and stood firmly by her words. It was refreshing. I wondered if she was always like this or if I influenced this side of her. They say people bring out different sides of you, so it's possible.

I think back to when the moment narrowed as I first kissed her at the bar, as if suddenly we were the only two people there and the bar was all ours.

Yet, another thing I remembered was her words and the way she said them: *"No last names, no exchanging of numbers, or even having any expectations."* They were light, flirty, but deliberate. Intentional, but firm. She was setting a boundary. But for whom?

If there's one thing I understand best in this world, it's boundaries. I respect them. I even have a few of my own. But boundaries aren't always obstacles that need to be challenged. The question is, do I really want to challenge hers? Better yet, would she even let me?

Something twists in my chest as I keep watching her sleep because last night didn't feel like just anything. It was more than the physical chemistry that erupted between us like a volcano. It was what happened when we finally caught our breath. It was the hours we spent talking until we passed out.

I never talk.

Yet with her, I did. I couldn't help wondering why.

Did I reveal too much? I'm not sure. But it's not like I can do anything about it now.

Her apartment is quiet as the early-morning stillness wraps around us like a farewell hug I wasn't ready to accept. Quietly, I swing my legs over the side of the bed, moving slowly so I don't wake her.

As I pick up my clothes from the floor, I can't help but glance back at her.

*God... She trusted me enough to sleep soundly.* That realization hits harder than expected, since most people who have met me only see what's on the surface: confidence, charm, a guy with tattoos, and someone who knows how to have a good time. They rarely see the parts underneath—the parts that know how quickly good things can disappear. Maybe it's my job that has distorted my perception on love. Still, I've learned that you can say the most beautiful things, make the most heartfelt promises to someone, and still have only a 50/50 chance of actually following through with them.

I lean against her dresser, running a hand through my hair. Stay, a voice suggests. Make coffee. Wake her gently. Take her to breakfast. Ask her about yesterday, today, and tomorrow. The thoughts hit me so hard I almost fall over laughing. Again, this goes against everything I believe in. Nor was it the agreement I had made with her. She didn't invite a tomorrow. She wanted one night. One. That was it. And me? I know better than to mistake one perfect night for a perfect future. I was always the guy who slipped away or had to "get up" early the next morning. I have enough excuses to tattoo another sleeve on my arm.

I make my way to her small galley kitchen, searching for something to drink. Her apartment feels lived-in and cozy. It's the kind of place where I could easily picture myself enjoying a lazy Sunday. She is obviously a lover of reading, as evidenced by the books scattered throughout each room. A SUNY Oswego sweatshirt is draped over a chair that still faintly smells of her perfume. Hell, even I smell faintly of her perfume. A coffee mug that says "I read Romance Novels—I know how this ends" sits in the sink. The sight of it makes me wonder how someone who clearly loves happily-ever-afters so much could want something so meaningless. Then I remember the cheesy joke I made at the bar: "Happily Everly after." I shake my head, slightly embarrassed with myself. Then again, who was I to judge her? She clearly knew how this was all going to end. As for me, I have bounced from one meaningless night to another without a second thought for years. I guess we'll both be fine.

I linger in her kitchen longer than I need to, staring at nothing and everything at once. Again, it feels like I'm trying to commit every detail about her to memory, as if I plan to revisit her file later. Then I grab a pen from the counter and, before I overthink it, pull the receipt from last night at The Last Chapter and sit down at her kitchen table.

The words come easily. They always do. I write quickly and with intention. My instinct guides me more than my pen does before I finally pause. I read it. My chest tightens because nothing about this note sounds casual or like me. It sounds hopeful. And hope was dangerous.

I head toward the bedroom doorway, imagining Everly waking up and reading the note. For a split second, I picture her smiling. I picture her calling me. I picture it as the start of something. But then what? Blow her off like I usually do before things get too serious?

I exhale slowly, releasing those thoughts into the air as if to be rid of them. She specifically said it was just one night, and I believe she trusted me to honor that. I doubt she saw me as the kind of guy she could build a life with—even if she doesn't know much about me.

I fold the paper once. Then I fold it again, as if I'm shaping my emotions into origami. I hold it between my fingers, thinking about what to do. After a long moment, I slip the note back into my pocket. It's better this way. Cleaner. Easier. Again, one perfect night doesn't mean I have to ruin it all the next morning.

I walk back into her bedroom when she shifts slightly, murmuring in her sleep. The pull is so intense, so magnetic, that I have to hold myself back from climbing back into bed with her.

"Yeah. You're definitely trouble," I whisper to myself before slipping on my shoes and heading toward the door. My hand rests on the knob, hesitant.

I have recklessness in my blood, but even this was too reckless for me. At this moment, I was considering putting curiosity over caution because I so badly wanted to stay.

But stay was not a word in my vocabulary.

Therefore, I open her door and close it softly behind me. It's best to walk away before I change my mind.

Trust me, it's better this way.

# Chapter Four
# Hide & Seek



For a few peaceful seconds, I stay still. My eyes remain closed as I try to soak in the last moments of an amazing dream. I'm lying curled up beneath my soft gray sheets, suspended in that hazy space between sleep and memory. For the first time in a long time, I feel wonderful.

Then I smile. Like, really smile. Because I remember EVERYTHING now, and I don't think I've smiled like this in a long time, either.

The memory flashes like lightning: the bar, the laughter, and the way Reese looked at me as if I were the only one there.

The way he said my name.

The way I screamed his.

My eyes stay closed as I stretch and turn toward the warmth beside me. But my hands find only cold sheets. I frown. Still half-asleep, I reach further. Still cold. Still empty.

I force my eyes open as sunlight spills unforgivingly into my room. It highlights the rumpled area on the other side of the bed, with half the duvet on the floor and the pillow's indentation showing where his head had been. Aside from that, there is no sign that Reese was ever here. And the evidence of our night quickly dissipates as the sun rises.

I push myself upright, hair falling into place. I look down, aware I'm still completely naked.

"Reese?" I call softly, clutching the sheets to my chest. But I get no answer.

I laugh quietly to myself. "Maybe he's in the bathroom?" I ask out loud, as if we are playing some naked hide-and-seek game.

I slip out of bed, grab one of my oversized Backstreet Boys concert T-shirts, and pull it on as I head into the main living area. I see my bathroom door is wide open. Empty. A small knot forms in my stomach.

"Maybe he went for coffee?" I mutter the suggestion to myself, trying to rationalize his absence. It makes sense, right? Reese seemed like the kind of guy who thrived on coffee—especially if he is a writer, as he claimed. So, he could have very well gone to the corner café for some coffee and muffins, sporting that devilish grin of his. My lips curl at the thought as I head into the kitchen, but there's no note to suggest this. After ten minutes of waiting, no one is knocking on my door with coffee in hand. I don't know exactly how long I stand like this, but it's long enough to realize that if he went for coffee, he would be back by now.

Everything around me feels quite still. Quiet. The only sound comes from the hum of my refrigerator. I just don't understand. Where did he go? Why did he leave? The space he once occupied feels strangely hollow, as if the air itself has noticed his disappearance. I nod as if I finally understand, as I settle on the quiet realization that he left because he wanted to.

Yet I continue standing here with my arms wrapped around myself like a pathetic hug.

He left.

My mind scrambles to find explanations it prefers to believe, justifying his sudden departure. Maybe he had work? Maybe there was an emergency? Maybe his grandma was sick, and he had to bring her soup?

*Why is it always a sick grandma and soup?*

*No, Everly, he left. He left because that's what you told him to do.*

It's my fault. I was the one who told him no last names, no exchanging phone numbers, and no expectations. Just thinking about that conversation hits me like a soft slap.

I let out a shaky laugh. "Why did you have to say that?" My palm gently touches my forehead. I'm a serial monogamist, and somehow I still kicked out the hottest guy I've ever been with because I'm an idiot.

I pour myself a glass of water, which I desperately need. "This is fine," I tell myself. This is what a one-night stand is all about. I should know; I've read enough one-night-stand tropes to last a lifetime. I will just have to accept that all we had was one night and try to get back to my normal life as if it never happened.

But it *did* happen. Twice, to be exact.

Still, I have no choice but to accept that this was to be expected (even without setting any expectations). This was a healthy way to leave things. There was no awkward goodbye. He didn't have to see my mascara all over my face as I shook his hand goodbye, thanking him for a nice time, which would have been worse. This is exactly what I wanted. *So, then why does my chest feel strange?* Even my stomach feels off. It could be all that liquor we drank. Heaven knows I haven't drunk like that since college.

I lean against my kitchen counter, replaying the night in short clips. One, however, stands out above the rest. It's the conversation we had in the middle of the night. I remember the way Reese listened to everything I said with genuine interest, and the unexpected gentleness he tried to hide beneath his tough exterior as he asked me questions. He was a secret golden retriever, and I doubt he even realized it. Not once did he make me feel like a temporary distraction. He made me feel seen—even in the darkness. And I liked it.

A lot.

Yet for one reckless moment, I can't help wondering what this morning might have been like if I hadn't said what I said. I'm so annoyed with myself. But then again, who's to say whether he would have stayed if I hadn't set those rules?

I walk back into my bedroom with the intention of stripping my bed and erasing all evidence of my impulsiveness, when something suddenly stops me in my tracks. It's his tie.

There it is, left by the foot of my bed.

I pick it up slowly, examining it as if it were a rare artifact from a one-night stand exhibit. It smells just like him, a mix of his cologne and bourbon. My fingers tighten around the fabric before I can stop myself.

"I have to stop romanticizing this," I tell myself as I fold his tie and set it on my dresser. The only good news about finding his tie is that it proves I didn't imagine everything last night.

Sunlight warms my shoulders as the world outside is already moving. It's May 6th. Cars drive by, and I hear laughter from the sidewalk below. Life goes on as usual. A siren blares in the distance. It's the city that never sleeps, yet I fear I may never sleep the same way again, without Reese invading my dreams.

Then again, I may have dodged a bullet. Maybe he was full of red flags that could attract a whole herd of bulls.

I should be happy. Everything was simple and straightforward. No strings attached. No promises of a phone call that would never happen. No plans for a date that would fall through. Not even an agreement to text later that would naturally go unsent—or unread. But true to my stubborn romantic nature, a part of me still said, "Just wait."

Reese looked like the kind of guy who broke the rules. Maybe after our conversation last night, he'd realize I was open to more, and then he'd turn around and come back. "Just wait," I tell myself again. Five minutes.

Ten.

Twenty.

With each passing moment, I quietly reaffirmed what I already knew but had been afraid to admit: He wasn't coming back.

I plop down on my bed, taking a deep breath. At least I had fun. My thoughts sound more optimistic than how I really feel. I roll onto my side, pulling my blanket closer and inhaling the scent he left behind. Somehow, for a reason I can't explain, disappointment presses gently against my ribs. Not heartbreak (because that would be ridiculous). Just an unfinished feeling. It's like reading a book only to be left on a cliffhanger with no promise of a sequel.

I close my eyes, feeling sleep tug at me again. But I have to get up and get on with my day. By the afternoon, I will tell myself that I won't think about Reese anymore. I will even promise my best friend, Morgan, who will want every salacious detail of my night, that once I'm done, I will never mention him again.

So that by tomorrow, I will have forgotten his laugh and how his eyes crinkled at the corners.

By next week, his scent will have faded from my sheets, and I will have put his tie in a box in my closet because I can't bring myself to throw it away.

By next month, he will become nothing more than a distant memory.

What I won't expect is that in a year and a half, I will be engaged.

# Part

## TWO

*One year and six months later*

# Chapter Five
## Roll with It

I'm pretty sure our waiter hates me. He was probably in the kitchen, complaining to the staff about me.

To be fair, I've asked quite a few questions. But in my defense, everything on the menu is written in French. And since I can't find either fries or toast, I end up choosing whatever option my finger lands on after I swirl it around the menu like an airplane searching for a safe landing spot. Not to mention, I've been trying (unsuccessfully) to hide a tiny bread roll I accidentally flung onto the floor for the past five minutes. To sum it up, I'm better suited for a McDonald's. At least I know I can order fries there.

"Sweetheart, just leave it," Carter whispers from across the table about the roll. He seems amused by the soccer game I'm playing under the table. Spoiler alert: the only one winning is the roll.

"I can't just leave it," I hiss. "People have eyes, Carter. They will know. They will see and judge. And then we will be put on a list that says we can never come back here."

"You're stressing out about a roll." He smiles, confidence and certainty visible in every line of his face. No wonder he's good at his job. I would give him all my money, too.

"Yes, but it's a fancy roll," I correct. "It's a roll that probably costs more than my light bill." I look pointedly at the enormous crystal chandelier that glitters above my head.

"Everly, it's fine."

Easy for him to say. Carter Jacobs is the kind of man who makes fancy restaurants feel like his second home. He's always calm, and I don't think I've ever seen him sweat, stumble, or spill anything, including dropping a roll and playing footsie with it all night. The man can navigate a Michelin-star menu as easily as I do at Taco Bell.

Meanwhile, I'm pretty sure I'm not using the right fork for my salad. In my defense, a fork is a fork. It's not like I'm shoveling it into my mouth with a spoon.

When I finish my salad, I move my cutlery around like a criminal tampering with evidence at a crime scene. No one has to know.

Carter's warm hand slides across the table and covers mine, calming my frantic rearranging. "Relax," he says in a smooth, gentle tone. "It's just dinner."

"Yes, but it's a very fancy, intimidating dinner," I reply. Honestly, I thought that after a year of dating Carter and all the wining and dining we've done, I would've gotten used to the "finer" things in life, but I haven't. I would've been just as happy tonight if he'd wanted to order a pizza. I'm really not hard to please.

"Everly." He tilts his head toward me. "It's still just dinner. With me."

My heart immediately softens because, if Carter is anything, he's always the person who grounds me. He's steady, kind, and comfortable—like a favorite sweater. With him, I always know what to expect. However, something about tonight feels off because he keeps staring at me with an expression I've never seen on him before.

It's not that I-want-you look or the you-are-gorgeous look. No, there's something else hidden behind those ocean-blue eyes. It's almost as if he's plotting something or working through a difficult math problem in his head.

I narrow my eyes. "You've had this silly grin on your face all night. Care to share what's going on in that handsome head of yours?"

"Silly grin?" he asks as the restaurant buzzes with quiet luxury. Men wear pressed suits, women wear cocktail dresses, sipping from glasses polished to perfection, while the comfortable hum of wealth and success surrounds us like a cocoon. "Although you did call me handsome," he smiles.

"I don't know," I continue. "It's like you're about to unveil a PowerPoint presentation or something. Carter, I swear, if you brought graphs to dinner again…"

He laughs. "No graphs tonight, I promise. Although I did bring something else with me."

But before I can even respond, I notice his knees bouncing up and down beneath the table. In all the time I've known him, I've never seen him so riled up. I've seen him calmer before a board meeting. I've never even seen him stressed about losing a case—and

definitely not during that one time when a pigeon landed on his shoulder in Central Park, like that lady in *Home Alone 2: Lost in New York.*

Yet something is up with him. Carter was not excitable. He has always been even-keeled. Cool as a cucumber.

"You're being weird," I finally say, taking another sip of my wine.

"Am I not allowed to be weird?"

"You? Weird? Never. You and I both know there is only room for one weird person in this relationship, and that spot is already taken," I smirk.

He chuckles as a violinist drifts closer to our table, playing a romantic melody. It sounds like the kind of music I associate with old movies and grand gestures. It would also make the perfect soundtrack for a romance novel. And I should know; I live for romance novels.

Then the lights dim slightly as our waiter appears to refill our wine glasses, smiling in a way that seems overly polite, considering I have been a huge pain in the ass all evening. This only confirms to me that something is indeed up.

My pulse skitters. *Oh. My. God. Is this really happening?*

Carter clears his throat, along with any remaining thoughts in my head. "Everly?"

"Yes?" My voice squeaks as if I just swallowed a hamster.

"As you know, I'm not very good at expressing my emotions…"

My lungs suddenly stopped working.

"I wish they had someone out there who could help with this sort of thing," he chuckles. "I tried writing them down, but I wasn't very good at that either. So I'm just going to wing it and hope I don't make a fool of myself."

I freeze. I no longer care about the wayward roll or which fork I need to use with each dish. I have tunnel vision, focused on Carter as he stands from his seat and drops to one knee in front of me. A woman at the table beside us clasps her hands over her heart as my brain begins to short-circuit.

"Everly Hart," Carter begins as he pulls a tiny blue box from his pocket.

I whimper.

"Just breathe," he assures me with a soft, supportive laugh.

*Was this really happening? We'd only been together for a year and a half. Eighteen months, to be exact. Was he sure he wanted to spend the rest of his life with me? Was I sure I wanted to spend the rest of mine with him?*

"Everly, you make everything in my life better. You're a ray of sunshine that has helped me become the best version of myself. You're the first person I've been with whom I want to share everything—even the ugly parts. What I'm really trying to say is that I want a life with you. I want a future with you. I want it all. And with you, I truly have it all," he says, never breaking eye contact with me.

Then he opens the box, and I swear the entire room gasps with me. "Everly Jane Hart, will you marry me?" he asks as silence falls over the dining room, and my pulse quickens.

My heart thuds wildly—not in the cinematic, fireworks kind of way I've always imagined proposals would feel like, but in a warm, steady beat that reminds me of soft blankets, Sunday coffee, and Carter's loyalty.

I love him.

Carter has been a breath of fresh air in my life, and he is the most dependable guy I've ever been with. He isn't chaotic or unpredictable. He doesn't leave me in doubt or uncertainty. He's stable. Secure. And with him, I know he will provide a future that makes sense. Yet as he and the room anxiously await my response, something feels…off. This moment feels different from what I expected.

Then again, *how* did I expect it to feel?

"Yes," I finally whisper. "Of course, yes!"

The room erupts into polite applause as Carter slips the ring onto my finger. It's a beautiful diamond that sparkles like a prism. *Was it me?* It's hard to say. Either way, I convince myself that it's perfect as I smile at him, feeling the weight of his promise settle over my hand. It's a promise I trust because it feels right. Love shouldn't feel reckless. And the one thing I know for sure is that Carter is far from reckless.

My eyes prickle. My cheeks blush. I lean across the table and kiss him, soft and grateful.

"Are you OK?" he whispers as we pull away.

"I'm wonderful," I reply, still smiling.

*Mostly.*

## Chapter Six
## Devilish Thoughts

Outside, the city lights shimmer against the evening sky. I'm lying in Carter's California king-sized bed, staring up at the ceiling as the ring glistens on my finger.

*Shouldn't I be floating on cloud nine right now? Am I not happy? Am I not lucky?* Yet I didn't make a single phone call to share the news of our engagement, nor did I even upload that celebratory social media post that all couples do. I did nothing. I simply told Carter I wanted to bask in our engagement before sharing it with the world. He didn't even question it. He didn't push or prod. He only said, "So, we bask." And he smiled and held my hand the entire drive home.

Turning to face Carter, who's now asleep beside me, I realize how incredible he is. He is everything I've told myself I should ever want—or need. Yet my heart is humming with a quiet ache, a whisper that I refuse to acknowledge or name.

Maybe this is what overwhelming happiness feels like? Maybe it's normal to feel stunned, as if being stuck in a state of shock you can't snap out of is part of the process. And maybe this is my brain's way of processing everything. Maybe. Maybe. *Maybe.*

The room spins as my mind processes the logistics of merging our lives. Was I moving too fast? Would I have to leave my beloved rent-controlled apartment for Carter's Manhattan high-rise condo?

It's funny because, as much as I appreciate his condo's spaciousness and luxurious amenities, there's something about my tiny apartment—with its exposed brick walls and a kitchen that could fit a hundred times over in his—that feels like home. It has a pulse. It's vibrant. It's a stark contrast to Carter's preferred neutral color palette. Would we clash? And why am I mourning the loss of my apartment hours after my proposal? Was it because so much life has been lived there? My mind flashes through memories before landing on one in particular that I thought I had buried…

It started with a laugh at a bar and ended with us tangled in overheated bed sheets, clinging to each other's sweaty bodies.

A wicked mouth of a tattooed stranger whose name rests on my tongue, begging for another taste. He was also a man who felt like a beginning, and a man whom I also told I wanted nothing to do with.

It's funny because Carter is nothing like *him*. He is the complete opposite of that bad boy writer who captivated me in ways I never knew I could be captivated. To be fair, I'm not comparing Carter, nor do I think any comparison is needed; it's simply about recognizing that two things can be true at once—you can be attracted to two different types of guys: the angel and the devil on my heart's shoulders.

Regardless, I have no choice but to set these thoughts aside. They don't belong here; they belong in the past. As for this one with Carter, I've decided it's part of my future.

So, the memory of that night softens. Edges blur. I now label it as a reckless chapter in my past. Still, there was a time when I believed I would see him again. I would scan crowded rooms, busy streets, and coffee shops for his face. There was also a time when I thought he might have been doing the same for me. He knew where I lived, but I never received a surprise knock on my door. Honestly, if it weren't for the tie he left behind, I would have thought I made him all up.

But I'm not that girl anymore. Better yet, I wasn't even that girl that night either. It was as if he awakened parts of me I didn't know existed. A fiery side I had buried deep erupted with wild abandon and no care, causing me to let my guard down in more ways than one. I've always considered myself a serial monogamist and have never ventured into the world of one-night stands. It was a foreign, uncharted territory for me—a place that required a special passport I never bothered to apply for.

For the longest time afterward, I thought maybe he was the one who brought out that side of me, as if he held the magical key (or paintbrush) to repaint a different version of the girl I thought I was. It was as if he saw me unfiltered and unedited, and he never once made me feel like a rough draft. But as time went on, I chalked it up to having too many espresso martinis, which made things seem better than they truly were. There's no way a guy could have this much power over me after just one night. Maybe I did romanticize it a little too much.

Fast-forward to now, and I find myself on the fast track to living in a glass-walled, mansion-sized condo overlooking the sparkling city. I dine at fancy restaurants, eating dishes I can barely pronounce. I wear silk robes that cost more than my couch instead of the oversized concert T-shirts I'd normally wear. Nick Carter is probably wondering why I'm playing games with his heart. I'm gradually becoming part of a life where structure, security, and a wedding hashtag will soon take center stage.

Truth be told, Carter and I almost never happened. Honestly, I could have written him off for two reasons. First, he stood me up on our first date. Second, I ended up meeting a handsome, devilish stranger in his place: Reese.

*Reese.*

Finally, his name breaks through its protective barrier. He's the guy I haven't been able to stop thinking about since he pretty much vanished off the face of the earth after what was literally the best sex of my life. Then again, it was me who told him I didn't want anything more (not that he pushed me). I said, "No names. No phone numbers. No expectations." Yet I scoured the internet and did enough social media recon I could stomach before deciding it wasn't meant to be. It was as if he didn't want to be found. So it was better to pretend it was all just a dream. One wild, passionate, WET dream.

Carter was the guy who stood me up that night at The Last Chapter. Apparently, he tried calling to let me know that his work meeting was running late and that he wanted to reschedule. But since I was too wrapped up in Reese's gaze to notice anything else, I ignored his call like it was spam or from some telemarketer trying to sell me an extended warranty on a car I haven't owned since college.

It wasn't until later that day, after Reese had left, that I checked my voicemails and found he had left two messages. The first was a request to reschedule, and the second was an apology, with a plea for a second chance. Feeling disappointed by Reese's departure, I decided to respond. I felt guilty for not answering the night before, but in my defense, I was used to guys texting—not calling. Carter, however, wasn't like most guys. He was old-fashioned in some ways. I couldn't help but give him a second chance (it's my favorite romance trope, after all). And I was glad I did, because we have been together ever since.

That's why these worries are worrying me.

If I love Carter as much as I do, why am I struggling to forget the memory of heat-soaked sheets, rough hands sliding down my hips, and a voice dark with hunger, as if saying my name were a challenge (trust me, he won every time)? It was a night I thought I had buried because I hadn't thought about it or him in months. So why was he now bursting through my mind's floodgates at a time I was supposed to be focused on my engagement?

*So, what gives?*

Maybe it's nerves. Or maybe it's the same feeling you have when you die, and your life flashes before your eyes. Only in this case, it's marriage, and the best sex of your life flashes before your eyes instead.

Then again, Carter is a good lover, too. He is attentive and caring. But there is nothing spontaneous about it—no hunger, no need, no pinning me against the wall or begging me to call out his name. Carter is his own flavor of ice cream, but sometimes I could use more sprinkles and a cherry on top, you know? A good old-fashioned sugar rush.

Does that mean something? Is that bad?

I slide my ring off and examine its sparkle. "It doesn't mean anything," I say softly. "This is the right thing."

But where are the sounds of upbeat music, the soundtrack to my happily-ever-after, playing in the background? Instead, real life lets my heart echo in the quiet. And I can't seem to convince myself that it's all just nerves.

# Chapter Seven
## More Money, More Problems



The next morning, Carter's voice carries down the hallway into the kitchen before he even appears.

"I understand," his voice echoes, "but the numbers from Q3 don't lie. If you want me to represent you, I need to know everything. Fine. Yes. Have the file sent to my office. I'll be there soon." He shuts off his phone as he walks toward me.

His suit jacket is slung over one arm, smooth and ready for business. His sleeves are smartly cuffed, and his tie is tightly knotted, as if he's worried his head might fall off. He spots me leaning against the counter with a cup of coffee and immediately softens. "Good morning, Mrs. Jacobs," he says, kissing me on the cheek as his other hand skillfully scrolls through his emails before slipping it back into his pocket.

"Mrs. Jacobs, huh?"

He smiles. "Just practicing. How did you sleep?"

"Great," I lie. The last thing I want to tell him is that I was up all night worrying about the future and obsessing over my past. "Busy day already?" I ask, changing the subject.

"Always," he says with a boyish grin. "So, my mother will be coming over tonight. She says she has an engagement surprise for us."

"Please tell me she hasn't already bought those monogrammed towels and napkins she loves so much. They are so…"

"Tacky? Pretentious?" he smirks. "Although I hardly doubt she would make a trip to Manhattan just for towels."

"You never know," I shrug.

"Do you think you will be able to stop by after work?" he asks.

"Yes, I think so. However, the real question is whether you'll be able to make it?" Carter is notorious for working late, whether he plans to or not. I've understood from our first canceled date that he has a very demanding job, but sometimes it's hard to make plans because of it. I can't count how many reservations we've canceled and how many dates we've rain-checked. However, I wouldn't mind rain-checking a few of his mom's visits.

I decided to leave work around lunchtime and head to the corner bodega to pick up some things for dinner. Carter had texted me to say that his mother planned to come around 7:00 pm and that he thought it would be nice to have dinner together. He suggested ordering something, but I offered to cook a meal for everyone instead.

So, for most of the day, I spent it making my mother's famous pot roast, only for Carter's mom, who came at exactly 7:00 pm, to barely touch any of it. I watch as she pushes her food around her plate like she is mining for gold. I'm extremely annoyed, considering how much time and effort I put into preparing this meal.

"What do you call this again?" she asks for the third time as if it would suddenly transform into something more suitable for her palette.

"And will there be a salad?" she also asks for the hundredth time, until I have no choice but to get up from the table and throw one together.

Once the painful dinner is finally over, we head into the living room with after-dinner coffee.

"You both are probably eager to know what the surprise is," she says, pursing her lips as if the words taste bitter. With my luck, she bought us a salad spinner instead of towels.

I have always considered myself the type of person who gets along with everyone. However, when Carter first introduced me to his mom, Margaret (or Mrs. Jacobs, as she forces me to call her), I could immediately tell she wasn't fond of me. Whenever I shared something about myself, she narrowed her eyes, as if trying to hold back any judgment.

Carter did his best to reassure me that she was like that with everyone at first, but deep down, I knew she didn't accept me. I was different from the girls Carter had previously dated, and she seemed perfectly happy to mention them along with their achievements, as if I were suddenly part of some weird dating show.

When she asked me which Ivy League school I graduated from, she almost fell out of her chair when I told her I had graduated from a SUNY school. She reacted as if I had just admitted to dropping out of college to pursue a career in underwater basket weaving.

It wasn't lost on me that Mrs. Jacobs had many reservations about me. I was a simple girl. I came from a middle-class family. I wasn't a lawyer like her son or a doctor like a few of his exes. I definitely didn't work on Wall Street or at any Fortune 500 company. I worked at a small literary agency, where I spent my days reading manuscripts and representing authors to publishers.

I'd be lying if I said her clearly low opinion of me didn't bother me. It also made me wonder what her successful son saw in me, since he clearly doesn't seem to share her opinions.

"Anyway, I wanted to do something I know you two will love and appreciate," Mrs. Jacobs smiles. "Not to mention, it helps to know the right people," she continues, reaching into her purse, which probably costs more than my rent.

I sit back nervously in my seat. I run through all the possible gifts she might give us just 24 hours into our engagement—an engagement I still haven't publicly announced. Suddenly, I notice her lift an envelope from her bag, its address in shiny gold letters.

Impossible. I gasp out loud before she even hands it over.

"Everly?" Carter turns toward me. "What is it?"

"Carter, it's Laurent & Co.," I say as he continues to look at me, confused.

"Who?"

"Genevieve Laurent?" I say, pointing to the envelope. "*The* Genevieve Laurent?"

However, he still looks at me like I grew a second head.

"I have to say, Everly," Mrs. Jacobs interjects. "I'm surprised you know who this is. I'm awfully impressed," she says pointedly.

Since I have never impressed this woman since the first day I met her, I'm willing to settle for the half-hearted, patronizing compliment. It's better than nothing.

"Now, who is this Genevieve Laurent?" Carter asks us both.

"She is only the most sought-after wedding planner in the industry," I answer before Mrs. Jacobs has a chance to.

"Now," Mrs. Jacobs cuts in, but only looks at Carter. "Your father and I pulled some strings. And by strings, I mean purse strings," she giggles as if she made a joke. "We want this wedding to be a wonderful event, the kind of wedding people talk about for years to come. We know this is the perfect company to make it happen."

I set my coffee on the end table. She isn't wrong. Laurent & Co. ranks among the top five wedding consulting firms in the country, and, lucky for us, it's based right here in the city. Long before Carter proposed, I visited their website out of curiosity and learned they were booked for the next five years. I wasn't the least bit surprised. Genevieve was known for making fairy-tale weddings happen.

"I can't believe it," I finally say. "But I thought they were booked?"

"They *were* booked." Mrs. Jacobs smiles.

"This is…" I struggle to find the words. Heat creeps into my chest as I wonder whether this gift will be something she holds over my head for years to come.

"This is wonderful of you and Dad," Carter fills in the words for me.

"Your father and I will spare no expense to make this wedding as elegant as a royal ball," she replies.

I press my lips together. This was such an overwhelming gift. Any bride-to-be would be jumping up and down if they were in my shoes right now. Yet somehow, I stay grounded.

"I don't know what to say, Margaret—"

"Mrs. Jacobs," she corrects.

"Mrs. Jacobs," I say. "Thank you."

"Your first consultation is scheduled for this Friday at 11:30 am sharp," she instructs, as if she has booked the Pope for lunch.

"I'll be there," I say, smiling as I hug Carter, suddenly feeling grateful because I know his mother wasn't one for physical acts of affection. But as I embrace him, a small, quiet voice in my mind whispers, *"Why are you not as excited as you should be?"*

Am I not as excited as I should be? Everything since the proposal has felt like a dream. Yes, I'm marrying a warm, dependable man who's wonderfully sweet, but I haven't been acting the way I expected. Or maybe this is how brides normally act at the beginning?

Before Carter's mom leaves, she says she will try to attend as many of the planning meetings as she can. Already, she begins discussing a few of her opinions on aesthetics and the guest list. It makes me worried about how much all of this will end up costing (in many ways). It feels just as wasteful as buying fancy napkins only for them to end up in the trash.

It's funny how much one night can end up costing someone.

# Chapter Eight
## But it's Still a Pothole



The next day at work, Morgan and I decide to take a break from the office and get lunch. After having spent most of my morning reading query submissions, my eyes are starting to burn, and my mind is racing. It's been a few days, and I still haven't told her (or anyone besides my mom, for that matter) about the engagement.

I check my reflection in the small mirror I keep at my desk. I do this a few times, trying to gauge my expression before finally telling Morgan the news. Do I look like I'm glowing? Should I be glowing? People don't get engaged without glowing. Am I smiling wide enough?

"Are you ready?" Morgan storms into my office—tall, dramatic, wearing sunglasses the size of planets. She looks like a modern-day Audrey Hepburn. "I'm famished."

Morgan and I have worked at the same literary agency for the past ten years. We both started as college interns and quickly became close friends. She's always there for me, no matter what, and I trust her completely. However, I'm not exactly sure how she'll react to my news. Part of me feels she hasn't been honest about her feelings toward Carter.

"Before we go, there is something I need to tell you." I glance over the pile of manuscripts stacked on my desk. I have always preferred reading printed copies to being glued to a screen. There is something better about holding a physical copy in your hands. It's more personal.

"What?" She cocks her head at me. "Shit. Please tell me you're not quitting. Fuck—are you quitting?" she asks, barely coming up for air. "Fine, I will quit, too. If you go, I go. Grab a box. Where are we going?" she keeps going as I try to interrupt her, to no avail. "A new agency? Are you opening your own?" Her eyes widen.

I laugh. "Calm down. I'm not quitting. I'm..." I slide my engagement ring onto my finger, which I've been secretly stashing in my bag ever since the engagement.

Morgan shrieks, slapping a hand over her chest. "Ev! That ring is..."

"Beautiful?" I try filling in the blank.

"No. It's in its own tax bracket," she replies, grabbing my hand for a closer look at the diamond. "It's truly obscene. I love it!"

"Well, tell that to Carter. He's the one who picked it out," I say with a smile.

"Next time I see him, I'll shake his hand—or his wallet. Whatever works. I'm not picky," she laughs. "But honestly, he did a really good job."

I look down at my ring, trying to see what Morgan sees. She seems more excited about it than I was when he first opened the ring box. "Yeah," I say.

"Uh, ok. What's wrong?"

I'm not about to get into this here, so I grab my bag and suggest we continue our conversation over lunch.

"OK. Give me the whole story. Did the proposal go wrong?" Morgan asks as she skims the menu. She and I have been coming to this café for years.

"No. The proposal was perfect," I say.

"Did you cry? Did he cry? Did he kneel? Or was it one of those progressive, seated proposals that everyone is in love with now?" she fires off her questions.

"He kneeled," I answer. "We were at a really fancy restaurant, and there was even a violinist."

Morgan clutches her heart. "Seriously? A violinist? You're telling me that Mr. Carter Jacobs, who only speaks in courtrooms and boardrooms, did a public proposal?"

I nod. When she puts it that way, it sounds even sweeter of him.

"Our Carter?" she says again, in disbelief. "Spreadsheet Carter?" I nod. "Emotionally controlled Carter?" she asks as I nod again.

"Yes. Yes. And yes," I chuckle. "It was very sweet."

"Sweet? Geesh!" Morgan fans herself with the menu. "Everly, he's a golden retriever with a hedge fund. Did you black out? I would have blacked out."

"I didn't black out," I say just as the waitress brings our drinks and takes our orders. "It was really...romantic."

Morgan narrows her eyes. "You hesitated."

"No, I didn't." I grab my glass of water.

"Yes, you did."

"I did not," I insist.

Morgan crosses her arms. "What are you not telling me?" she asks just as the waiter brings us our lunch.

I take a quick bite as Morgan's question lingers in the air, heavy yet soft.

"There's nothing to tell," I shrug.

She leans back in her seat. "Come to think of it, you're not acting like someone who just got engaged. Are you not happy?" She looks at me with concern, as only a best friend could.

"I am," I finally say. "I really am. I just think… it all feels so surreal—like I can't even begin to process everything that's happened."

Morgan's expression softens. "OK. That's normal," she says. "But if he ever hurts you, I'm ready to ruin his credit score or seduce his boss and persuade him to get fired." She tosses her hair back.

I laugh so hard that I almost choke. "You are unhinged."

"Correction. I'm loyal." She points her fork at me. "So, let's talk wedding." She opens the Pinterest app on her phone and starts pointing to some ideas she's already pinning to a board titled "Everly's HEA."

"I should probably stop you while you're ahead. No need for all this planning," I tell her.

"Why? Are you eloping?"

"No…"

"Wait, is it because I'm not your maid of honor?" Her eyebrows arch into Botox territory.

"Of course, you are my maid of honor," I say as she lets out a sigh of relief. "But I think we should leave the planning to the professionals."

"Please tell me you're not talking about Carter's mom?" she scowls.

"Nope." I shake my head. "I'm talking about Genevieve Laurent."

"Shut your mouth. *The* Genevieve Laurent? From Laurent & Co.? Are you serious?" She practically shoots up from her seat like a rocket blasting into space. "Is she planning your wedding?"

My stomach flutters. "She is. We have our first meeting with her on Friday."

She shrieks. "This Friday? As in, two days from now?"

"Yep." I smile.

"And Carter's going, right?" she asks, knowing he has unintentionally canceled on so many events with me in the past because of work.

"Of course," I say. "He wouldn't miss it."


**A soft knock on** my apartment door freezes me in place. After work, Morgan and I decided to head back to my place to tackle a few more queries and, of course, discuss more wedding details to help me prepare for the first planning appointment.

Morgan whispers, "Is that Carter? Or is someone about to break in and kill us?"

"If someone is here to kill us, do you think they'd knock?" I laugh. "It's probably just Carter, although I'm not expecting him," I say just as the door opens. He steps into my apartment, fresh and polished as if his workday was nothing but a breeze. Not a hair is out of place, and there isn't a wrinkle in his shirt. He is still dressed and ready for business.

Morgan lifts her glass of wine, which she insisted we open to celebrate my engagement. "Congratulations on your handsome face and your bank account."

He laughs. "Good to see you, Morgan. Thank you. I've never been congratulated like that before."

As Morgan refills our glasses, I get up to meet Carter in the kitchen, which is really one stone throw away.

"You're here early," I say as he hugs me.

"Actually, I came by to tell you I'm sorry," he begins, "but I have to cancel dinner tonight because I need to meet with a client."

"You seriously came all this way to tell me you can't make dinner? Why didn't you just call?" I ask.

"Well, we are meeting nearby, and I thought it would at least give me a chance to see you before I have to spend the night going through a bunch of case files." He kisses me on the cheek. "How about I treat you, girls, to a night out? Pick a place." He reaches for his wallet as Morgan instantly materializes between us.

"Is this pick a card, any card?" she laughs. "Because if so, this is now my favorite magic trick."

"That's very sweet of you," I say. "Morgan and I have been prepping for Friday. I want to be fully prepared for our meeting."

"Oh, are you signing a new author?" he beams as if I'm about to announce good news.

"You're kidding, right? We have that meeting at Laurent & Co., remember?" I smile, hoping he's joking. But when his smile flatlines, mine does too.

Carter exhales, rubbing the back of his neck, his tell when he's nervous or anxious. "Marcus moved our meeting again, and the Partners asked me to be there. They are not confident that it can be closed without me."

"But it's our first meeting," I sigh.

"Do you think we can reschedule?" he asks, but he and I both know it would be in poor taste—especially after whatever "strings" his parents pulled.

"There is no way I can be in two places at once," he frowns.

"It's OK." I force a smile, watching Morgan's mouth slowly gape in shock from the corner of my eye.

"I won't miss another one." He takes my hand in his and gently squeezes it. "I promise."

"It's OK," I repeat, this time more quietly.

"Listen, I have to go now, but I hope you two have a good night. Spare no expense." He kisses me on the cheek. "When the meeting ends, I will call you so we can sort this out."

After he leaves, the silence fills the room the moment the door closes behind him.

Morgan turns toward me. "He's a sweet guy—a lovely guy. He has great arms and a trust fund. But I'm just going to be the bad guy and say it: missing the first wedding-planning appointment? That sounds like a red flag to me."

I fold my arms. "His job is demanding. I've known that from the start. Trust me, he would never miss something on purpose. He also promised he wouldn't miss another one. You heard him.

"I also heard him having to miss your dinner tonight, which he threw money at to solve the problem." She looks at me crossly.

"Do you want him just to hand you his credit card every time he misses something in your lives?"

"He doesn't throw money at me. He offered us dinner because he was trying to be nice," I reply.

"And you said so yourself that his job is demanding, so, like it or not, it can happen again," she pauses. "And it will."

I take a breath. "OK. Fine. Yes, I'm upset. I'm concerned, but it's a minor concern—like a tiny pothole in the road," I confess.

"But it's still a pothole. Even the smallest ones can cause damage."

I let out a laugh. "You need to calm down. He works really hard. It wasn't as if he did this on purpose."

"Like your first date?" Morgan tilts her head. "I just want you to recognize a pattern when there is one. It's not going to stop just because there's a ring on your finger. There will just be more at stake. Family dinners, soccer games..."

"You're overreacting, Morgan," I say.

"Or are you not reacting enough?"

Morgan, if anything, is loyal, and she doesn't sugarcoat anything. That's why what she's saying is sucker-punching me in the gut right now. I don't want her to know that this is being added to the mountain of worries I've already been collecting. "We all make compromises in relationships," I finally say.

"Is this a compromise or a sacrifice?"

"Either way, I really don't want to go to this appointment alone," I say, staring down at my ring. The ring that's supposed to symbolize comfort, stability, and commitment. Yet something flutters beneath my ribs. It's a strange, unsettling sensation I try to shake off. Was it about Carter missing our first appointment, or something more?

"I don't suppose you would like to go with me?" I ask her.

"I wouldn't miss it for the world," she says, smiling.

# Chapter Nine
## But First, Coffee



The universe woke up and chose violence this morning as my phone started vibrating uncontrollably at 9:30 am. Seeing that it was only my sister, I hit ignore and closed my eyes again. Whatever it's about, it can wait.

However, as soon as I settle back into my dream, my phone begins vibrating again. If I know my sister, she won't stop calling. She is relentless. Ignoring her will only encourage her more.

As soon as I answer, her voice crackles over the phone. "Reese? Tell me you're not still asleep?"

I crack one eye open and groan into my pillow. "I'm not anymore."

"Well, get up. I need you."

"Ask someone else," I mumble into the phone.

"There is no one else, which is why I'm calling you," she says.

"Weddings or something personal?" I ask, rolling onto my back.

"A wedding," she answers, a bit too quickly.

"And you called me? You must be desperate," I say with a chuckle.

"Shut up," she huffs. "Meet me at my office in an hour. Don't be late."

"Genny, you have planners, coordinators, and enough interns to build a wedding army. What the hell do you need from me? Some wedding vow emergency?" My yawn is laced with sarcasm.

"Just don't be late," she repeats before ending the call.

I rub the sleep from my eyes and get out of bed. My studio apartment is cluttered with pages scribbled in red, while others are crumpled into balls that didn't make it into the trash. Last night's dishes are still in the sink. My single-serve coffee maker is out of coffee, and I just remembered that I haven't done laundry in weeks. Soon, I will be out of clean clothes. Still, I take a quick shower, put on the cleanest clothes I can find, and head out the door. But first, coffee.

There is already a line at The Last Chapter, one of my favorite spots in the city. Oftentimes, I bring my laptop here and pretend I am Ernest Hemingway, transported into modern times, desperately trying to work through (or suffer through) writing the next Great American Novel.

As I wait in line, I notice the *Beauty and the Beast* table. It immediately triggers a memory that loves to sneak into the forefront of my mind from time to time. In its wake, it always leaves me with a trail of "what-ifs." They force me to question whether I should have done things differently. Either way, when the memory appears, and the trail goes cold, I'm left with nothing but a sea of regret.

After ordering my coffee to go, I head toward my sister's office. Genny, or Genevieve, as others call her, owns a wedding-planning enterprise that occupies two floors of a historic building near Times Square. Everything inside is decorated in bright whites, marble, and an abundance of candles that likely violate the fire code.

As I walk inside, the entire place is buzzing with activity. Assistants hurry past, carrying colorful fabrics, swatches, fragile items, and delicate towers of macarons. Vision boards are being carried around from left to right as I'm passing billboards on the freeway, while the air smells like a mix of fresh flowers and printer ink.

Reception, which is kiddy-corner from Genny's office, is painted an off-white shade with a fancy name, suggesting that, even though the color is technically white, it didn't want to be associated with such a commonplace color.

Lila Bennett, with her strawberry-blonde hair and green eyes, who works as Genny's assistant, sits at the reception desk. As soon as I enter, she lights up, as if my presence flipped a switch inside her.

For the past few years, I have resisted her advances. She has made it clear she likes me, and while I'm flattered because she is very attractive, I don't see how dating her would lead to anything good. I wouldn't want a relationship that would only cause problems at work, and that's the last thing Genny or I would want. So I promised myself I would never date anyone from the office. Still, it hasn't stopped Lila from trying.

"You're late," she says as I pass her desk on my way to Genny's office.

I smile. "I'm on time."

If someone had asked me five years ago whether I saw myself working here, I probably would have laughed my ass off.

For most of my adult life, I have been a struggling writer. I took on a few journalism gigs here and there, but I have always wanted to be an author—a novelist. However, after years of rejections and bills piling up, I decided to walk away from my nom de plume, R.E.M (Reese Edward Myers), and focus on a paying gig I never imagined in my wildest dreams: vow writer.

At first, it was just a favor for my sister, but it somehow turned into a full-time job. Who knew people desperately needed help writing their vows? So I became the in-house vow writer. That's right. I have now garnered a reputation for writing the best vows—those that make your guests tear up and remember for years to come. I craft vows that people frame on their walls and that go viral on social media. The only unfortunate part is that this kind of writing doesn't come with accolades or awards. Once the bride and groom speak my words, they no longer belong to me. I basically make promises for other people to keep. And that, I have found, is much safer than making them myself. Even if I've never been one to believe in marriage or happily-ever-afters, I have the power to convince other people of their existence.

Yes, I'm *that* good.

That's not to say I've never been in love. It just wasn't the kind of love movies and books have led us to believe exists. In the end, how can you promise someone forever? It's always been a gamble I've never been willing to take.

Kenny, one of the top planning consultants, stands by Genny's door, waiting anxiously with his tablet in hand. He looks more frazzled than usual because he runs on caffeine and anxiety pretty much on a daily basis.

"Is she here?" I ask Kenny, who shakes his head as I brush past him and walk into her office.

"Shouldn't you wait until she gets here?" Kenny looks at me as if he's about to have a heart attack as I toss my leather bag onto the velvet settee in her office.

"It's fine, Kenny. Relax," I say, plopping down beside my bag. "She doesn't bite."

"She might," he says just as Genny bursts through the doorway, arms full of files, which she offloads onto her marble desk. "You're late."

"I believe I was here before you," I say with a smirk.

She rolls her eyes. "I've been here all morning, and you're fifteen minutes late." She glances at her watch. "Kenny, get in here. Stop loitering by my door."

"In my defense, I needed coffee," I continue, raising my paper cup as proof.

"We have coffee here."

"Not like this."

"Either way, I'm glad you're here," she says.

"How about I let you know if I feel the same way after you tell me *why* I'm here," I reply as she tosses one of the files at me.

I flip it open. It's a wedding consultation file. "What's this?"

"As you know, we are booked solid. However, I have to squeeze in another client. They came in as a special request from a very prominent New York City family," she explains. "So my hands are tied."

"OK? Again, what do you need me for?" I ask.

"They want to plan a wedding this year. And as you know, we are booked out for the next—"

"Five years," Kenny interjects.

"So? You have plenty of planners and interns who can help out. Or you can plan this one," I say.

"You know I don't plan every wedding. I oversee the entire execution. It's impossible for me to give all my clients that special touch if I have to attend every planning meeting. My business would never work," she huffs. "Luckily, I have very capable planners," she continues as Kenny straightens his tie.

"Again, what do you need me for?" My eyes narrow on her. I suspect I won't like where this conversation is headed.

"I need you to step in." She winces, bracing for my reaction as Kenny nearly chokes himself with his tie.

"You have got to be kidding me, Genny. You know I have nothing to do with wedding planning. It's bad enough I write vows for a living, but now you want me to plan weddings, too? You know how I feel about all this crap," I say as Kenny gasps in horror.

"Personal feelings aside, this is business, Reese. You have been to enough wedding-planning meetings to know what goes on. And I promise you will be compensated for your…troubles." She rolls her eyes.

"How much? Because I am *very* troubled."

"It's more than you make writing vows. And don't worry, you won't be working alone." She winces again, which signals that my problems are about to get worse.

"And who exactly am I working with?" I look at her.

"Kenny," she says with a smile as he throws his fist into the air like he just won the world championship.

"You have got to be kidding me." I shake my head. "No offense, Kenny," but definitely offense. Kenny is literally Genny's shadow—her mini-me. He's way too enthusiastic and tends to be over-the-top about anything related to weddings. It's not that I don't like Kenny; it's just that where he sees rainbows and butterflies, I see clouds and bees. We are not the same. And I'm definitely going to need something stronger than coffee if I'm going to be working with him.

"Since you are less experienced than Kenny, he will be the frontrunner for this wedding. I just need you to tag along and ensure everything runs smoothly," she says.

"Wait a second. If this is such a high-profile case, why are you putting Kenny and me on this? It doesn't make sense." Another thing I know about Genny is that she isn't someone who puts her business in any compromising position, and this feels very compromising to me. Something isn't adding up.

"I'm booked…" Her words hang in the air before she snatches them back and replaces them with: "And I'm pregnant."

I did not expect this. "You are?"

"Yes, and it doesn't leave this room. Got it? That goes for you, Kenny. So please stop announcing that I'm glowing every time I enter a room." She glares at him.

"Well, you *do* glow," he says quietly enough for only me to hear.

"And Kenny knew this before me?" I ask.

"I made the appointment." Kenny points proudly at his chest.

"Yes, and I've had the worst case of morning, noon, and night sickness ever," she whines. "Don't get me wrong, I'm ecstatic and blessed, but they weren't lying about how awful you may feel at the beginning."

"Well, I'm happy for you and Kyle," I say, knowing there's no way I can deny her request for help—even if it means working with Mr. Wedding himself. "Kyle does know, right?"

"He's my husband. Of course, he knows." She rolls her eyes.

"Fine, I will do this," I cave.

"Thank you, Reese." She lets out a sigh of relief.

"Just one wedding, right?"

"Just one. Then you're free to go back to writing vows and that novel you refuse to admit you're writing." She smiles.

"OK, just let me know when you need me to start," I say, pulling out my phone.

"Right now," she says.

## Chapter Ten
## Here Comes the Bride

I start walking toward one of the consultation rooms with Kenny trailing behind me. He reminds me of an excited puppy eager for me to pet him or give him a treat. He's getting neither from me.

"This will be fun," he says with a smile. "The infamous vow-writing god and the wedding-planning extraordinaire are teaming up."

"We are no A-team," I say.

"What's an A-team?" he looks at me.

"Never mind," I say as I keep walking.

"The ladies must love you, though," he continues.

"Oh, yes. I propose to someone new every night." I roll my eyes as I open my sister's file, scanning the insane wedding to-do list. It's baffling how much goes into one day.

"So, how are we tackling this?" Kenny looks at me for guidance. "Who's playing the fun, laid-back planner and who will be the more serious one?"

"Kenny, we're not interrogating this couple. No one is playing good cop or bad cop."

"Right." He nods as if the thought had never occurred to him. "Sorry, I spend most of my time with Genevieve. Some people might call me her second-in-command." He looks at me as if I'm supposed to salute him.

"Kenny, this is your show. Consider me a shadow or a fly on the wall." I hand him the file. "I'll just be on the sidelines, ready to jump in whenever you need me. Sound good?" I ask. To be honest, it's a little selfish of me to dump most of the responsibility on Kenny, but judging by the expression on his face, you'd think I'd just told him Christmas came early. "It's your time to shine."

"Dreams really do come true here," he beams. "If this wedding goes well, Genevieve will definitely promote me."

"I can't see why it wouldn't," I say as I swing open the consultation room door, only to be sucker-punched in the throat by the universe. Apparently, nightmares come true here, too.

I was expecting a bride—an ordinary bride. A bride I have worked with a thousand times before. What I didn't expect was *her*.

Yes. *Her.*

She stands by the window, gazing down at the city below. One hand rests on the back of a velvet chair, and a soft pastel dress drapes smoothly over her curves, which I vividly remember seeing from every angle. Her hair spills in loose waves, a shade much more golden than before. Still, I know that hair. I have had my hands in that hair.

How long has it been? It was a long time ago, but not long enough for her to be standing in this room, planning her wedding.

Out of all the women I've been with, she, for some reason, has stayed with me. She became the one-night stand I haven't been able to forget, and I still fantasize about her at 2:00 am on some nights. Not that I would ever willingly confess this, but she has made me question countless what-if scenarios about what I should have done that morning. Should I have stayed? Should I have left her that note? In the end, it probably wouldn't have mattered. She would have most likely ended up here regardless of whether I had left a note.

She turns. Our eyes lock. And the only combination is a key that neither of us possesses.

Her hair is slightly longer. She's less tan than she was on that May night we met. Even her eyes seem a bit softer, as if the fire I had seen in them had gone out, like extinguishing a candle's flame.

The only logical explanation is that I'm hallucinating. It's the only thing that makes sense, since I was thinking about her this morning after visiting The Last Chapter for coffee. But I should know better. Of course, it would be her standing in this room. The universe fucking hates me.

As for Everly, she glares at me from across the room as she slowly takes a seat at the table. I imagine it looks like we are both seeing ghosts from our pasts that we have each denied were haunting us. The room immediately fills with an awkward silence and tension so thick you could iron clothes on it.

I decide to play it cool, but as soon as I spot that enormous rock on her finger, my pulse spikes. My signature smirk twitches as something sharp stabs my chest. It's not jealousy. No, it's pure denial.

"Hi, everyone," Kenny pipes up, oblivious to my reaction. I need to teach this guy how to read a room.

"You're not Genevieve," a girl seated beside Everly says. I almost didn't realize she was in the room.

"Ugh, I wish!" Kenny chuckles. "I'm Kenny Howard, and this is Reese Myers. We'll be working with you to plan your dream wedding."

"And Genevieve?" the girl asks again.

"She will work with you on the overall vision and execution as we approach your ceremony date," he replies.

The girl leans back in her seat as if Kenny just pissed in her Cheerios. I watch her for a moment, wondering why she looks so annoyed.

"So, which one of you is Everly Hart?" Kenny asks, looking up from the wedding file.

*Everly Hart.* What a perfect name.

Everly smiles and waves her ring finger at us. "That would be me."

"You're getting married?" I ask, forcing my jaw to unclench as Kenny ushers me into the seat beside him at the table.

Her tone is tight. "I am."

"Wait," the girl sitting beside Everly whispers to her. "You're Reese?" She turns to me next.

I raise a brow. "The very one." I keep trying to play it cool. Maybe if I play it off like I don't remember Everly or that amazing fucking night, it will make this entire situation feel less like a kick in the balls.

Everly swallows hard before whispering to the girl beside her. "This…can't be happening." I make out the words as they leave her soft pink lips.

"Oh, it's happening, girl," Everly's friend doesn't bother whispering back. Instead, she crosses her legs as if she's about to deliver some salacious news.

"Morgan? Kenny? Would you mind giving Reese and me a minute, please?" Everly's eyes lock onto me again. Hearing her say my name after all this time sends a trickle of sweat down my spine.

"Oh, no. I'm staying for this." Morgan reaches for the carafe to pour herself a cup of coffee.

"Morgan? Please," Everly asks again.

"Fine." She stands. "But Kenny and I will be back in exactly five minutes," she says, practically dragging a very confused Kenny out of the room.

"You do remember me, right?" She looks at me. Her eyes have always given her away. There is not much she can hide behind them.

How could I forget her? But I can't tell her that. Instead, I change the subject. "I'm not trying to be that guy, but your fiancée is not the person I would have expected," I say.

She rolls her eyes. "Morgan is my best friend."

"And you're marrying her?"

"No, you fool. I'm not marrying Morgan. She's here because my fiancé couldn't make it," she explains.

"Well, it sounds like you two are off to a good start." I cross my arms and sit back in my seat.

"What I don't understand is why you're here," she says, flustered. I won't lie, seeing her like this is a total turn-on. I need to be careful not to stand up too fast.

"For starters, my sister owns this circus. I just work here," I say.

"Your sister is Genevieve Laurent?" she asks.

"She is."

"But your last name is—"

"Myers? Yes. So was hers before she married. However, Laurent is her middle name," I say.

"And you're a wedding planner?" she asks, as if the words are foreign to her tongue.

*Ugh, her tongue. I remember where I felt that tongue.*

"Sort of," I reply. "However, vow writing is my specialty."

"Vow writing?" she repeats faintly.

"Remember how I told you I was a writer? Well, I write vows professionally. And when I say I write them, I mean I *write* them—not say them," I clarify quickly. "Just so we're clear."

"Just so WE'RE clear, I'm not doing this." She stands up from the table. "I *can't* do this."

"Fine." I stand up as well. "I don't have to do this either."

"Typical," she laughs.

"Typical?" I look at her. "What are you talking about?"

"You. Running away again." She glares at me.

"I didn't run. If anyone is running, it's you right now."

"You left before I even woke up. You didn't even leave a note or anything," she says, as if I've been the bad guy this whole time. Yet she was the one who laid down all the ground rules I reluctantly followed. Still, now I know she expected a note. She expected more—even though she said there were NO expectations.

So I remind her of this. "What was I supposed to do? Leave you a note thanking you for great sex?" I counter. "If anyone ran, it was you. You ran before we even got started."

"I didn't run."

"I did exactly what you asked of me, Everly. You're just mad you didn't get the chance to have me wake you up properly." My tone shifts as my gaze deliberately drops to her mouth. "Tragic, really."

She turns pink.

PINK.

I can feel it in my spine.

I should know better than to flirt—especially with a bride. I shouldn't even be smirking at her discomfort. Nor should I be imagining throwing her on the table and reminding her exactly how it felt that night. Either way, I don't get the chance to explore any of these options because she snatches her bag off the table and leaves the consultation room.

"Shit," I mutter. I didn't exactly expect her to leave. My sister is going to kill me for losing her high-profile client. *Wait. Who exactly is Everly marrying?*

I run a hand through my hair, staring at the door she just walked through. It feels like an ache I once thought buried has been dug up and reexamined like an archaeological artifact.

I'm sincerely fucked—and not in a good way.

# Chapter Eleven
# Runaway Bride



I burst through the front door of the building as Morgan calls after me.

"What the hell happened in there?" she asks.

"I don't want to talk about it." I stare up at the sky, then back toward the third floor of the building, where I thought I was about to receive the ultimate fairytale.

Memories crash over me. Goosebumps cover my body. Yet standing in that consultation room felt as if I were struggling to breathe. It was as if someone quietly removed the oxygen and replaced it with the sound of me saying his name over and over like I did that night.

Reese.

After all this time, after all the fantasizing and longing, of course, he would be standing five feet away from me under these circumstances. Just over a year ago, he was in my bed—well, he was in more than that. The universe is one cruel bitch.

Everything Morgan is saying to me now sounds like it's coming from underwater. All I can focus on is how calm Reese seemed, as if he weren't affected by seeing me again. Did I overromanticize that night? I can't decide which hurts more.

When Kenny first introduced himself and Reese, I pretended my pulse wasn't detonating in my throat. For so long, I've kept a piece of his memory alive, wondering what would have happened if he had stayed that morning. All he left behind was his tie, and I don't think he even meant to leave it.

Then, when Reese's eyes flicked briefly to mine, and his crooked smile appeared, it felt as if no time had passed at all. That smile is what romance novels are made of. He was truly a book boyfriend, if I had ever seen one in the flesh.

His voice hadn't changed at all. A low, controlled tone—familiar in the way that made my ribs ache. He was still trouble in a well-fitted shirt.

After everyone left the room, I was left with nothing but his arrogance. Reese showed not a single ounce of remorse or regret. It was then that I realized I was truly just another of his countless one-night stands. It was as if he never once thought of me after that night, while I spent more time obsessing over it and him than I care to admit.

"*Sounds like you two are off to a good start,*" he said to me.

It was in that one comment that he created a microscopic crack in my confidence, one only I could feel, making something spiral in my chest: uncertainty. Great, just what I needed, more uncertainty.

I no longer cared about my wedding vision, my color palette, the guest list, or the dream ceremony setting because all I could think about in that moment was that one night and how he felt and tasted.

Suddenly, I feel guilty for having all these thoughts as an engaged woman. But seeing Reese was a shock, and it's not my fault that my mind reacts that way to shocks.

"You look pale," Morgan says, bringing me back to the present.

"I'm sorry, I had to get out of there." I frown. If I had stayed, I would have had to explain how I felt after he left. I would have had to explain why tears wanted to spill from my eyes and drown us in that room. And if he had pressed me, I wouldn't have been able to give an explanation that didn't sound crazy, because he was right. I was the one who said no to last names, phone numbers, and expectations. Yet here I am, blaming him for letting me down, even though he respected each one.

The first time in my life I wanted a guy to break a rule—to push a boundary—instead, he followed and respected them.

The cold air hits my face. My heart races. I know my reaction is ridiculous. It was just one night. One! One reckless, impulsive, martini-soaked mistake. Now I'm engaged to a wonderful man who loves me. He is the kind of man who doesn't disappear before sunrise.

But just before I get the chance to say anything else, the door behind us opens, and I refuse to turn around. From Morgan's expression, I know who it is. However, I'm in no condition to face him.

"Everly?" Reese's voice travels with the wind. "Are you OK?" He is closer now, just as Morgan steps between us like an emotional shield.

I close my eyes. "I'm fine."

"It doesn't seem like you're fine."

I spin toward him. "Who are you to tell me how I'm supposed to feel, huh? It's not like you know a single thing about me."

"That's not entirely true…" he begins, just as Morgan cuts in.

"Let's just go, Everly." She reaches for my hand.

"This is just not right. It's…" I try to find the word. "Inappropriate."

"What is inappropriate?"

"You!" I shout, startling a few passersby. "You being here!"

His jaw tightens. "I told you I work here."

"That's not what I mean, and you know it." I look at him.

"Then why don't you say what you do mean?"

His question would be easy to answer if I actually knew what I meant. "I'm getting married," I finally say, as if that's the answer to everything.

He nods. "I'm aware." However, the calmness of his response infuriates me even more.

"I just don't think it's right given our…history," I say.

"What history?" His words hit harder than I expected, cutting through whatever tough exterior I had left.

"That night," I whisper to him, as if I'm letting him in on a secret.

He studies me carefully, I can tell. He looks at me as he did that night, as if he were preparing for a test he would never take. "I hardly call one night a 'history,'" he replies.

And now I'm furious. If it was just one night, why did it matter so much to me? Doesn't he remember how we laughed? The way we connected on nearly everything? How perfect it felt to be with each other—effortless? Or how we talked until we both fell asleep?

Then my anger turns inward. I have no reason to be mad at him. I was the one who set the conditions for that night, which, in my defense, I did out of fear of rejection. He's so out of my league, so I thought that setting a safe boundary to protect myself would keep me from getting hurt. Funny how that turned out. I still ended up getting hurt.

In this moment, I am finally facing him after months of only imagining him and conjuring images of that night. I was afraid those memories would soften and fade over time. I have to gather myself. This cannot affect me. But it does. He knows it. I know it. I wouldn't have walked out of that meeting if it didn't. I wouldn't be standing here on the sidewalk, practically confessing how much it doesn't "affect" me, if it didn't.

"This is ridiculous. I just don't see how I can plan my wedding with someone who—"

He looks at me. "Someone who *what?*"

*Who knows how I taste? Who knows how I sound when I lose control? Who saw me unedited—in my true rough-draft form? That night, I didn't care that I wasn't a polished version of myself. He made me feel seen in the best way.*

"Who isn't neutral?" I finally say.

He exhales slowly, glancing at Morgan, then back at me. "I can be neutral. I am neutral." The way he says it, as if it were a promise, makes my stomach twist in knots.

"We are going to go," Morgan pipes up, taking hold of my hand.

As we walk away, I realize it's the best decision. Had I stayed, I would have been tempted to ask him the one question I can't seem to let go of: *Why didn't you stay?*

But then, was leaving the best thing he had done? Had he stayed, would he have put himself in a position he didn't want to be in?

Later that night, I head over to Carter's place. After the appointment, I went back to work and stayed later than usual, letting fiction take over rather than face the reality of my current predicament. Instead of going home, I needed to be somewhere where I could distract myself from my thoughts.

His warm smile greets me as I walk through the door. His tie hangs loosely around his neck as he leans over the kitchen island, leafing through a stack of paperwork. "Hey, sweetheart. How was your day? How was the meeting?"

I walk toward him and kiss him, inhaling his scent as I try to forget the day's events. "They were both fine," I lie.

He looks at me as if he notices I'm not being completely honest. "Just fine?"

"OK," I cave. "It was overwhelming."

At that, he laughs. "According to everyone I've spoken to, wedding planning is intense. But this planning company is apparently the best. They'll handle everything so we don't have to."

Of course, they are the best. And of course, the universe would throw one hell of a wrench into my wedding plans. Carter tucks a strand of my hair back behind my ear before walking over to a cabinet and pulling down a couple of wine glasses.

"But are you happy?" he asks, though the question feels heavier than it should. I doubt he understands the weight of his question, nor should he.

"I'm not sure," I say carefully—which isn't a lie. It's just not the whole truth.

"Why is that?" he asks.

"Like I said, it's just a lot," I say.

"Well, I only want what's best for us." He smiles, pulling me in for a hug.

*Us.* The word echoes through my heart and settles softly in the center. Carter and me. Me and Carter. We are the only ones who matter—not some one-night stand that meant nothing from the start.

"Actually," I say as he reaches for his phone. "I think we should reschedule."

He looks up from his screen. "How come?"

"I just think you need to be there," I explain. "It feels strange making all these decisions without you." At least that part is true.

He smiles again. "You're right. When's the next appointment?"

"Not sure," I say, feeling the awkwardness of how I left things with Reese creeping back in. I try to shake off the memory of storming out of one of the most prestigious wedding planning companies ever. I redden at the thought. "I will email them tonight and let you know."

"Sounds good." He kisses my forehead. "But you're right. I should be there."

I rest into him, knowing he means every word he says. He is a man who stands by his word. He's the one who stays.

After we part from our embrace, I take my laptop out of my workbag and take a deep breath. I have no idea how to begin this email. I'm so embarrassed. There's no justification for my reaction to seeing Reese. But I have to swallow my pride.

Just as I'm about to type an email, I notice I've already received one from Laurent & Co. Before I overthink it, I open it.

# Chapter Twelve
## All is Fair in Love & Weddings

**Reese**

My sister is going to kill me.

I head back into the consultation room and find Kenny still there, twirling in his seat as if he expected me to return with the bride. Unfortunately, when he sees that I'm alone, his face drops.

"Where is the bride?" he asks.

"She left," I say.

"Oh, no, no, no," he shakes his head as if I just admitted that weddings are canceled everywhere. "Your sister is not going to be happy. In fact, she may kill us," he sobs into his hands as I plop into the seat beside him.

"Relax. We'll figure this out."

"Relax? Have you met your sister? She doesn't relax!"

"You think I don't know that?" I groan loudly, realizing the room still smells like Everly. It's a scent I haven't forgotten.

Sensory memory has the power to take you back in time, and there was a time I didn't mind the trip.

But Everly was right. This is ridiculous. It was just one night. One night—that's all. And now she's engaged. Chapter closed. Book shut. So, for the love of book puns, why are we still keeping our page bookmarked?

It wasn't like we owed each other anything. And yes, the city is huge, so the chances of running into someone you had mind-blowing sex with were slim, but it could still happen. And it did. But we are adults. We should be able to handle this and move on. Right?

"So, do you mind telling me what happened? She looked pissed. What did you do?" Kenny looks at me.

"Why do you think I did something?"

"Because she looked pissed off at you. Do you know her?" His eyes narrow, anticipating my response, when my sister storms into the room.

"Why did Kenny message me that the bride walked out?" She glares at me. "What did you do?"

"Why does everyone think I did something?" I play dumb.

"Never in my company's history has a bride walked out of a wedding planning meeting. Now, somebody had better start talking." Her tone is sharp enough to cut. I quickly look down to make sure I'm not bleeding.

By the look on Kenny's face, I can tell he feels bad about messaging my sister, but he shouldn't. He's just doing his job—a job that matters more to him than to me.

From across the table, Genny opens Everly's portfolio to find that nothing was written down. "Nothing was written down," she says. "Why wasn't anything written down?"

"We didn't get that far," Kenny stutters.

Then, as only my sister can, she begins assembling pieces of an invisible puzzle to figure out what happened. She may not have the whole picture yet, but I can tell from how laser-focused she is on me that she has a pretty good idea. "You know her," she says. It isn't a question. She knows I won't lie to her.

"Yes," I confess.

Kenny's eyes widen. "I knew it!" he says, delighted, while my sister looks mildly irritated.

She settles back into her seat. "Well, I knew this day would come sooner or later," she sighs. "Spill it, Reese. What's the story?"

"There is no story," I say.

"Just so you know, her fiancé is a Wall Street lawyer and comes from a family in the oil business. I told you this was an important client. So, you'd better start talking," she orders.

I release a deep breath into the air. "It's complicated."

"Oh, it's complicated, huh?" she mocks me, then tosses her hands up in defeat. "Of course, it's complicated. Why did I even ask? Everything with you is complicated, Reese." She looks at me like she's about to cry or yell even louder, and honestly, I could do without either. "So, I need to know if this is going to be a problem. If it is, I need you off this wedding."

I look toward the doorway where Everly disappeared through not long ago. She looked pale and shaken, again as if she had seen a ghost. Maybe she did, because the man she met at the bar that night isn't the same man standing here now. That version of me doesn't exist anymore; he can't exist.

"No," I say evenly. "It won't be a problem." I want to kick myself for not jumping ship when I had the chance. My sister literally gave me an out, and I didn't take it. But I knew she must have been desperate to ask for my help. So I don't know if it's because I have something to prove to her, to myself, or, worse, to Everly.

Genny holds my gaze before accepting my response. "OK. Good. If we pull this wedding off, it will do wonders for the business. It will be the kind of wedding we build like architecture. Perfect groom. Perfect bride."

*Perfect bride.*

Suddenly, I find myself back outside the building. I'm standing before her as the cold air and the city's noise flood my senses. She looks at me as if she's holding back so much—like she's about to cry. Why would she cry?

I had asked her if she was OK. She told me she was, but she wasn't. We both knew it. Even her friend knew it.

She even alluded to our "history." But there is no history to allude to. So, yeah, I was right to tell my sister it was complicated. Because it was. It *is*.

Out of everything she said, she accused me of running away. It sounded like a grudge she has harbored since we met, waiting for the chance to turn it against the villain in her story: me.

Her memory must be selective. How could she have forgotten a very important detail: no expectations? Did she not remember how she set those boundaries, making it clear she didn't want me to cross them? Was it all just a game? Was I a pawn, used to see how far I could get across her board? Well, I don't play games. Not in life. Not in love.

Then she said how she couldn't plan a wedding with someone who wasn't neutral. And to be honest, I almost smiled. *Neutral?* I write vows for strangers almost every week. I watch men promise forever to women they only met six months prior. I am excellent at being neutral. So, if she wants to establish yet another boundary, then game on. Wait—I don't play games.

Whatever.

"I trust you both will fix this," Genny says, pulling me back to the present.

"We will," Kenny replies, like an obedient student.

After she leaves the room, I stare at nothing and everything all at once. How the hell am I supposed to fix this? I can't beg her to have her wedding here.

"Any ideas?" I ask Kenny for advice—even though I'm pretty sure my sister wanted me to handle this myself. But if we have a chance at saving this wedding, then Kenny stands a better chance than I do.

"I will reach out to her and do some damage control. Unless you think you should?" he offers.

"I think it's best if you do it," I say as I get up from my seat and grab my bag. "I trust you'll fix this, right?" I wink before heading out of the room.

It probably wasn't fair of me to do that. But as I'm starting to learn, all is fair in love and weddings.

**I drop my keys** into the bowl by my apartment door, then collapse onto my couch. The lights are off, and my place is quiet. I desperately need a drink after today.

Three fingers of straight bourbon in, and my mind already betrays my sworn neutrality, replaying the night I met Everly.

I recall the way she looked at me at the bar when we kissed. When I was inside of her. The way she said my name when she laughed. When she talked. When she moaned.

I reach into my pocket and pull out my wallet. The folded receipt is still there. I have kept it all this time. It's a little worn and rough around the edges, so I have to unfold it carefully to prevent it from tearing in two.

I read every word because that's what I do. I'm a word guy. I'm an observer. I consider myself a witness to the world, documenting what others can't seem to put into words. However, that morning was the first time I ever put *my* feelings into words. Now, it's just a painful reminder of what could have been and what will never be.

It's 3:00 am, and my laptop sits open on my kitchen table, which also serves as my desk. My manuscript stares back at me. I can't count how many versions of this book I've written or how many I've considered sending into the world. But I've never been ready. I was afraid of crickets. I was afraid of hearing that the project wouldn't be right for whoever I was pitching to. I was afraid of rejection.

So, this book lives in unfinished Purgatory. I will just keep rewriting it until it bears no resemblance to any version before. I know there is a story worth telling here, but I'm just not sure I'm telling the right one yet.

I started with a collection of stories from weddings I have been a part of over the years. They are a collection of vows I have written for others, professing love to those I have never loved. Since love seems more believable in a fictional setting, I am more likely to buy into meet-cutes, the idea of soulmates, and even the fragility of vows and promises. That's when the idea hits me: What if I never write my own?

I open up a new page and decide to write:

*Today I met a bride who didn't believe in expectations.*

I immediately delete the line. It's too personal. Too honest. Then again, aren't writers more honest on page than in real life? I lean back in my chair and rub my face.

But the truth? Everly is getting married. And apparently, to some guy who is in a league of his own. Someone considered "high-profile." I read the bios they submitted about each other on my way home from the office earlier. Everly described him as someone who "shows up." Was that code for "someone who stays?"

Fuck this. I can't become the cautionary tale in everyone's love story. Why does listening to what she wanted make me the villain? But just as I'm about to close my laptop, I notice I have a new email. It's from Laurent & Co. Kenny must have reached out to Everly after I had left.

After I skim through it, I see that there's already a reply. It's from Everly. My stomach tightens as I click on it.

*Thank you again for meeting with me today. I apologize for leaving abruptly, but something came up...*

Yeah, like our past.

*I would like to reschedule so that my fiancé, Carter, may attend. Please let me know your earliest availability.*

*Best,*
*Everly*

She wants to reschedule? *This is good, right?* At least, my sister and Kenny will be happy. As for me, I promised to be neutral. So, I will be.

However, something inside me quietly whispers the answer I've been hiding since that faded night. I didn't leave because I wanted to. And I definitely didn't leave because I didn't care. I've never known that side of me—the one who saw more than the morning after. So I didn't know how to handle those unfamiliar feelings. I left because I saw myself caring too much, and I thought that made me dangerous.

## *Chapter Thirteen*
## *Neutral Grounds*

*Everly*

For the entire week, I spent each day dreading the next wedding-planning appointment. I threw myself into my work and tried not letting my nerves get the best of me. As of right now, I'm sitting in my office when Morgan walks in. She's holding two cups of coffee and hands me one.

"I gave you some time to cool off. Now, it's time for you to spill." She sits down in the armchair in front of my desk.

"What's there to spill?" I say, avoiding eye contact. I turn around and start rearranging the books behind my desk—something I do whenever I'm stressed. It's my tell, and Morgan doesn't miss a beat.

"I obviously know the answer to this, but I think it's best we say it out loud," she begins, as if this is the start of some trust exercise. "Reese is the guy you had that one-night stand with and then obsessed over for months afterward. Right?"

"I wouldn't say I was obsessed with him…" I start as she smiles back at me mischievously.

"What are the freakin' odds, though? Who knew this would be your romance trope?" she laughs.

"It's not funny, Morgan. This isn't a romance novel. This is real life—my life," I groan.

"But you love, Carter. So none of this should matter, right?"

"Of course, I love Carter. That shouldn't even be up for debate. I want to spend forever with him, which is why I said yes to marrying him. Reese being part of this doesn't change that. It just made it…awkward," I say, holding back the full truth as I did with Carter. Although I have a sneaking suspicion I'm also hiding it from myself.

"Uh-huh," she replies, noticeably unconvinced. "So, are you going back?"

I nod. "I have to. His mother paid for all of this, and I can't exactly explain to everyone that I refuse to go back because a guy I slept with over a year ago is working there. I doubt it would go over well."

"Sounds admirable. When is your next appointment?"

"This afternoon," I wince.

She chuckles. "Well, a word of advice? You'd better find a way to make things less awkward. Carter knows you very well and can sense any tension or discomfort you try to hide. So, if you don't want him thinking there's more to this, don't act like there is."

"There isn't anything more to this," I say, pausing. "Do you think I should tell him?"

"I don't know. Reese vanished after that one night, and it's not your fault he resurfaced at your wedding-planning appointment," she says.

"It's not like we dated for months, and he's a true ex of mine. I was just taken off guard when I saw him, that's all," I add.

"Can I ask you something without you getting mad at me?" She takes a sip of her coffee, waiting for my permission.

"Go ahead," I wave her on. It can't be any worse than what she's already asked me.

"Has your guard ever really been up with him?

**I promise myself during** the entire two-block walk to Laurent & Co. that things will go smoothly this time. I will keep my emotions under control. Since Carter will be joining the meeting, I know his presence will make it more official. Concrete. Impenetrable. I'll be much safer if I don't let anything affect me. I repeat this three more times in the elevator and again when I walk through the office's glass doors, only to forget it all as soon as I step into the waiting area.

When the door opens, I see Carter sitting on a white sofa. His phone is in his hand, and he's typing away on it, either a message or an email. He had offered to call me a ride to the meeting, but I insisted on walking. I needed to clear my head. When he sees me, he tucks his phone back into his pocket and kisses me on the cheek.

"I'm so glad you're here," I say, relieved. Part of me worried that something would come up at the last minute and prevent him from attending the meeting.

"I haven't checked us in yet," he says. "I will do that now." He walks to the receptionist, who immediately rises from her seat and offers us champagne as if we were royalty. This is far from the welcome I received on our first visit. Either way, the champagne is a nice touch. It will certainly help take the edge off.

"My name is Lila. If there is anything else I can get for you, please let me know," she says as she hands us our glasses.

A few minutes later, she brings us back into the consultation room, and I quickly realize I'm not the only one who came prepared with a plan.

Reese is seated at the table, looking completely stoic as I walk in with Carter. He shows no signs of awkwardness or any indication that we've met before.

"Mr. Jacobs, we are so glad you could join us." Kenny reaches for Carter's hand.

"Please call me Carter. Thank you. I'm sorry I missed the first one."

*No, you don't.*

He steps forward with a polished smile on his face before his gaze falls on Reese.

As for Reese, he looks exactly the same as he did last time. He's wearing a dark button-down shirt, sleeves rolled up to reveal his tattooed arms. His rugged notebook sits beside his leather bag. In contrast, Kenny could easily be mistaken for a groom. He's ready for a wedding at any moment. Not to mention, he's even wearing a boutonniere. As for Reese, he looks like he's ready for a wedding night.

Carter extends his hand to Reese. "Carter Jacobs," he repeats.

"Reese Myers." Their handshake is firm and confident. Neither man squeezes too hard nor breaks eye contact too soon. It's subtle, but it's not casual (at least on one side of the shake). Maybe I'm reading too much into it, or into the fact that they appear to be sizing each other up. Maybe men just naturally do this without a reason. However, Carter is not one to get rattled. This is probably all in my head.

Yeah, it's definitely in my head.

At Kenny's insistence, we begin reviewing venue mockups, which are just images from previous weddings they have planned. "We basically want to get a sense of your ceremony vision," he says as he goes through a few boards he brought with him. "It helps us get an idea of your taste and preferred styles, which makes the planning process much easier."

Out of the corner of my eye, I see that Reese doesn't let his gaze rest on me longer than professionally necessary. In fact, he barely looks at me at all. Which, oddly enough, somehow makes things even worse.

As we start discussing a specific color palette from a previous wedding, the receptionist, Lila, enters the room with fresh champagne and chocolate-dipped strawberries. They are really going all out this time.

"And here's your coffee." Lila smiles as she hands Reese a cup. But there's something in the way she smiles at him that makes me wonder if there's something more there than her just delivering him coffee. Either way, it's not my business, nor should I care.

"Many couples are adding champagne towers to their décor to complement the room's romantic lighting. It looks great in photos, especially for an evening wedding. Even better, it's multi-purpose," Kenny suggests.

"I love it," Carter says without hesitation. "It's both elegant and celebratory."

"I know we're a few meetings away from this, but do you have a general sense of the guest count?" Reese interjects after jotting something down in his notebook.

"I would say around two hundred," Carter answers confidently as Reese turns his attention to me.

"And does that feel right to you?" he asks me directly. It's a small question, but it lands like a boulder. His tone doesn't change when he speaks to me. It almost sounds like a punishment. He would call it neutral.

Carter glances at me. "Of course it does. Right, Everly?"

*But does it?* Honestly, I always imagined a more intimate wedding. Then again, I never imagined I'd be marrying someone like Carter, so I guess if he wants a bigger wedding, it's a small (or, in this case, a large) sacrifice I'm willing to make.

Still, having two hundred people staring at me as I walk down the aisle is already making my palms sweat. How can I possibly sign off on a decision that isn't exactly what I want? It feels excessive and makes the wedding feel like a spectacle. I wouldn't even know half of these people, yet they're about to witness one of the most important days of my life. Something about that doesn't feel right.

I reach for my glass of champagne. "Or maybe a bit smaller?" I say carefully before taking a sip.

Carter hesitates. "Smaller? Are you sure?"

Reese remains silent as his pen hovers over his notebook, suspended like a secret it isn't ready to tell.

"You know," Carter clears his throat, "we don't need to settle on a headcount today. We can revisit this, right?"

"Correct," Kenny answers.

"Well, whatever we end up deciding, I want to make sure that Everly gets exactly what she wants," Carter says, smiling as he gently squeezes my hand.

My shoulders relax. Since Carter and I started dating, he has repeatedly shown how kind, flexible, and accommodating he is to my needs. Nevertheless, Reese sits across the table as if he isn't convinced of Carter's chivalry. He watches me as if he wants to see what I would choose if no one else had a say—as if I had no voice of my own.

But before I can add anything more to the conversation, the tension in the room suddenly spikes when Kenny brings up the vow-writing discussion.

"Carter, you suggested adding the vow-writing services to your wedding package," Kenny acknowledges, looking down at our portfolio. "So I will hand this over to the expert. Reese?"

In a neutral tone, Reese asks, "Do either of you have an idea of what you want your vows to reflect?"

Carter smiles as if wanting me to take the lead.

I clear my throat. "Our future," I say.

"Can you define that?" Reese asks gently.

"A future with stability, partnership, love, commitment, and of course, family," Carter speaks up. What he adds are all good things, yet Reese won't stop looking at me. Whatever happened to him avoiding me from across the table? Let's go back to that.

"And you, Everly?" he asks as if Carter's answer wasn't sufficient for us both.

I swallow, feeling my throat tighten as if I'm having an allergic reaction. Hearing him say my name sparks a visceral response. "I agree with Carter," I reply. "And I think the idea of us being fully seen."

With my words, the air in the room shifts like the wind. Reese's jaw tightens as Carter reaches for my hand. "You *are* seen," he says without hesitation.

I know Carter believes what he is saying. He truly does. But the question I wish I could ask him without offending him is: *What do you really see?*

I do my best to focus on Kenny because he's the least emotionally threatening person in this room. Still, Reese is watching me like he knows I'm holding back. He's relentless! Just like that night when we were up late talking in bed, he wouldn't let me dodge the hard questions. He pushed for the truth. He valued it. And I can see that part of him hasn't changed. With a subtle glance, I notice Carter fidgeting. He shifts as he adjusts his cuff. He only does this when he's nervous.

*Why is he nervous?*

Reese closes his notebook, keeping his professional mask intact. "I think we made good progress today. Wouldn't you agree?" he asks the room.

I nod. Too quickly.

For the next few minutes, we discuss the timelines and agenda items moving forward. However, Carter has to step out of the room to take a work call. When he leaves, it feels like the room exhales, as if it's been holding its breath the entire time.

Kenny stands up from the table. He hands a chocolate-covered strawberry to Reese. "You good?" he asks.

"I'm fine," he says, swatting the strawberry away with a hint of irritation he doesn't bother to hide. "Just tired."

Kenny's eyes narrow. He looks at Reese, then at me, as if something is clicking into place in his mind. For a moment, I worry he suspects why I left that day. But his expression suggests something else, like recognition. However, I'm sure Kenny has seen countless couples in his career and has studied them as if each wedding were another test of love. Carter and I will be no different. And we will pass with flying colors.

But something in my gut tells me this isn't about Carter and me. *Does he know? Did Reese tell him?* He had to. How could he not? Not to mention, he does look like the kind of guy who knows the difference between attraction and history. And regardless of what Reese says or not, one night *is* history.

As for me, I pretend to be absorbed in something on my phone when Kenny leans in close to Reese and whispers to him. Reese doesn't react. All I can see in my peripheral vision is his fingers tightening slightly around the coffee cup he's holding.

# Part
# THREE

# Chapter Fourteen
## Say Yes to the Address!



I always thought choosing a wedding venue would feel magical. Instead, I'm standing in four-inch heels in the grass as Carter stands perfectly relaxed, while I feel like I accidentally scheduled an emotional ambush.

The castle-like estate rises before us, its white-stone façade and ivy-climbing walls bathed in sunlight, and the manicured gardens look as if they were filtered through reality. It's truly breathtaking. It looks exactly like the place Carter's mom would frame on a Christmas card. And why wouldn't she? She chose this place.

"This place is incredible," Carter says, slipping his hand into mine. Behind us, Kenny rushes up, carrying his tablet with the energy of someone personally responsible for romance worldwide. "Welcome to forever, people!" he announces.

I laugh despite myself, but I've kinda grown to like Kenny. His enthusiasm is contagious, and I'm hoping some of it rubs off on me.

Then, Mrs. Jacobs gets out of her car as her driver parks and waits. "Isn't this place marvelous? You have no idea how hard it is to reserve, but your father and I pulled some strings again." She clasps her hands together in triumph.

I'm starting to get really tired of all the "strings" she's been pulling.

"I have to agree, Mom," Carter says as Reese steps out of a black SUV. Now I feel like I have to filter my feelings, too.

*Ugh, look at him. He looks like he just stepped off the cover of GQ.* He's wearing sunglasses today, along with another button-down shirt. Does he own anything else? Either way, he wears it with effortless confidence. I can't help but feel like the universe has deliberately placed temptation in this entire wedding-planning process. But if Reese can stay neutral, so can I.

Reese politely nods to both Carter and me before taking Carter's mom's hand. "You must be Mrs. Jacobs. It's nice to finally meet you."


## Reese

I decided that if I'm going to survive this wedding, I would need to set a few ground rules for myself. The first rule is that I can't let her see me react to anything. I have to show no emotion. Zero. Even when I see her walking down the paved driveway in skinny jeans and heels, scanning the property, her hair moving in the breeze as a touch of excitement battles a hint of uncertainty etched across her face, I do not react.

I can't be the only one noticing these subtleties. Carter stands beside her, wearing that same air of confidence I sometimes wear. It's all too familiar, but there's something else beneath it. He's grounded. Solid. Trustworthy. He also seems like the kind of guy who could buy her the world. I don't dislike him at all, which isn't convenient given the circumstances.

Kenny appears at my side. "You look emotionally constipated," he mutters.

"Well," I scan him up and down for a good comeback, "you just look constipated." I take off my sunglasses and tuck them into my leather bag. "And besides, I look professional."

"Or doomed," he shoots back, but I ignore him. I know what he's trying to do, and he's not getting anything out of me. Fort Knox here.

Kenny quickly takes charge and outlines the logistics. "Ceremony options include the garden terrace or the indoor ballroom, depending on the weather. However, the indoor ballroom will be your reception space either way. The catering is handled in-house by a Michelin-starred chef, and the estate can host about fifty overnight guests, including your wedding party. I should also mention that there are 5-star accommodations nearby for any additional out-of-town guests."

As we all head toward the estate's front steps, Carter starts asking smart questions about the budget, timeline, guest flow, and amenities. I can tell he's really engaged in the process, as if he wants to be part of it rather than just going through the motions (unlike some grooms who prefer a more hands-off approach). I respect that. While it's not an indicator of a couple's success rate, it does paint a picture. Then, as Everly turns down the garden path while Carter and his mother discuss money, I instinctively follow her without thinking.

## Everly

The garden terrace overlooks a large pond with a fountain at its center. A wooden sign asks people not to feed the fish. A soft wind blows as I watch white chairs being set up for another event. For a moment, I can almost picture my wedding. I can even hear the music. I can see the guests standing as I walk down the aisle.

Well, almost.

But before my mind wanders any further down the garden path, Reese appears beside me. He's not close, but close enough.

"This is where most couples fall in love with the venue," he says.

"I can see why," I reply.

His eyes cast off into the pond. "Close your eyes," he says suddenly.

I hesitate at his instruction. "What? Is this some wedding trust exercise?" I chuckle.

"More of a venue exercise," he says. "Just trust me, OK?" The words spill out of his mouth, landing solidly between us. There is so much I don't trust about this man, or about myself when I'm near him. Yet I still close my eyes.

"Now," he begins once my eyes are closed, "imagine the moment you walk down the aisle." His voice is calm and soothing, as if he's guiding a meditation. "What do you want to feel?"

The question hits me in a way I didn't expect. I picture what he has asked me to do. I see my dress brushing the ground as everyone watches. I see Carter waiting for me at the altar.

"I want to feel at peace. Calm," I admit.

I open my eyes to see Reese nodding. "That's a good answer."

"What's a bad one?"

He glances at me then. "Usually, it's anything that sounds like you're performing for an audience. You know, putting on a show for everyone else's benefit rather than your own."

Instantly, my stomach flips.


## Reese

I am no stranger to one-night stands. I have had a few. OK, I have had more than a few. So, I know how it all works—it doesn't. Whether you go in with the best of intentions or none at all, someone always gets their feelings hurt. But what I can say is that it's never been me. I have never had my feelings hurt because I don't allow myself to feel more than I should. I compartmentalize. It's been one of my superpowers.

Until Everly.

With Everly, things were different. It's not that my feelings were hurt or my ego was shattered. I was just left confused about why I would want to put myself in a position where I could be hurt. I did not compartmentalize with her. I did not separate. I was left wondering what I should have done differently, which is something I had never done before.

I had one night with this girl, and that was all it took for me to see all sides of her. It was as if she put them all on display—a buffet of Everly's personality. To be honest, there wasn't a single thing I sampled that I didn't like. She was a kaleidoscope of colors and flavors, and I was given the chance to see (and taste) every last one. I even came back for seconds.

The interesting part of experiencing each other the way we did is that I notice what she doesn't realize I notice. For example, she doesn't realize that she tells the truth in fragments. Only I doubt anyone has taken those pieces and put them together to understand what she's really saying.

And what kind of answer was calm? I didn't want to say more because it wasn't my place, but normally, brides tell me they want to feel excitement, fireworks, something louder than everyday life.

*Should I have written down her answer?* Perhaps. But I didn't. Some things don't need to make it onto paper. I believe that was one of them.

Across the lawn, Carter waves us back over. He looks genuinely happy. Despite being as "high-profile" as I've been told, he doesn't seem to have an inflated ego. He's humble. He looks like a man excited to build a life with the woman he loves, and I don't blame him.

When we all come together again, I take a small step back from the group. I have to remind myself of my role. I am an observer. I am a witness. I am a neutral party in all this wedding-planning nonsense. Neutral. Neutral. NEUTRAL.

As Carter goes over a few details he had discussed with his mother and Kenny in our absence, I notice one more thing. Out of the corner of my eye, I see that Everly is not looking at Carter.

She's looking at me.

*Everly*

Carter drapes his arm over my shoulders. "What do you think, sweetheart?" he asks.

I look around again. It's perfect. "I love it," I say because I truly do. What's not to love? It's more than I could have ever imagined. The only concern I have is whether more is really better.

But then Reese clears his throat, and all the confidence I had in my answer disappears. "Do you love it for you?"

Carter lets out a light laugh. "He asks the intense questions, doesn't he?"

Reese faintly smiles as Kenny nervously shuffles his feet on the pavement.

"I'm sorry, but this is how I get to know you both," Reese says. "It also helps set the tone of your vows."

Carter nods. "Perfect. I love the attention to detail."

"OK!" Kenny claps his hands together. "Let's take a logistical break and head inside. Shall we?"

As we head inside the estate, we are greeted by a waiter carrying a tray of sparkling water. Kenny hands me one, which I gratefully accept. Then he grabs another glass and practically shoves it at Reese.

*Reese*

As the estate manager begins the tour, Kenny pulls me aside. "You lied," he whispers.

"About what?" I ask.

"About her," he whispers more loudly this time. "There *is* a story there."

"What?" I laugh. "You're crazy. I think all of this wedding stuff has gone to your head." I point to his forehead.

"Seriously? I'm not the one who followed her into the garden like some Victorian poet," he snickers.

"I honestly have no idea what you're talking about. I was just assessing sightlines and helping her picture the big day," I reply.

"You were assessing feelings," he corrects as I keep staring straight ahead.

"Listen, Kenny, I think you should just drop it. The last thing either of us wants is to piss off my sister again. No need to destroy a wedding because you think you know something," I say.

"Or is it because I'm right?" he says, looking at me knowingly.

"She's happy," I say, because it's true and hopefully enough to end this conversation.

"I didn't ask if she was." His expression shifts to pity, or maybe it's concern. Either way, I don't want to find out.


*Everly*

Kenny gathers us back outside after we finish the tour. The indoor ballroom was stunning. Everything looked like it belonged to the Gilded Age. Even the rooms were perfectly decorated. It's a place I could never afford to stay on my own.

"So, what do you think?" Kenny asks. "It's amazing, huh?"

"It's the one," Mrs. Jacobs says first. "I don't think we need to see anything else."

Carter squeezes my hand. In his eyes, he looks so excited and hopeful. I can tell he loves this place and is waiting for me to say the same. In fact, everyone is looking at me for the same reason.

This is the first item we need to check off the wedding planning checklist. I look up at Carter, who keeps smiling, then at Reese, who gives the tiniest nod, as if signaling me to respond. No emotion. Neutral.

"Yes. Let's reserve it. It's perfect," I say as everyone smiles. I honestly think it's the first time I've ever made Carter's mom this happy. Yet for reasons I can't explain, my heart races as if I just made a bigger decision than just the location.

"Wonderful!" Kenny exclaims. "Now we have to figure out a date. This place tends to book up quickly."

"What about a spring wedding?" Carter asks. "Preferably in May?"

"What year?" Kenny asks as he begins swiping through his planner like he's on a speed-dating app.

"I was thinking *this* May," Carter says without hesitation.

"This May?" I repeat, doing the math in my head. This May was only six months away. I would have thought we would get married in a year, not six months. This feels too soon. Rushed.

"This May?" Kenny echoes me, as if he, too, wasn't expecting the wedding to be this soon.

"Let me speak with the estate manager. Sometimes there are cancellations," Kenny says as he heads back inside.

But just as I'm about to ask Carter why he wants the wedding this soon, his phone rings. "It's work," he says, walking a few feet away, while his mother announces she's late for her spa appointment.

As for me, I linger near the terrace railing, staring back out toward the pond when Reese walks up beside me. His leather bag is slung over his shoulder, and his notebook is tucked under his arm. It's kind of old-school that he writes everything down rather than resorting to a tablet, as Kenny does.

"Big decision day," he says as a light breeze blows in our direction.

I nod. "Yeah, it is," I say as the silence between us stretches uncomfortably.

"Great news!" Kenny's voice soars from across the lawn. "We have a date! May 5th!"

May 5th. It takes my brain a moment to register the date before my heart does. It settles somewhere deep and familiar—at a bar with a literary theme. Espresso martinis. A stranger who took me by storm and left me in emotional devastation. I remember the scenes from my bedroom. Clips of passion that replay in my mind from time to time. I can still hear him say my name over and over. And the way I said his…

My breath catches, but I don't move. I don't react. I simply stare out at the water as the realization unfolds slowly—like opening a text message you dread reading.

Reese shifts beside me. He is silent. Does he remember? No. There is no way a guy like him would remember the day we met.

I swallow. "May 5th?" I say quietly as if it were an answer to a question.

"Yeah," Reese replies, but says nothing more.

And somehow, in that one-word response, he has said it all.


*Reese*

May 5th? Seriously?

The date hits me like a thrown brick. I tell myself I can't react, so I'm not. I can't look at her or let her know I remember. It's best not to say anything. I have to stay motionless. E-motionless. May 5th may have been our night once upon a time, but now it's about to take on a whole new meaning—one that will completely wash away any lingering memories tied to it. It will wash me away.

The universe is a piece of shit.

"Perfect," Carter says once we regroup. "That date is perfect. Kismet. It's as if the universe is giving me a second chance to rewrite that date in our history." He turns to Everly and takes her hand. "I never want you to feel like I won't show up for you. Never again."

It's clear he's not posturing. He loves her the only way he knows how. The only question I have is: what is he trying to rewrite?

Kenny smiles as he confirms the date in his planner. Then, for the first time since this whole shitshow began, I consider the possibility that fate doesn't care who deserves what.

My pen lingers over my notebook just long enough for Kenny to notice, though there's not much he doesn't notice. I jot down the date anyway. Ink steady. Hand steady. My breathing is uneven, but no one seems to notice. It takes everything I have to block out Carter's speech about why the date is so important, but then something catches my attention. He says he was the one who stood her up that night. Now he's turning that failure into a promise—a chance I will never get.

For someone who writes happily-ever-afters for others, this one truly takes the wedding cake. After hearing him speak, I think he might give me a run for my money. So, why does this man need help writing his vows? He seems perfectly capable of expressing his own feelings.

A part of me wishes I could speak up and tell him that May 5th was also the night Everly laughed into my shoulder. The night she kissed me with such hunger and passion, as if nothing could ever quench it. It was the same night he stood her up, allowing me to talk with her for hours until we both fell asleep…naked.

I wonder if she remembers all that was said.

Because I do.

Every word.

Later that night, I open my wallet. The folded note I've kept is still there. As I expected, the date reads May 5th. I trace the ink with my finger, realizing the day is now becoming one she promises someone else forever. Funny how that works. It's a true sliding-door moment.

Had I stayed, she probably never would have called Carter back. She probably wouldn't have ended up dating him. And they certainly wouldn't be planning their wedding right now. However, I was never the type to stay. Even if I had stayed in that moment, would I have stayed for the long haul? Maybe everything is as it should be because she is marrying someone she never has to doubt. I'm riddled with so much of it.

I've always been told I'm too much of a risk—a liability. People see me as the kind of guy you can't trust with your heart. But the truth is, I've never trusted mine. Somehow, someway, she did. That night, she saw something in me that others usually miss—maybe even something I've missed myself. I've always doubted my ability to love, as if I can't give or receive properly. Maybe too many weddings have jaded me further. Or maybe I've been projecting my own insecurities, and she was the first to show me that they could actually be my strengths.

None of that matters now. What's done is done.

# Chapter Fifteen
## Mood Boards & Mixed Signals

*Reese*

Two weeks later, we are all seated back in the consultation room, with vision boards, several color palettes, fabric swatches, ribbon samples, and more spread across the table as if a Pinterest board had exploded. Kenny is standing near an easel-looking thing, looking like a flight attendant ready to show us how to buckle our seatbelts before takeoff. All I really care about is where the exit signs are.

Kenny was ready for this meeting several hours ago, eager to show off the vision boards he designed himself. It's obvious he has a knack for this—like he was born to plan weddings. As for me, it probably looks like I've been dragged here against my will.

We are all seated around the table, except for Kenny, when Lila enters with a tray of fresh coffee and chocolate croissants. Usually, she just leaves the tray, but this time she pours cups for all of us. When she hands me mine, she touches my arm as I say thank you. She smiles as if the gesture means something more.

Carter's mom arrives ten minutes later, dressed in a beige suit and diamond earrings, with the posture of someone who is confident they belong in the room.

Unlike her son, Mrs. Jacobs' warmth feels very calculated. She acts as if she has a limited amount to give and has already decided how much to allocate to each person.

"I apologize for my tardiness," she says to the room. I pretend not to notice Everly's shoulders tighten. It's clear she wasn't expecting her to come. Still, instead of sitting down right away, Mrs. Jacobs positions herself in a way only someone with generational wealth could, surveying the room as if she's assisting with a merger—and not the kind that involves the merging of two lives.

Carter stands to greet his mother. "Mom, thank you for coming," he says as if he were clearly expecting her.

"Oh, I wouldn't miss it," she says smoothly. "This is a family event." The word family lands with a soft directive, making me wonder if I'm the only one who picked up on it.

But just as Kenny is about to start for the second time, we're greeted by another surprise guest: my sister. I wonder whether she's here to see how our vision is coming together (well, Kenny's) or just wants some face time with our "high-profile" clients. But I know my sister. She's here to check whether I'm behaving as she instructed. Either way, I'm just sitting back and watching the show. Kenny has this fully under control.

"So," Genny announces to the room, "how is everything going? Have we decided on our wedding design aesthetic?"

Mrs. Jacobs immediately interjects, "I don't want anything too trendy. Everything we choose must be timeless."

It's amusing how Mrs. Jacobs acts as if this is her wedding. As for Everly, she nods politely, but I don't write anything Mrs. Jacobs says down. The only thing I do write is:

*Bride defers when uncertain.*

Because I honestly believe that's the part that really matters.


## Everly

It's not that I oppose timeless choices; I just prefer to choose what looks and feels good. I couldn't care less whether our wedding photographs are featured in a magazine. This is the start of my life with Carter, yet Mrs. Jacobs feels entitled to decorate it from start to finish.

I wish I had more backbone to oppose her, but since she is paying for all of this, I almost feel handcuffed to her decisions. So I politely nod and choose my battles. Maybe I can talk to Carter later about limiting the number of meetings she is invited to.

After Kenny shows us a few more vision boards, I say, "I love the soft champagne tones and how light and romantic it feels. It definitely speaks to me."

"I have to agree," Carter speaks up. "Mom?"

She shrugs. "I was thinking of something grander. It's hard to call it intimate with how big this wedding is going to be."

"And how big do you think this wedding will be?" I ask, knowing full well that even though the aesthetics topic was a pain, the guest-count discussion will be even worse.

"Given the estate's occupancy limit, I think if we're around two hundred and fifty, that should be plenty," Mrs. Jacobs says lightly, as if she's planning a lunch for five people. "There are colleagues, extended friends, and family to consider."

"Did you just say two hundred and fifty guests?" I almost choke on the number. "I thought two hundred was too many."

Mrs. Jacobs smiles as if I'm just an impressionable child. "Oh, dear. Anything less than two hundred is too small for this scale," she says, as if we're launching a business rather than a wedding. Not to mention, it isn't even her wedding!

Noticing my discomfort, Carter gently squeezes my hand under the table. "We can find a middle ground on the guest list, right, Mom?"

Before she can respond, Reese clears his throat. "May I ask you something?" he asks, drawing everyone's attention. Genevieve's head spins toward him as if Reese shouldn't be asking anything at all. "Who do you want to look out and see when you're both standing at the altar?"

"Um," I hesitate, unsure whether the question was meant for me, Carter, or both of us. "I don't know…"

"Who do you want to see?" Carter encourages me with a smile.

"I guess the people who actually know me." I swallow.

## Reese

I sit back, watching as Everly glances at Carter. He doesn't dismiss his mother, but he doesn't override her input either. He simply smooths it over. A tactic he must use repeatedly in his professional life, as if he'd rather reach a settlement before anything goes to court.

"As for me, I just want everyone we love there," he says at last. "I think we can all agree on that?"

I have to admit, I'm a bit surprised. It's a good answer, and the right one, if I'm judging, because I instantly notice Everly's anxiety easing. I open my notebook and write:

*Groom equates love with inclusion.*

My notes rarely focus on the wedding-planning aspect of this gig—that's Kenny's job. I concentrate on the vows. I observe everything and use it to my advantage in writing. It helps me craft meaningful sentiments that people often struggle to express or put into words. Trust me, I get paid well to deliver. And I definitely deliver.

Genny masterfully shifts the focus back to the meeting's agenda. "Now, let's discuss the budget. I think that once we have a general idea, it will help with the other planning items."

Mrs. Jacobs relaxes. Money is clearly a language she speaks fluently. However, it's Carter who explains the budgeting projections with more confidence. Again, it must be something he is accustomed to in his professional life.

But dollar signs don't reveal what a person is truly like—only how they respond to them do. So, I sit back and watch how each of them reacts to the pile of money being tossed around the table like a strange game of hot potato. The only person clearly opposed is Everly, who seems shocked at how much Carter and his mom are willing to spend on one single day.

"OK, I think I have a general sense of where your budget is," Genny concludes the discussion. "However, there is one more item to discuss, and then I will leave you in Kenny's capable hands," she says, shooting a subtle glance in my direction.

"As you probably already figured out, Kenny is your lead planner. He will handle all the planning, logistics, and design for your big day. I will oversee everything to make sure it's executed flawlessly. As for Reese, he will join Kenny in all these meetings to get to know you, since you elected to use our vow-writing services," she says.

"Did you say vow-writing services?" Mrs. Jacobs' eyebrows lift slightly, as if Genny just told her that a wizard has been hired as the officiant. "What do you mean by vow-writing services?"

"It's a way for the bride and groom to express how they feel without the pressure to find the right words themselves," Genny clarifies. "We believe in providing deeply personal ceremonies, so Reese will begin working one-on-one with Carter and Everly to craft vows that are authentic and true to their relationship."

"Think of him as a wedding anthropologist," Kenny says.

Carter nods. "I am all in favor. It certainly takes the pressure off. And, Reese, I trust you will take our feedback into consideration?" He looks directly at me.

"Of course," I say. "I won't finalize anything without your approval."

"And you're the one who writes the vows?" Mrs. Jacobs asks, sizing me up and down.

"Yes, ma'am. That is correct," I reply. I can't entirely fault her skepticism, since I don't look like someone who writes vows for a living, but she didn't need to be so obvious about it.

"And exactly how long have you been doing this?" she peers at me from across the table.

"Long enough to know that no one remembers the centerpieces or the color of the linens. They remember what was said and how they felt. And I help create that moment," I say evenly.

"And the cake," Kenny whispers. "They also remember the cake," he says as I hush him.

Mrs. Jacobs holds my gaze a second longer than I'm comfortable with, as if trying to assess my abilities. "Well, then, let's just hope they are as memorable as you're claiming."

Everly quickly looks over at me, and I notice something flicker in her eyes. Relief? Curiosity? Fear?

Perhaps all three?

*Everly*

"While we're here, I'd like to ask you two a few basic questions. I know you answered them in your introductory paperwork, but I'd like to hear from you," Reese begins. "Tell me how you two met."

"Well, our first date didn't go exactly as planned," Carter answers first. "I was caught up in a huge meeting—"

"He was closing a very important case," Mrs. Jacobs interrupts as Reese jots something down. I stiffen at the thought of what it might be.

"And then what happened?" Reese asks Carter.

"I tried calling her, but she never answered. I didn't want to text her to say I couldn't make it because I thought it would come across as insensitive. I actually thought my chance with her was over," he chuckles. "Turns out she watched a movie and fell asleep early. But she called me the next day, and, well, the rest is history."

"Interesting." Reese looks me directly in the eyes. "And what movie did you watch?"

"I don't remember?" I say, feeling the heat rise in my chest.

"*No Strings Attached? Friends with Benefits,* perhaps?" Reese continues to egg me on.

"I said I don't remember," I sneer.

"Well, tell me what made you give him a second chance?"

I smile, maybe a little too quickly. But in my defense, Reese is trying to trip me up, and I won't let him. "Well, Carter left me several messages and seemed genuinely apologetic. If he intended to stand me up, he wouldn't have tried so hard to reschedule," I say, noticing Reese's pen pause over his notebook.

"Well, how about saving the rest of the vow questions for your sessions?" Kenny interrupts, holding up a few color swatches. "I, for one, loved *Friends with Benefits*," he says as Reese rolls his eyes.

"Anyway, Everly, you get to choose between Champagne Elegance and Billionaire Gatsby."

"Cute names," I say as Carter's mom immediately picks Billionaire Gatsby. I doubt she even looked at the color and just picked it by name.

"I prefer Champagne Elegance. It's beautiful," I say.

"I agree." Carter reaches for my hand again. "I want whatever makes you happiest." His words make me smile.

Half an hour later, Carter's mom finally leaves the meeting, and I couldn't be happier. I was getting tired of her constant interruptions and her opinions on everything. It felt like she was drowning out my voice. I'm grateful she arranged these meetings for us, but I need to make decisions without her constant input.

"So, tell me about these one-on-one vow sessions?" Carter asks Reese as soon as Genevieve leaves the room as well.

"Well, I will arrange individual sessions with both of you, and then we will finish with a joint meeting. My role is to ask questions most people don't think to ask before they promise forever," he explains.

Carter smiles. "Well, fire away! There is nothing we haven't asked or told each other."

"That's good to know," Reese says, looking at me. "Who wants to go first?"


*Reese*

I honestly doubt they've shared everything. Judging by her movie excuse, that night has been a secret in her life. It was kind of fun watching her squirm in her seat. I'm surprised she didn't fall off it.

"Why individual sessions? It seems unnecessary," she says.

*Of course, she would ask this.*

"Your vows should be a surprise at the altar," I say, feeling the atmosphere in the room shift again. Kenny coughs as he reaches for his glass of water.

"Reese is right, Everly. We have to trust the process. He is the expert," Carter unexpectedly comes to my defense.

Suddenly, I feel as if I've been put under a spotlight—a microscope, even. I'd better write the best damn vows ever, or I'm likely to get scathing reviews or need to start a new career altogether.

"When do we start?" Carter asks. "I know we have a tight timeline given our wedding date."

I look down at my planner. "We should start as soon as possible. How does Thursday evening sound?"

## Everly

I hesitate. Why does this feel so personal? So...deliberate? "This Thursday?" I ask, as if he might have picked a random Thursday next year.

Reese nods with a hint of arrogance. It's as if he knows he's making me uncomfortable and is savoring every minute of it.

"Thursday is a busy day for me, but maybe Everly can start first?" Carter suggests.

I can no longer feel my legs. My throat is parched as I reach for my glass of water, which I nervously chug as if I just crossed a desert to get here. "Yeah. Sure," I finally say as my heart races out of my chest. The thought of being alone with Reese doesn't sit well with me.

Once we confirm the time for the first solo session and the next planning meeting, everyone stands to leave.

"Take these with you," Kenny says, handing me a few design images. "They will help you brainstorm when we meet again."

As I reach for the designs, one slips off the table. Reese goes to pick it up at the same time I do. Our fingers brush. A surge of electricity runs through my veins, but I do not react. If he can stay neutral, so can I.

But when I look up, Kenny is staring at me. I may fool Reese, but I think I may have a harder time fooling him.

*Reese*

Kenny leans against the wall after everyone leaves, watching me. "Individual sessions, eh?" he murmurs.

"Yes. It's part of the process." I shrug him off.

"Is it, though?" he asks quietly, afraid someone might overhear us beyond the consultation room walls. "Why do I feel like this is the beginning of the end?"

"Most weddings are," I say.

"Not the wedding." He glances toward the doorway. "For someone…"

I close my notebook and tuck it into my leather bag. "Kenny, I think you've been sniffing way too many color swatches. I've written more vows than I can count. This isn't a new process."

"No, it's something old. Something borrowed…"

"Shut up."

# Chapter Sixteen
## Neutral Grounds Round 2

Everly

I read romances for a living, which makes it deeply ironic that I can't write my own vows. I literally have the best prose at my fingertips, yet I have no idea how to turn it into something I could say to Carter on our wedding day.

I'm at work, sitting at my desk with a new manuscript in front of me. It has sharp dialogue, sexual tension, and a huge emotional payoff in act three. But for some reason, none of it holds my attention. I think I've read the same paragraph ten times without absorbing a single word.

Why? Because I'm meeting with Reese tonight.

Alone.

Outside my office door lies the literary bullpen. Phones ring, assistants chatter, and keyboards clatter. It's the white noise of a typical literary agency. Yet everything sounds too loud. Distracting. Overstimulating. I can't seem to focus, so I close my office door.

Why does it feel like my life has shifted off course? As if I'm no longer standing on solid ground. It's as if I took a detour somewhere, and I have no idea how to get back onto the main road.

I sit back down, trying to refocus on the manuscript, when I decide to text Morgan to say I need some coffee and fresh air.

Ten minutes later, she slides into the café chair across from me, wearing her huge sunglasses even though we are indoors.

"You look like shit," she says.

"Well, it's nice to see you, too," I say as I quickly check myself in my phone's camera.

"Are you tired? Maybe you need to go home and take a nap," she suggests. "So, tell me about Mr. Hot Wedding Planner?" She quickly changes the subject.

I nearly choke on my latte. "Excuse me?"

"Reese? Girl, he's hot enough to scorch fabric. I'd give my left leg for the night you spent with him."

"He's not my wedding planner," I say, ignoring her comment.

"OK, then, *assistant* wedding planner."

"Wrong again. He's a vow writer," I correct.

Morgan freezes. "You're joking, right? Tell me you're joking."

"I stare at her. "Apparently, he is a professional vow writer and is very sought after."

Morgan takes off her sunglasses. "And you're OK with this?"

I open my mouth, then close it because the truth sounds reckless even in my head. "It's really no big deal. We shared one night over a year ago. It will be fine."

"Then why are you sweating?" she asks. "That's sexual-guilt sweat. And trust me, I know sexual-guilt sweat when I see it."

"OK. I'm not totally fine with it," I admit. I figured that since Morgan is my best friend, I should be able to unload some of my feelings onto her. I can trust her. It felt like a small puncture in my Reese-inflated balloon. It felt good to let some of the air out. "I notice him too much."

Her grin softens instantly. "That's usually how it begins—and how it began for you two that night at the bar."

"Nothing is starting, Morgan," I insist. "Or will ever start again. I'm marrying Carter. I love Carter. End of story."

"Calm down," Morgan says. "I know you love Carter. No one is saying you don't. But can I be honest with you without you hating me too much?"

I sigh. "Go ahead."

"You seem to react to Reese physically in a way I've never seen you react to Carter."

"What do you mean?" I ask, my stomach twisting into a knot.

"When I mention their names, your body just reacts differently. That's all. And it's just an observation," she explains. "So, I'm not saying it's a good thing or a bad thing per se, or that it even means anything at all, but…"

"But what?" I look at her.

"It's definitely a dangerous thing if left unchecked."


*Reese*

Neutral grounds.

If I have to meet Everly alone, I'm not taking her anywhere. Having her return to Laurent & Co. is about as neutral as it gets.

Kenny, like the stalker he's become, stays back at the office as if I need to be babysat. I don't say anything to him because I don't want to give him the impression I'm hiding anything. He may have his suspicions, but that doesn't mean he knows the full story. I want to keep it that way.

Regardless of what Genny thinks, I wouldn't mind if Everly decided not to go through with these meetings. In my opinion, it all feels like one colossal mistake. Yet Everly isn't leaving. She finally sits across from me, curiosity in her eyes. I recognize that look. It doesn't excite me the way it did that night. She seems, I don't know, different. She doesn't carry herself the way she did when we first met. Still, I know that girl is somewhere inside her. The question is, does she?

I open my notebook before engaging in a professional tone. The Reese she once knew can't be present or detected at all.

"Just so we're clear," I say as her eyes meet mine. "Tonight isn't about Carter. It's about you."

## Everly

Reese was already seated when I approached the consultation room. As expected, he's wearing his signature dark button-down shirt, sleeves rolled up, and that devilish smirk I so desperately want to wipe off his face.

Once I sit down, he opens his notebook, his pen resting between his fingers like a starving writer begging for inspiration. But when he looks up at me, I freeze.

I could run.

Yes, I could. I should. I've done it before. But I can't. I have to be OK with this because I'm marrying Carter. I can't let some foolish night tarnish what will be an incredible future with an amazing man. So whatever effect Morgan thinks Reese has on me, I must put it to bed. No, wait. I've already done that. Scratch that. I must put it aside. I can't react. If Reese can stay professional, so can I.

I sit at the table with my arms folded. I quickly unfold them when I realize how aggressive it may seem—like a toddler pouting in the corner because I didn't get my way.

But just as Reese is about to ask me something, there's a knock at the door. The receptionist, Lila, peeks her head in and smiles.

"Excuse me, Reese. Do you need anything before I leave for the night?" she asks, looking at him as her smile widens by the second.

"I'm OK, Lila. Thank you."

She nods as if disappointed she couldn't be of service. "A few of us are going out for drinks tonight if you'd like to join us."

Without making eye contact with her, he declines. "I have plans. Sorry," he says. "But Everly, is there anything Lila can get you before she leaves?"

"I'm fine." I turn toward her. "Thank you."

However, she doesn't say much as she slips back behind the door and leaves. I recognize the look of rejection when I see it, and this girl looks rejected.

"She seems disappointed," I say to Reese, though it's truly none of my business. He doesn't say anything in response. Instead, he shifts the conversation back to the questions he wanted to ask.

Not logistical ones, but more human ones. The kind of questions he definitely didn't ask me the first time we met, or the ones he whispered to me until morning.

"What do you admire most about Carter?" he asks next.

"He's dependable," I respond. "He's sweet and always makes an effort to show he cares."

"What was the moment you realized you loved him?" He looks at me. But there's something about the way he watches me from across the table—steady, intent, and a little dangerous. I'm suspended in this moment, which feels like the kind you don't breathe through because you're afraid of what might happen if you do.

I pause, unsure how to respond. I wonder whether the pause is too long.

"We can go back to that." Reese looks down at his notebook. "What scares you most about marriage?"

I laugh. "Are you serious? Did you get these questions from Google?"

"If these are such easy questions, I expect easy answers," he says. His tone takes me back to that night when he used a similar, dominant tone with me. *Should I be asking for a safe word?*

"To answer your question earlier, there really wasn't a specific moment. I just knew," I say, and Reese only nods in response. "And as for what scares me? Nothing. How could marrying someone you love be scary?"

"Fear doesn't have to come from a negative place," he explains. "For instance, you can love your job yet fear failing."

"I guess, if anything, I would be afraid of disappearing," I say as my chest tightens. I wasn't expecting to say this.

"Can you explain?"

*Do I have to?*

"Have you ever seen those couples who lose themselves by getting lost in each other? Not in a good way, but in a way that makes them lose their individual identities and become something different—someone entirely different," I explain.


## Reese

As I'm about to write down her answer, she tries to deflect by asking me a question.

"What about me?" I ask.

"You write vows for people all day. You must have an opinion about all this," she says.

I set my pen down and lean back in my seat. "I don't write fairy tales, Everly," I say as she tilts her head at me. A strand of her blonde hair falls across her face. It takes everything I have not to reach over and tuck it back into place.

"No?"

"No." I tap my notebook. "I write promises for others to keep, not the other way around," I say as I suddenly feel the weight of my note to her in my pocket. It weighs on me like lead.

An hour later, Everly and I are still in this meeting, which is longer than I expected. But she doesn't answer my questions right away, nor does she give me complete answers, so I guess I can't be too surprised it's taking this long. Everyone in the office has already gone home. The lobby lights are dim, and the only sign of life is when Kenny bursts through the door carrying pastries. "Surprise! I brought emotional support croissants!"

"I want to go back to a previous question," I say, mindful of Kenny lingering beside me with his tray of croissants. "When did you know you loved Carter?" I ask, and Kenny nearly loses control of the tray, sending a stray chocolate croissant onto my lap.

Acting as if the stray croissant didn't throw me off, I pick it up and take a bite. "You can set the tray down, Kenny. No need to throw food at us."

Everly giggles. Just hearing her laugh and knowing I caused it is the highlight of the session.

"It's been a long day," Kenny says as he sets the tray down. "Maybe I should sit down? Just pretend I'm not here."


*Everly*

Saved by the Kenny.

I let out a silent sigh of relief because he saved me from having to answer Reese's question again.

"So, tell me," Kenny says with a mouthful of croissant, "have I interrupted a vow-writing session or a slow-burning enemies-to-lovers subplot?"

"Ugh, I love those tropes, I say.

"Don't we all?" Kenny winks at me.

After a few more questions, Reese leans in slightly. He's not flirting or crossing some professional vow-writing line; he's just closer. And yet, I have no idea how I feel about it. Is Morgan right? Does Reese make me react physically differently than I do with Carter?

"So, what would the perfect vow sound like?" he asks.

I take a sip of my drink, which has been untouched throughout the session. I know these vows are Reese's way of getting to know the bride and groom so he can write them, but part of me wonders if it's also his way of getting to know me. There are so many things I could say right now. So many answers would work. Yet he looks at me like he's the kind of guy who could wait all night.

Too bad he can't last through the morning.

"Knowing someone chooses me even when it's inconvenient," I finally say.

## Reese

My composure falters slightly. I doubt anyone notices, but I feel it. That's the thing with tiny cracks—they go unnoticed until they cause foundation problems, breaks, tears—you get the idea. Then what might have been easily fixed becomes unmanageable. I refuse to let it come to that, so I'm determined to smooth it over. But then I look at her, desperate to say something dangerous— things I once whispered to her in the dark.

Instead, I tell her it's a nice bow as my knee accidentally brushes against hers under the table. For a split second, I don't pull away as that touch ignites the memory of that night ever so slightly.

It burns. Slowly.

I finally understand the trope.

I clear my throat quickly before reaching for my glass of water. "Last question, and then I think we are good for now. What do you want your marriage to feel like?"

Everly thinks. Kenny watches.

Then she says quietly, "Like I'm exactly where I'm supposed to be."

I swallow because the last time she said something like that, she was in my arms.

"I think we're good for today," I say, shutting my notebook a little too quickly. I didn't even bother to write anything down.

Kenny nods with a mouthful of croissant again. "I think so, too."

"Kenny, why don't you go grab Everly's coat?" I ask, hoping he will leave so we can have a few moments of privacy. When he finally leaves the room, I know he is running down the hallway at full speed, so I will have to make this quick.

"Everly, just so you know, I'm not trying to complicate your life," I say. I don't know why I say this, but I don't regret the words. I believe we say what we mean; it's just that sometimes the meaning of our words is different for the person they're directed to.

"You're not," she says very matter-of-factly. Her tone goes for blood.

"You just deserve vows that sound like the truth, not like some Hallmark greeting card," I continue.

"What do you mean by that?" she asks, her voice nearly trembling.

"I think you know." My response comes too quickly, but I don't regret my words or the fact that my earlier attempt to mend the fracture has now widened the divide. There is a reason Everly and I are sitting on opposite sides of the table. I have to remember that. However, there really isn't much more I can say because Kenny is back with her coat.

# Chapter Seventeen
## Save the Last Date for Me

*Everly*

The stationary studio smells like handmade paper and rich ink. Rows of samples cover a linen-draped table, including various wax seals and embossed lettering. The scent of lined paper and cardstock comforts me as aromatherapy would. It gives me the same feeling as sniffing an old library book.

Carter is beside me, relaxed, considering he has to rearrange his schedule more often than I do to attend these planning meetings. I almost feel bad about it, but he keeps assuring me he can make it work—and he has. He flips through a stack of sample cardstock as if he's about to shuffle a deck of cards, while Kenny dramatically spreads the rest out like tarot cards. I wonder if he can see our future in what we choose?

"Ladies and Gentlemen," Kenny announces, "today we decide how aggressively we want to intimidate your guests."

I laugh. Carter smiles. Reese leans against the corner wall with his notebook open, just watching. Even when he's relaxed, he carries this restless energy as if he's made for movement. And even though he's the quiet, observant type, he also enjoys being part of the action.

"Are we ready to get started?" Kenny beams as Carter reaches into his briefcase and pulls out a sleek folder.

"My mom actually had an idea for the save-the-dates," Carter says, surprising me. All week, and even during the car ride here, he didn't mention it at all. He slides the design across the table to Kenny, who eagerly takes it.

From what I can see, it's elegant. It's printed on heavy cardstock with gold foil lettering. The font is romantic—something I'd see on the cover of a romance novel. Not to mention, the color choices fall within the champagne family I selected at a previous planning meeting. Still, I'm a little upset. She stole my thunder. Anything I choose from here on out won't make the same boom.

"It's very nice," Kenny says, examining the sample. "Let's keep it as an option. First, we should decide on a design direction. Your save-the-dates will be the first indication of what guests can expect at the wedding and should coordinate with the invitations you select."

"Makes sense," I say.

"Option one is a classic, formal design." He holds it up for all of us to see. It's very plain, with nothing special about it. "See, no pizazz. It basically screams, or in this case, whispers, that you're invited to a regular ol' wedding."

"Option two?" Carter asks.

"Option two is a more romantic watercolor. It's dreamy and timeless," Kenny says as he passes it around the table.

"And what does it scream?" I ask him.

"Consider this one as having a more soothing voice—the kind you'd hear from your masseuse at the spa," he says. "As for option three, we have a very modern, minimalist approach. It may lack frills, but it's rich and elegant and screams black tie."

"Based on what I've seen here, I think my mother's option is best. What do you think, Everly?" Carter asks me directly.

While I mostly agree, I still want to have a say. I want the decision to be mine, not Carter's mom's. So, I need to decide: do I fight her on this, or let her win? Or does letting her have this win give her the impression she will win at everything else?

"What if we combine the look of option three with the design elements from the one Carter's mom has chosen?" I ask.

"Which font do you prefer?" Kenny asks.

"I have to admit, I do like the font on the sample from Carter's mom. Could we use a variation of that, like the one used in option two?"

"You certainly have an eye for this," Kenny beams with pride.

## Reese

"The wording is important," I chime in from the corner. "It will set the tone for the entire wedding. So, the question you should be asking yourselves is what tone you want to set."

"Elegance," Carter speaks first.

"What about something more personal?" I press.

Kenny tilts his head. "Personal, how?"

"Something that reflects who you are as a couple, not just the venue or the event itself." I glare at Kenny.

Everly inhales, then looks at Carter. I notice she does this often, as if she is unsure of herself. However, Carter doesn't seem like the type of guy who would suppress her voice. "Even though I want the feeling of an intimate wedding, it should still be warm and inviting."

I write that down because it's important.

Soon, the designer prints up a few mockups as everyone gathers their things. Carter wraps his arm around Everly's shoulder.

"Are you ready to begin our registry?" he asks her. In response, she smiles. She doesn't say anything in return. Just smiles.

I open my notebook and write down one line.

Just one.


*Some promises are written before anyone realizes they've made them.*


## Everly

The bridal registry department at Harrington & Cole feels less like a store and more like a place curated for the wealthy. I slow my pace, taking it all in. Crystal towers under glass lights reflect off strategically placed mirrors, creating the illusion of an even larger space. To my right, porcelain plates in nearly every design and color are either displayed on velvet stands or hidden behind locked cabinets. Even the silverware choices seem overwhelming, with different finishes and designs. Immediately, I feel unprepared for this. Take me to Macy's.

As we walk to the counter, my heels clack against the marble floor, and I wonder if they can tell by the sound that they are not designer.

"Mr. Jacobs! Welcome back!" A young sales associate approaches Carter as if he were a celebrity. In the time I've dated Carter, we've never visited this store together. So, I'm a little taken aback that they know him by name—and by face.

"How do they know who you are?" I ask him.

"Mom and I shop here all the time," he whispers back to me as if it's some secret he's finally letting me in on, while Kenny grabs the registry scanner like it's a toy.

"Now, listen up. This is a very dangerous weapon," he warns us as he scans a gold salad bowl. The screen immediately lights up with the item and its price.

"How much is it?" I ask as I approach the scanner, which Kenny flips around, and I almost choke. "For a salad bowl?!"

"I told you it was dangerous." Kenny hands me one scanner and another to Carter. "Now, keep in mind, not everyone will purchase everything on your registry, but it's good to have a variety of items in different price ranges to give your guests a better selection."

Standing in this massive store, where a simple salad bowl costs more than my light bill, the knot in my stomach tightens. If that's how much one freakin' salad bowl costs, I can't imagine what everything else will cost. How can I expect my guests to buy items I can't even afford myself? The whole concept doesn't sit well with me.

## Reese

Everly runs her fingers along a display plate. It's thin porcelain and looks hand-painted. It doesn't seem like something you can put in the dishwasher, which makes it a pointless purchase to me. If I'm going to spend that much money on a plate, it better be safe for everything a plate is designed to do. Not melt in hot water like the Wicked Witch of the West.

From a distance, I watch her walk off, peeking at another price tag on a plate. As soon as she reads it, she heads off in another direction. I follow closely behind her as Kenny and Carter run around the store, scanning everything they like, as if they are playing a department-store version of laser tag. As for Everly, I don't think she's scanned a single item.

"What about this?" I ask, picking up a champagne flute as she approaches the stemware.

Everly immediately glances at the price. "It's beautiful," she says. "But no."

I gently take the scanner from her and scan the set of champagne flutes.

"What are you doing?" she raises her voice at me, snatching the scanner back.

"We've been here for about an hour, and you haven't scanned a single item. At the very least, you can pick something," I say.

"So, you decided to pick one for me?" she asks, looking at me crossly as I take down an amber-colored martini glass from a display case.

"These would be perfect for espresso martinis, don't you think?" I smirk.

**Everly**

A few minutes later, Kenny joins us, carrying what appears to be a waffle maker.

"This one makes heart-shaped waffles," he sobs into the box. "How romantic is that?"

"A waffle is a waffle, Kenny," Reese says.

"Yes, but shouldn't all marriages begin with breakfast-themed symbolism?" Kenny continues.

"Nothing says true love like a heart-shaped waffle," I say with a chuckle.

"Exactly!" Kenny exclaims.

"Heart waffles, it is," I laugh, realizing that if I had turned Kenny down, I might have ended up breaking his heart.

"Awesome!" he shrieks. "I need to find Carter so I can show him this, too."

After he leaves, I wander through a simpler, less intimidating area filled with plain white ceramic plates. There is nothing hand-painted or seemingly "special" about them, yet they are still not inexpensive.

Reese follows me quietly like he's auditioning to be my shadow. He picks up a random plate. "This one is nice."

I exhale. "It's simple. I like simple."

He gestures toward the scanner. "Scan them."

"Shouldn't I ask Carter first? He'll be eating from them, too," I say.

"You do realize that he and Kenny have been scanning pretty much everything in this store without asking you. Do you honestly think he's going to object to you scanning a plate?" Reese's eyes narrow.

I shrug, unsure what to say.

"Everly, you are half of this wedding—half of the relationship. There is give and take. Compromise." He looks at me as if I needed a reminder of these things. "Get the plates."

"Spoken like a man who writes vows for a living," I chuckle as Carter suddenly appears behind me.

"What have I missed?" he asks, kissing my cheek as I quickly scan the ceramic plates.

"Just these," I say with a smile, pointing at the plates.

"Perfect. I love them!" he says, smiling broadly. There is no hesitation or second-guessing of my choice—just acceptance.

I finally relax.


## Reese

Carter takes Everly by the hand and leads her toward a neighboring department full of linens. I linger back, checking my phone when Kenny's voice appears in my ear.

"I noticed something," he says, still hugging the waffle maker as if he's afraid to let go.

"Yeah? And what's that?" I ask. "Is the waffle maker on sale?"

He laughs. "There is nothing on sale in this store."

"Then what is it?"

"She seems different around you. I can't describe it, but I've noticed it." He peers over the waffle box at me. "Why is that?"

Luckily, the registry appointment is nearly finished. The sales associate from earlier prints out a summary of all the scanned items. She hands a copy to each of us. However, I don't bother looking at mine. Carter, on the other hand, examines it like a business proposal, while Everly's eyes widen as if she's been handed a bill.

"You've picked some lovely items. After you review everything, you can access your online registry to edit quantities and remove or add anything else," the sales associate says with a smile.

I quickly glance at their list, filled with crystal and gold stemware, luxury cookware, gadgets, and silver serving trays. There are bowls for everything, gold silverware, and more. Then I remember the coffee mug in Everly's sink. It's not part of some curated set. It's personal to her, and I can tell she uses it almost every day. I doubt Carter has anything like it in his cabinets. Yet tucked away among the items I deem unnecessary luxuries are the heart-shaped waffle maker and white ceramic plates.

"Well, I have another meeting to attend. I will see you both next time," I say, knowing Kenny will schedule the next meeting in my absence.

I walk out of the store before anyone can say anything else. Not that they would. They seem too busy reviewing the registry list. As the store's doors close behind me, a feeling hits the pit of my stomach, one I don't understand or have ever felt before.

*Everly wants simple.*


## Everly

Later that night, I'm sitting in my bedroom, avoiding another glance at the registry. A half-finished glass of wine sits beside my laptop. I tell myself I'm too busy to look at it. I have emails to catch up on, including replying to an author about a publishing contract. Eventually, the sounds from the city street below drift into my apartment. I check the time on my phone. I've been sitting here for hours, accomplishing nothing.

I pick up the registry. The pages feel heavier than they did in the store. Embossed at the top is the store's elegant logo. As I take a closer look at the scanned items, I realize how many on the list seem as pretentious as a monogrammed towel. Crystal bowls, sterling silver trays, and even a fancy coffee machine that costs more than my first car. I exhale slowly. When will we even use this stuff?

Everything on the list feels rather extravagant. Not that there's anything wrong with extravagance, but I would be afraid to touch half of this stuff. My clumsy fingers would probably break the crystal, and I have never polished silver in my life. These are the kinds of things I have safely admired from behind glass cases and in window displays, but I have never wanted to own. But now? I'm asking people to buy them for us.

My phone buzzes with a text message from Morgan.

Morgan: You still up?

Me: Yep.

Morgan: How did it go today?

Instead of responding, I sent her a picture of the registry.

Morgan: Holy hell! It's like a manuscript LOL. Did you accidentally register at the royal palace?"

I laugh softly.

Me: Apparently, this is normal?

Morgan: Maybe for Carter. Or billionaires. I'd be happy just registering at Target.

I glance down at the list again. I run my finger along each page as the items blur together. Gold-rimmed china? Crystal decanters? Monogrammed linens (which annoy me because Carter knows how much I dislike them)? At least there are the ceramic plates I picked. The simple, white ceramic plates. If you blink, you might miss them on the list altogether. All the other items almost outshine them—lost in a sea of crystal and gold. I can't help but wonder if my fear of losing myself is starting to unfold. Am I the ceramic plates in Carter's life? But when I take a look at everything again, I feel like they're the only items that are made to last.

I lean back in bed, staring at the ceiling. My apartment feels smaller tonight, as if it were filling with all this useless clutter. But I can't tell Carter any of this. Can I? It makes me wonder what place my mismatched mugs would have in this new life we're building together. What about my books? Or even the worn-out couch in my living room, my first adult purchase? Carter is the crystal decanter. He is the champagne flutes and silver serving trays. He is what I'm afraid I might accidentally break.

My phone lights up again. This time, it's a meeting invite from Laurent & Co. for our next planning appointment: florals. I set the registry aside, wondering if I'm making a big deal out of nothing. Carter may be used to the finer things in life, but that doesn't mean I have to chastise him for it. It's no different if he chastises me for the things I like.

I look at my ring. I am truly lucky to have found someone as supportive as he is. Carter is the kind of man anyone would dream of building a life with. Yet I'm still clouded by doubt. Maybe this is what cold feet feels like? I always thought it happened on the day of the wedding, not during the engagement.

And what was up with Reese leaving the way he did? He just walked out. He didn't linger or say goodbye. He didn't even look my way. It was almost as if he refused to stay another moment. Typical. He always leaves—no matter the circumstances.

# Chapter Eighteen
## Something is Blooming

*Everly*

My apartment smells like coffee and nerves. I check my phone again—no new messages from Carter. This isn't unusual since he's working on a tough case right now, which doesn't leave him much free time. A week ago, he sensed this was going to happen and told me. His job is volatile and unpredictable. So, during times like these, date nights and random texts fall by the wayside. I'm not upset about it. I know he works very hard.

I look at myself in the bathroom mirror. Why am I so nervous? It's just a meeting about flowers. Oh, wait. I know why! I have to go alone. Carter can't make it. Thank goodness for Kenny, because the last thing I want is to pick out flowers alone with Reese, whether he's professional or "neutral." Yet my pulse contradicts that.

An hour later, I arrive at the florist's studio. It's bright and airy, with the scent of spring. Buckets of peonies, roses, and eucalyptus spill from tall glass vases. I pause just inside the door, taking it all in. It's like a secret garden.

Kenny spreads his arms dramatically. "Welcome to the botanical part of your wedding journey. This is the part where you can," he taps his feet, "stop and smell the roses. Get it?"

I laugh. Maybe this won't be as bad as I originally thought.

"Will Carter be joining us today?" Kenny asks.

"Nope, it will just be me," I say.

"Well, it's just me as well, it seems. I'm not exactly sure where Reese is," Kenny says, then checks his phone in case he missed a message from Reese.


## Reese

I'm late. I know it. But I'm not moving. Instead, I'm sitting on my couch with my notebook open to a blank page. I will soon start Carter's solo session, but instead, I'm replaying Everly's answers from our session.

*Knowing someone chooses me even when it's inconvenient.*

I press my thumb against the edge of the page until it cuts into my skin. I desperately want to feel something—anything—rather than the memories swirling in my mind. As for Carter, he deserves something real, and I should treat him no differently than I would any other groom.

I write:

*I promise not only to stand by you when it's easy but also to choose you even when it's hard.*

I pause. I cross it out and wonder whether it's something that Everly would actually say. At this point, it's hard to say. She'd probably just ask Carter.

Not to mention, she's much harder to crack than she was that night. I wonder if I'm up against a protective barrier. If so, I'm doomed.

Eventually, I close my notebook. As I head to the next wedding appointment, I can't help but wonder if she is telling herself the same lies that I'm telling myself.

I doubt it.

Everly is clearly in love.

When I arrive at the florist studio about twenty minutes later than I should have, I see Kenny is already touching things he shouldn't. If my sister thinks I'm a liability, this guy can't handle himself around anything wedding-related.

"Now, these are aggressively romantic. Don't you think?" Kenny asks as he holds up a bouquet to Everly like he's proposing.

Everly laughs that easy laugh of hers. I think this is the first time since the wedding planning began that she seems so relaxed. That's when I notice it's just her and Kenny. Carter isn't here, and neither is his mom.

"Sorry, I'm late," I say as the florist steps away from behind the counter. "Miss Hart? Your fiancé sent these flowers to apologize for missing the meeting."

*How fitting.*

As if on cue, the florist places a vase of white orchids on the table. I watch as Everly touches the card and smiles. "He didn't have to do this," she says softly.

"He's very thoughtful," I say without any bitterness. Just a fact. He *is* a thoughtful guy. I probably wouldn't have even thought to send flowers if I were in his shoes.

I probably couldn't afford his shoes.


## Everly

Soon, the florist begins arranging flowers on a large wooden table, creating a makeshift garden of soft pink roses, cream garden roses, wild white anemones, and more. But I reach for my favorite of them all: peonies.

"Peonies are my favorite," I say.

"The peony is a wonderful choice," she says. "It symbolizes romance, good luck, and a happy marriage."

Kenny nearly sobs. "It's perfect," he says, holding up a bunch of wildflowers. "Whereas these symbolize eloping in Tuscany with a poet."

"Shall I ring those up for you?" the florist teases Kenny.

"A poet in Tuscany? Hell, yes!" he exclaims.

"So, tell me, Miss Hart, what mood are you envisioning?" she asks me.

I hesitate as I consider her question. I know Carter's mom wants classic and timeless. Carter would say something along the lines of elegance. But what do I want? What do I picture? I've always imagined my wedding filled with white peonies. I see a library setting with sheets of poetry and old books stacked at the center of the tables, surrounded by flickering tealight candles. I quickly shake those thoughts from my mind as I stare longingly at the peonies, reminding myself I'm having my wedding at the estate.

I'm not sure how long I've been quiet, but my thoughts are suddenly interrupted by Reese's voice. "Everly?" he asks. "She is asking what you want the day to feel like."

*Why am I constantly being asked questions like this? I don't even know what I want to feel like TODAY.*

I take a deep breath. "I want warmth—nothing stuffy or overly fragrant. I want the feeling of reading a good book and receiving that…"

"Happily ever after?" Kenny finishes my sentence, his hand resting under his chin.

"Exactly," I say.

"Just the idea of having an evening wedding with candles and a variety of neutral colored flowers seems romantic and intimate." I realize it's a weird thing to say, considering there are supposed to be over two hundred people attending this wedding.

The florist nods. "I think I know what you want." She smiles.

## 𝓡eese

I watch as Everly leans closer to the flowers. The soft light catches her blonde hair. I remember the night she leaned across the table at the bar like that. Only then was she leaning toward me.

The florist drapes a garland mockup over Everly's shoulders. Spotting a stray stem, I step closer to adjust it. Maybe I'm too close, but since I would have done the same for any other bride out of courtesy, I think I'm fine. What I wouldn't have done is let my hand brush her collarbone and linger there a second too long.

In my defense, it was completely accidental. But it still happened anyway. And by God, that touch was electrifying.

"Is something blooming over here?" Kenny asks, shoving a bunch of lavender between Everly and me. "Now, this flower represents devotion and smells divine, much like me."

Everly takes the lavender from Kenny. "Sorry," she says to me.

"For what?" I ask, since nothing happened.

And nothing ever will.

"Well, I think we have all our selections, right?" Kenny asks as Everly nods. "I will inform the florist, and then I think we are all set." He steps away as the florist prepares a few sample arrangements for Everly to take home. For everything else, Everly takes pictures to show Carter later.

She gently touches a rose petal from an arrangement that probably costs more than a week's worth of takeout. "They're beautiful," she says, admiring the arrangement.

"Yeah, but they're temporary," I say as she turns to face me.

"Well, that's a depressing take on flowers, Mr. Vow Man."

I shrug. "Most things worth keeping seem to be."

*Everly*

The florist gives me my samples to take home. She even made a small one with peonies because, apparently, Carter's mom was adamant about white roses. It's not that I have anything against white roses; it's just that I prefer peonies.

As the floral appointment comes to an end, I carry the samples out the door, with Kenny following behind me with the arrangement Carter sent.

"Everly?" Reese calls out to me just as my cab pulls up to the curb. "Can you remind Carter that I will still meet with him tonight?"

"Of course," I say before climbing into the cab with my miniature garden of flowers.

When I get back to my apartment, I decide to change into comfy clothes and turn on Netflix, but nothing looks good enough to binge. So, I settled on reading a new book. But with each page I turn, I keep thinking about how Reese's hand brushed my collarbone and where that hand had explored before.

Knowing that Reese is meeting with Carter right now, I can't help but feel guilty for never telling Carter the truth about Reese. It's starting to feel like betrayal, and the last thing I want is to start a marriage with any secrets between us. If the situation were reversed, I wouldn't like it either.

I really wish I had been upfront and honest with Carter from the beginning, because I don't know how he would react if I admitted everything now. It would seem like I was trying to hide something, but to be honest, there isn't much to hide.

*Right?*

In most of the romance books I've read, the main characters present themselves differently in front of their romantic interest. But when they're in front of the one they truly love, their best selves come out. It's easy for me to see that Carter brings out the quieter, more reserved side of me. It's not that I feel he has dimmed my light, but it's just a different side of me, that's all. With Reese, in one night, I let my guard down and shared so much of myself. I didn't hold back. Maybe that was part of the magic of a one-night stand? Or was it the magic of Reese? I think that because I debated that question for so long, I allowed myself to be so hung up on that night—on him. To be honest, it's easier to blame it all on having too many martinis.

I decide to call my mom.

"Here comes the bride!" she sings into the phone as soon as she answers. "How is the wedding planning going, sweetie? I hate being so far away."

"It's going," I say. "There are just so many details to consider."

"I wouldn't know. Your father and I had a simple backyard wedding. No frills. No fuss. Just the stars above, a few lightning bugs, and a string of twinkling lights he hung from a tree," she says with a chuckle in remembrance.

"Honestly, that sounds more enticing—bugs and all. Next week, we have our first wedding party meeting, and then it's time for cake tasting," I continue.

"Well, just keep me posted before you go dress shopping and when you plan your shower. I don't want to miss any of it," she sighs. "I wish I didn't have to miss any of it, honestly."

"You know I would love to have you here for anything you can be, but if you can't swing it, Mom, please don't feel like you have to," I say.

"Oh, hush," she says. "I will be there no matter what."

"OK," I sigh. I don't sigh because she is coming; I sigh because there is so much on my mind, and it's starting to weigh me down.

"What's wrong, Everly?" she asks. She knows me too well.

"Nothing. I'm fine," I reply, wondering what is actually wrong with me.

"Are you sure? Because it sounds like you're trying to convince us both that you're fine."

"It's just nerves and the stress from all the planning. It's like another full-time job," I say.

"And Carter?" she asks.

"He's fine. He is at his vow-writing session as we speak," I say.

My mother's voice softens. "Everything that is supposed to work out will work out. Trust the process," she says.

"OK," I say. I honestly don't understand why she sounds so worried about me. I really am fine.

*Right?"*


## Reese

I end up meeting Carter at a quiet lounge near his office. The setting sun streams through the windows, illuminating the edge of my notebook, which rests on the small wooden table before me. I flip to a fresh page, ready for Carter's arrival. I'm a bit early, but

I like to get a feel for a place before starting an interview. And that's essentially what this is: an interview.

As for Carter, he arrives right on time. Compared with the other grooms I've worked with, he's very different. He's always composed, no matter the situation. His suit jacket is draped over his arm. He carries himself with perfect posture, dressed as if he's here to hand out business loans, while I look like I could use one. He messaged me after the meeting with the florist, saying it would be easier to meet here since it's closer to his office. I didn't object. It would be nice to see how he behaves on his turf.

Somehow, after the day he claimed to have had, he seems very relaxed. No hair out of place, no wrinkle in his suit. For a split second, maybe in a different timeline under different circumstances, he and I could be good friends. But there is no way in this universe that could happen now.

"I hope I'm not late," he says, shaking my hand. "Did I keep you waiting long?"

"No, you are right on time," I say, releasing his hand.

After we order a drink and Carter loosens his cufflinks, he leans forward. "I want our vows to be an honest representation of both Everly and me. I don't want them to sound manufactured, as if I'm reading from someone else's script."

"I would never let that happen," I say.

"I just wish I had it in me to write them on my own. Everly deserves that much. It's just that I'm afraid I won't get the words right," he continues.

I observe him carefully. He seems comfortable enough to open up to me, even though we hardly know each other. I've learned that when I work with people who are too closed off, it limits how expressive I can be with their vows. So, in order to make them better than reality, I have to fictionalize them. I've never had any complaints, since it elicits emotional reactions from people. I just don't have time for unnecessary obstacles.

"So, tell me, when did you realize you had fallen in love with her?" I begin. It's a simple question, but it's one that tells me a lot about a couple. A bride once told me she fell in love with the groom when he remembered what she liked on her pizza without her having to remind him. It wasn't that she loved pizza; it was just the fact that he remembered. He listened. It was a simple moment like that that made her realize that love didn't come with grand gestures; sometimes it came with peppers and onions.

Carter smiles faintly. "I think it took me longer to get there than it did for her, but I'm not sure."

I look up from my notebook. "What do you mean?"

Carter chuckles before taking a sip of his port wine. "I'm not great at reading emotions. I've always been all business, no fun. But with Everly? She has brought out that side of me that can be more spontaneous and live a little."

"Tell me more about her," I probe.

"Well, Everly is the kind of girl who can walk into a room and make everything change," Carter begins as I set my pen down to give him my full attention. "She talks to people as if she's genuinely curious about them. She once told me she's obsessed with people's stories and always roots for the underdog."

I write:

*She is curious about people—a hopeless romantic.*

"She also edits the world," Carter says with an unusually loud laugh for a man so reserved. He loosens his tie slightly as he continues. "She sees people's potential before they even see it themselves. She did that for me."

*And me.*

But I don't write that down.

"Again, I'm the least spontaneous guy, but I show up. When we first met, she had her guard up, as if she'd been hurt. I thought for sure she'd never agree to another date, but she did. I think it's because I didn't give up." He smiles as if he's recalling the memory perfectly. "As I said, I kept showing up."

I stare at Carter. The man literally did what I couldn't. Then again, was he given the same rules as I was? Either way, it sounds like she made the perfect choice. The right choice.

"That matters, right?" He looks at me for reassurance, as if I have a crystal ball to see into their future.

"Yes, it matters greatly."

"Did you know that Everly works at a literary agency? She's so creative and passionate about her work in a way I never am about mine—the only creativity I have is how I use information to win my cases. But Everly? She takes chances on authors when she believes in them and their stories. She sees potential where others don't," he says.

"I didn't know that about her," I say, because it's true. Everly and I never shared what we do for a living. If we had, she wouldn't have been so surprised to learn I was her vow writer. Either way, somehow learning this piece of information about her makes sense.

"The trouble is, I'm the exact opposite of her," Carter says with a warm smile as I raise an eyebrow.

"I'm focused on my work in a completely different capacity," he explains. "I love my job, but I'm not as passionate about it as she is about hers. She can talk for hours about a book's premise, while all I can think about is how I'm going to win my next case." He shakes his head. "I build strong defenses. I fix problems. I'm a closer," he says, as if making a confession.

"So, she makes you see that there's a life outside the courtroom," I say.

"Exactly." He points to me.

At this moment, I realized something about Carter I hadn't noticed before. Carter doesn't love Everly because she fits neatly into his curated life; he loves her because she expands it. She is the mismatched mug. She adds color to his neutral surroundings.

I've been doing this job long enough to know he truly loves her, as he talks about her—how he sees her. No, there would be no competition, but if there were, I would lose.

"Does anything scare you about marriage?" I ask, but it takes Carter a few minutes to find his answer.

"To be honest, I'm scared she'll realize she deserves someone better," he says before downing the rest of his port and signaling the waiter for another.

"Why would she realize that?" I ask because that is not a common fear.

After his second glass of port is poured, he shrugs. "Sometimes people just jive, you know? They understand your quirks and flaws better. And while I love everything about her, it's like learning a different language I'm not fluent in. When you're not fluent, the dialogue feels stilted and needs translation. With her, I feel like I'm constantly in need of translation, and sometimes that scares me."

His words feel heavy. I take another sip of my bourbon, letting everything he's told me sink in.

"So that's why these vows matter." He looks at me. "I want them spoken in her language."

"That makes perfect sense," I say.

After we finish our drinks, Carter is the first to stand and leave. He pays for everything, even though I tell him it's covered by Laurent & Co.

"One more thing," he says as he puts his suit jacket back on. "I want you to tell her that no matter what, I choose her. All of her."

I catch myself frowning. "You should tell her that anyway. Don't wait until the vows to say it."

"You know, this felt more like a therapy session than a vow-writing one," he laughs.

"I've gotten that before." I smile.

We stand outside the lounge entrance while Carter flags down a taxi. He offers me a ride, but I choose to walk instead. I need some time with my thoughts, and the longer I'm with Carter, the more I find myself rooting for him.

But is he the underdog in this story, or am I?

Either way, I open my apartment door and head inside. Carter is a good man—a truly good one. That fact alone makes this entire situation worse.

*Chapter Nineteen*
*Sweet Decisions*

*Everly*

Kenny schedules us an appointment at one of the most prestigious patisseries in the city. It's the kind of patisserie that isn't open to the public and operates by appointment only. And, according to Kenny, it's by special appointment only. They are that exclusive. However, if there was one item on the wedding-planning checklist I was most excited about, it was this. I have quite a sweet tooth.

The walls are pink, which pairs nicely with the golden accents throughout. Tiny sample forks are arranged around a circular table like surgical instruments.

I inhale. "This is heaven."

Kenny nods. "To me, this is one of the most important appointments for the entire wedding." His eyes are wide, taking in all the cakes and pastries. Looking at him, I finally understand the expression "people eat with their eyes first." "It's like my Super Bowl," he says.

159

"Just think of this as competitive eating under emotional surveillance," Reese interjects, as if cake tasting were a sociological study.

Carter laughs, squeezing my hand as he takes in all the cakes and baked goods around us. He never had much of a sweet tooth, but I can tell he is up for the challenge.

"Welcome to Le Bella Créme!" the baker announces when he enters the room. Once he spots Kenny, he kisses him on both cheeks. "So happy to see you again, Kenneth! Now, who's ready to taste?"

Immediately, Kenny's hand shoots up in the air. "You know I am!"

"Are you going to be OK?" I tease him.

"Some do this job for money, Miss Evely," the baker answers. "But Kenneth here does it for the cake."


## Reese

I remember the first rule I set for myself: Don't get emotionally involved. But I realize that if I want to survive this, I need another rule, such as not noticing how happy she looks when she laughs.

Ten minutes in, I completely fail to follow both of these rules.

"Now, this is an appointment I understand," Carter says, taking a seat beside Everly.

"I've been training my whole life for these appointments," Kenny says, a mini fork at the ready. I'm a little worried he might eat everything before Carter and Everly get a chance to try a bite.

The baker returns to the room with a large serving tray full of sponges in various colors and textures, all arranged on sleek gold plates. Flavor cards are propped up next to each one, and Everly takes it upon herself to read them aloud.

"This one is champagne-vanilla," she announces as everyone reaches for their forks, but Kenny raises his instead.

"A toast!" he exclaims. "To romance and sweet decisions!"

Everly is smiling and laughing more than I've seen her since all this wedding nonsense started. It reminds me of that night at the bar when we were laughing uncontrollably at jokes that other people probably wouldn't have found funny. Because of this, I find myself caught up in the nostalgia of it all.

She leans toward Carter before they sample the champagne-vanilla sponge. She gently tucks a strand of her blonde hair back behind her ear, a gesture I vividly remember from a time when she wore less clothing. We never needed a translator that night. We spoke to each other fluently.

Then again, if that truly was the case, why didn't we realize we both wanted the same thing?

"Just so everyone knows," Kenny says, mouth full of cake, "I take this part of my job very seriously."

"Kenny, you already ate the frosting off the display cake," I say, laughing.

"That, my dear sir, was research," Kenny says, pointing his tasting fork at me.

Everly laughs—loud and completely unguarded. The sound hits harder than expected. So does it when Carter grins back at her, wrapping his arm around her.

"I haven't heard you laugh like this in a long time," he says as I watch her blush. It takes everything I have to tear my eyes away. Screw the cake, I want to taste her…again.

Next, we sample the chocolate espresso. Everyone grabs their forks at once, as if it's some kind of cake-tasting race. Kenny grabs his fork a little aggressively, then defends himself by saying he didn't skip lunch for this experience to be mediocre.

At the same time, Everly and I accidentally reach for the same fork. Our hands collide. Our fingers touch. There's a pregnant pause that lingers too long, as if we're suspended in an emotional void between panic and something dangerously close to hope. Her fingers are warm against mine, yet I freeze at her touch.

Kenny pauses mid-bite. I can feel his eyes fixed on me as if he's watching some reality TV show involving love and cakes.

"Well, isn't this delicious?" he says as we both release the fork simultaneously.

"Sorry," Everly apologizes.

But before I can say anything, Carter chuckles. "This is clearly the most popular flavor so far," he says, handing Everly another fork without a hint of suspicion. He's trusting. And it's clear that Everly isn't the only one in the relationship who sees the good in others.

## Everly

I try to focus on the cake. I really do. But Reese keeps making quiet cake commentary with Kenny, and I can't stop laughing. I had almost forgotten how funny he can be.

"Now, Kenny, what do you think this one tastes like?" Reese faces Kenny, holding his fork like a microphone.

"Well, Reese, thank you for asking. This particular flavor tastes like a motivational speech," he says, speaking into Reese's fork after taking a bite of the vanilla almond sponge. Just as my slice was set in front of me, Reese moved it aside with a wink. Did he remember my allergy? Of course he did. Why else would he move my plate?

Although I'm a bit surprised that Carter takes a bite of his, I always have him brush his teeth if he eats a tree nut before kissing me. It's not foolproof, but it's better than nothing.

"And do you feel motivated?" Reese continues his fake interview.

"Motivated for more cake!" Kenny answers, and I can't stop laughing.

"What does that even mean?" I chime in, trying to play along without making it too obvious. "How could a cake taste motivational?"

"It's like it's really trying hard to be inspiring," Kenny explains with a dramatic tone.

"You two are funny," Carter laughs. "But I have to agree, it's trying too hard. Now, let's hear what you have to say about this lemon one." He holds up his fork to Kenny as we each get plates. It's kind of cute how he's trying to play along, too.

"Well, Carter, it's a bit tart—like someone in this room is trying not to feel anything," Kenny laughs. For a moment, I swear I saw him nudge Reese's shoulder, but I'm not sure. It happened too quickly.

Now the slices of cake are coming out faster than the cake game show Kenny is playing.

"The red velvet is good," I say after taking a bite. "What do you think of the flavor?"

"I think it tastes like it has secrets." Kenny waves his fingers as if he's trying to be mysterious, which makes me laugh even harder.

"What's its secret?" I whisper to him.

"Well, you would never know from its color that it's made from cocoa powder."

"What about you, Reese? What do you think?" Carter asks Reese directly.

"I really don't have an opinion," he says.

"Oh, come on," Carter urges. "You must like one sponge flavor more than the others."

"I guess if I had to pick," he says, his eyes darting to mine. "I would choose the espresso."

I know exactly what he's trying to say without him actually saying it. But I don't give him the satisfaction of knowing.

"And do you, Kenny, have anything to say about that flavor?" Carter asks. It's apparent he's having way more fun at the game than the rest of us.

"It tastes like it could write vows and ruin lives."


## Reese

I don't want to be here any longer. Because I can't just abruptly leave, I sit back and watch everyone debate flavors.

Everly's head tilts back slightly. She wipes the cake crumbs from her fingers. She looks happy, and it's hard not to notice. She has the kind of warmth that draws people in without them realizing it. And I'm like a moth to her flame.

Kenny leans in toward me as Carter feeds Everly a bite of cake. "You're smiling," he says to me. "I didn't know you could do that."

Luckily, the baker interrupts us by bringing out a variety of frostings and fillings to try with the sponges. "I think if you experiment with different flavor combinations, you might find that your sponge preference changes."

Carter takes the champagne-vanilla with a bite of strawberries. It's simple but classic—a very Carter choice. "I like this combination," he says, "but your opinion matters more, Everly. You have a better taste for this than I do." He reaches for her hand. Even with all the cake around us, Carter still tries to be the sweetest thing in the room.

Then, just as the chocolate ganache touches Kenny's tongue, he declares it a winner just before cake chaos erupts.

Forks fly every which way. Plates are tossed back and forth, each loaded with different fillings and frosting combinations; it's like a swinger's party for cakes. Everyone is laughing and having a good time until someone accidentally bumps into the table, leaving a tiny streak of frosting on Everly's cheek. But somehow, she doesn't notice.

But I do.

I notice.

## *Everly*

Just as I'm about to take a bite of cake, Reese's hand reaches toward my face. His thumb brushes gently across my skin, wiping away a bit of frosting I didn't even know was there. Everything in the room stops. I no longer see forks flying or plates of cake being swapped back and forth, nor can I hear the laughter and chatter from everyone around the table. I can't even taste the bite of cake in my mouth. I can easily blame this on a sugar rush because there is no way this is happening. I am one hundred percent sure I'm imagining this.

Yet his hand lingers on my face, letting me know I'm not imagining a single thing. My breath catches in my throat. Heat floods my face. Only then does Reese realize what he's done, and he pulls his hand back instantly. His professional mask snaps back into place. It all happens so quickly that it leaves me with emotional whiplash.

"You had frosting…" he says, trying to justify his actions.

As for me, I say nothing because I'm completely focused on not combusting.

## *Reese*

And of course, Kenny doesn't miss a fucking beat. He watches the entire interaction as if witnessing a moment in history. I turn to him as he slowly lowers his fork.

"What the hell was that?" he whispers to me as Everly and Carter are having a side conversation.

"What are you talking about?" I shrug him off, a little worried that Carter might have seen what happened, too.

"You're lying about something. I can smell it—and it's not the cake," he says.

"You're crazy." I roll my eyes once he and I are alone at the tasting table. Everly and Carter are off discussing something with the baker.

"Listen, here bucko—"

"Bucko?"

"I have seen enough romance movies that start exactly like this." Kenny tilts his head at me, making me fear it might roll off his shoulders and land in a bowl of frosting. "So, for someone who claims to be emotionally gluten-free, you sure seem to be taking a lot of bites."

"You've obviously eaten way too much cake. You're delirious." I brush him off.

"And do you think your sister has ever had one of her staff wipe frosting off a bride or groom's face before? Maybe I should call her and check?" He reaches for his phone, which I swat away. It lands in a bowl of raspberry filling. Kenny picks it up and practically licks it clean.

"I should be mad about this, but it tastes good," he says.

I hate myself right now. *Why the hell did I touch her?* I shouldn't have touched her! I had two simple rules. Two simple boundaries. And now look at me. My neutral, Switzerland-like wedding plan has collapsed like an underbaked cake.

Eventually, Carter and Everly make their way back to the table. "You're a mess today," Carter says, noticing a little more frosting on Everly's face. "Hazards of cake tasting. Am I right?" He smiles as he addresses the table. He seems unaware of the moment I had with Everly. Thank the cake gods for that.

## Everly

Outside the patisserie, Carter drapes his arm around my shoulders. "That was really fun," he says.

"It was," I agree as he kisses my temple. I close my eyes to his touch and am reminded again of why Carter is such a good man. He is warm, safe, and truly cares about me.

"Everly, are we still on tonight for your next vow session?" Reese asks as he follows Kenny out onto the sidewalk.

"And don't forget we need to start the bridal party draft. Let's plan for early next week," Kenny adds.

"Sounds good," I say to both of them just as I catch Kenny whispering to Reese before they climb into their company's SUV.


## Reese

"Well," Kenny leans over the passenger seat toward me. "How about you just tell me the truth? Friends don't keep secrets from each other. We are not red velvet."

"What's there to tell?" I huff.

"There's obviously more to your past with Everly than what you've been letting on," he says.

"There is nothing going on between us. There is nothing more to our 'past.' And there is nothing to say about it," I say.

Kenny shakes his head, knowing I'm lying. "Reese? Can I call you, Reese?"

"What?" I groan.

"As your friend…

"We are not friends," I say.

"I'm going to ignore that comment, but as your friend, you're doomed."

But this time, I don't argue with him. I just stare into the rearview mirror, watching Everly laugh with Carter in the sunlight, and realize that happiness sometimes looks exactly like something you can't have.

So, no, I'm not doomed.

I'm fucked.

/ Chapter Twenty
The Truth Between the Lines

Reese

Everly chooses the spot for our session this time. It's a small indie bookstore I've visited many times. I used to walk into bookstores, imagining what it would feel like to see my book on the shelves.

She arrived before I did. From the window, I see her running her hand along the book spines. The doorbell chimes as I enter. She looks up as I walk in.

"You're early," I say.

"I thought I'd do a little shopping beforehand." She smiles, pointing to a small pile of books in a basket on the floor.

"What made you choose this place for our session?" I ask as we walk to the back of the store, where there are tables and chairs and a small café serving coffee and pastries. Before she can answer, I head to the counter and order two espressos for us.

"It feels like home," she says as soon as I sit down with our drinks. "Anywhere you can be surrounded by books is the best place to be. Not to mention, I love seeing the books by authors I helped get published. It's like visiting old friends."

"I heard you were a literary agent," I say.

"I am," she responds, very matter-of-factly. "I represent contemporary romance, romcoms, well, pretty much anything in the romance realm that catches my attention." She takes a small sip of her espresso. "It's funny because I never would have guessed in a million years that when you told me you were a writer, you wrote vows for a living. I had you pegged as a novelist."

"Common misconception," I say.

"Have you ever thought about writing something beyond vows, like a novel?" She looks at me as if I'm the one being interviewed. But there's nothing for me to say. I don't need to explain myself to her. My life and career don't matter.

"How about we focus on your vows?" I change the subject. "Tell me about your proposal."

### Everly

I tell Reese about the restaurant, the décor, and how everyone was dressed as if it were a black-tie event, and how everything on the menu was written in French.

"How did you manage to order?" he asks, trying hard not to laugh. "I wouldn't know what to order besides—"

"French toast and french fries," we say simultaneously.

"Exactly!" I say before telling him about the wayward roll.

"You seriously cared that much about dropping a roll?" he laughs.

"You have no idea how embarrassed I felt! I felt so out of place there. I'm more comfortable at a—"

"Longhorn Steakhouse?" he smirks that crooked smile of his.

"Pretty much," I chuckle.

"If it makes you feel any better, same," he says to me. "Although I wish they would cut the bread before bringing it out. I always end up squishing it."

I nod. Part of me wants to tell him I do the same exact thing, but it seems we've already expressed that sentiment too many times. The last thing I want is for this to feel like a bonding moment. Or worse, a date.

"Did you know prior to him proposing that you wanted to marry Carter?" he asks as if eager to get straight to the point.

I stare down into my espresso mug as images of Carter's proposal flash through my mind, like the way he held my hand and looked deeply into my eyes. But I also remember how he missed our first date and how I spent the evening at The Last Chapter, sitting right across from the man I am with now.

It's funny how much time can change things. I was so determined to find Reese again, but I never could. He was a mystery that defied solution, no matter how hard I tried. But once I stopped looking, he reappeared in the one place I least expected. He's like my apartment keys.

I blink hard, trying to focus on Reese's question, but it's difficult. I honestly don't know when I realized I wanted to marry him. To be honest, I still don't know—and that scares me. The only thing I do know is that I love him.

Reese leans back slightly. "How about we revisit that? What does Carter do that makes you feel like the luckiest person on earth?"

I laugh at this. "That's a very specific question."

"It's all for the vows," he says.

"For starters, he listens to me," I explain. "I never feel like he forgets how I feel in any given moment."

"Hmm," Reese says, flipping to a fresh page in his notebook. "Let's try this from a different angle."

"OK?" I say, crossing my arms.

"What does loving him feel like?" he asks, locking eyes with mine.

I freeze because no one has ever asked me that before. I want to answer Reese. I really do, but the words feel slippery, as if hard to hold onto. "It feels…" I start. "It feels right."

Reese, however, doesn't write anything down.

## *Reese*

This isn't my relationship. But if I were in her shoes, I would clearly see that there are a lot of safe words being used—and not the good kind. Still, it's not my place or my business to share my opinions. I'm neutral, remember?

Against my better judgment, I can't keep the next question from slipping out of my mouth. "Everly?" She looks across the table at me again. "What does it feel like when you are happiest with him?"

The silence stretches so long it hurts. *Why is it so hard for her to answer me?*

"When he meets me halfway," she finally says. As before, I'm having a hard time writing down her answers. They are, if nothing else, incomplete. There is so much she is not saying. The words are hidden between the lines, in her true feelings. I want to decipher them, but I fear what would happen if I do.

"You don't like my answers." She leans back in her seat.

"I never said that," I say.

"You don't have to. I can tell by the way you're not writing anything down," she points out.

I sigh. "I'm taking it all in," I lie.

"And exactly what have you been taking in?" Her tone turns accusatory.

I study her carefully. I also need to choose my words carefully because the last thing I want to do is offend her. Nor do I want Genny yelling at me for Everly running out of another meeting.

"Just be honest, Reese. Is it really that hard?" Her eyes shoot daggers in my direction.

*Shouldn't I be telling her that?*

*Whatever. Fine. If she wants the truth, then she'd better be able to handle it.*

"It seems like you're trying to tell me that you chose the safe option," I say.

She flinches at my words. Apparently, I wasn't too careful, but then again, she asked for it.

"That's not fair of you to say."

"You're right," I soften. "I'm sorry."

She exhales. "Carter is the kind of man people build lives with. He is dependable. He shows up. He never left, even after I told him I didn't want anything serious. He has never stopped trying."

And there it is. The truth is stacked high between us like the mountain of books she bought. However, I know she was selective with her answer because it was not meant for Carter. It was meant for me.

"So, that makes him the kind of man you promise the rest of your life to?" I ask, refusing to acknowledge how much her words affected me.

## Everly

"Tell me again why you're marrying Carter," Reese asks me as if he refuses to let go of the question.

"You've already asked me this," I say, annoyed.

"I did. But you didn't give me much of an answer," he replies.

"He's good to me," I say. "He shows up. Is that enough for you?"

"Is it enough for *you*?"

"What is that supposed to mean?" I ask.

"It almost sounds like you're trying to convince me," he says with a chuckle. "Or yourself."

"How dare you say that to me?" I snap.

Then he says calmly, "Answer the question again, without convincing yourself or me."

My chest rises and falls. "I'm marrying Carter for those reasons. They aren't going to change, so you might as well write them down."

"No." Reese shakes his head. "Because that's not a vow. They aren't even real reasons."

My breathing intensifies. What the hell is going on here? This meeting was supposed to be about my vows to Carter, but for some reason, it's starting to feel like something else. I don't like it one bit.

I gather my bag of books. "I think it's best that we finish the vows another time."

"If that's what you want," Reese says without emotion—not a single shred of guilt for making me upset.

As I start to leave, something makes me turn back. "For what it's worth," I say to Reese, "I love Carter, and that's reason enough."

Monday arrives, and I'm back at work. I've reviewed fifteen queries since the start of the day, but nothing has caught my attention. I'm searching for something I can't quite describe. Morgan stops by my office as I read a few of them aloud.

"I don't understand. That one sounded good!" she says. She's not wrong; it does sound good, but it's not what I'm looking for. I wonder if it's because I'm not in the mood for the usual tropes. Maybe I need a good palate cleanser—something most publishers would deem "hard to market" because they don't know where to place a book on a store's shelves. However, those books are often the most magical. They possess qualities readers have never encountered before. So my stance has always been that if there is no space for these books, create the damn space.

"We should probably get going. The meeting starts in less than an hour," she says, glancing at her watch.

I can't explain how relieved I am that Morgan will be joining me for this wedding-planning meeting—especially after the way I left things with Reese. I needed someone other than Carter to serve as a buffer.

When we arrive, the conference room at Laurent & Co. looks less like a wedding-planning meeting and more like the start of game night. Kenny has already commandeered the whiteboard and written across the top:

### *The Official Wedding Party Draft*

I pause in the doorway beside Morgan. "What in the world?"

Kenny turns proudly at the sound of my voice. "Welcome to the draft party!"

Morgan breezes into the room, dropping her bag on the table. "This is already looking a lot more fun than the first meeting I attended."

Carter arrives shortly after, apologizing that his meeting ran a bit long. "You made a draft board, Kenny?"

"Of course, I did," he replies. "Every major life decision should involve charts. I once made one when I wanted to change fabric softeners."

Is it sad that I never wanted a huge wedding party? I never wanted a bridal party or even a bachelorette party. I love intimate gatherings. I hate it when the attention is all on me because I never know what to do with it. I feel responsible for how everyone feels and for their sense of fun and enjoyment. I'd rather have small events where I can easily enjoy the people I'm with, not make rounds just to say hello, thank you, and goodbye.

"Morgan, you are currently the number one draft pick for maid of honor," Kenny cheers. "Congratulations."

"Was there even a competition?" Morgan smirks.

"And for the best man, we have your brother Daniel. Is that correct, Carter?" Kenny asks as Carter straightens his posture.

"He is. Unfortunately, he lives out West and can't attend all the festivities, but he will definitely be here for the big day," Carter says.

"Perfect!" Kenny claps, then pretends to use an invisible lasso. "I love a good cowboy!"

## Reese

"I would also like my college roommate, Tyler, to be in the wedding party, along with my business partner, Marcus," Carter says when I enter the room. "And if we go bigger, I have quite a few colleagues and friends I'd like to include."

"And for you, Everly?" Kenny asks as I sit at the far end of the table—the farthest I can get from Everly and all this wedding shit. "There should be an even split among the parties."

"Honestly, I just considered having a maid of honor," she says as Morgan bows to her.

"It will be an honor to serve you," Morgan teases. As much as Morgan is a spitfire, I like how she and Everly balance each other. It's clear they have a good relationship.

"I guess I could add my cousin Karrie. She lives in the city, so it won't be too hard for her to participate," Everly says, as if weighing her options for a real sports team. "And my friend Jenny from back home."

Kenny writes their names on the whiteboard with an unnecessary flourish.

I decide not to say much. Or maybe it's best I not say anything at all. I've learned that the more time I spend in a room with Everly, the more I find myself saying things I shouldn't. The last thing I want is to put myself in that position again. I don't trust myself.

Interrupting my thoughts, Kenny suddenly taps the whiteboard. "Only one more question remains," he says. "What is your stance on having a bridesman?" He grins so wide it almost looks creepy.

Everly laughs. "*You* want to stand with my bridesmaids?"

"At no extra charge, if you need a fill-in, I'm your guy. I bring emotional support and impeccable style." He turns around to give us a 360-degree view of his outfit.

Morgan claps. "I approve."

"Don't encourage him," I say before I can stop myself. "He's only in it for the cake."

Kenny shrugs.

"Hang on. I forgot," Morgan pipes up. "Do I have to give a speech?"

"Right now?" asks Kenny.

"No, Mr. Bridesman, at the wedding," Morgan says.

"Well, of course you do," he answers. "Traditionally speaking."

Morgan groans. "This sucks. No offense, Everly."

"I can help with that," I offer to Morgan, who raises a suspicious eyebrow at me.

"You write bridesmaid speeches now, too?" she asks, still peering at me.

"I've done it before. Besides, I write vows for a living; it's not a huge leap," I say.

"OK," she says, hesitating as if considering my offer. "I may take you up on that," she says just as Lila enters the room with a fresh carafe of coffee. She fills my cup without me asking.


## Everly

I'm staying at Carter's tonight. It's been a while since I've stayed over because of his busy work schedule, so I'm excited to have dinner and enjoy a relaxed evening. He's not home when I walk in. My footsteps echo through the large space, which is very different from my apartment, where the floorboards creak under my feet.

His apartment is spotless. Not a single item is out of place. There are no dishes in the sink, and there's no mess to suggest someone has been working long hours and can't keep up with their chores. Even his laundry baskets are empty. It must be nice to send laundry out to be washed. I have to carry a basket down the street and wait until it's done. I refuse to make the same mistake again by leaving the laundromat mid-cycle. It's not fun to return to find someone has stolen all your linens.

My phone lights up with a message from Carter saying he is on his way. So I order us some takeout, pour a couple of glasses of wine, and wait.

I stand in front of his floor-to-ceiling windows, wine glass in hand, listening to the city's soft hum far below, barely noticing when Carter walks through the door.

"You're staring out the window like you're critiquing the skyline," he teases, setting his briefcase by the door.

I smile. "Just thinking."

"About work?" he asks as he approaches me, hugging me gently from behind.

"No, about everything. There seems to be so much going on all at once," I say.

He kisses the top of my head, calming the swirling thoughts inside. It's been a while since we've had a nice night in. Between his schedule and the endless wedding-planning meetings, we've mostly been two ships passing in the night. I just feel like I haven't docked yet.

As we make our way to his living room couch, he loosens his tie and signals for me to sit closer. He pulls me into his arms and kisses me gently. It feels practiced yet sincere. I melt into it as his hand rests at the small of my back, grounding me. This is where I feel safe, and I know what loving Carter truly feels like. It feels like this.

He presses his lips to mine and says, "I've missed you."

"You saw me at the meeting earlier," I say, chuckling at how cute he is.

"Yes." He kisses me again. "But not like this."

Later that night, the city lights glow through his bedroom windows as we lie tangled in his Egyptian cotton sheets. Carter traces circles along my bare arm.

"You're quiet," he says.

"I'm just tired."

"I know. This wedding planning has been tough and time-consuming, and I feel like you've been carrying most of the load. For that, I'm sorry," he says.

"You've been helping." I turn toward him.

"Yes, but at times I feel like I could be helping more." He kisses me on the forehead.

This moment with Carter feels right. It's the kind of scene I love in romance novels. It's sweet and intimate. But it's also expected. Sometimes, I want to be surprised, though. I want a little spontaneity that makes me wonder what will happen next. Yes, it's comforting to know, but there's something about not knowing that keeps the flame ignited.

My mind shifts to a different night when I didn't know what to expect from one moment to the next. Music drifts through a busy bar, and I'm sitting across from a stranger with an irresistible smile.

That night felt chaotic. It was unpredictable yet electric. The kind of scene in romance novels that makes you flip through pages faster than your eyes can read. But it was also reckless.

And I loved every second of it.

I come to as Carter brushes a strand of hair from my face. "Did I lose you?" he asks, looking deep into my eyes, but I have no idea what he means. "You know, if there is something else going on, you can tell me anything," he continues.

"I know," I say, guilt rising like bile in my throat. I kiss him softly, letting him know that everything is OK, because it is.

"You're going to be a beautiful bride." He pulls me closer.

"You're biased," I tease.

"Guilty as charged," he laughs. "But I'm also right."

I rest my head on his bare chest, feeling the steady rhythm of his heartbeat until I drift off to sleep.


## *Reese*

Since the first vow meeting, I haven't written much at all. I plan to spend some time this evening working on things, but I can't seem to put anything into words. My laptop screen glows in the dim light of my apartment. A half-finished glass of whiskey sits beside me. The only sounds, besides the city's white noise, are the slow taps of my keys.

Type.

Delete.

Type.

Delete.

My cursor blinks at me as if judging whether I can stay neutral. I lean back in my chair and run a hand through my hair. "Fuck," I mutter. I thought I was supposed to be good at this. People tell me their stories, and I shape them into promises. It's that simple.

But this has been anything but simple.

Talking with Carter, it's like he knew he loved Everly from the moment she walked into his life. And he has fought to stay in it, no matter how hard she resisted.

As I'm about to try to formulate another sentence, a knock rattles at my apartment door. I don't normally have uninvited visitors, so I can't imagine who it could be.

I open the door and find Kenny standing there with a bag of takeout. "I thought I'd stop by and cheer you up," he says with that goofy smile of his.

"How do you know where I live?" I ask.

"I asked your sister. Told her it was related to wedding planning."

"I will be chatting with her tomorrow. And who says I need cheering up?" I lean against the doorway, blocking him from coming in.

"Lately, you've looked like a man on the verge of an emotional breakdown. So I figured I'd do anything a friend would—"

"We are not fr—" I try to interject, but he immediately hushes me.

"I brought emotional-support dumplings," he says, moving me out of the way as she enters my apartment.

"You're overreacting," I say.

"And you're in love with the bride," he says, peering at me.

"What?" I say flatly, but I don't have any words to counter him.

"This isn't my first rodeo—or wedding," he says, setting the bags on the counter. "But relax, friends don't judge."

"We are not fr—"

"Quit kidding yourself, Reese. We are friends."

# Chapter Twenty-One
## Double, Double, Tulle & Trouble



I wait patiently outside the bridal boutique, Ivory & Veil, for my mom's taxi to arrive. She surprised me by not only coming into town for my dress shopping but also by planning to stay with me the entire week.

When the cab kisses the curb, and my mom gets out, I run to her.

"My baby is getting married!" She squeezes me, and I squeeze her back.

The bridal boutique that Kenny chose operates by appointment only, just like the bakery. Once we are all let inside by someone who looks like a boutique bouncer, the scent of roses and fine fabric energizes my senses. I am quickly guided to the middle of the showroom, where I am surrounded by racks upon racks of gowns in various colors, styles, textures, and lengths.

My mother, Morgan, and Mrs. Jacobs sit on a large cream-colored sofa as a young girl in a blush-pink cocktail dress serves us champagne.

"Isn't this wonderful?" My mother takes the glass in her hand. "I can't remember the last time I had champagne."

Mrs. Jacobs turns to my mother. "It's a very sophisticated drink," she says. "And by the way, I'm Carter's mom. I wasn't sure if anyone was going to introduce us." She glances at me, which I know is a dig.

"Annie." My mother returns the sentiment as Morgan sprawls across the sofa, sipping complimentary champagne. If someone showed up with a box of donuts, Morgan would be in heaven.

Kenny, who practically begged me to attend this appointment, brings along Genevieve's receptionist, Lila, who used to work in the fashion industry. She's the same girl I saw at the last meeting, paying a little too much attention to Reese. Not that I care. I just noticed. That's all.

Kenny and I start walking through the showroom as he helps me examine the options like a seasoned hunter. "I want you to relax." He rests his hands on my shoulders. "If the dress isn't an instant yes, it's an instant no, OK?"

"OK," I nod. "I'm really glad you're here."

"Sweetie, that's what a bridesman is for," he winks. "And besides, as I told you on the phone, Lila has an eye for fashion. You're in excellent hands."

Not long after, the three of us gathered a good selection of dresses for me to try on. I head into the dressing room, which looks like a glamorous hotel suite. It has a chandelier, a couch, and refreshments that seem to be more for show than for actual consumption while trying on gowns. Soon, I'm greeted by a few dress consultants who are ready to button and tie me into the first dress.

I step out of the fitting room and am led onto a small platform surrounded by mirrors and the best lighting I've ever seen. The couch where my mom, Morgan, and Carter's mom wait sits directly in front of me, as if I'm on stage and they are my audience.

The dress I am wearing is too fluffy for my taste. Fluffy may not be the right word, but I feel like one of those 90s Barbie dolls—and not in a good way.

Morgan bursts out laughing. "You look like a wedding cake," she snickers, which noticeably offends one of the consultants, who ends up defending the dress, noting that only a few were made by an exclusive designer.

Kenny nods in agreement. "I have to agree with Morgan, and it's sad, because you know how much I like cake. Who picked this dress out?" He charges toward the dressing room only to be escorted back into the viewing area.

Looking down from the podium, I can tell by the look on Mrs. Jacobs' face that she is the guilty party. Yet she doesn't admit to picking out the dress. She keeps sipping her champagne, ready to judge someone else's choice but not her own.

Six dresses later, I try on one made of creamy silk, but it's rather uncomfortable to move in. I'm afraid that if I turn too quickly, it will tear at the seams. "Nope." I shake my head as one of the consultants helps me off the platform.

"Remember," Kenny says from the couch, "if something isn't an instant yes, it's an instant no." His tone makes me wonder whether I should apply that sentiment to more than just dresses.

## Reese

I'm back at the office at my sister's insistence. Apparently, she's caught up in two weddings this weekend and feels a little overwhelmed trying to ensure everything goes smoothly. She is usually someone who works well under pressure, but by the looks of her, she seems defeated.

I walk into her office and see her resting her head on her desk. "Genny? Are you OK?" I ask.

"I'm just exhausted. I'd give anything for a nap," she groans.

"Then why don't you go home and take one?" I offer, as if I'm the boss of her. But I've learned over the years working here that the week of any client's wedding is all hands on deck. She wouldn't have time for a nap, even if she wanted one.

"I need you to do me a favor. I know today is technically your day off, but I need you to go to the Hart appointment at Ivory & Veil."

"The bridal boutique?" I ask her as she lifts her head from her desk. A Post-it is stuck to her cheek, which she quickly peels off.

"Yes. I couldn't catch Kenny before he ran off to attend," she says, yawning.

"Kenny went?" I ask.

"You know, Kenny. You would think he's the one getting married." She smiles. "Anyway, Mr. Jacobs' mother has been planning a surprise engagement party for the couple this Friday, and I need her to sign off on the final invoice. Please let her know that the guest list has been contacted and that she only owes the amount charged to her open bar tab."

"Where's the party?" I ask.

"The Olive Branch in Manhattan. It's a very posh five-star establishment that's even harder to book than we are," she laughs, as if the level of exclusivity among businesses is now an unspoken competition. "But we made it happen."

"So, what do you need me for?" I ask as she shuffles through a stack of paperwork on her desk, then hands me a large envelope containing Mrs. Jacobs' invoice.

"I need you to go down to the boutique and have Mrs. Jacobs sign this. I also need you to remind her that she needs to finalize her plans for the bridal shower as well."

"Anything else?"

"That's it. I already informed the staff at Ivory & Veil, so they will be expecting you when you ring the doorbell," she says.

"I have to ring a doorbell?" I laugh. "What is this, some speakeasy bridal boutique? Do I need to whisper a password to them as well?"

"Yes, the password is 'sign this invoice.' Now, please go." She shoos me out of her office.


## Everly

I'm now on the eighth dress after taking a break, which still isn't the one. Who knew this would be so exhausting? During the break, Morgan helped me pick out the bridesmaid dresses. I snapped a few pictures to send to them for input. Finally, we unanimously chose a soft pink that complements gold jewelry. Morgan is very pleased with the choice because she didn't want a dress with too much tulle or lace. This dress is the perfect balance.

Once I resume my dress shopping, I am hoping the ninth is the one. The dress is a white lace mermaid gown with a plunging neckline that's still modest. Beneath the lace is a champagne-colored slip. The dress hugs my curves as if it were made for me. The dress consultant even ties a jeweled belt around my waist, completing the look.

The dress is simple yet elegant. It moves with me, and I have honestly never felt more beautiful.

My mom gasps the moment I step onto the podium. "Oh, honey, it's beautiful!" she exclaims, wiping away a tear.

Morgan, Kenny, and Lila begin clapping and yelling various things to let me know this dress is the one.

I turn toward the mirrors and, for the first time since getting engaged, see myself as a bride. I finally feel excited about this wedding—about my future.

Just as I'm about to announce that this dress is the one, Reese walks into the viewing room.

## Reese

I feel like an intruder. I really shouldn't be here. I hope I can get Mrs. Jacobs to sign this invoice so I can leave as quickly as possible. Even though I knew what kind of boutique this is, I never considered what I might actually walk into.

I stop dead.

I don't think my heart is beating anymore, and I'm almost sure my lungs have stopped working too. From ten feet away, Everly is standing in a wedding dress.

I can't move. I just stare. Seeing her like this confirms that this wedding is really happening.

It's real. Painfully real.

She turns around slowly. Our eyes meet.

A consultant, blissfully unaware of the emotional chaos brewing inside me, smiles brightly. "I hope you're not the groom!" she says to me just as I notice Everly's lips part to correct her, but no words come out.

"You should know it's bad luck to see the bride in her dress before the wedding!" the consultant continues as Kenny steps forward.

"Don't worry, Angela. He's not the groom," he says a little too loudly, as if to make a point.

*I got it, Kenny.*

"Oh, thank goodness!" sighs the consultant, Angela, with relief.

I nervously run a hand through my hair as I quickly pass Kenny, then head over to Mrs. Jacobs.

"Genevieve asked me to come down so you could sign this," I say to her.

"Oh! Of course." She sets her glass of champagne down and reaches into her bag for a pen, even though I have one already extended to her.

Out of the corner of my eye, I watch Everly as she stares at herself in the mirrors while the room suddenly empties.

"I appreciate you bringing this down," Mrs. Jacobs says as she finishes signing the invoice. "Oh! And you caught me just in time. Looks like I'm running late for my next appointment. Everly, dear," she calls over to her. "You look wonderful,' she says with the same enthusiasm one would have for a colonoscopy, and then leaves the room.

Now it's just Everly and me. Do I need to say something? Professionally speaking, shouldn't I say something nice? Compliment the dress?

"You look…" is all I can say before I stop myself. No words feel safe.

*Fuck it. I'm not safe.*

When she moves, the fabric of her dress brushes the floor. I'm trying hard not to stare, but I can't help it. She looks like she belongs in that dress. And that dress belongs on my floor.

"Terrible? Not the one?" She turns to face the mirror again, as if to confirm the dress isn't as spectacular as she thought. But she knows she looks stunning. How could she not? Yet something in her eyes suggests uncertainty. The only question is what she's uncertain about.

"No." I shake my head. "You look like someone I could ruin my life for."


## Everly

*Did he just say what I thought he said?*

For a moment, neither of us moves. Neither of us says a word. He looks at me the way he's never looked before—like he's trying on something, too. But instead of a dress, it's his feelings. Something about this whole exchange doesn't sit right. It almost taints the dress I'm wearing. Am I worried no one else will look at me the way Reese is looking at me now? And by no one, I mean Carter.

"I have to go. Enjoy the rest of your appointment," he says as everyone funnels back into the room. As for Lila, she heads straight over to Reese.

"Are you heading back to the office?" she asks him.

"Yes." He nods.

"Perfect." She smiles. "I will head back with you." She walks to the couch and grabs her purse.

My eyes may be playing tricks on me, but I think I saw her reach for his arm.

## Reese

Back at the office, Kenny confines me to one of the consultation rooms. I am essentially being held against my will.

"What the hell was that?" he asks the moment the door shuts.

"What is it now, Kenny?" I roll my eyes.

"Just stop it, Reese. You literally walked into the showroom and stopped breathing," he says to me. "You look like someone who—" He stops, taking a step back as if to create space between us, or maybe even between his words.

"I looked like someone who, what?" I ask.

"Who saw their future," he answers softly, but I still hear him loud and clear.

I stare down at my feet, unable to meet his gaze. "Well, we both know that that future doesn't include me."

"How about you try being honest with me about everything for once?" Kenny asks as he pours us a couple of glasses from an unopened bottle of red blend on the table. I'm not much of a wine drinker, but anything that takes the edge off right now is fine with me.

"So, spill the tea." He sits down at the table.

"Kenny, there is nothing to spill. How many times do I have to tell you this?" I take a large sip of wine.

"Then explain why you left the bridal boutique like someone pulled the fire alarm?" His eyes narrow.

I rub my jaw. "It was a long day. I had things to do."

"Wrong. Try again."

Looking at Kenny, I realize I truly have no one else to confide in about any of this. At least among my friends, Kenny would be the only one who could understand it better. Most of my friends are still happy living the single life, so I doubt anyone would get where I'm coming from. So, against my will, I tell him. But I make him promise first that he won't say a word.

"So, let me get this straight." He sets down his glass. "You have been pining for this woman for over a year, and the next time you run into her is when she comes in to plan her wedding?"

"That's correct. Please don't say anything. She is happy, and the last thing I want to do is ruin that," I say.

Kenny raises an eyebrow. "*Is* she?"

"What do you mean?"

"As I said before, she acts differently when she's around you…"

"Yeah, she acts differently around you, too." I cross my arms. "That doesn't mean anything."

"Reese, don't you watch movies or read books? It means *everything.*"

# Chapter Twenty-Two
## Champagne Problems
## & Kool-Aid Dreams

### Everly

Carter's parents live out in the Hamptons. It's a huge house run by a small staff. It's downright intimidating to be greeted at the door by someone who doesn't live there. Even my mom, who is as simple as I am, finds it a bit strange to pay someone to do something as basic as opening a door.

The first time Carter brought me here, I felt out of my league. I was underdressed for what I was told was a casual family dinner. However, I quickly learned that nothing Mrs. Jacobs does is casual. She looked like she was heading to an upscale night out, while I was in jeans and a blouse. I was upset with Carter for not telling me to change. But he kept assuring me that I looked fine. Either way, he never made me feel out of place, even with his opinionated mother, whom I have also learned to take in stride.

We are led into the dining room, which looks like something straight out of a magazine. Candles flicker along the table, their flames dancing off the crystal glasses strategically placed at each place setting, while perfectly folded (and monogrammed) linen napkins rest on each plate.

My mom and I look around the room as if we're gazing at the eighth wonder of the world, holding our breath, afraid that if we breathe too hard, everything might shatter.

"Well," my mom says brightly, "this is fancy. I'm almost afraid to touch anything."

Carter enters the room holding a couple of glasses of white wine. "My mother has strong opinions about table settings, but I promise," he says with a chuckle, "nothing in this house is considered a museum artifact."

"Presentation matters," Mrs. Jacobs says as she enters the room.

My mom leans toward me and whispers, "My presentation usually involves pizza boxes."

I laugh. To be honest, I think I would prefer a pizza night to a three-course meal prepared by the Jacobs' full-time chef.

"Thank you for having us," my mother says, kissing Carter on the cheek. "I hope we are not too late. Everly was showing me around the city."

"You are not late at all. I'm happy you two had some quality time together today," he says with a smile.

As we take our seats at the table, it's funny to see how different Carter's mom is from mine. While Mrs. Jacobs sits perfectly upright with pearls resting neatly on her collarbone, my mom wears jeans and enthusiastically butters her bread.

"So," my mom says, playfully pointing her butter knife at Carter, "how did my daughter convince you to marry her?"

Carter laughs. "Well, she didn't have to try very hard."

"Good answer." My mom nudges me on the shoulder. "I like him."

Mrs. Jacobs clears her throat. "Good dinnerware should be appreciated," she says, as if my mom's knife display were beneath its rightful purpose.

"Well, my dinnerware is usually paper plates," my mom teases as Carter's dad walks into the room.

I've always liked Carter's dad. He's always been kinder and warmer to me than his wife could ever be.

"Now, I like her," Mr. Jacobs says, pointing his butter knife at my mom. "She's honest and not afraid to be herself."

His comment brings a smile to my mother's face while an audible sigh escapes his wife's mouth.

"I was happy to hear that you'll be staying with Everly all week," Carter says to my mom.

My mom beams. "I wish I could come here more often. I'm just sad Everly's father couldn't be here, too," she says, a tear sliding down her cheek. I immediately reach for her hand.

"We are sorry for your loss," Mr. Jacobs says as the first course is being served.

"It's been four years, but it feels like only yesterday," my mom says, blotting her cheeks with her napkin.

I try to hold back as well, but they come just the same. I don't talk about my dad much because I haven't reached the point where talking about him isn't so painful. I instantly become a sobbing mess whenever I do. He was the one who made me fall in love with reading. When I got my job at the literary agency, making peanuts as an intern, he told me I still hit the jackpot. *"Any career where you get to be surrounded by books makes you rich."*

"Well," Mrs. Jacobs sets down her glass. "I was also hoping to share another surprise with you both tonight," she says, as if the moment about my father was interrupting her dinner agenda.

I blink. *Dear God, I hope she isn't planning to come on our honeymoon.*

"Another surprise? You and Dad have already done so much," Carter says.

Mrs. Jacobs smiles, pausing for effect. "I secretly planned your engagement party," she says as the room falls silent. "I know we should have had it right after the proposal, but I figured that if I didn't plan it, it probably wouldn't happen."

"You planned an engagement party for us?" Carter asks, clearly surprised, as I am.

"I did. And it's this Friday night," she replies as I chug the rest of my glass of wine.

*Why does it feel like she's hijacking this wedding? Can't she find a damn hobby instead?*

Already, I am starting to feel the effects of too much alcohol today, from the champagne at Ivory & Veil to the wine now, all on an empty stomach.

"A proper celebration seemed appropriate," Mrs. Jacobs continues as my mom claps her hands.

"That is so thoughtful of you, Margaret," she says as I pour another glass of wine. Mrs. Jacobs then shares that it will be at The Olive Branch in Manhattan.

"That place is impossible to book," I say.

"Yes," Mrs. Jacobs says. "It was. I also took the liberty of planning your shower, since it appears you haven't planned it either." She looks at me.

"My shower?"

"Certainly, dear. What did you think your registry was for?" She shakes her head as if I'm too clueless for words. "So, we will have brunch here the morning after the engagement party."

"Well, that was very thoughtful of you both," Carter says, smoothing out the small ripple of tension spreading across the dinner table, which I'm pretty sure is only coming from me. But how could it not? I'm starting to get concerned about how much Carter's mom likes to involve herself in her son's life and how much she plans to do so after we're married. She has already taken significant control of the wedding. And while I appreciate everything she has done—like booking us with Laurent & Co.—it doesn't give her the authority to make all the decisions. The day is for Carter and me, not her.

"To the happy couple!" Mr. Jacobs raises his glass, and everyone follows suit. However, it takes me a moment to remember what I'm toasting to.

"So, how did dress shopping go today? Did you find the one?" Carter asks when the main course arrives. By then, the conversation has thawed, though I'm still exuding ice.

"It was…an experience," I begin.

"She looked stunning," my mom adds.

"I never doubted that." Carter smiles, causing my cheeks to warm slightly.

Dinner soon comes to an end, and I step out onto the back deck for some fresh air while Carter gives my mom a quick house tour. I rest my hands on the railing, gazing out into the bay. Behind me, the door slides open, and Carter's dad steps out with a couple of glasses of wine.

"I thought you might like a refill," he says.

"You read minds now?" I chuckle before thanking him.

"After forty years of marriage, you learn a thing or two." He hands me a glass as we stand side by side, looking out over the bay. "My wife, as you know, loves to be in control," he says, breaking the silence.

I laugh. "You don't say?"

"She always has. Ever since I met her, she has been structured, organized, and strategic in everything she does. She can run circles around me." He smiles.

I nod, taking a sip of wine.

"But we are different people," he continues. "Where she likes to plan everything and is usually two steps ahead of me, I spend most of my time improvising as I go."

"That sounds familiar."

"Does it?" he chuckles. "But that's also the point. If I can tell you one thing about marriage, it's that sometimes you need to marry your opposite, and sometimes you don't. It all depends on how the pieces fit."

I stare out into the bay, processing his words. Thinking. Unaware that my face is giving away how much his words resonated with me more than he realized.

"Marriage is interesting," he says quietly. "You don't just choose the person, you also choose the life they bring with them, too."

"I know this," I say.

"Carter is my son, and I have raised him to be a fine man. He will always give you stability." He smiles. "But I ask only that you make sure the pieces fit."

I freeze for a second, wondering what he's getting at and where this is all coming from.

"I do love your son," I say.

"I know you do, kid."

"So, why are you telling me this?"

"No reason." He winks.

But I know there is a reason. There is always a reason.


## Reese

I'm bringing my laptop to the office because I need to start putting together the beginning of Carter's vows and now his engagement toast. He messaged me about an hour ago, asking if I could quickly get something ready for Friday's party.

The office is quiet, but it's a restless quiet that settles in your mind and keeps replaying the moments you'd rather forget—like Everly in her wedding dress.

*God, she looked so beautiful.*

I've always thought she was beautiful since the moment I spotted her reading at the bar. But seeing her this way felt like looking at something behind glass, something you can only admire from afar, never touch.

And I'm so mad at myself for what I said to her. I know she heard me. How could she not?

I rub my hand over my face because I can barely stomach writing their vows, and now I have to write a last-minute toast he requested.

I'm toast.

My cursor blinks on an empty document as my memory flashes with the lacey fabric that draped her body. That familiar hunger I felt for her that first night begins coursing through my veins again. But this time, I have no release.

I instantly remember how my tongue searched her mouth.

The way she tasted.

The way it traced along the nape of her neck, down to her breasts, then to her stomach, until she opened wide for me.

I remember how she tasted then, too.

I could never forget how she felt when I was inside her and how she kept saying my name over and over, as if she wanted to make sure she'd never forget it.

I don't want her to forget it. Ever.

But she has. She has replaced my name with someone else's.

What saddens me most about these recollections is how uninhibited and free she was.

Now, it seems her sense of adventure is lost.

But that isn't my problem to fix. Instead, I focus on the task at hand. Carter's toast doesn't have to be complicated. Carter is the kind of man who speaks, and people listen. It just needs to be short and sweet.

Just as I'm about to type something, my phone buzzes beside me. It's Kenny.

"What?" I answer.

"Well, hello to you, too," he says. "Are you still here?"

"Let me guess, you're somewhere in the building, tangled in ribbon and drunk on chocolate?" I laugh.

"Ugh, I wish!"

A few minutes later, Kenny tracks me down and sits beside me in the conference room. Other than finding an empty room, I don't have a desk here like Kenny's. I never want my place here to feel permanent. Funny how that's working out for me.

"Let's recap. You're writing an engagement speech for the guy marrying the girl you're in love with. Sounds like a piece of cake," he says. "Ugh, cake sounds so good right now."

"Focus, Kenny." I rub my temple. "And I never said I loved her."

"You didn't have to."

"What about this?" I ask him as I move my screen in front of him.

"The best relationships aren't built on grand gestures. They're built on little things, like simply showing up. And if you're lucky, you find someone who reminds you every day why you chose them in the first place," Kenny reads my words aloud.

"What do you think?"

"They're good..."

"But what?" I ask.

I can't imagine what could be wrong with this toast. What I wrote was honest and thoughtful—short and sweet. It was something I could picture Carter saying. But just after I reread my words, I realized the problem: it's something I could picture myself saying as well.

Outside, the traffic noise grows louder. I shake my head as if to clear my mind. Then, before I can stop myself, words spill out of my mouth. And not just words, but feelings.

"You know how Carter said he missed their first date because his meeting ran long?" I ask.

"Yeah?" Kenny looks at me.

"It was the same night I met Everly. It was the same night we—," I pause, "well, let's just say that night has haunted me ever since."

"What happened between you?"

"She told me she wanted nothing more, and I thought I was doing the right thing by respecting that. So when I woke up the next morning, I left while she was still asleep."

"Yeah, you forgot to mention this when we first talked about it." Kenny shakes his head. "I thought I sensed a plot hole."

"And now I hear she pretty much told Carter something similar, but he wasn't deterred. He stayed and then fought to remain in her life from then on."

"Which is why you said you're filled with regret?" I nod as he continues. "And why you look like someone stabbed you in the soul every time you're in the room with her?" he sighs.

"This isn't even like me!" I groan. "I never get attached. I never regret anything, and I've never doubted my actions. But with Everly? I've doubted so much, and now…"

"You realize you love her," Kenny says, as if he just solved a mystery.

"But it's fine. She's marrying a good guy," I say.

"But have you told her any of this?" he asks.

"How? When? I haven't seen her since that night, and, like I told you, the first time I do is when I walk into the room and realize I'm writing her marriage vows. It's not something I can easily slip into the conversation," I say. "Plus, you and I both know Genny would kill me. And I'm also very aware that some guys just don't get the girl."

"And you think you're *that* guy?"

"I've always been the guy who can get the girl, but I never stayed around long enough to know if I could keep them," I say, the words punching me hard in the gut. "I guess I never cared too much about it until now."

"So, what's the plan?" he asks, pulling himself upright in his seat.

"Nothing. There is no plan," I say. "But if I show you something, will you promise not to say a word?"

"Until death do us part," Kenny says, crossing his heart.

And that is when I show him the note.

# Chapter Twenty-Three
## Rules of Engagement

*Everly*

Strings of light glow above polished marble tables. Champagne towers are strategically placed around the rooftop lounge like crystal castles. A small jazz band plays softly in the corner beneath a perfectly clear night sky. Waiters in black ties walk around with trays of fancy hors d'oeuvres as the skyline stretches endlessly around us.

My mom stops walking, taking it all in. "I have to say, this is quite stunning," she says. "I should go find Margaret and thank her for putting this together. I just wish I had known. I would have loved to help," she says, her shoulders slumping slightly.

"It's OK, Mom. If it makes you feel any better, she never lets me help." I smile, but it bothers me that she never thought to include my mom. I also wonder whether she will exclude her tomorrow. I make a mental note to talk to Carter about it.

As predicted, everything looks expensive and carefully chosen for the event. I feel like I'm watching everything from outside my body, as if I'm observing this party from a distance rather than actually being present.

Morgan walks up beside me, holding two glasses of champagne with strawberry garnishes. "You look like someone who just learned they are marrying into royalty," she teases.

I laugh. "Is it that obvious?

"Just relax." She hands me one of the glasses. "This is supposed to be fun. Not to mention, there's an open bar."

"Well, if I could, I'd drink my weight in champagne, but we have my shower in the morning," I sigh. "I can't be hungover for that. I'll be miserable enough already."

"I can't believe she planned all this without even telling you. She did it so you wouldn't have a say," Morgan points out.

"It may come from a nice place, but it makes me feel left out of my own events. You know?"

"Well, it's almost over." She takes a sip of her drink.

"Is it? I have a feeling she is going to do this for baby showers, birthday parties, and who knows what else?"

"Don't let her," she says.

"Have you met her?" I tilt my head toward her. "She doesn't exactly listen to anything I say."

I survey the room, filled with Carter's mom's invited guests. I see a few of Carter's co-workers mingling near the bar, and some of his immediate and extended family are scattered throughout. Even his brother Daniel, whom I've met only a handful of times, flew in for the event. But as I keep looking around, I realize that not many people are from my side. Where are my aunts? My uncles? My grandparents? Besides my mom, Morgan, and my cousin Karrie, there's no one else.

"Looks like Karrie is already flirting with some guy who works on Wall Street with Carter," Morgan mutters into her glass of champagne. "Should I stop her?"

"No." I take a sip. "Let her have fun," I say as I watch Mrs. Jacobs directing waitstaff as if she were trying to land a plane.

"Are you going to have some fun, too?" She looks at me.

## Reese

From across the room, I see Everly standing at the edge of the terrace. She's wearing a white dress and holding a glass of champagne, laughing at something Morgan said. Her hair falls in loose waves down her back like a waterfall of blonde. My chest tightens at the sight. I really don't want to be here.

"Take a deep breath," Kenny says, already noticing my discomfort. "I'm here, so everything will be OK."

"I see you also brought Lila, so doubtful," I say as I order a drink at the bar, happy to find my options aren't limited to champagne and white wine. I order a bourbon on the rocks and take a big sip as I watch Carter approach Everly. He wraps his arm around her waist and kisses her on the cheek.

"I had no choice but to bring her," Kenny says to me. "Your sister has two weddings this weekend, and everyone else is working alongside her."

But I'm not listening. I keep staring until I feel eyes staring back at me. However, they are not Everly's. They are Carter's.

*Fuck! Did I just blow my neutral cover?*

Carter stares at me curiously, though I may just be imagining it. If he says anything, I can tell him I was watching their interaction to help me with their vows. I just hope he buys it if I need to sell it.

"I'll try to keep Lila at bay," Kenny continues. "But she's feisty and apparently has a crush on you."

"People don't say 'crush' anymore."

"Sure, they do," he says as I roll my eyes.

I do feel bad about how many times I've turned Lila down, but she keeps coming back as if she can't take the hint. One of these days, I'm afraid I might really hurt her feelings, and I'm sure I'll end up making Genny mad at me as well.

I take another sip when I turn my attention to where Everly's mom, Annie, and Carter's mom are standing side by side at a nearby buffet table. They couldn't look more different if they tried. Carter's mom is polished, elegant, and composed, while Everly's mom is relaxed, expressive, and very humble.

"These look adorable!" Annie exclaims as she studies the hors d'oeuvres.

"Those are truffle crostini." Mrs. Jacobs smiles as if everyone should know what they are.

"So, tiny toasts?" Annie says, popping one into her mouth as Mrs. Jacobs blinks in shock, nibbling away at hers like a squirrel.

A few minutes and a second bourbon later, their conversation turns to the wedding. "I'm sure the seating arrangements will reflect the importance of our guests," Mrs. Jacobs says to Annie, as if she's planning a networking event rather than a wedding.

Annie frowns. "What do you mean by importance?"

Mrs. Jacobs gestures calmly toward some of the people gathered on the rooftop. "Business partners, longtime friends, and other professional relationships we've maintained over the years," she explains, her tone suggesting that what she said should have been obvious.

"And what about family?" Annie asks.

"We'll figure all that out when we finalize the seating arrangements. Don't you worry." Mrs. Jacobs taps Annie on the shoulder as if to appease a small child, which makes me feel offended by the exchange.

And sure enough, I was right. Annie's cheeks flush as if she suddenly realized this wedding is being treated like a paid show rather than a special moment. It's as if Everly's family doesn't matter. They would be relegated to the nosebleed section.

I can't help but interrupt the conversation. "I can assure you, Annie, that the seating arrangements will reflect your daughter and Carter's preferences," I say.

Mrs. Jacobs raises an eyebrow. "Is that so?"

I shrug. "I think the seating arrangement is up to the bride and groom. Don't you agree? It's their day, after all."

"Oh, and please let me know if I can be of any help tomorrow. It is my daughter's bridal shower," she says, grinning as Mrs. Jacobs walks away in a huff.

"Thank you for that," she says to me. "But who exactly are you?"

"I'm with Laurent & Co. I'm the professional vow writer," I say.

"I didn't even know that was a thing," she says curiously.

"Stand in line." I smile.

"So, you basically write other people's happily ever afters?"

I nod. "You could say that."

"You know, my late husband, Everly's dad, was really big into reading. He had more books than a library," she chuckles. "He especially loved stories that gave readers happy endings. That's where Everly got her love of romance and why she is so successful in the literary space."

"Really?" I ask as I marinate in a piece of Everly's life I hadn't been privy to before.

"And that's how she got her name: Everly."

"I don't follow?" I set my bourdon down.

"She doesn't like to talk about it since her father's passing, but he used to call her 'Happily Everly After,'" she says as I instantly recall the joke I made at the bar that night. The one I thought was cheesy.

And suddenly, I recall the moment she went quiet, and I can no longer feel my legs.


## Everly

My mother appears to be chatting with Reese. They are both smiling and laughing, something I have never done with Carter's mom. Curious, I walk over and join their conversation.

"Are you married?" my mom asks Reese.

He smiles. "No, ma'am."

"Well, is there a lucky lady in your life?" she asks.

"Mom!" I try to stop her, but Reese only smiles.

"What?" my mom shrugs. "Or lucky guy?"

"No, lucky lady," Reese answers.

"Well, she's out there." She offers him an encouraging smile as my fingers sweat around the stem of my glass. "But you know what? My husband would have liked you. You both have an affinity for words."

"That's very nice of you to say, Annie. I'm sure I would have liked him, too," he says just as my mom excuses herself to where more food is being brought out.

Just as I'm about to say something to Reese, I notice Carter looking across the rooftop at me. A strange, inquisitive look crosses his face. I stare back at him and smile, but the way he keeps looking at me is unlike any expression I've ever seen on his face. For the first time, I wonder if he suspects something, though I have no reason to think so. I haven't done anything wrong.

*Right?*

Then he makes his way over and takes hold of my hand. His expression softens. "I'm nervous," he says, which explains the look I tried to dissect a minute ago.

"What are you nervous about?" I gently cup his face in my hands.

"I can speak in courtrooms and boardrooms just fine, but other than that, I'm terrible," he admits.

"You'll be fine," Reese assures him. "Why don't we take a walk and practice?

## Reese

The rooftop terrace hums with conversation. Music drifts through the warm night air as the city skyline sparkles like a romantic backdrop.

Carter stands in front of me, loosening his tie.

"Too tight?" I joke.

"You're lucky you're not wearing one," he says.

"I used to, but I lost my favorite one and haven't worn one since," I say. "But let's get you a drink. It looks like you could use one."

"I have one." He points to his glass of champagne.

I laugh. "I was thinking of something a bit stronger," I say as I order two shots of whiskey for us.

Carter rests his elbows on the bar. "I don't know why I'm so worried about a toast. I rehearsed what you sent—I even have it memorized."

We both turn our attention to the terrace, where Everly is standing with Morgan, Kenny, and Lila. Carter watches her for a moment longer before turning back toward the bar. "I tend to make things sound too…corporate," he admits.

"You don't say," I chuckle.

"If we were negotiating or arguing a case, I'm the guy for that. But this? This feels different." He rubs the back of his neck.

"Because there's more at stake?" I ask as I swipe a napkin from the bar.

"Exactly," he says. "You're a smart man, Reese."

"So, trust me, OK?" I look at him, feeling more two-faced than I have ever been. But right now, I only focus on him. I want to help him. He deserves my help. Better yet, he deserves Everly. "What's the one thing you want her to know tonight?" I ask.

"That choosing her was the easiest decision I have ever made."

I nod. It's a great answer. I grab a pen from the bartender and start writing.

"Wait," Carter stops me. "Are you changing my toast?" His eyes widen with fear.

"I am," I affirm.

"But I've already memorized the other one. This seems too risky," he says.

I shrug. "The best speeches always carry a little risk," I say, sliding the napkin toward him.

Carter reads it, then, after a few silent moments, he looks up. "I don't know how you do it. I loved the other one, but this is perfect."

"Carter, word of advice? If you can't focus on the words, speak from the heart." I place my hand on his shoulder.

"You always know the right things to say…for other people, that is." He smiles as he orders us another round of shots.

"I'm really good at reading people," I reply.

Carter nods slowly. "You'd make a good lawyer."

I laugh at this. "Not my thing."

"Well, either way, you certainly write like a man in love," he says as he carefully folds the napkin and slips it into his jacket pocket. "I hope I don't embarrass myself."

I smirk. "You'll be fine. You can never embarrass yourself in front of the one you love."

"I'm really glad you're here. You're a great guy. To you," he says, raising his shot glass to me.

*You're a great guy.* I repeat his words in my head as I take my shot. However, I can't help wondering whether it's the liquor or Carter's words that burn the most.

"Go get her," I say as Carter notices Everly waving him over. "Go get your girl. I'm here if you need me."

He shakes my hand before making his way to Everly.

If I've learned anything tonight, it's that Carter isn't the villain here. Maybe in this story, I am. Or I could be if I keep letting my feelings for Everly cloud my judgment. But I can't let that happen. I won't let that happen. Just as much as Carter believes I'm a great guy, I think the same of him.

Carter, now full of confidence (and maybe a little too much whiskey), taps a fork against his glass to get everyone's attention. "I want to thank you all for coming tonight—especially my brother Daniel, who took the redeye to get here."

I swear I heard Kenny yell "Yee-haw!" as I turned to see a younger version of Carter raising his glass to Carter.

"It will probably shock some of you to know that I'm not very good at making speeches," Carter chuckles as a ripple of laughter spreads through the guests while he pulls the folded napkin from his jacket pocket.

"I've always been the man who believed that if you plan things carefully enough, they'll work out as you planned," he continues as some of the crowd nod knowingly. "But Everly doesn't live that way," he says, pulling her closer to him while trying his best to keep his eyes on the napkin. "She talks to strangers like they're already friends. She reads books as if they were conversations. And she keeps reminding me that the most important things in life aren't the ones you plan."

The crowd quiets as he reaches for Everly's hand. "Everly, you have changed my life in ways I never expected." His voice softens. "And I want to thank you for reminding me every day how truly lucky I am."

Everly's eyes glisten at Carter's words. My words.

"I promise that no matter where life takes us, I will always show up," he says as the crowd erupts in cheers.

I take in the moment. They both look genuinely happy. She is beautiful as ever—if that were even possible. Then, Carter lifts his glass. "To Everly. Choosing you was the best decision I've ever made," he toasts as someone in the crowd whistles. I think I even see Morgan dramatically wiping away a fake tear.

Carter scans the crows, and when his eyes meet mine, he raises a glass to thank me. In response, I raise mine to him just as Kenny materializes beside me.

"That's not the toast you wrote," he says to me.

"I know. I wrote something different for him," I say.

"No. You wrote something different for *her.*"


## Everly

The music resumes as people gather around Carter and me. They shake his hand and clap him on the back as if congratulating him on winning a game. As for me, they hug me and kiss me on the cheek as if I had just accomplished something of equal importance.

When we are finally alone, I hug Carter. "That was beautiful," I say.

He smiles. "I had a little help."

I raise an eyebrow. "Oh? Is that so?"

He taps his jacket pocket, where he pulled out his speech, written on a cocktail napkin. "Reese," he says.

My heart drops into the pit of my stomach. It's the first time I've heard Reese's words put into action. Now that I have, I can't help wondering whether it changes how I perceive them. Has anyone else felt this way, with their professions of love written by someone else? Does it affect the sincerity? Then again, it's not like every bride has had a one-night stand with their vow writer. Dear God, I hope not.

I tell myself that Reese didn't come up with all of this on his own; he had to have had input from Carter. So, in that case, it's Carter's feelings—just a little polished.

I walk toward the edge of the rooftop deck as Carter shares a drink with his brother. I stare out over the city, which glows beneath the rooftop lights. The music fades behind me as I take a deep breath in, then out. I think again about Carter's toast. It was perfect.

*But were those really his feelings?*

"I thought I'd bring you something to drink." Reese suddenly hands me a martini glass. It's an espresso martini. My breath catches. "It's no Java & Juliet," he says, but I think it will do the trick."

"You remembered my drink?" I ask softly, afraid my words might be carried off by the night breeze. I look down into my glass and notice the three beans.

"For good luck," he says. "Congratulations."

"I have to say, Carter's toast was beautiful." I take a sip of my martini.

Reese nods as he leans against the rooftop railing, reminding me of that night at The Last Chapter when he leaned against the bar. He always looks as if he were sculpted to stand wherever he leans.

I glance at him. "Did you have anything to do with it?"

"A little," he says, which makes me wonder if he's unwilling to confess the whole truth.

"Don't lie to me, Reese. Did you write the entire thing?"


*Reese*

I chuckle because I refuse to play this game. "It doesn't matter," I say. "I'm not the one marrying you."

As my words hang between us, I look up at the twinkling lights. *How did I end up here?*

Either way, I'm here. Yet, strangely, it feels like we are back at The Last Chapter—just two strangers sharing a drink, getting to know each other. But as quickly as that feeling appears, it vanishes. Now, we are nothing more than two strangers desperately trying to pretend that it all meant nothing.

I step back, creating space between us. We say nothing. We do nothing. It's not until the sound of approaching footsteps breaks the uncomfortable silence eating away at me.

"There you are," Carter says as he appears before us. "I was wondering where you'd run off to."

"Well, you two go celebrate. Thank you again for the invitation, but I should be heading out," I say before downing the rest of my drink.


*Kenny*

I'm halfway through my delicious cosmopolitan, like I'm Carrie Bradshaw at some random NYC party, when I notice Reese is leaving. He doesn't announce his departure. Doesn't even come over to say goodbye. He just heads to the elevator like a man who would rather be somewhere else. And because I understand why, I don't try to stop him.

But you want to know who stops him?

Lila Bennett.

Great. I told Reese I would keep her at bay, but to my defense, I lost track of her. I thought maybe she found another eligible bachelor and abandoned her mission to pursue Reese.

Apparently, I thought wrong.

I'm great at reading lips. But it's tough to make out what Reese is saying to her because his lips aren't in direct view. As for Lila, I could have sworn I saw her tell him to stop pretending.

"Stop pretending, what?" I ask myself out loud.

"Talking to yourself?" Morgan asks as she suddenly appears beside me.

"No. Just reading lips," I confess over my cosmo as she looks in the direction I am facing.

"Yeah, she has it bad for him," Morgan says. "Or she wants his job."

"No. Just him," I snicker just as Reese steps into the elevator, and the doors close in front of Lila. Her face is red, as if she is embarrassed by whatever exchange just took place.

"Does he like her?" she asks.

I shrug. I refuse to get into this conversation with her. It's unprofessional, for one. And two, I have to be careful about treading this close to Reese's secret.

"Oh, come on," she says. "Spill the tea—or the cosmo."

"I'm not spilling anything," I say.

"But there is something to spill, isn't there?" She locks eyes with me until I'm sweating through my dress shirt. This is not a good look for me.

I force a yawn. "Oh, look at the time. I really should be going."

"Why do you have this strange look on your face? What is wrong with you? You're all sweaty and flushed." She studies me.

"I'm just tired and perhaps had too many drinks," I say, even though I down the rest of my cosmo.

"Cut the theatrics. That's my department," she snaps.

"Is it now?" I ask.

"It is. I had a double major in theatre and English," she looks at me as if this is some form of competition.

"Were you cast as one of the witches in Macbeth?" I peer at her.

"No, *I* was Lady Macbeth." Her eyes narrow more.

"Seriously?" My shoulders slouch. "Lucky,"

"So, what do you know? Because it looks like you are trying not to burst," she says.

"I know a lot of things." I wave dismissively at her.

"You're the wedding planner, and you spend a lot of time with the bride and groom," she says, more as a statement than a question.

"What's your point?" I ask.

Morgan laughs so loudly that I worry she'll draw attention to us. "You're the worst liar I've ever seen."

"Oh, yeah? And what would I be lying about, Miss Sherlock?" I tilt my head at her. Two can play this game, and even though I think I've finally met my match, I can't help but feel equal parts excited and terrified.

"Have you noticed how she acts differently around him?" she asks, trying not to lose eye contact with me. I know that the minute I look away, she has me where she wants me.

"Who does? Lila?" I play dumb.

"So, you're playing dumb?"

*How the hell is she doing this?*

"Well, playing dumb is not a good look on you. And I can see on that face of yours that you know exactly what I'm talking about. The question is," she takes hold of me by the shoulders, "what are we going to do about it?"

"I'm sorry, *we*?"

She crosses her arms as if I'm deliberately making things harder than they should be. But I made a promise to Reese, and I refuse to break it.

"I've just seen some things, and I guess I was hoping I wasn't the only one," she says.

"Listen, I'm not getting involved in whatever scheme you're obviously… scheming," I say.

"Oh, Kenny," she says, resting her hand against my cheek. "You're already involved."

# Chapter Twenty-Four
## Bride, Interrupted



So this is my nightmare: Mrs. Jacobs planned my bridal shower. She decided to host it at her home in the Hamptons and serve brunch and mimosas. Everything looks nice, but I don't know more than half the people in the room. I feel like I just walked in on someone else's party.

My mom even feels out of place.

This is not a bridal party for me. It's a party for Mrs. Jacobs. She is throwing a party for the version of the bride she wants me to be. And suddenly, this kind gesture feels like manipulation.

"You're late, darling," Mrs. Jacobs says as she approaches me.

"You said the party is at 11:00 am. It's 10:45 am," I say.

"Well, yes, but you should know enough to arrive before your guests. This is *your* party after all."

*Is it?*

"Is there anything I can do to help?" my mom offers.

"No, Annie. Everything is taken care of. Please relax and enjoy yourself," she says as she guides me into her large sitting room, where more guests I have never met are seated like they are part of Ladies Who Lunch.

For the next hour, everything is a blur. I am so upset that I'm being introduced to all my guests that I am longing for a familiar face just to feel comfortable.

I am now seated in a high-backed chair, being told to smile and say thank you for gifts from people whose names I've already forgotten.

Fine china with a gold rim.

Monogrammed towels with *Carter & Everly* stitched across the fabric.

A crystal serving tray that probably cost more than my wedding dress.

"Beautiful, right? Absolutely timeless!" Mrs. Jacobs prompts me to give more of a reaction to the gifts I'm receiving.

"Yeah," I say, echoing her. I try my best to smile, but none of this is me.

I scan the room, my smile tightening just a fraction.

There are at least forty women here. I know maybe five?

My mom is now standing near the mimosa bar, talking politely to a group of women wearing various pastel-colored shirts who look like they have to schedule fun six months in advance. Karrie and Morgan came late because they were told the party started at noon, which I know was Mrs. Jacobs' doing.

Morgan leans against the gift table, arms crossed, eyes sharp as she watches everything unfold, as if making mental notes for a crime documentary.

Kenny, somehow, is here, too. Morgan tells me she called him for a ride because she and Karrie had trouble finding transportation out of the city. He is now hovering over the dessert display, as if planning his attack.

And then there is Mrs. Jacobs. She is still floating from room to room like a social general, greeting guests and orchestrating everything. Never once including my mom in even the simplest tasks.

"Everly, dear?" Mrs. Jacobs calls, clapping her hands lightly. "Let's continue with the gifts."

*There's more?!*

I am forced back into the high-backed chair, where I fold my hands in my lap as another elegantly wrapped box is set before me.

"This one is from Catherine," Mrs. Jacobs says.

I blink. *Who the hell is Catherine?*

I open it anyway.

Lingerie.

*Are you fucking kidding me?*

And not just lingerie, but delicate, lacy, and not something I would have ever picked for myself.

"Every bride needs something special for the honeymoon!" Catherine beams from across the room. "It is hand-stitched from a boutique in Paris."

*Of course, it is.*

I set it aside carefully, my fingers lingering on the tissue paper as if I might disappear if I close my eyes and wish hard enough.

Another gift from another name I don't recognize, which is just another reminder that this isn't my party.

This is a performance featuring Mrs. Margaret Jacobs.

"Next!" Mrs. Jacobs chirps.

I exhale quietly as I reach for the next box.

"Wait."

The voice cuts through the room like a subtle shift in whatever lullaby music is playing.

I look up, and for a second, the room tilts.

Standing in the doorway—poised, polished, and entirely too composed—is a woman I have never met but somehow recognize.

*How do I know her?*

She is tall. Effortless, Familiar in a way that she moves through the room as if she belongs here or has been here before.

Mrs. Jacobs lights up as she sees her.

"Oh, thank goodness, you made it," Mrs. Jacobs says as she nearly runs to her. "Everyone, this is Charlotte."

It's one of Carter's exes.

I quickly text this to Morgan, who straightens across the room. I swear she nudges Kenny, who mutters something under his breath.

Charlotte smiles, graceful and warm. "I wouldn't miss it, Margaret."

*Margaret? So they are on a first-name basis?*

Mrs. Jacobs rests a hand lightly on Charlotte's arm, turning toward me as if unveiling something important.

"Charlotte and Carter dated for years," she says, almost casually. "We always thought—well," she laughs softly. "Life has its own plans."

The room hums.

My fingers go still on the edge of the gift box.

*The one who got away.*

Carter has told me about Charlotte. They dated for three years before breaking up when Charlotte decided to move to California. After living there for a year and deciding she missed the city, and I guess, Carter, she moved back. Only by then, Carter was dating me.

Charlotte steps forward, extending a beautifully wrapped package. "Congratulations, Beverly. Truly."

"It's Everly, I correct her as I take the gift. "Thank you."

"Open it," Mrs. Jacobs encourages me as I slowly unwrap the gift, painfully aware that every set of eyes is on me.

Charlotte walks around the room, greeting everyone as if she knows them, because more than likely, she does.

Inside the package is a sterling silver frame. It's classic and elegant. The bottom is engraved with the words "The beginning of Forever."

"You and Carter had one just like it, right?" Mrs. Jacobs says, and my throat immediately tightens.

"We did," Charlotte smiles. "Maybe you'll have better luck."

"Well, Charlotte, you have always had impeccable taste," Mrs. Jacobs says, satisfied with the gift.

*I am not OK.*

But I have to pretend to be.

"Maybe we should take a break so Everly can eat?" my mom cuts in gently.

Bless her heart.

"Yes, of course," Mrs. Jacobs agrees, though she doesn't sound thrilled.

I stand, smoothing out my dress, immediately feeling untethered.

"Mom, I'm going to go outside to get some air. OK?"

"Would you like me to join you?" she asks, her expression concerned.

"No, I will be OK." I kiss her on the cheek. "I'll be back in a few."

I slip through the front doors, and the noise (if you could even call it that) fades behind me as I step out onto the front porch.

The moment the door closes behind me. I breathe.

My shoulders drop. My fake smile disappears.

"I hear this is one hell of a party."

I freeze. I know that voice. Of course, I do. I turn slowly and see Reese leaning against the porch railing, sleeves rolled, a look that says he couldn't quite commit to being here but showed up anyway.

"Why are you here?" I ask.

"Kenny," he says simply. "He was afraid he would drink too many mimosas and wanted me to drive."

"Oh, I thought he drove," I say—not that it matters. "Well, he's going to get himself disinvited from social events," I say with a laugh. "The women in there are brutal."

"He's tough." Reese's mouth curves slightly as silence settles between us, softer than it has any right to be. "Are you OK?" he asks me.

I swallow. "Yeah. I just—" I glance back at the door. "It's a lot."

He nods as if he already knew. Then he reaches down and picks up a small gift bag. Nothing extravagant like the gifts I unwrapped inside. No gold foil or ribbon. Just simple.

"What's that?" I frown.

"Open it," he says, handing it to me.

Inside is a mug. White. Slightly imperfect as though it were handmade. The words printed on it in soft script:

*Happily Everly After*

My breath catches.

My heart stops.

Out of every gift, no matter the cost, this one was me. *For me.*

Reese shrugs as if the gesture is no big deal. "I had it made."

I run my thumb over the lettering, feeling a rush of tears that I prevent from falling.

I shouldn't feel like this.

This gift shouldn't matter this much.

But it does.

*God, it does.*

"Thank you," I say as he watches me a second longer with something unreadable flickering in his expression.

"I had a feeling you would get a bunch of gifts that didn't feel like you, so I wanted to at least give you one," he says.

I look up at him. Really look. Suddenly, I'm reminded of the shower. My vows. My wedding. Everything.

"This was the cheesy joke you made that night—"

"Although a little birdie told me it wasn't exactly cheesy," he cuts in.

*So, he knows.*

My grip tightens around the mug as someone inside calls my name.

"You'd better go back in, or they'll wonder where you are," he says, but I don't move toward the door right away.

Because for the first time, I don't know if I want to go back. Instead of trying to explain this to him, I turn the mug in my hands slowly when it hits me: *Is this really my happily Everly after?*

*Chapter Twenty-Five*
*A Fork in the Road*

*Everly*

I hug my mom outside the grand entrance of the estate. The late afternoon sun reflects off the tall windows behind us. The grand staircase is adorned with flowerless vines that we have been told will bloom in time for the wedding.

"Do you really have to go?" I ask.

Since my father's passing, I've been urging my mother to move to the city to be closer to me, but she never agrees. She says she prefers the quiet. She loves our hometown and knows where everything is and who everyone is. She tells me it would be a pity to leave the comforts of a place that already feels like home. I can't exactly fault her for that, but I sure miss her.

My mom squeezes my shoulders affectionately. "I'll be back before you know it."

"I can't wait," I say with a smile as the town car Carter called pulls up to take my mother to the airport. She came out to the estate so I could at least show her where the wedding would be held.

I'm still reeling from the bridal shower, and I would give anything for my mom to stay longer—especially since tonight is our menu-tasting appointment.

Just as I reach for another hug, a black SUV pulls up alongside the town car. Through the semi-tinted windows, I see it's Reese and Kenny. Kenny steps out with his tablet, and I swear I saw him tuck a bib into his pocket. As for Reese, he looks the same as usual. At this point, his entire appearance is borderline cliché.

My mom looks in their direction. "That one." She points to Reese.

"Who?" I ask, pretending I don't know who she means.

"The vow writer," she says, watching him. "There's something about him. He's very intuitive. It's as if he observes the room before speaking."

I frown. "That's oddly specific."

My mom smiles. "I can tell he tries holding onto that tough exterior of his, but deep down, he's a big softy. I just don't think he trusts that part of himself."

"I think that's part of his job, Mom," I say, shrugging off her comment.

"Either way, he sees you. Doesn't he?"

My stomach flips unexpectedly. "What do you mean by that?" I ask as she kisses me goodbye.

"Oh, nothing. I'm just a little sappier now that your father's gone. But can you do me a favor?" she asks as she heads toward the car. "Call me later and tell me about everything you ate." She smiles as she gets into the back seat of the car.

A part of me wanted to tell her about the mug from Reese, but I didn't. In fact, I didn't tell or show anyone. I feel like if I did, it would require an explanation I'm not emotionally prepared to give.

**The tasting room overlooks** the venue's gardens. The setting sun pours through the floor-to-ceiling windows, which offer the most stunning view. A long table is set in the center with polished silverware and bone china. Carter stands as soon as I walk in. He had to take a work call while I was outside, saying goodbye to my mom. As much as it would have been nice for him to see her off, I still appreciated that he called a car to take her to the airport and made this menu-tasting appointment while in the middle of a high-profile case.

"Did the car arrive for your mom?" he asks as he greets me with a kiss on the cheek.

"Yes," I say. "Thank you for arranging that."

"Who's ready to eat our way through this wedding?" Kenny bounces into the room with his tablet. Only then do I notice that Mrs. Jacobs has been seated at the head of the table and is already examining the place setting. I wonder if she is comparing it to hers.

"The menu is extremely important," she announces to all of us. "Guests will always remember the food."

"The menu *is* important, but I always remember the cake," Kenny says while Mrs. Jacobs scowls back at him.

# Reese

Genny decided to come. She walks in, places her bag in the corner, then picks up her tablet and signals for Kenny to come over so they can review tonight's selections.

As I take a seat at the table, I am suddenly overwhelmed with nerves. I think about the mug. Yes, it was a simple mug, but there was a level of intimacy attached to it that didn't register until she held it in her hands.

I never told Kenny about it because I was afraid he would talk me out of it. Sure enough, when I told him on the drive home, he nearly had a heart attack. He kept telling me that we don't give out gifts, especially not one that references the one-night stand I had with the bride.

He's not wrong. But after I learned the true meaning behind my cheesy joke, I thought maybe I could make it more sentimental. After seeing her reaction, I could tell I had failed.

Truth is, I wanted to fail.

"Hello, everyone," Genny greets the group. "Tonight is all about curating the perfect menu for your guests. It's important to choose options that pair well together. Your chef, Dominic Russo, is a Michelin-starred chef. I'm sure you will be pleased with the samples presented to you this evening," she says as several waiters pour out of the kitchen to serve us the appetizer options. Each plate holds several miniature appetizers for us to taste.

"Chef Dominic has prepared the following selections for you," Genny begins. "Going clockwise, you have mini lobster rolls with lemon aioli. Next to that is a burrata crostini with heirloom tomato and basil. Then there's a prosciutto-wrapped pear with fresh basil and cream cheese, drizzled with balsamic reduction. Lastly, there's a mushroom tartlet with a thyme dressing. Enjoy!"

Kenny leans back in his seat, gazing down at his food. "This looks like heaven."

Carter immediately tries the burrata. "Wow. This tastes amazing," he says as Mrs. Jacobs sniffs the food on her plate before going for the wild mushroom tartlet.

As for Everly, she starts with the pear. So, I do the same.

"How many appetizers do we choose, Genevieve?" she asks as I notice a tiny drizzle of balsamic glaze at the corner of her mouth. I wish I could lean across the table and lick it off myself.

"I would recommend picking two," Genny answers. "Any ideas which ones you like so far?"

I watch as Everly takes a bite of everything. She savors each bite, and I start to feel a hunger I know this food won't satisfy.

"I really like the pear with prosciutto," she says, "but I'm torn between the crostini and the lobster roll."

"I have to agree," Carter says. "What do you think, Mom?"

She clears her throat as if she's about to give a speech. "I was hoping for less messy options. This isn't a backyard wedding."

Suddenly, Everly's head snaps toward Mrs. Jacobs. Her reaction is so quick that I feel a gust of wind. "What's wrong with backyard weddings? My parents had a backyard wedding."

The sad part is that Mrs. Jacobs doesn't even apologize for clearly offending Everly. Instead, she simply dismisses her with a wave. "You know what I mean," she says as if that justifies her comment.

## Everly

I'm on edge. How dare she? Even if she didn't know about my parents' wedding, the least she could have done was apologize for her insensitive comment. But she doesn't. Because she never does. And the fact that Carter completely missed that comment because he was too busy sampling his food makes me even more pissed. I really only have him to defend me against his mother, and I know it's still his mom, but I will be his wife. Don't I deserve some respect here?

By the time the salad options arrive, I feel like I'm losing my appetite.

"For your salad course," Genevieve says, as the waiters present each of us with three options. "You have an arugula salad with shaved parmesan and a lemon vinaigrette."

"It's delicious," Kenny says. He dove right in before the other two salads were even described.

"Next is a roasted beet salad with goat cheese and pistachios." But just as I'm about to ask them to take the plate away, Reese pipes up.

"She can't have that," he says as Genevieve looks over at him. "She's allergic to nuts."

"You are?" Genevieve rushes to her bag and pulls out our wedding file. She frantically flips through the pages, checking her notes on any dietary restrictions. "All that was listed here were no heavy carbohydrate options." She looks up at the table, slightly relieved that she didn't make a grave mistake. "I wasn't aware of this! I am so sorry, Everly."

"Honestly, I don't remember ever telling you about my dietary restrictions," I say as she hands me the form. As soon as she does, I can tell by the handwriting who filled it out.

"Again, I apologize, Everly, but I did speak to Carter as well. He never once told me you had a nut allergy; otherwise, I wouldn't have ordered any nuts on the menu."

I look at Carter, who immediately reddens at his mistake.

"I'm sorry, Everly. I forgot." He looks as guilty as if I had caught him cheating. "But thank you, Reese. You saved the day. How did you know about her allergy?"

Reese clears his throat. "She mentioned it at one of the meetings," he lies.

"Candace," Everly says to one of the waiters, "can you tell Dominic to omit the beet salad? The last thing we need is for the bride to have an allergic reaction on her big day. Apologize to him for my oversight."

"Of course, Genevieve," she says, instructing all the waiters to remove the beet salad from in front of us.

"Well, the only other option is the baby greens salad with heirloom tomatoes and a champagne vinaigrette," Genevieve says.

We all take a bite and unanimously agree it's the one. And since we only have to choose one, it was a slam dunk.

"As I said," Mrs. Jacobs says, setting her fork down, "the food is one of the few things guests talk about after the wedding."

"She's right," Kenny nods. "I still think about the taco bar at my cousin's wedding in 2018. Best guacamole I've ever had."

All Carter's mom can do is sigh.

*Reese*

The waiters return to refill our drinks and hand each of us a palate cleanser: bread. Mrs. Jacobs nearly faints when it's placed in front of her, as if it might reach out and bite her.

*I can't say I'd be upset if it did.*

"I'm really sorry, I can't stay for the final course, but I have to head to a wedding and check on how things are going," Genny says as she stands from the table. I offer to walk her out, and she tells me that the smell of all the food is making her nauseated.

"Are you sure you don't want me to come with you?" I offer.

"No," she shakes her head. "Just keep an eye on Kenny and make sure he doesn't eat off anyone's plate."

When I'm back inside and seated at the table, Candace advises us to pick two meat options and one vegetarian option.

"All of your guests will receive menu selection cards with their invitations. I will order them after you make your final selections," Kenny says.

The first option is filet mignon with truffle fries. I'm not going to lie, it looks fucking amazing. But just as I'm about to cut into my steak, which I can tell will slice like butter, I see Kenny putting on his bib.

"Tell me you're joking." I look at him, trying hard not to laugh.

"What? I don't want to ruin my shirt." He looks down at his bib.

"Then eat like a normal person," I say.

"I knew you were carrying a bib!" Everly exclaims. "That is hilarious. By any chance, do you have another one?"

"Oh, honey, I always carry a spare." Kenny reaches into his pocket and pulls out a second bib.

"You two are unbelievable," I laugh as Everly puts on the bib.

"Very cute," Carter says as he helps tie the bib around Everly's neck, while his mother looks on in horror.

The next option is herb-crusted salmon with a lemon-butter sauce. I'm not much of a seafood guy, so I pick at the vegetables while everyone else devours their salmon.

Lastly, we were served a chicken roulade with truffle cream sauce and potatoes, made for Kenny's bib. The sauce is a little messy, which only makes Kenny and Everly eat like total slobs. It's kind of cute to see her let her hair down this way. It's even cuter that she doesn't care what anyone in the room thinks of her.

After the vegetarian options are brought out, we're all too full to speak. I'm starting to consider renting a room for the night just to sleep off all the carbs.

## Everly

As much as the menu tasting was fun—and delicious—I'm still upset about how the night played out. Why didn't Carter remember my allergy? Was that why the almond cake was at that tasting as well? Should I be alarmed that the man I am choosing to spend the rest of my life with forgot that detail—that life-threatening detail?

After our plates are cleared and we finalize the menu options, Kenny leans back in his chair as if he's desperate to unbutton his pants. "Well, this was an excellent day at work," he says as Carter's mom gets up from her seat.

"I trust that you both made the right decisions about your menu," she says, looking at me before kissing her son and heading out of the estate.

"Carter?" Reese suddenly asks from across the table. "Since we are here, would you mind if we squeezed in a quick vow session?"

Carter nods. "Of course. Lead the way," he says as he and Reese walk out of the room.

I stay back with Kenny as one of the waiters surprises us with after-dinner treats.

"I know we are stuffed…" I say, looking down at the mini pastries.

"But we have the bibs," Kenny says, as if that changes anything. "And where there's a bib, there's a way."

As I take a bite, a tightness spreads through my chest. At first, I think I might be having an allergic reaction, but I know I'm not. It's a different kind of reaction, one medicine wouldn't fix.

Suddenly, my mom's words echo in my head:

*"He sees you. Doesn't he?"*


## Reese

The sitting room Carter and I venture into is more like a fancy parlor. Still, I can easily picture myself here with a glass of bourbon and a good book. I settle into one of the club chairs while Carter sits in the one directly across from me. One of the estate's workers enters the room with after-dinner espressos and a few pastries.

*I could get used to this.*

I reach into my leather bag and pull out my notebook just as the outside light casts long shadows across the tall windows and the polished wood.

"I feel terrible," Carter sighs, leaning back in his seat. "How did I miss her allergy? What if she ate something and had a reaction?"

"Don't beat yourself up," I say. "It was just an honest mistake."

"Yes, but you don't know Everly, and yet you remembered," he says to me. "I'm about to marry her, and I forgot."

"The good news is that she didn't eat anything she wasn't supposed to," I reassure him. "Just explain it to her. She seems like a very forgiving woman."

But I do know Everly, and I don't think she easily forgives—at least, not to me. Then again, she doesn't love me; she loves Carter, so anything is possible.

"For this session," I get us back on topic. "I want to focus on what you want your marriage and life with Everly to look like," I say, tapping my pen lightly against the page.

Carter straightens his posture. "That sounds rather philosophical."

"Perhaps, but it helps paint a picture," I say as Carter takes a moment to think.

"Well, I want stability," he answers before taking a sip of espresso.

I write that down. "Can you explain?"

Carter folds his hands. "My whole life has been moving toward something bigger—a bigger career, a bigger client, bigger expectations." He glances out the window as if the answer is looking in on us. Then he adds, "Everything is always moving fast. But I have found that with Everly, things slow down a bit. And I enjoy that."

"What does she do to help slow things down for you?" I ask.

Carter tries to conceal his smile as if I've broken through a barrier of his. "She reminds me that there's more to life than winning."

I nod. That does sound like Everly. "What does she challenge you on?"

Carter laughs. "Everything."

I raise an eyebrow because, from what I've seen, she doesn't seem to challenge him about much of anything. It's almost as if she's more reserved around him. "Can you give me an example?" I ask.

He leans forward as if he's about to let me in on a secret. "I once told her that my calendar was my most valuable asset."

"And what did she say to that?"

"She told me it was sad," he frowns. "She was right."

I smirk. "She would say that," I say, realizing my words were not meant to be spoken aloud.

"You seem to know her pretty well," he says, taking another sip of his espresso.

My pen stops moving. "I'm good at my job."

"I certainly can't fault a guy for being good at his job." He sets his espresso cup aside. "But do you want to know what I admire most about her? It's that she doesn't care about the things most people do—what I normally care about. You know what I mean?"

"Money?"

"Not impressed by it at all," he says.

*No. She's intimidated by it.*

"She loves the simple things," he continues.

*You love extravagance.*

"Tell me, Reese, you've been doing this job for a long time. What makes vows work?" he asks, as if there were some secret about them that only I know.

"Honestly? It's just plain honesty," I answer.

"It's that simple?" He looks at me.

I shrug. "It's that simple. Most people overthink them. A good vow isn't about sounding impressive or trying to sell yourself to the one you love. It's about telling the truth about the person standing next to you and the kind of life you want to build with them."

"That's exactly what I want," he says.

"What about this?" I say, quickly jotting something down and showing it to Reese.

He takes my notebook and reads aloud, "Everly, you make my life feel less like a race and more like an incredible journey." He hands it back to me. "It *is* honest."

"See? Simple. Don't overthink it," I say as he hands me back my notebook. "And that's what I plan to do with your vows."

"I'm really glad you're helping me with this. I don't know how I'd manage without you." He sighs with relief.

"Well, that's my job," I say as I close my notebook.

"You'll have the vows ready in time for the wedding?" he asks.

I nod. "I won't let you down. Trust me."

After he leaves the room, I feel trapped by my words. If Carter even knew half the truth, I've already let him down more than once. And I certainly don't think that makes me someone he could trust.

*But does that make me a terrible guy?*

I sit back for a few minutes. The room is quiet. I open my notebook again and flip to the last page, where I wrote the beginning of his vows. They are taking shape as the best vows I've ever written. And in just a few months, I will hear them spoken aloud. The sad part is, I may not survive hearing them when I do.

# Chapter Twenty-Six
## Picture-Perfect Disaster

*Everly*

I don't know what I'm searching for. I don't even know if I'd recognize it if I came across it. My usual optimistic attitude seems to have soured.

I was raised to believe that happily ever afters were as simple as "…and they lived happily ever after." I never really thought about what happened after the prince and princess rode off into the sunset. What comes next? Did he snore, keeping the princess awake all night? Did she have an odd sense of humor he didn't quite understand? Did he forget her damn food allergies?

I also struggle to understand why I'm letting these intrusive thoughts disrupt my work. It's pushing me to want something more genuine—real, not the usual tropes. I'm searching for a main character who doesn't just see rainbows and butterflies.

*Maybe I'm searching for someone like…me?*

I stare down at the manuscript on my desk. Then I shift my attention to my laptop screen, where I've started several emails but haven't finished any. In moments like these, I miss my dad the most. He would be the one to help me see the fairy-tale forest through the wedding-planning trees.

"What's wrong?" Morgan asks as she steps into my office.

"Nothing. It's just that none of these submissions are what I'm looking for," I sigh, motioning to the stack of papers on my desk.

Morgan walks over and sits in the chair in front of my desk. "Tell me about them."

"Well," I say, grabbing the first one on top of the pile. "This one is about how two people meet on a train."

Morgan nods. "And then what happens?"

"During the ride, they get to know each other and eventually fall in love, but because they live far apart, they never see each other again after they disembark. They remain in love, never reaching out or making contact with each other for fear of disrupting the other's life. Then one day, ten years later, they reunite on a plane."

"OK. Classic romance formula," she says.

"That's the problem." I set the submission aside. "It's a good story, but not the one I'm looking for. I want something different."

Morgan smiles knowingly at me. "Different, huh? Interesting problem to have."

"What do you mean?" I ask, stifling a groan.

"You're searching for a love story that doesn't follow the usual formula." She casually gestures toward the shelves of romance novels around my office. "You want something with a more unexpected emotional arc."

"Yes," I agree. "That's right."

"Interesting timing. Don't you think?"

## Reese

I really don't want to be here, which is something I've said more times than I care to admit. But it's true. I don't want to be here.

However, Kenny apparently needs a chaperone just as much as I do, and Genny was very clear that we stick together because she somehow thinks we will get into less trouble. Still, it can't hurt being here. It will help with the vows.

Fuck that. *Everything* hurts for the vows.

We are all in Central Park in the middle of the day, as Everly stands holding a bouquet of flowers she doesn't know how to hold on to naturally. Her arms are stiff as if she's holding out a bag of garbage she doesn't want to smell.

As for the photographer, he bounces around her and Carter as if he's trying to conjure rain.

"OK, Carter, I want you to stand behind Everly and wrap your arms around her waist," the photographer instructs.

"Like this?" Carter asks as if he's never been in that position with Everly before.

*I can list plenty of positions that I've been with her…*

"Perfect!" the photographer exclaims just as Kenny arrives with a hot dog.

"Want one?" he asks.

I shake my head as the photographer begins snapping pictures. Everly smiles as his assistant holds up a reflector to improve the lighting. However, her expression looks staged. I can tell she's uncomfortable. She prefers candid shots to a typical photo shoot, where she has to pretend to react to something that isn't actually happening. Plus, she looks too distracted by people walking by with their dogs, kids being pushed in strollers, and random runners zipping past, making it hard for her to focus on the camera.

How do I know all this?

It's amazing how many things are whispered in the middle of the night. She revealed more of herself to me than she had when she tore off her clothes.

"Why do these shots look like stock photos?" Kenny asks, mouth full of hot dog.

*Everly*

Reese is standing off to the side with Kenny, who appears to be chowing down on a hot dog. *I would give anything for a hot dog.* And then my mind starts to wander further...

Reese isn't wearing his standard Reese uniform today. Instead, he's wearing a fitted black T-shirt that not only showcases more of his tattooed sleeves but also highlights the definition of his arms. I remember those arms. And I remember how they felt wrapped around me.

*Why am I having these thoughts in the middle of my engagement photo session?*

I'm starting to think I'm a terrible person. Does it make me a terrible person to find myself drifting back to thoughts of that night? Or to feel a flutter in my stomach whenever I see him or hear his name?

I'd be lying if I said it doesn't scare me. It makes me feel deceptive—as if I'm emotionally cheating on Carter, even though I've never actually crossed the line with Reese (only my mind has). But as I stand here, smiling for picture after picture, I glance over at Reese, who is looking toward us in his aviator sunglasses, his leather bag slung over his shoulder, looking like he should be posing for the camera instead of me. I wonder what allure he has that has tethered me, even loosely, up until now.

Carter is a good man. He's not perfect, but he's good. He's oblivious to the feelings stirring within me, smiling as if I'm 100% in this moment, but I'm not. We've been moving so fast through the wedding-planning process that I haven't had time to process how I feel about anything. I'm still getting used to the ring on my finger.

As for today's event, engagement photos always seemed cheesy to me, which is why I didn't want to do them in the first place. But with the assistance of Carter's mom (surprise, surprise), who told me I would regret not doing them, she paid for everything before I had a chance to argue.

As the photoshoot continues, I think about my conversation with Morgan. Her words ring in my head like a warning bell: *"Interesting timing, don't you think?"*

I'm barely paying attention as the photographer continues directing us through the next couple of shots. He's determined to capture us at the right angle and in the right pose, all while urging us to adjust our smiles. Adjust our smiles? This is why I prefer candid shots. There's nothing to adjust.

"Carter, I need you to stand right here." The photographer directs Carter through several poses before Carter excuses himself to take a work call.

"Need any help?" Kenny asks the photographer as he wipes ketchup from his mouth with the back of his hand.

"Actually," the photographer perks up, "my assistant had to run to the restroom. Would you mind holding the reflector for me? And you!" he points to Reese. "Can you help me with the veil? We want to get a couple of shots of Everly wearing it."

"Kenny might be better at that," Reese counters. "Why don't I handle the reflector?"

"Nah, I'm good," Kenny waves him off. "You can help Everly with her veil."

I stand there, watching as Reese steps closer. Each step is cautious, as if he's walking on eggshells or hot coals to reach me. We haven't said much to each other since my bridal shower. I haven't thanked him properly for the gift, which turned out to be my favorite.

"I promise not to ruin your veil," he says.

I smile nervously because no words come to mind.


*Reese*

I gently adjust Everly's veil, which she tells me is chiffon. But honestly, I have no idea what I'm doing or what chiffon even is.

"It's a little tricky," Everly says as she reaches toward her veil.

Our hands brush briefly. Compared with other moments we've shared, this one happens so quickly that I doubt she even noticed. As for me, I do. The sensation of her skin on mine ignites another memory that burns against my skin. At this point, my entire body is covered in invisible tattoos dedicated to her, like a shrine.

"You must be having the time of your life," I tease her. It's easy to get her going—and I love doing it.

She smiles. "Everything feels unnatural."

"I get that," I say because I do.

Soon, we begin bantering just like we did that night, which now feels like a lifetime ago. Since she told me everything feels unnatural, I decided to make her feel, in her words, more natural. She tells me how much she loves cinnamon rolls and wishes that her wedding cake could taste like one. She even confesses that she has always wanted a library-themed wedding, but knows it would be out of the question. She says that Mrs. Jacobs would probably call it as classless as a backyard barbecue. But just as I'm about to tell her that what she wants is important, I look up and notice that the photographer has been taking pictures of us this entire time.

"Wow," he exclaims as he approaches us to show us a few raw images.

Everly's smile is genuine. It's bright, unfiltered, and unstaged. As for me, mine is unrecognizable. Have I ever looked like this before? The smile on my face is foreign, yet it looks like it has finally found its way home.

The pictures of Everly and me are great, but there is no Everly and me. Therefore, these pictures will never be framed or shared with family and friends. They will most likely end up in a folder on the photographer's computer.

Maybe one day I will see them again and be reminded of what happiness looks like on me.

## Everly

They say a picture is worth a thousand words, but this one is a picture-perfect disaster. When the photographer shows us the images he captured of Reese and me, I am at a loss for words. I can't even come up with one, let alone a thousand.

Then, when Carter rejoins the shoot, the photographer shows a few images of him and me. They came out equally stunning yet different.

I have taken dozens of pictures with Carter, and I'm starting to question my smile in a way I never have before. Does it belong there? Right now, I'm questioning everything. Again. To me, it looks like someone took another woman's smile and photocopied it onto my face. Yet everyone else sees a happy bride-to-be. They keep saying how happy we look. If they can see it, why can't I?

I just don't get it! I *am* happy.

Maybe the stress of everything is weighing more heavily on me than I realize, and it's starting to distort the way I think and feel—maybe even what I see. I've always been the one telling Carter to loosen up and not take life so seriously, but somehow, as soon as he slipped that ring on my finger, we switched places.

We only have two more months until the wedding, and it feels like it's moving both lightning-fast and glacially slow. I'm starting to think that this is more than just cold feet. But I love Carter, so I'm sure my feet will warm up by the time I walk down the aisle.

The photographer's assistant reappears just as he starts packing up. Apparently, she got lost and couldn't find her way back, so she missed half the shoot. At least Kenny did a good job as a substitute.

"My face hurts from all the smiling," Carter teases.

"So does mine. Imagine how they'll feel the day of the wedding," I say.

"Given how happy I'll be, it will be worth the pain." He leans in and wraps his arm around me. We decide to sit for a minute on a nearby park bench, watching people walk and run past us. One older couple catches my eye. They look so in love—so carefree and lost in a world that only they belong to.

When I turn toward Carter to point them out, as if to ask, "Do you think that will be us in the future?" I notice he's not even looking out into the park. He's looking down at his phone. By the time he looks up, the couple has disappeared.

"Did you say something?" he asks me. "I'm just checking messages to make sure nothing exploded at work while I've been gone."

"No big deal," I say.

"Well, I should head back to work. I have a meeting in an hour that I need to prepare for. Marcus wants to rehearse before the deposition." He stands, stretching. "If we land this, it will be huge for the firm. One step closer to seeing my name on the door." He bends and kisses me on the forehead. "Would you like me to walk you back to the agency?"

"No, I think I will hang out here a bit longer," I say.

"Are you sure?" he asks, visibly worried about leaving me alone in the park. But it's daytime, and my work is only a short walk away.

After Carter leaves, I feel a sense of doom hanging over me like a dark cloud. A completely overwhelming, hopelessly doomed dark cloud. But when I try to define this feeling, I come up short. I have the words—just not the definition.

In the distance, I see Kenny and Reese talking near a hot dog stand while I'm sitting here alone, wondering why these feelings are hitting me on a Tuesday, on a park bench in the middle of Central Park.

Then, Reese looks over, and the park tilts like I'm on one of those carnival rides.

Was what I once felt for him lust? Because what I'm feeling right now doesn't feel like nostalgia. Maybe a little. But it's wrapped up in something slow and terrifying.

*Does he always notice me?*

"Hi," he says as he approaches me. "Did Carter leave?"

"Yeah," I reply. "He had a meeting to get to."

"Is everything Ok?" he asks as he takes the seat beside me.

I look out into the park at all the passersby. "Can I ask you something?"

"Sure," he replies.

"Strictly professional," I add.

He laughs. "Got it. Professional."

"You've done a lot of weddings, so you've probably seen it all, right?" I face him. He's wearing his sunglasses, which makes it hard to read his expression.

"Relatively speaking, I suppose," he says, as if choosing his words carefully.

"Are brides supposed to feel a certain way? I always thought I was supposed to feel one way, but I find myself feeling differently." I swallow the uncertainty lodged in my throat. "Is that normal?"

He looks at me as if the question I ask scares him. "Depends on the situation," he finally says. "And what you're feeling."

"Can you explain?" I ask.

"Can you?" he asks, but I say nothing. "Well," he clears his throat, "people have expectations about everything in life—and they also attach the feelings they're supposed to feel to those expectations. That doesn't mean it's right. Right means something different to each of us," he says.

I look at him as my chest tightens. My heart pounds so hard I'm afraid he might see it—feel it.

He watches as I fix my necklace, which somehow got tangled in my hair during the photoshoot. When I keep struggling to free it, he leans over to help.

And I think—

*I could love you, couldn't I, Reese?*

*I did love you, didn't I? That one night?*

My stomach drops because even thinking these thoughts feels awful. I can't ever fall for him because allowing myself to do this would be like stepping back into The Last Chapter and back inside my bedroom.

I suddenly feel the heat.

The danger.

The truth of everything.

And then I remember, with such horrifying clarity, what his voice sounded like against my neck.

"What if you have no expectations?" I ask, immediately reminded of the words I told him that night. I didn't plan to say this, but when has anything gone as planned for me?

"Don't be silly, Everly. We both know there's no such thing."

# Chapter Twenty-Seven
## Flirty Dancing



You have got to be kidding me.

Moments before I'm about to leave my apartment for our dance lesson, Carter messages me that he has a work emergency that he can't get out of and asks to reschedule.

But we can't reschedule. We are supposed to be there in thirty minutes, so canceling on such short notice would be wrong.

I sigh. *Why does it feel like we are off on the wrong foot?* No pun intended.

When I arrive at the dance studio, which smells faintly of lemon floor polish and feet, Morgan is already waiting for me. I walk over to her, sit down, and swap my sneakers for heels, trying hard not to stare at the wall-length mirrors lining the entire wall in front of me. The lighting is rather harsh, making me afraid of what it may reveal—pores and all.

Morgan takes off her jean jacket and appears to be wearing a dance leotard underneath. "What are you wearing?" I ask, trying to stifle a laugh.

"I had zero notice and no idea what to wear," she says.

"We are practicing for the wedding—not auditioning for *The Nutcracker*," I tease.

"Is Carter really not coming?" she asks.

"Work emergency," I say, worried about how often I might have to say that in the future.

She nods but says nothing, just as the instructor announces that all the happy couples should gather around her.

## Reese

This is the first night I've had off in weeks, maybe even months. I want nothing to do with vows or weddings. I want to spend the evening doing what I want—writing what I want to write. But just as I'm about to leave my apartment, my phone buzzes. It's Kenny.

He fakes a cough as soon as I answer the phone. "I think I have the flu," he says before I have the chance to say hello.

"No, you don't," I say.

"I do, which is why I need your help," he says as I hear a ding on my phone. He posted a picture of himself holding a pitcher of margaritas on his social media about fifteen minutes ago. Had he not forced me to follow him, I would not have found out.

I'm not a social media guy, but I only recently decided to join after considering how to promote my book. But what book? I have nothing to promote, so my page has remained empty except for one picture of a glass of bourbon and another of the New York Library.

"You poor thing. You must have that margarita flu going around." I roll my eyes.

"Wait—how did you? Crap!" he says when he realizes I caught him.

"What do you need, Kenny?" I ask.

"Everly's maid of honor, Morgan, just texted me. Apparently, Carter flaked out on tonight's dance lesson, and Morgan wanted to see if I could fill in," he says.

"OK? Have fun. Break a leg," I say as I'm about to hang up, but he stops me.

"But I can't go, Reese. I've had way too many margaritas, and I'll be doing the Cupid Shuffle or Cha Cha Slide like it's the early 2000s. I'm in club-dancing condition, not ballroom," he says. "Which leaves you."

"Leaves me for what?"


Kenny is dead to me.

That little cake-eating rat set me up. Instead of a quiet evening of writing, I'm forced to fill in for Carter at what's supposed to be his wedding dance lesson. How is this even right?

I open the studio doors about twenty minutes later, when all eyes turn to me. It's clear I've interrupted something because the instructor glares at me as if I'm the mayor in *Footloose*, here to tell her that dancing is outlawed.

"OK," I mutter under my breath. "You help write vows for couples all the time. You can certainly survive a waltz."

*Everly*

*What the hell is he doing here?*

I watch as Reese stands in the doorway, wearing a leather jacket and jeans, looking as if he has no business being in this room, or as if he's about to announce he's auditioning for *Grease*.

I lean into Morgan and whisper, "Did you call him?"

"No," she whispers back, and my heart flutters. "I texted Kenny, but he said he has the flu and didn't tell me he was sending Reese." She shrugs as if it's no big deal.

*But it is a big deal!*

As Reese makes his way over to me, Morgan asks whether she is free to go.

"I guess so?" I say, more of a question, because I don't want her to go. I may actually need her to stay, but there's no way I can tell her that.

After she walks away, leaving Reese standing in front of me, I fold my arms as if assessing the situation I'm stuck in. "Can you even dance?" I ask him.

"Shouldn't matter either way. These are dance lessons, right?" he smirks.

"So, basically, you're saying that you don't know how to dance?" I stare back at him.

"That's a bold assumption coming from someone who scheduled a dance lesson." Reese raises an eyebrow at me. "You strike me as someone who trips over air."

I try not to laugh, but I do. Then Reese offers me his hand, and I hesitate for a second before taking it. I feel like this is a bad idea—an undeniably electric bad idea. I'm literally dancing with the devil.

"Now, your other hand," Reese says as he gently guides my one hand to his shoulder.

Like muscle memory, my hands remember being here before. The only difference is that they can't get as comfortable as they once did.

"How wonderful!" The instructor claps her hands together, smushing Reese into me. "The groom has finally arrived!" The last time Reese and I were this close, we were… well, less clothed.

However, I have no time to correct her because she turns the music up louder, as if that will help everyone find their rhythm.

"What exactly are we practicing?" Reese asks as he tries to follow the instructor's directions.

"Our first dance," I say, then correct myself. "I mean, Carter's and my first dance."

That's when I remember how upset I am with Carter for missing our appointment. He should really be here. Of all the appointments, this one is especially important.

I wish I could say I was surprised, but things like this happen all the time. His job is intense and unpredictable. It's not like he purposefully missed being here. Now I'm here without him, practicing a dance that was supposed to be shared with him—and it's difficult to practice a dance when your partner isn't here to learn the steps.

The music starts again, this time soft and romantic. I force myself to look everywhere else but at Reese.

## Reese

The instructor walks over to us again and pushes us even closer. If she does it again, I'm going to have to peel Everly off me.

"You both are dancing as if you've just met," she teases us. "Mr. Jacobs, please place your right hand on her waist."

I freeze. I can't touch Everly like this. I know it's just a dance, but still. Then, without a moment to waste, the instructor takes my hand for me. Everything within me stills as I become aware of everything. The curve of her. The way she inhaled just slightly when I touched her. And the fact that I would give anything to move my thumb an inch more. But I don't.

"Five, six, seven—" the instructor counts.

I step left. Everly steps right, but somehow we collide. We can't help but laugh, and I'm grateful for it because it eases some of my tension and brings me back into focus.

"This is humiliating," Everly groans.

"You're the one with two left feet," I say teasingly.

"Well, you keep stepping on my toes," she says playfully.

"You were in the way," I say. "But seriously, relax. I can actually feel the tension radiating off you."

"Relax?" she huffs. "You're holding onto me as if I might run away."

My mouth twitches as I loosen my hold on her.


## Everly

This time, I manage to take three steps before slipping slightly into Reese. His hands instantly tighten around my waist to steady me.

"See?" he smiles. "You have to hold on."

My breath hitches. "I'm trying."

*I'm trying not to enjoy this as much as I actually am.*

After a few tries, we find our rhythm. It's not awkward—it's more about us trying to navigate around things we cannot see, like conversations we've shared that remain unresolved—mini cliffhangers that make me too scared to turn the page.

Reese spins me softly, and for some strange reason, I can't help but give in to how much fun I'm having. Even the instructor nods at us approvingly.

"You're doing great," Reese whispers quietly.

"Don't jinx it," I chuckle. "So, tell me, why are you here?"

"Kenny has the flu," he answers as he suddenly pulls me closer to match the instructor's demonstration. His hand slides slightly lower on my back, and I forget the choreography. I can't help but remember how those hands once felt. I recall every place they traveled to (and what they did when they got there). It feels like we are the only two people in the room, just like that night at the bar.

*God, that night was pure magic. We vibed. We connected. Our chemistry was the kind that would have me flipping through pages of a romance novel at lightning speed.*

Then, when he made what he thought was a cheesy joke at the bar about happily ever after and how it affected me, because only one other person in my life has made that reference. And then, the mug...

I look at Reese now and wonder if he remembers that night at all. I could be imagining things, but the look in his eyes tells me

I'm not the only one who hasn't forgotten how we felt. It lingers inside us like a pilot light waiting to be fully ignited.

I spin too early, but Reese catches me just as we fall back into sync. We no longer count our steps. We aren't overthinking our moves. We just go with the flow until I notice his fingers curl around mine.

His eyes drop briefly to my lips as my heart races. Our faces draw closer until only breath separates us. In this moment, he shows no teasing or smugness, which I suspect might be a mask for his golden retriever nature. Yet I see something in his eyes I haven't seen since that night I fell asleep in his arms. It's the look of someone trying to figure me out.

Or to see me.

My stomach flips in a way that feels dangerous as his thumb shifts slightly at my waist. It's a small movement, yet powerful enough to send shockwaves through my body. I can barely catch my breath.

"Reese..." his name slips out like a whisper as I grip his shoulder.

His gaze drops again to my lips, and that's when my world flips upside down. *What the fuck is gravity, anyway?*

His face hovers too close to mine, and my pulse thunders in my ears.

"Everly..." he whispers softly. "You're going to ruin me."

We are even closer—closer than necessary, closer than safe. I need to press the reset button and start over.

*What did he just say to me?*

*Should I say something back?*

*Should I back away?*

They all sound like good options, but instead, I do nothing. For one reckless, impossible second, I want him to kiss me. I want to know if everything was as amazing as I have remembered it. I want to find out if this has all been in my head because I overromanticized things. I want to be proven wrong. I so desperately want to be wrong.

But then Reese suddenly steps back, as if he almost jumps out of the way. The moment passes, and once again, another cliffhanger is added to the pile.

## Reese

I step back because I know that if I give in to whatever is happening here, it will be a mistake I could never undo. I can't do that to her or to Carter, for that matter. If I kiss her, it would be under false pretenses, and I wouldn't deserve any redemption.

She fucking scares me.

She scares me because so many thoughts and feelings are surfacing that I can't even begin to express. No one has ever sparked even a fraction of what she evokes in me, and knowing she will soon be starting a life with someone else only reminds me that mine will be ending as hers begins.

But every time I look into her eyes, I'm instantly transported back to that night…

*Her bedroom was quiet—not completely silent, as the city hummed faintly outside the window. Everly lay on her back, staring up at the ceiling. I was beside her, one arm tucked under my head and the other around her.*

*Somehow, the moment feels more intimate than those before. She turns her head slightly toward me.*

*"That was..." her words trailed off and faded into the darkness.*

*"Life-changing? Mind-blowing?" I teased her.*

*She giggled. Yes, giggled. Then another pause settled between us as she pulled the sheets up around her. "So, what's your story?" she asked.*

*I raised an eyebrow. "That's a bold question for someone who said no last names, no phone numbers, and what was the last one? No expectations?"*

*She smiled lazily. "I didn't say we couldn't talk."*

*"I feel like this is a trick," I said.*

*She groaned. "Absolutely not."*

*I laughed because I still didn't believe her. "Well, you started this with your rules."*

*"Yeah, because I don't trust you yet," she said.*

*I smirked. "Didn't seem that way a few minutes ago. Felt like you trusted me just fine."*

*"That was different," she said, looking at me.*

*"How so?" I asked, keeping my gaze on her.*

*But she doesn't respond. Instead, she deflects. "So, you're a writer?"*

*"That's correct."*

*"And what exactly do you write?" she studied me carefully.*

*"Things people have a hard time saying out loud," I said as she nodded, as if she understood what I meant. "People are bad at being honest sometimes."*

*"Or afraid of it." She smiled again.*

*"Which one are you?" I asked. "Bad at it, or just afraid of it?"*

*She frowned slightly. "Tonight? Strangely, neither."*

*Then something inside me stirred. I watched her reach for a glass of water from her nightstand.*

*"Do you ever think people choose the wrong partners just because they believe they're supposed to make that choice?" she asked.*

*It was a strange question, indeed. "That's a loaded question," I laughed.*

*"Just answer it." She nudged me.*

*"I think people choose partners who make sense given where they are in life, and sometimes what makes sense doesn't feel right."*

*"What do you think feels right?" she asked.*

*"I'm not sure," I said, because everything I thought I knew was quickly thrown out the window. "What about you?"*

*"I think if you have to convince yourself of something, it's not right," she answered.*

*"That seems risky."*

*"I think that's why people avoid it," she yawned. "People are sometimes too afraid to pursue what is right because it contradicts what supposedly makes sense. You know what I mean?"*

*The Reese I was that night transformed into a version of myself I never knew existed. I wasn't looking for a quick escape. I wasn't making excuses to leave. I was just thinking about her. I wanted to understand how she thinks, and out of all the questions she could have asked me, I wonder why she chose the one she did.*

*I glanced at her one last time as she was starting to close her eyes.*

*"What I said earlier made sense, but I don't think it's right,"* she said as she fell asleep.

She told me to stay.

FUCK.

*How did I forget this?*

How could I have missed this moment after replaying that night and the morning after in my mind so many times, yet forgotten this major detail? I blew it. I don't even deserve to be standing here.

And now I can't be around her. I don't trust myself. I was seconds away from showing her how much I've missed her—how much I wanted her—and how I regret walking out that morning.

She was justified in storming out of the meeting that first day. In her defense, I did run. She told me to stay, but I fucking left anyway.

Either way, it's too late. *I'm* too late. She's getting married, and I refuse to ruin anyone's life because I failed to commit.

I had a year and a half to find her. Even though I tried, we never reconnected. Yes, I knew where she lived. I even walked past her place now and then, hoping to run into her, but I never saw her. I can't tell her any of this because it's too late.

"That was very good, class!" the instructor announces to the room just as I look up and see Kenny standing by the door, holding a bottle of water and looking very healthy.

"You did great, Everly," I tell her.

She laughs. "You weren't so bad yourself."

*No, Everly. I was bad. How is it that I'm part of a dance not meant for me, yet I'm the only one who knows the steps?*

Everly walks toward Kenny, smoothing her dress. "I thought you had the flu?" she says.

"I did," he answers. "It was an emotional flu, but it passed."

Everly smiles. "Well, I'm glad you're feeling better," she says, walking over to her bag to change her shoes.

As Kenny walks toward me, all I can focus on is the dance lesson. I can still feel the movement. Her hand. Her waist. The way she looked me in the eyes. And worse, the way I looked back into hers.

I'm growing more fearful as the wedding date gets closer that what I'm feeling isn't just some silly distraction or temporary emotion. I know for sure it's not because I romanticized or became obsessed with her like some lovestruck teenager. It's not a feeling I can easily shake off.

There was a problem—a HUGE problem. A very specific, very persistent, very Everly-shaped problem. And this was the first time in my life that I had faced a problem I couldn't fix.

I'm not equipped for this.

I'm not equipped for her.

### Everly

I slide out of my heels and put my sneakers back on.

Just like when the effects of alcohol wear off, and you start thinking and seeing things more clearly, I'm now mortified and embarrassed that I almost crossed an unforgivable line. Fortunately, nothing happened. What did happen was that I let my guard down with him, and I refuse to make that mistake ever again.

After I grab my things and thank the instructor, the three of us step outside the studio, where we are greeted by a chill in the evening air. It feels refreshing after an hour of dancing.

"Would you like us to walk you home?" Reese offers.

"No, that's OK," I say, "I already scheduled a cab." But just as I'm about to reach for my phone, I look up and see Morgan walking toward us.

"Morgan? I thought you had gone home," I ask.

"I was going to, but then I figured I would hang out here and enjoy the show," she says, gesturing toward the windows into the studio, where you can clearly see inside.

"You stayed outside and watched?" I ask her.

"Not the whole time. I went and got a little margarita flu myself," she laughs as Kenny shrugs. "How about you and I get a drink? My treat."

**I'm halfway through my** second glass of wine when Morgan finally says, "So..." as if she's been waiting all night to say that one word.

"So?" I echo.

"Really?" She shoots me a look. "Let's not do this dance."

I laugh. "Would you rather do one of the dances I learned tonight?" But she doesn't laugh back. "Seriously, what's wrong?"

She sits across from me, running her fingers along the stem of her wine glass. "Are you OK?"

"Of course," I say. "Why?"

Morgan hums. "Are you sure?"

"Is this about Carter missing tonight's session? Yeah, it sucked, but I'm fine," I reassure her.

She takes another sip of wine, then reclines in her seat. "OK then."

I glance back at her. "That's it?"

She shrugs. "You said you were fine."

I frown. "But you don't believe me, do you?"

She smiles at me the way only a best friend can. "I don't think you believe yourself."

A beat passes before I break the silence, saying, "You saw everything. Didn't you?"

"I did," she says. Yet she doesn't argue her point. She doesn't push. She doesn't even judge.

"Are you trying to tell me something?" I ask because her silence is affecting me more than she knows.

"No, we're not there yet," she says, reaching across the table to hold my hand.

# Chapter Twenty-Eight
# This Could Have Been an Email

*Reese*

I like control. I thrive on it. In my personal life, I've maintained a certain level of control over my relationships. To do this, I've always used a "get in, get out before anyone gets hurt" approach.

Throughout the week before the final planning meeting, I needed to regroup. I needed to reassess. I tried to come up with a plan to let go of any lingering feelings I have for Everly, which is way easier said than done. I said it, but I haven't done it. But I have to keep reminding myself that she is getting married. She made her choice, and I had to respect it whether I agreed with it or not.

I could kick myself for being so close to crossing a line. I can blame it on the forced proximity, since she and I have been working closely together. And because there have been some unresolved feelings, it might have sparked a wildfire of emotions that could have been misplaced for both of us. Chemistry happens. It doesn't necessarily mean anything.

I walk into Laurent & Co. and notice Kenny fanning his face. "Ugh, I burned my tongue on this coffee." He holds out the mug he just poured.

"You'll be fine," I say. "Am I late?"

"No. Everyone is with your sister now, discussing the ceremony setup. She wants to make sure the layout, décor, and finishing touches match their vision," he replies. "I'm not worried. I know I killed it."

I'm not a fan of any wedding-planning meeting, but this one is always a logistical nightmare. It's like taking puzzle pieces and trying to assemble them into a clear picture of what the wedding day should look and feel like. Luckily for me, I don't have any involvement in that nonsense. I just need to schedule their last vow session, and then I can walk away from this entire wedding for good.

Kenny leads us to one of our showrooms, where Genny sets up all the mock displays for the brides and grooms to review and approve. It also allows her to make any adjustments before the big day without scrambling to make last-minute changes.

She stands off to the side, her tablet resting almost on the baby bump she now proudly advertises. She has even allowed Kenny to finally announce that she is glowing whenever she enters the room. She points to a few things as she begins reviewing the details, while Carter and Everly listen closely. Carter whispers something to Everly, and a smile spreads across her face. She tilts her head back slightly, and her golden hair catches the light from the chandeliers above. That smile always appears before she even realizes she's smiling. It's a surprise to her as much as it is to everyone else.

Carter leans toward her, pointing at something on a table. She smiles again as a strand of blonde hair slips loose, which she casually tucks back behind her ear—something I've seen her do many times. Yet there's a shift in the energy I haven't felt before. A sick feeling settles in my gut as a sharp, unexpected pain strikes my chest. I refuse to acknowledge it. I will only focus on the job at hand. Nothing more. Nothing less.

But then Everly looks up and kisses Carter. It's a sweet, simple kiss between them, one I've seen countless times from couples. Yet never have those kisses made my heart drop out of my chest, as if I just walked into a life I thought was mine, only to find it had been given to someone else.

So, this is it. This life isn't mine, and it never will be. I had my chance, and I blew it. So the almost kiss we shared doesn't matter. Nothing we ever shared will matter again.

And I hate it.

Because I want it to mean something.

And I have never wanted something this bad…ever.

*Everly*

After the dance lesson, I learned more than a few new steps. I realized I can't let myself get carried away by fantasies. I must avoid crossing the line I nearly crossed that night. That's why, from this moment on, I am focusing solely on the wedding and my future life with Carter. Nothing more. Nothing less.

During this final planning meeting, I will stay composed. By composed, I mean I will absolutely, definitely, and without question pretend I didn't almost kiss Reese.

Genevieve places her tablet on the table just as Mrs. Jacobs and Morgan walk into the room behind us. Kenny and Reese are nowhere to be found.

"OK," Genevieve says to us all. "All that is left is your final vow session. Afterward, Reese will produce your drafts so you both have enough time to make any changes before the big day. From there, we need to finalize your seating chart and finish the last few details of your rehearsal dinner."

"After seeing the mock-up, I'm very pleased with how everything is coming together," Carter's mom says, as if she's speaking for everyone.

Just as Genevieve is about to move on to her next agenda item, Reese and Kenny walk into the conference room. Reese carries himself as if nothing happened. Yet there is an invisible thread taut between us. He refuses to look at me just as much as I refuse to look at him. That tells me he came with a plan, too. His plan is the same as mine.

"Sorry, we're late," Reese apologizes. "Kenny burnt his tongue on his coffee and claims he can no longer feel joy."

A laugh escapes me as Kenny sits beside Morgan, who appears calm yet strangely watchful. Her eyes flick around the table. Since the night we went for drinks, we haven't spoken much, and I doubt we will do much of that here.

"Did we miss anything?" Kenny asks.

"We're just finishing up the final few items. I trust everything is ready for the final stretch?" Genevieve looks at both Kenny and Reese.

"We are so ready that we could have this wedding tomorrow," Kenny winks.

Thank goodness he's not being serious.


## *Reese*

After Genny leaves the room, Kenny begins discussing the flow of the ceremony, the timing of the reception, and whether any last-minute adjustments are needed. I have to admit, as much as I thought Kenny was scatterbrained, he has thought of every detail and executed everything to everyone's expectations. Had it been left to me, I would have written enough to fit on a Post-It.

"If I may interrupt for a second?" Morgan raises her hand. "I still need help with my speech. The wedding is a month away, and I'd like to have it completed."

I had completely forgotten to help Morgan with her speech. I lean back in my chair as I scroll through my phone's calendar. We have another wedding starting in a couple of weeks, so with the overlap, things will be total chaos. "Can you do this Saturday?" I suggest. It's the only day I have nothing important planned.

Morgan shifts in her chair as she checks her schedule. "That will work. Just let me know the time and location," she says. "Oh, and by the way, I would really like my speech to have a touch of humor. Can you do that?"

"Be funny?" I ask her. "I can be hilarious."

Everly laughs, which she quickly cuts off as if she were crossing another line.

"Great," Morgan continues. "I just don't want anything too sappy. I'm not much of a cryer."

Kenny snorts. "Didn't you just post on social media that some dog food commercial made you cry?"

We all sit back and watch the two of them bicker. Kenny only bickers with his friends, so maybe they're friends now? That's news to me.

"Structure matters," I interrupt them before they end up taking over the meeting. "With all speeches, you want to start with a strong opening—something that grabs the audience's attention. Then, you can add a personal touch and a bit of humor before closing with an emotionally packed ending."

Out of the corner of my eye, I see Everly glance at me as if I just explained a scientific equation. She seems impressed. She smiles.

And there it is again. I feel it like a gentle breeze sweeping through the room. It's an awareness that tension still bubbles beneath the surface, and if we're not careful, it could erupt. Again.

"As for your vows," Kenny picks up where he left off, "we will want to build in a pause after they are spoken."

Mrs. Jacobs nods with approval as Carter asks additional logistical questions.

"Please also make sure you've already scheduled your final fittings. We don't want any wardrobe issues on the wedding day," Kenny adds. "Other than that, we will see you all the night of the rehearsal."

"I have to say, this process has been wonderful," Carter says as he stands. "Everything looks great and appears to be on track." He shakes Kenny's and my hands. "Unfortunately, I have to get back to the office, but Reese, please let me know about the final vow session."

I nod. "Will do," I say as he kisses Everly on the cheek.

## *Kenny*

Mrs. Jacobs quickly leaves with Carter, as if she doesn't want to be left in the room any longer than necessary. As I'm about to add a few last notes on my tablet, Morgan speaks up.

"This was…productive," she says slowly as I realize Reese and Everly have also left the room.

"I'm glad you think so," I say.

"To be honest, it could have been an email." She rolls her eyes.

"Yeah, but then you wouldn't have had the pleasure of seeing me," I smirk. Why does it feel like she and I have reached the point where we communicate without actually saying anything? "Plus, you learn more."

"I've definitely learned that wedding planning creates a lot of tension." Her brow lifts.

I exhale sharply. *Here we go again.*

"Kenny, look at me." She grabs me by the chin, but I still try my best to avoid meeting her gaze. "You see it, too, right?"

"See what?" Morgan really needs to drop this.

From inside the room's glass enclosure, we look out and see Reese and Everly talking. Morgan tilts her head, watching them as if she is studying something more interesting than wedding logistics.

Morgan's lips twitch. "Work with me here."

"On what, exactly?" I narrow my eyes at her. There's absolutely no way I'm telling on Reese.

She leans back in her seat before getting up and grabbing her bag. She does so slowly—almost intentionally—as if she is stalling.

"I'm worried," she finally says. "I'm worried that no one is going to do anything about this." She slings her bag over her shoulder. "Can I ask you something?" she lowers her voice.

"Maybe…"

"How well do you know Reese?" Her eyes bore into mine as if trying to weed out any lie I might tell.

"He's my friend and co-worker. Why?"

"Does he have feelings for anyone?"

"Why do you want to date him?" I laugh.

"If you're his friend, tell me what we do," she asks as I nearly choke on my cold coffee.

"We? What are you even talking about?" Unfortunately, I do know what she's talking about, but I can't tell her.

Morgan smirks. "Oh, there's definitely a 'we.'"

I shake my head and set my coffee down. "I'm sorry, but this is outside my professional boundaries."

"Is that so? And does everyone in the company follow the same professional boundaries?"

I let out a sigh. "What do you want?"

"The same thing you do," she says.

"Professional boundaries," I say through clenched teeth.

"Oh, Kenny. We are totally going to break those," she says, walking out of the room.

And then I realize that the perfect wedding I've planned is about to turn into a perfect disaster.

# Part FOUR

# Chapter Twenty-Nine
# Something Borrowed,
# Something Hidden

*Everly*

By Friday night, my apartment smells like candles and indecision, which, if I'm being honest, feels fitting. Morgan and I are sitting in my living room, with magazines scattered across my coffee table and Pinterest open on my laptop. Morgan refills our wine glasses as we keep planning my bachelorette party.

"I want nothing crazy," I tell her for the hundredth time.

"OK, so you're going for boring? Basic?" she fakes a yawn.

"It doesn't have to be boring, but I don't want anything over the top," I say, sitting cross-legged on the floor, sipping my wine.

"Are penis party favors over the top?" she asks me. "I need to know where the line is drawn here."

"Minimal penis party favors," I say. "But what if we did something literary-themed?" I figured that since I can't have the wedding I always pictured, this might help fill the void.

"That sounds fun! A penis for each trope," she laughs.

I shake my head. "Sure," I say, since it's obvious I won't win the penis fight.

"I can create some fun games, and maybe we can get drunk and go book shopping? Oh! And we definitely need to stop at The Last Chapter because it's a literary-themed bar," she says.

"The Last Chapter?" I ask.

"Yeah? Why? Is that a problem?"

There isn't a specific problem, per se. It's just that I haven't been back there since that night with—well, you know. And it wasn't exactly a place Carter ever suggested we visit. Knowing Carter now, it definitely wouldn't have been a good first-date spot.

"Well, we can iron out those details later," she says, moving on to other ideas she found online. "What about sharing ex-stories while wearing comfy pjs or matching robes?"

"Absolutely not," I laugh. "There is no way I'm rehashing those messy memories."

"Oh, come on! It would be so much fun, not to mention hilarious. Imagine the drama." She tilts her glass of wine at me.

"I *lived* the drama," I say. "I don't need a reenactment."

"Think of them as survivor stories," she grins as I reach for my glass of wine but miss it by a hair. "You seem… distracted. What's going on with you?"

"I'm not distracted. I've been participating all night," I say.

She raises an eyebrow. "You literally just tried to grab your wine glass, which was six inches away from where you were reaching."

"So?" I huff as Morgan walks over and plops down beside me.

"Wedding stuff?" she asks.

I nod because it seems like the safest answer.

She leans back into the couch. "You know, you don't have to convince me of anything. I've been to a few of these meetings, and it's a war zone."

I smile, but just as quickly as it appears, it falls into an unexpected frown. "It's also…" I start, staring down at my hands, twisting my engagement ring as I try to remember everything it's supposed to symbolize. "It's weird, you know? Everything is happening exactly as it's supposed to."

"Oh, you poor thing," she replies sarcastically. "What's wrong with that?"

"It feels like I'm having an out-of-body experience—watching everything happen outside myself." I shrug. "Yet nothing feels the way I expected."

She takes a deep breath, as if savoring fresh air. "Nothing in life ever feels the way we've been told it's supposed to feel. That's why we live in fictional worlds—at least we get to feel it there." She nudges me on the shoulder. "But as your best friend, I want to remind you that you're allowed to feel anything you want, even if it doesn't match the plan or other people's expectations."

I look at her. "Even if the plan is good?"

Morgan smiles. "Especially then."

"Carter is…" I begin, but I have no idea where my words are headed. Morgan looks at me knowingly, as if I don't need to finish that thought.

"He's great," she says for me. "And Reese?" she asks. The name hits like dropped glass. It shatters before me, and I'm afraid that if I move, I might cut myself.

"Why would you ask me about him?" I look at her. "You know he's just part of the process—nothing more. Not to mention, I thought we had talked about all this after the dance lesson?"

"And you and I both agreed that he's a very intense, very attractive, very tattooed obstacle in this process." She winks as if to make light of it all.

I groan. "Can we not do this again? We're supposed to be planning my bachelorette party, not talking about him."

"If I may, I'm pulling my BFF card," she says, pretending to draw a card from her pocket. "With this card, nothing leaves the room. OK?"

I hesitate for a moment before pretending to accept her card. "Fine. He still makes things complicated. Are you happy?" I roll my eyes.

"Reese makes you fly that freak flag of yours. A flag I have honestly never seen you wave with Carter. Not that it means one is better than the other. I'm just more concerned with who you're waving your white flag for, because that means more," she says.

"I don't know what to say to that. Do you think I'm settling with Carter?"

Morgan sighs as she stands, then places her empty wine glass on the coffee table. "Everly, listen, you don't have to say anything or even have it all figured out. I just want you to know I support whatever you decide."

"What's there to decide? There's nothing to decide, Morgan. I'm with Carter. That decision was made a long time ago," I snap.

"As I said, you don't have to say anything. I just wouldn't be a good friend if I stayed quiet," she says. "But I have to get going. I have my maid of honor speech appointment tomorrow, and I need my beauty rest." She playfully flutters her eyelashes as she picks up her bag and heads toward my door.

"You know," she pauses briefly. "You deserve everything in this world, and I want you to be happy no matter what that looks like or what the plan is."

I sit here for a long time after she leaves. My eyes drift back to my ring, and for the first time since it was put on, I start to wonder whether it fits.

*Reese*

It's Saturday morning, and the office is just as hectic as it is on Monday morning. During wedding season, the business never slows down.

Soft music plays beneath the low murmur of conversation filtering through the consultation rooms. The scent of freshly brewed coffee and lavender room spray permeates my senses. It lingers in the air, intense.

Lila walks by the room and lets Morgan in.

"Come in," I tell Morgan, but for a moment, it seems Lila thinks I'm speaking to her. Her face brightens with hope, then quickly darkens. She walks away, disappointed.

"She's pretty," Morgan says, referring to Lila.

"Yeah," I say because she is. She's just not my type. Then again, I wonder what my type will be, since Everly pretty much knocked it out of the park in every category.

"So, do you normally write the bridal party speeches, or is this more of a favor?" she asks as she slides into the seat across from me.

"I don't usually, no. But I don't mind helping out," I say.

The session with Morgan starts light and easy. She jokes a lot, but most of her jokes seem like a defense mechanism, as if she likes to hide truths behind them. Like Kenny, it's hard to get her to focus, which is proving to be an unexpected challenge.

"Let's start with something real," I say, trying to reel her back in. "Don't think about the guests' reactions. Just think about what you want to say if it were just you and Everly."

Morgan pulls a notebook out of her bag. She came prepared. As for me, I not only brought my notebook, but also my laptop in case I have time to write what I want.

"Just so you know, I'm not great with emotional vulnerability. I like it in my characters, but not for me." She looks at me as if I have the antidote to her problem. However, I'm the worst person to help her with that. The only thing I can do is help her fake it during her speech.

"Emotional vulnerability is where the interesting stuff lies," I tell her. "Let's see what we can dig up."

"So, you really know what you're doing." She studies me. "Like they didn't just plant you in this position for show."

I laugh. "Was that supposed to be a compliment?"

"It can be," she says with a smile.


## Morgan

A few minutes later, Kenny is waving to Reese outside the glass door. "Your sidekick really needs to see you." I point to where Kenny is now jumping up and down like a toddler eager to go outside and play.

"I can't leave him alone for five minutes," Reese chuckles. "I'll be back in a few minutes. Help yourself to coffee or anything else on the refreshment table," he offers as he pushes his laptop aside and leaves the room.

As I sit in my seat, a surge of curiosity washes over me. I get up and grab a bottle of water, wondering whether I should do what I'm considering. I glance back at the door and see that Reese and Kenny are nowhere in sight. Then I look at Reese's laptop. I know I shouldn't, but the screen is still on, and a document is open. Would it really hurt if I took a quick peek? Seriously, what's the worst that could happen?

Before I can talk myself out of it, I quickly walk over, eyes flicking to the screen. I see he has started crafting my speech. I have to admit, it has a pretty strong opening. But just as I feel my curiosity satisfied, I notice he has another document open as well. I click the tab, and it opens…

*She said no last names, no phone numbers, and no expectations. I agreed because I believed it was the right thing to do. I thought I was respecting her boundaries.*

*Now, I've been left trying to survive that choice.*

I scroll to the bottom of the page and read more:

*Romance is dead. True love? Soulmates? I think they are just commercially marketed labels we're supposed to buy into, like the dreaded Valentine's Day. I've never taken any of this seriously, yet I get paid to convince others that, yes, they all exist.*

*What's marriage without true love? And how can romance be dead when two people look into each other's eyes and feel what they feel? Like butterflies.*

*But there is always a morning after. You know, when the dust settles. Or, in this case, butterflies. And that is what my 80,000-word novel, The Last Chapter, is about—the real-life happily ever afters. What happens after the couple rides into the sunset? What happens after the curtain falls on the movie and the final page is turned in the book?*

*We have been led to believe that it's real life, and as a result, our expectations about love have been skewed.*


I skim what appears to be a draft of a query letter, then head straight to the first chapter. My palms sweat. My chest tightens. I know this is wrong as I glance toward the door to make sure I'm still safe. But the only thing I can't stop thinking about is: Reese wrote a novel?

*Chapter One*

*The strange thing about love is that sometimes you meet someone who feels like someone you've known long before you're brave enough to stay. So he told himself that one night meant nothing— that people meet strangers in bars every day and, come morning, carry on with their lives. Unfortunately, as he's learned, the night doesn't always end when the sun comes up. Some nights follow you home and lead you back to their doorstep a year and a half later. And if you're lucky, you won't find someone else answering the door.*

My heart pounds in my ears. I'm reading faster now—pages, moments, a girl, a bar—caught in a night that didn't feel like a mistake. The knife the universe drove in the main character's back at the precise moment his cynical heart finally believed in love, tore me up.

The sad part is that he never wanted to be right about how much he cared for her. He wanted so badly to be wrong, so it wouldn't hurt as much to know she was in love with someone else.

So, I take another quick look at the doorway, and the coast is still clear. I open my email browser and decide to send the file to myself before erasing my history by the time Reese returns.

Now, I sit quietly in my seat as if nothing happened. But everything did, and I feel like so much more is about to happen.

## Reese

I usually don't write the full speech in front of the client, but Morgan is insistent that I finish it today so she can review, practice, and modify it if necessary. However, one of the perks of this job is that I get to sit behind the words, shape them in private, and polish them without watchful eyes.

"We've been here for two hours. Are you stalling? Are you at a loss for words?" she asks, tapping her pen on the table.

I glance up at her. "I'm editing. If you would let me handle this part on my own, you could have left already."

"Editing is crossing out the same sentence four times?" She looks at me.

"Who says it's the same sentence?" I reply. She's not wrong, but there's no way in hell I'm going to admit it to her. The sentence I'm unsure about just sits there, half-formed, as if it's waiting for me to be honest about it.

*Everly is the kind of friend who...*

I drag my pen through it again as Morgan leans forward, elbows resting on the table. "You're very good at this," she teases.

"Flattery won't make your speech better," I roll my eyes. "How about we start with a moment?" I suggest. "Don't summarize, though. People get bored with long, drawn-out stories."

"A moment with Everly?" She taps her pen against her lip, thinking. "OK. How about this? Everly once cried in a bookstore after accidentally reading the last page of a book and ruining the ending for herself."

"That's good." I write that down.

"You write like you're trying to fix something," she says to me. "What I've learned from my authors is that the right words never fix anything. They just make certain pages harder to ignore. They carry a reader through a book."

"What do you mean?" I look at her.

"For example, words create plot points, Easter eggs, or subtle hints that resurface with greater force when the truth is revealed. They make the book's revelations more powerful," she explains.

"When readers notice the small details, those details become more significant."

After Morgan leaves, I decide not to hold the final vow session with Carter and Everly because the wedding is so close. Given Carter's limited schedule, I decide to do things differently.

For one, I refuse to meet with Everly alone. Next, I am just going to email them some last-minute questions to help me fill in the gaps in their speeches. This was the safest way for me to officially separate and detach. I know I will end up giving them the best vows in the world because, regardless of my role in this story, the one thing I know I can give her is the words she deserves to hear.

The *right* words.

And I may throw in an Easter egg or two.

# *Chapter Thirty*
## *Fiction isn't Fiction*

*Morgan*

Later that night, I sit cross-legged on my apartment floor. I made a quick pitstop at work after leaving Laurent & Co. and printed Reese's entire manuscript. Now, it's spread before me like evidence in a case I'm desperate to solve.

His manuscript reads like a confession. I know it's wrong of me to have taken it, but I needed to read it. I needed to know the truth. And this is the closest I could get to it.

I read every line, feeling the ache he poured into his words, which were so beautifully and delicately crafted that if I hadn't known the subtext, I would have signed this book immediately. This wasn't written as a simple attraction or lust (although some parts had me sweating). It also wasn't nostalgic or written out of a need for closure. It was pure, unfiltered love.

It feels like I'm peeking behind the curtain and seeing a side of Reese he has successfully kept hidden from the world. But what I can't understand is why he wants to hide that part of himself.

*No one has ever made me want to stay. Usually, I find any excuse to leave. This time, I just want to lie back down and ignore the door completely. But she asked me to leave. She made that very clear.*

*...She laughs as if she believes the world is full of possibilities.*

*...The problem with one night is that it can sometimes ruin the rest of your life.*

*...She doesn't have to love me in return, but she at least deserves to know how much she is loved and how deeply I regret not staying.*

When I reach the end, I exhale slowly. It says it's written by R.E.M., which I find to be a clever name.

The last page of the book feels heavy, as if I'm holding a bag of bricks.

"He loves her," I say out loud, as if I'm announcing my discovery to a room of fellow detectives.

And this discovery changes everything.

*Reese*

I'm scheduled to meet with the new bride and groom this morning, and I'm already feeling wedding-fatigued. As for Kenny, he's on his second cup of coffee and stretching in the corner as if he's about to run a marathon.

As I set my bag down, the doors to the consultation room swing open, and Morgan is standing in the doorway, looking for…

*Me?*

"I read it," she frowns.

"What? You don't like your speech?" I ask. I'm actually quite surprised because I thought it turned out great.

"No. Your manuscript," she corrects as I almost fall over.

"I'm sorry, but how? How the hell did you manage to read it?" I look at her, then back at my leather bag, as if trying to piece together the mystery. "Wait—did you go through my laptop?" I ask as Kenny stops stretching and falls to the floor. The silence in the room is sharp enough to cause irreparable damage. I feel cornered. I don't like it. I want to defend myself.

*But how?*

"I didn't have to go through anything," Morgan fires back. "It was right there." She points to the table where I left it behind to go tend to Kenny's wedding distress.

My jaw tightens. "But it's *my* laptop."

"Which you left open," she says as if that excuses her behavior.

"That still doesn't give you the right to go through my things," I snap.

She softens. "I know. And you have every right to be mad at me, but I needed to know the truth," she says as Kenny tries to tiptoe out of the room, but she stops him. "You're not going anywhere, Kenny boy."

"You're right. I am mad." I run my hand through my hair. "There is nothing for you to know or find out," I say as Morgan steps closer, calmer now.

"But what about her?" she asks, as if begging me to come clean.

I shake my head. "I have no idea what you're getting at. You read a story. Stories are fiction."

"Fiction is never just fiction," she says.

"Well, there is a wedding happening, and I think we all need to focus on that," I say.

"But you wrote an entire book about her," she cuts in, like a knife through my armor.

"That doesn't mean I get to have her," I say, as Kenny and Morgan look like I just canceled Christmas.

Her shoulders tremble. "Confessing your feelings doesn't make you the bad guy. In some stories, it makes you the hero," she says, twisting some of the words she took from my book.

The room is quiet when she leaves. Or maybe it's just me. Kenny hasn't said a word, which is very unusual for him. He never shuts up—especially about feelings. Because of this, I find myself hoping he would say something. Anything.

I remain frozen in place. My coffee has gone cold in my hand as I stare at the spot where Morgan was standing, hoping that the conversation might rewind itself if I wait long enough.

"This is fucking great," I mutter. Of course, this is how it happens. But this isn't some kiss I can't take back or a comment I shouldn't have made. This is a confession wrapped in a story to sugarcoat the truth. But this book wasn't meant for anyone to read. At least, not yet. My words were private, and I feel invaded.

I don't know Morgan well enough to know whether she would run and tell Everly or, worse, show her.

*That doesn't mean I get to have her.*

I said that. Me. I meant every word. I still do. But every time I promise myself I will put my feelings on hold—to take a step back—I get pulled back into the ring to fight for something I can never win—or have.

I close my eyes. There's no outcome here that wouldn't make me the bad guy, no matter what Morgan said. I don't have the right to say or do anything. I can't just ruin other people's lives because I failed to take the lead in my own.

If I left once, I can do it again.

# Chapter Thirty-One
## Good on Paper



It's Wednesday afternoon, and I'm looking at the calendar invite for Carter's and Everly's final vow session, which has been canceled. Carter had declined it due to a work conflict before I had the chance to cancel it on my own. My cursor hovers over the email, wondering how best I'm going to wrap this up.

I guess it's good timing because, according to Kenny, it's Carter and Everly's bachelor and Bachelorette parties this weekend. I doubt they're thinking about their vows.

I lean back in my chair. This isn't how I normally do things. It's not my process, nor is it how I've become successful. Either way, it's the only way to get the job done. And that's how I'm approaching this situation because I have zero desire—personally or professionally—to be alone with Everly.

Subject: Final Vow Session Questions

Hello,

Due to scheduling conflicts and the tight timeline, I have decided to move our final session to a written format. I have attached a list of questions. Please answer them honestly. Don't overthink them. Vows are not meant to be perfect; they are meant to be genuine.

Send your responses back to me separately.

Best Regards,
Reese Myers
Professional Vow Writer
Laurent & Co.

After I hit send, I realize I have effectively removed myself from the situation. Distance is the only way I can survive this.

## Everly

I read Reese's email once. Then twice. Then a third time. My chest, in turn, feels… strange. Off. Like I've been rejected or something. No, that feeling isn't right or appropriate.

So, there won't be a final vow session with Reese. I knew Carter wouldn't be able to make it, but I didn't expect Reese to cancel the whole thing and turn the meeting into an email. Then again, maybe it's for the best. The last thing I need is to be alone with him again. This should make things simpler, but instead, I feel almost cheated, as if a part of the process was taken from me.

Fine. If this is the way he wants things, then so be it. My fingers hover over my keyboard and begin responding.

Q: What made you say yes?"
A: *Because it made sense.*

I stare at my answer before deleting it.

Q: What made you say yes?"
A: *Because Carter is everything I've ever wanted in a partner. He's stable, kind, and always there for me.*

My cursor blinks, waiting for me to add something more, but I don't.

Q: **When did you first know this was something real?**

My fingers slow. *How am I supposed to answer that?*

Q: **When did you first know this was something real?**
A: *Because Carter shows up for me. Consistently. Without question.*

Q: **What does forever look like to you—with them, specifically?**
A: *Safe.*

That feels like the loudest answer yet. One word says it all.

Q: **What do they give you that no one else ever has?**
A: *Peace.*

I lean back and close my eyes. It's true. It's honest. But it's not the same.

**Q: What would you regret if you didn't say it out loud?**
**A: ….**

This one stings.

## Reese

Surprisingly, both Everly's and Carter's responses came back to me within a couple of hours. I open Everly's first, knowing I probably shouldn't. But since I'm a masochist and a glutton for emotional punishment, I do.

I'm also not surprised to find her answers are once again basic. Safe. Generic.

As for Carter, he responds with more gusto but remains very matter-of-fact. At the end, he invites Kenny and me to his bachelor night. When I tell Kenny about it, he says it would be rude to decline. So I guess we're going.

An hour later, I'm sitting at my kitchen table while Kenny relaxes on my couch with a stack of notebooks I've kept from past weddings. I also have a bookshelf full of poetry to help me overcome writer's block whenever it strikes. Still, nothing is helping me write Carter and Everly's vows. It's as if I physically and emotionally can't do it. My body outright rejects the idea.

"We've been at this for hours, and you haven't written more than two words," Kenny says, scrolling on his phone. "I'm starving. I'm ordering delivery."

This was supposed to be easy—like every other wedding I've done. By now, I would have written the vows and delivered them to the bride and groom. Instead, I'm barely close to a rough draft. I can't speak for Carter without speaking for myself, and I can't speak for Everly without wishing the words were being spoken to me.

"Does this happen often?" Kenny looks at me with a worried expression. "You know, writer's block?"

"Vows are promises people make when they are certain, but I'm not sure anyone involved is." My words hang in the air, as if waiting to be affirmed.

"I would leave that part out," Kenny snickers.

"How about this?" I clear my throat, looking down at my notebook. "Love isn't about choosing the person who looks perfect on paper. It's about choosing the person who feels like home… even when everything feels uncertain."

Kenny shakes his head. "Nope. That sounds too clunky. Not to mention, it's a total dig at Carter."

"You're right," I agree. "What about saying that forever isn't a feeling; it's a decision you make again tomorrow?"

As Kenny considers my words, I think of other words—words I had written in my book. I wonder whether the bravest, most selfless thing I can do is to use something I wrote about her for her. It's the greatest gift I can offer Carter. I don't want to be the bad guy.

*Everly wasn't the kind of woman who looked fragile or perfectly put-together. She just looked vibrant.*

*Ever since I met her, her blonde hair fell in soft, loose waves that never quite stayed in place. And there's one strand in particular that always seems to have a mind of its own. As for her smile? It was effortless. And if you had any part in bringing it out, it was pure magic. Hearing her laugh? You'd count yourself lucky to hear it.*

*As for her eyes, they could shift between green and gold depending on the light. When she laughed, they crinkled at the corners in a way that made my knees go weak.*

*She is beautiful, yes. But there is so much more to her than beauty—things you can only learn by whispering from your pillow in the middle of the night. She's honest in the best way. And every emotion that crosses her face is like a story you wish you could decipher.*

*I did.*

"Could you end on that quote?" he finally says. "I would just be careful that your words don't sound like your words."

I close my notebook. "They may be my words, but they are his feelings. I'm only sprucing them up."

"Well, if it's that easy, why aren't the vows written?" he asks, leaning forward with his elbows on his knees. "Let me guess… You keep writing the wrong love story?"

I sigh, opening my notebook again. After several hours of ripping out notebook pages and a stomach full of Chinese takeout, I finish. "I'm done," I say.

"This to Carter or from?" he asks, yawning.

"From," I answer.

Everly,

I don't think there's a perfect way to describe what it feels like to stand here with you, mostly because anything I say feels too small for something that has shaped my entire life.

But I will try.

From the very beginning, you've been the kind of person who makes the world feel... fuller. Brighter—like there's always something just around the corner worth believing in.

You perceive things differently from most people. Where others see endings, you see opportunities—beginnings. Instead of settling, you ask for more, not just from the world but from the people you love.

And I have learned that loving you means rising to that.

Therefore, I promise to keep showing up for you, not just on the easy days but also on the days that don't seem to fit into our story. You know, the messy, complicated, real ones. The ones that test us in the best ways.

I promise to listen when you speak, even when you don't.

I promise to notice the little things, like how you get lost in bookstores, how deeply you care about everything, and how you pretend you're fine even when you're not.

I promise to remind you that even if we don't have everything figured out, we are still worthy of this love.

And that _YOU_ are worthy, just as you are today, tomorrow, and forever.

*I vow to build a life with you that isn't just good on paper, but one that feels right, something we would both choose.*

*And if there are times when the path feels uncertain, when things don't look or feel the way they should, I promise never to let go of your hand. Loving you isn't a decision I made once. It's one I will keep making again and again for the rest of my life.*

Kenny is quiet. I can barely hear him breathe. My fingers rest on the keys as he stares at the screen. He turns to face me. "Reese, those are not Carter's vows," he says.

I look back at the screen. "What do you mean? It's a perfect summary of everything he and I discussed."

When I look back at him, I swear I saw him wipe away a tear. "It's good. Isn't it?" I ask.

"It's beautiful," he says, noticeably choked up. "But as I said, they are not Carter's vows."

"But you said…"

"Listen, I say a lot, but I want you to hold onto this because someday, someone will want you to say these words to them."

I chuckle. "That's never going to happen," I say as a bead of sweat trickles down my forehead.

"Before I head home, I'm going to ask you one last time: what is the plan?"

"I don't have one, Kenny," I say. "There is no plan."

*Chapter Thirty-Two*
*Plot Twist*

*Morgan*

I sit on my bed with Reese's manuscript in my lap. I've read it four times. I know I shouldn't have read it the first time, but here we are. What's done is done.

This time, I read it slowly, as if digesting each word to ensure I truly understand the truth behind his words. I need to be certain—not for the story, but for Everly. I'm not searching for plot points. It's all about proof. Proof of feelings I never realized were there. Proof that if I decide to say something to her, I won't ruin my best friend's life on a guess or a hunch.

But every page confirms my greatest fear. Fiction actually contains more truth than most people realize.

My fingers press into the pages as I contemplate what to do next. Because, like any good high-stakes emotional plot, this is the moment when a single decision can make or break everything. I pace my apartment, aware that so much could go wrong. It could literally blow up so many lives, and I will be the one to blame. Then there's the question of whether Everly would want to know. Would she be happy and content where she is, never knowing Reese's true feelings? And what if one day she discovers I knew the whole time? And that I was the one who kept it from her?

The one thing I do know is that I've seen a look in her eyes that tells me there's something she isn't being honest about.

Or worse, she's not being honest with herself about.

I think about what I would want. Would I want to walk into a marriage blindly? Or would I want to know all the facts before committing my life to someone? Would the facts even matter? Or should they? Then there is the biggest question: if the facts change the plan, was there really a plan to begin with?

I stack the pages neatly this time. I grab a large envelope and slide the manuscript inside just before sealing it. I've read all I need to. Just as I'm about to set it aside, I receive a text:

### Fine. You win. What's the plan?

## Everly

I could tell something was off with Carter as soon as the waitress brought us our menus. The last time he acted like this, he proposed, so I have no clue what it could be about.

It's the night before our bachelor and bachelorette parties, so we decided to revisit the restaurant where our engagement began. This time, I'm paying closer attention to my roll. That bitch isn't going anywhere.

"OK," I say, gnawing away on my roll as if I haven't eaten in weeks. "Either you closed a huge case for the firm, or you're about to ruin my life."

Carter laughs as he reaches for my hand. "I received a promotion today," he says, glowing. "Managing Partner," he says, as if he still can't believe it. "It's everything I've been working toward for years. My name will finally be on the door."

"Carter! That's incredible!" I exclaim, realizing my voice was a little too loud. I really have bad luck at this restaurant.

"It is," he agrees as we place our orders and the waitress brings our drinks. "Although this promotion does come with some…changes," he says, pausing to take a sip of his drink.

"What kind of changes?" I ask as I reach for another roll. I don't care about obsessing over calories. If I'm hungry, I'm going to eat.

"For one, there's a lot of travel involved. I'll be going to places like London, Singapore, and probably even Zurich by the end of the year. And the best part is, I get to take you with me." His words land on the table between us with a thump.

"With you?" I repeat.

"Of course," he says, as if he has already figured out the logistics of all this. "We can definitely make this work. You can take a step back from the agency—temporarily, that is. Or you can pivot. You're brilliant, so you can do whatever you want," he continues.

I blink as he continues planning my future. I know it will soon be our future, but it doesn't seem like what I want is being taken into account.

Honestly, it all sounds like a dream. His, maybe, but not entirely mine. Still, agreeing to all of this right away feels like a trap. I need time to process everything. In just a few weeks, my whole life is about to be flipped upside down, and now I find out it's about to be turned inside out.

Finally, I say, "I love my job, Carter. I don't want to leave it."

"I'm not asking you to give it up forever. You said yourself you haven't read anything good in a while. Maybe taking a break would be good for you?" he says, as if my job is too stressful and I need to step back.

"But you're still asking me to give it up," I say.

"No," he shakes his head. "I'm asking you to build something with me," he sighs, as if he expected me to react differently.

"Well, I'm building something here, too," I say, fighting back tears that are desperate to fall. "This is my career. You know I love it. And you also know that one day I'd love to have my own agency."

"So, you're basically saying you won't come with me?" he looks at me as if this was supposed to be an open and shut case.

I falter. "I'm not saying I won't come with you. I'm telling you that I love my career, and it's not something I'm willing to give up, even temporarily."

"That may be true," he says as the waiter brings us our entrees. "But I feel like there's something else you're not saying. I'm not going to lie. I'm a little surprised by your reaction. I thought you'd be happy. And I thought this was what we wanted."

"We?" I echo as the room starts to blur. I feel like I'm on a rocky boat and about to be sick.

His jaw tightens in a subtle way I have never seen before. He has never been a man who rattles easily. "Yes. *Us,*" he says to me.

I take a sip of my wine.

*How am I supposed to answer all of this?*

Instead, I force a smile—a smile that feels all too familiar.


## *Reese*

Kenny looks like he's dressed to blow his life savings in Las Vegas. I'm wearing what I normally wear because I really couldn't care less about attending Carter's bachelor party.

"Just so you know, I'm not staying long," I prewarn Kenny.

"What you need to do is let loose. You should have a night out and have some fun," he says, as if a couple of drinks will fix all my problems. Spoiler alert: a couple of drinks got me into this mess.

We end up taking a cab to a swanky, expensive lounge in Upper Manhattan that costs more than a couple of drinks at a nearby dive bar. The lounge features jazz and looks like the kind of place that requires a membership.

Kenny claps me on the back the moment we step inside. "We have arrived." He smiles as wide as the Cheshire Cat. "This is going to be fun!"

Across the room, we spot Carter talking to a group of guys, exuding his usual effortless, magnetic charm that keeps everyone's eyes on him. He's the kind of guy people naturally orbit without even trying.

"It's my favorite wedding planners!" Carter announces when he sees Kenny and me approach.

"But this guy?" He waves me over before putting his arm around my shoulder. "He is a professional vow writer."

"A professional vow writer? I've never heard of that before." An older man in a suit shakes my hand. "And that's your career? This is really a thing?"

"That's correct. We do exist," I say with a smile.

"He's going to make me sound like a man worth marrying." Carter raises his glass. I can already tell he's had a few before we arrived.

"Depends," I say. "Are you planning to be one?" I ask, which draws a laugh from the group.

"Well, tonight? I plan to be a problem," he lets out a raucous laugh.

From there, the night swirls like a tornado of shots, stories, and laughter, making me believe, for a moment, that these are the kind of people I could surround myself with. Kenny, however, has already taken charge of the group, handing out business cards and cracking jokes as if he were the hired entertainment for the evening.

A few shots in, Carter leans in and says to me, "So, how are my vows coming along?"

"They are perfect," I say, even though Kenny's feelings about the vows came from a good place. I still plan to give them to Carter. He can certainly put them to better use.

"Good, because I'm in the doghouse right now," he slurs. "I got a promotion with a chance to see the world, and she's upset about it. I don't get it."

"Well, it's simple," I say. "What would she have to give up?"

**A few hours later**, the bar is quiet. I take a breath and another sip of my freshly poured bourbon, feeling no pain. Maybe Kenny was right. Maybe I did need a night out. Well, I had it. Now I'm ready to go home.

"I'm heading out, too," Kenny says. "I'm off to another party."

"What party?" I ask.

"Everly's," he says, hiding behind his glass of wine. "Are you mad? I'm a bridesman, so I have to make an appearance."

"You're not a bridesman," I say. "But no, I'm not mad. Have fun."

"We can share a cab if you'd like?" he offers.

"No. That's OK. I'm going to finish my drink, and then I'll head out," I say as he heads toward the door, his expression suggesting tonight is more fun than tasting cakes.

As I down the rest of my bourbon, a familiar voice whispers in my ear. "Leaving so soon?"

I turn to see Lila standing behind me. She stands in a black minidress, wearing a sharp smile. Her eyes look as though they don't ask many questions but give away too many answers. "Looks like you're in need of a little distraction," she says.

"Lila, I don't sleep with people from work. I've told you that," I say. It's just one more mess I'd like to avoid.

But then she looks at me with eyes that tell me she could help ease some of my pain. I should tell her no again, but for some reason, I don't.

## *Everly*

The night begins exactly as Morgan promised: unhinged but literary.

We begin the night at an indie bookstore, where we pick books featuring our favorite tropes. Then we head to The Last Chapter, where we drink literary-themed cocktails. If it weren't for Morgan distracting me every few seconds, I would have fallen into a pit of nostalgia. This place is bittersweet to me. It holds so much, yet it has lost an equal amount as well.

Morgan holds her phone and starts reading the questions she prepared for some games. She instructs us that if we get a question wrong, we have to take a shot.

"OK," she announces. "Game one is Guess the Trope!"

Kenny, who arrived a few minutes ago, immediately raises his hand. "I was born for this!"

I laugh, already feeling a little buzzed. "Of course you were," I say.

"They hate each other, yet they are forced to work together," Morgan begins.

"Trick question!" Kenny stands as if to object. "That's two tropes: enemies-to-lovers and forced proximity."

"Next question!" Molly from our agency yells.

For the next couple of hours, we drink and dance before calling a few cabs to take us back to the agency, where Morgan had it decorated with bookish decorations and, of course, penis paraphernalia. We all stumble inside, tearing off our shoes.

"My phone is almost dead. I'm going to grab my charger in my office," I tell the group before I head down the hallway.

The agency is quiet. It's more like a library than a buzzing literary agency. Not going to lie, I kind of like it. If I were a writer, I could probably pump out a few books in this setting. But then music starts playing, and I hear laughter carry down the hall.

I push open my office door, which creaks at the hinges, and I love it. My office has always felt like an extension of my home because I've never considered what I do work. It brings me joy. And the fact that Carter doesn't know that about me (or worse, cares) makes me sad.

As I round my desk to grab my charger from the drawer, I notice a large envelope on my desk. It's not addressed to anyone. There's no label or stamp. It's just a plain envelope.

For a moment, I wonder if this is an unsolicited manuscript. But no one mails in printed manuscripts anymore. It may save paper, but it's a lost art.

I sit down at my desk and slide the heavy envelope in front of me. I open it, and just as I suspected, it's a manuscript. I open it to the first page:

*The strange thing about love is that sometimes you meet someone who feels like home long before you're brave enough to stay. So he told himself the night meant nothing—that people meet strangers in bars every day and, come morning, carry on with their lives.*

My breath catches. I begin reading, forgetting where I am or how long I've sequestered myself in my office. The writing consumes me. I turn the pages faster. My heart races. For some reason, I break my cardinal rule and skip straight to the end, and I read it:

*He didn't choose her out loud. Instead, he chose her in every way that mattered. And should he ever be lucky enough to cross paths with her again—if fate allows such a chance—then he would stay as he should have that morning after.*

I stop breathing. This story isn't another cliché. It's everything I've been looking for. It's far from perfect, but what it lacks in a polished draft, it makes up for with its unpredictable, honest prose. It's the kind of love story I've been dying to read. It's genuine.

Morgan suddenly appears in my doorway, a glass of wine in hand. "There you are."

I slowly look up, holding the manuscript in my hand. "This is it."

"What is?" Morgan asks.

"This is the book I've been looking for," I say as she steps toward my desk. "It's not perfect or well-structured, and it has some major grammatical errors, but it's real," I continue.

"What's it about?" she asks as she sits in the chair in front of me.

"It's about a guy who meets a girl one night, and they have no expectations going into the evening. They just enjoy their time together. But then, come morning, he leaves. Here's the kicker, though—he doesn't forget her! He actually wanted to stay, but he thought she didn't want him to. And—" I stop mid-sentence because something suddenly clicks in the story. I resonate with it so deeply because I connect with it. It's familiar.

I sit back down and search for the author's name. It's written by someone named R.E.M.

*R.E.M?*

I'm silent for several minutes until Morgan leans forward. "Reese," she spells it out for me.

"Reese?" I look at her. "*He* wrote this? How?"

"He wrote it," she exhales as if a weight has been lifted from her shoulders.

I shake my head. "No. This isn't possible. This isn't happening." But it is. Every moment. Every line. Every feeling I couldn't name, he did. And he did it beautifully.

My voice drops. "He never forgot me."

Morgan watches me closely. "No. He didn't."

"He loves me?" I ask, but Morgan says nothing. My hands are shaking now. I feel like I'm losing control of my life.

"Everly, I'm not going to tell you what I think you should do or who you should be with, but I figured you had the right to know. I felt horrible for not saying anything to you," she says as she pulls out her phone and types what looks like a message.

My phone buzzes on my desk, and I look to see it's Morgan. She texted me Reese's address.

"I support you no matter what. I love you no matter what. There's no rule that says you can't break the rules. If something doesn't feel right, you shouldn't have to force yourself to go through with it just because of other people's expectations. Weren't expectations what got you into this mess?" She tilts her head at me.

"And if I ruin everything?" My voice cracks.

"Then ruin everything. So what? Happily ever after can be whatever the hell you want it to be. Sometimes the princess just runs off into the sunset, alone."

I look back down at the manuscript, then at the address on my phone. For the first time, I'm not wondering which choice is right. I'm wondering if I'm brave enough to make it.

## Reese

It's well past midnight when I hear a knock on my door. I climb out of bed, assuming it's Kenny looking for a place to crash. But when I open the door, barefoot, in sweatpants, shirtless, I find Everly standing there as if she is lost and has no idea how she ended up on my doorstep.

I freeze. Why is she here? Several thoughts pour into my head until it overflows with possibilities. Either Morgan showed my manuscript to her, or something happened with Carter. He did say he was in the doghouse, so that's quite possible. Yet the fact that she is standing here at all feels like a dream. I have pictured her in my apartment many times, but having her here is too surreal to put into words.

However, reality crashes into me when she reaches into her bag and pulls out my book. Her grip is tight around the pages. "Did you write this?"

I can feel my expression transform from surprise to worry, like it made a quick costume change.

"You wrote a book about me, and that is your first question?" She looks at me, her face a storm of anger, sadness, and confusion.

She is a tornado of emotion, and I have no clue which emotion will cause the most destruction.

I step back, running my hand down my face. "Everly…"

"No," she cuts in. "Just don't." She tosses the manuscript into the room. The sound of it landing wakes whatever parts of me were still tired.

"It's me. It's…" she hesitates. "Us."

I don't even try to deny it. "You weren't supposed to read it," I say. "In fact, no one was."

She stares back at me through the darkness of my apartment. I'm afraid to turn on any lights in case they reveal something more.

"Why?" she asks.

"Why? Because it's easier to pretend nothing happened—that it meant nothing. That's why," I say, sharp and to the point.

"Based on what I read, it doesn't sound like you're pretending nothing happened," she says as the air shifts in my apartment. "Or that it meant nothing."

I swallow. My heart races. Too fast. Too loud. I'm not made for this. Yet I don't bury the feeling as I normally would. If it's going to erupt, I'm going to let it. But I can't be to blame for what happens when it does.

"Why didn't you say anything?" she asks, walking into the room and then leaning against my kitchen counter, defeated.

"Because you're engaged."

"That didn't stop you from writing that." She points to my manuscript.

"No, but it could have been taken as fiction if Morgan hadn't stolen it from me," I say.

She shakes her head. "That's not fair."

My eyes shoot daggers at her. I suddenly feel overwhelmed by emotions I have shoved so deep inside me, but only anger makes it to the surface. "You want fair?" My voice rises. "Fair would have been never seeing you again. Fair would have been me not writing the vows for your fucking wedding."

"You don't get to act like this is all on me," she says.

"I'm not," I fire back. "You're the only one here about to get married, not me." My words hit harder than the manuscript she hurled.

She flinches. "You think I don't know that? You think everything is all rainbows and butterflies here? You think I haven't felt anything?" She looks at me the way she did that first night, a hunger in her eyes I haven't seen in so long.

I still at her words. "What have you felt?" My question dangles between us, dangerously. I doubt she will be brave enough to catch it.

"It just feels like I made a decision before I had all the information," she says, unable to meet my gaze. "I didn't forget you either. I tried. And for months, I tried to find you," she laughs, as if what she says is ludicrous.

"Don't," I stop her.

"What?" She finally meets my gaze. "Because it complicates things?"

"Yes," I say.

"I have a choice, you know?" Everly stands, rattled, as I put my professional mask back on, even though it's been dunked in too much bourbon.

"You always have a choice, but you're about to walk down the aisle and promise the rest of your life to someone who is a good man, Everly. And I can't stand in your way," I say.

"But I have a choice," she repeats.

"Then make it," I say. But instead of answering me, she deflects.

"You didn't choose me," she says.

I run a hand through my hair. "I did."

"But not in the way it mattered," she cries out.

My lungs almost collapse. "Well, you know everything now. There's nothing left for me to hide."

We stand, staring at each other. No words are exchanged until she finally says what we both already know: "I'm getting married."

I nod. "I know."

"And you want me to blow that up?" She looks at me as if I'm the one at the helm.

"I never said that, Everly. It's your life. You have to choose what's best for you. Forget about me. Forget about Carter. Think about you."

"I hate you for this."

*This is ridiculous!* But I can't help but smile. It's a nervous twitch that has landed me in more trouble than I care to admit. "Then hate me if it makes everything easier for you," I say. "I'm just trying to be the kind of man who doesn't take what isn't his."

"You're right. I'm not something to be taken," she whispers to me through the darkness. "I'm something to be chosen."

"Just so you know, I *did* choose you," I whisper back. "Just not out loud."

"Then choose me now," she says, as if her entire life depends on my choice, which I find completely unfair.

"No," I say. "Carter chose you. You chose him. There is nothing left to choose," I say his name because he deserves a fight in this conversation.

"Screw you, Reese," she says as she walks toward my apartment door to leave, but she abruptly stops. She doesn't look back but says, "You should have left a note."

But before I can say anything more, she pulls open the door and closes it behind her.

*Everly*

I feel caught in an internal earthquake. I can't stop shaking. My hand is still on the door handle. Our words hang in the air like mist.

This is dumb. This isn't over. Just as quickly as I shut Reese's door, I open it again to find him standing in the same spot. He hasn't moved. He looks as defeated as I feel.

"Reese, I…" but just as I'm about to reopen the conversation, his bedroom door creaks open. We both turn to see a girl step out, barefoot, wearing nothing but Reese's dark button-down dress shirt. Her hair is a mess, as if she has just woken up or something worse.

"Reese? Is everything OK?" She walks over to him as I realize who she is. She is that girl, Lila from Laurent & Co. She just smiles at me and then back at Reese.

"Are you coming back to bed?"

Reese looks as if the rug has just been pulled out from under him. "Lila," he starts, but I don't give him the chance to finish. All I can do is laugh, because, of course, this is how our story ends—with another one-night stand. I guess the saying "how you get them is how you lose them" rings true.

This time, I charge toward the door, ignoring Reese as he calls out my name to stop me. "This is not what it looks like!" he yells.

"No. It's exactly what it looks like. It looks like you write stories about one woman and then sleep with another." I gesture toward Lila, who has been caught in the crosshairs of our fight.

"You're twisting this," Reese continues.

"Regardless, I have my answer now," I say as I pull the door open again. "Thank you for making it easy for me."

"Everly, please." He walks toward me, but I don't allow him to get any closer.

"Maybe everything happened the way it did because that's how it's supposed to be. Let's just leave it at that," I say as I close the door behind me.

This time for good.


## *Reese*

Sadness, regret, and fury flood my apartment. I stand motionless. Beside me, Lila shifts awkwardly.

"Wow," she says softly. "What was that all about?"

I don't look at her. "Lila, please get dressed. I will call you a cab," I say, trying not to sound too harsh or unkind.

"Over before it started," she says, even though it looks like something happened between Lila and me. Nothing did. We didn't sleep together. I couldn't bring myself to do it.

"I'm really sorry," I say to her, because I am.

"You like her?" She looks at me.

I nod. Everything is out in the open now. I can no longer hide behind neutrality. Even though it's nice not to feel like I'm in hiding, it somehow feels worse. It's soul-crushing.

*"Maybe everything happened the way it did because that's how it's supposed to be. Let's just leave it at that."*

Her words won't leave my head. They play on a loop I can't turn off. So I grab my phone and call the only person I know who'd understand.

### Everly

I take a cab to Carter's apartment. I should have gone home, but I didn't. I couldn't. When I walk in, he's in his kitchen, drinking water. His tie is off. His dress shirt is unbuttoned as if he had a great night. I wish I could say the same.

"Everly?" he asks, looking at me, clearly surprised to see me. "I wasn't expecting you." He reaches for me and pulls me into a hug. "Did you have a fun night with the girls?"

"Yeah," I say, but I don't elaborate. It's not a lie, but it's certainly not the whole truth.

He holds me closer, solid. Steady. Safe. His embrace suggests he means it and that, no matter what, he'll always be there. For a moment, I try to sink into the beauty of his comfort. I tell myself it's enough.

321

*Why isn't it enough?*

His hand runs through my hair with a gentle caress.

"Are you OK?" he asks.

I nod.

"Are you still upset about the promotion?" He looks down at me, but I don't say anything because, at this point, I have no idea what I'm upset about. Throw a dart at something, and you'll hit something I'm upset about.

"How about we talk more about it in the morning? I want to know how you feel before I make any final decision with the firm," he says.

"But it's what you've always wanted. It's your dream," I say.

"It is, but you're also my dream." He kisses me on the forehead.

A few seconds later, he pulls me into his bed. We shed our clothes. He is on top of me, watching as if he's trying to make sure everything he does feels right.

"Tell me what you want," he says softly, and I freeze at his words because I honestly don't know what I want anymore.

But after everything that happened tonight, I have to move forward. "Just you," I say, and Carter smiles as if he were worried I might have said something else.

He brushes his thumb across my cheek as I close my eyes to his touch, but when I do, I don't see him.

# Chapter Thirty-Three
## Vanishing Act



I deleted the manuscript. Not that it matters because Morgan emailed a copy to herself, and who knows how many she had printed. However, I don't just delete the file, I delete it where it matters most: my heart.

Cheesy, I know. But I think that's what love does to you—it makes you crack jokes in a bar like "happily Everly after."

Kenny shows up at my apartment with coffee, ready for me to tell him everything—even the details I deliberately left out before.

"You look like you've been hit by a truck," he says, setting the coffee and a bag of muffins on my counter.

"I'm fine," I say.

"Right," Kenny deadpans.

"I still have to write Everly's vows for Carter, and then I'm done with this whole thing. I should have been done with it from the start," I say.

"As your best friend..." Kenny sighs.

"So, you're my best friend now?" I interrupt.

"Just accept it. We both know it's true." He winks. "But isn't disappearing still you doing something?"

"Maybe, but it's me choosing not to ruin someone else's life." Kenny softens. "Or your own?"

But I don't answer. Instead, I tell him I don't want anything more to do with this wedding. I'm going to finish Everly's vows and be officially done with it.

I spend the next hour finalizing everything, then I have Kenny help me tweak it. Once I'm done, he reviews the final product.

"Life is about being spontaneous, living in the moment, and having no expectations," he reads aloud. "No expectations, huh?"

"You caught that, didn't you? I doubt anyone else will," I say.

"If I did, Evelry will," he replies.

But I don't care. I hit send.

"Yeah, but the vows you've written are basically telling her to pick Carter. You literally wrote vows with subliminal messages. Why would you do that?" he asks.

"Kenny, it's not about me telling her to do anything. She already picked him. She's already made her decision. I'm just tying the bow on it," I say.

He stands to stretch. "Are you coming to the rehearsal planning meeting tonight?"

"No," I say. "My work here is finished."

He nods as if he understands. Maybe he is my best friend after all.

*Everly*

We decided to hold a last-minute rehearsal-planning meeting at Carter's mom's request. She insisted we needed a meeting to plan the rehearsal logistics. It's literally like having a meeting about the meeting.

It's almost bittersweet to think this will be the last meeting and the last time I set foot through these doors. So much has happened since that first meeting, and it only accelerated when Carter chose such a quick wedding date.

Kenny and Genevieve walk into the room while Carter, his mom, and I are already seated at the table. Our wedding is literally a week away, but after all the last-minute dress fittings and finalizing details with the vendors, I'm starting to panic more than I normally do. And if I'm not panicking about something, I'm panicking that I'm not panicking.

As for Reese? He's nowhere in sight. Again, bittersweet.

Genevieve quickly reviews the place settings for the rehearsal dinner and what to expect logistically. We will also be staying there the night of the rehearsal and the night of the wedding, before Carter and I head off to our honeymoon. Carter and I are going to Italy.

Genevieve also confirms that the hair and makeup appointments will be handled at the estate, so I won't have to go anywhere. She also notes that Carter and I will have separate rooms the night before the wedding and share the royal suite the night of the wedding.

"Here is the rendered drawing of your rehearsal dinner," she says as she passes it around the room.

"Well, the flowers are all wrong," Mrs. Jacobs pipes up. "No one asked for peonies. I wanted soft ivory roses with a hint of pink."

Genevieve looks at me before I finally say that they are my favorite flowers. "They stay," I add. I didn't ask for the flowers, but I can't explain how pleased I am that they are making an appearance.

"We have classic romance-novel-inspired centerpieces, sheets of poetry, and paper flowers made from book pages, scattered across the table runners like confetti," she continues as my jaw drops to the floor.

"We are also serving small plates instead of a full-course meal. And the chef made a special three-layered cinnamon roll cake," she says as I almost lose it.

"He did what?" I interject. "This is all so perfect. How did it happen?"

Genevieve looks down at the planning sheet, then back at me. "Didn't you ask for all of this?"

## Morgan

"We have to do something, Kenny. We can't just sit back and let our best friends make the worst mistake of their lives." I pace around Kenny's cubicle as if I belong here.

He tells me that since he hasn't earned an office yet, he's stuck out in the open like a fish in a fishbowl. Lucky for us, no one is around to overhear us as we contemplate not only blowing up a wedding but possibly his career.

"Does he love her?" I ask him point-blank. "We are not imagining things, right?"

"Yes," he nods. "He does."

"And he's a good guy, right?"

"Reese isn't one to show his feelings, or even to have them, for that matter. So the fact that he has done both speaks volumes about what he feels for Everly. It's not like he runs around the city writing books about other women, if that's what you're asking," he replies.

I lean against his cubicle. "This is bad. This is really bad."

"It's worse. I like them both, but Reese is my friend…"

I sigh. "She won't tell me what happened the other night. Do you know?"

"It wasn't good," he says. "It obviously didn't go as either of them would have wanted."

"And now what? He just vanishes into thin air?" I cross my arms as if Kenny had something to do with his vanishing act.


*Kenny*

"Well, what the hell is he supposed to do? She's getting married. And he didn't vanish," I say. "He's just…hiding. He's lying low until this is all over."

"But then it will be all over." She looks at me.

"There's a wedding happening," I remind her.

"You know, the strange thing about love is that sometimes you meet a person who feels like home long before you're brave enough to stay. So he told himself that night meant nothing—that people meet in bars every day and, come morning, carry on with their lives. Unfortunately, as he's learned, the night doesn't end when the sun comes up. Some nights follow you home and lead you back to their doorstep a year and a half later."

"What, did you memorize his book?" I roll my eyes.

"Well?"

"A best friend would crash this wedding, right?" I ask her.

Morgan hesitates because she and I both know this is a make-or-break moment.

"But I swear on all the wedding gods that if we lose our friends over this or if I lose my job..."

"Stop worrying so much," she says.

"I think we both have a lot to worry about," I counter.

"The rehearsal dinner," she perks up. "That's it!"

I blink. "What's it?"

"That's the last moment we have before the wedding to do anything," she says.

"Not exactly. The priest does ask the guests to speak up if they don't think a couple should get married," I reply.

"We are not waiting until the last minute. That's terrible and too risky," she says.

"I honestly don't like where this is going. I'm going to be really pissed if I miss out on that cinnamon roll cake," I say.

"Shut up about the cake. Listen, you find a way to get Reese to the estate, and then we can put them in a room together to hash this out. They need to face whatever this is before it's too late," she says.

I scoff. "He will never go there unless I blindfold him and drag him there against his will, but that's a whole other romantic trope."

"He will if you make up a good enough excuse. Tell him his sister needs him. You said so yourself; he would never say no to her."

"You're absolutely terrifying," I say.

"Thank you." She bows.

"But what exactly happens when we get them in the same room?" I ask.

"They talk. They figure this out. They choose."

"You realize this plan will not go as planned," I say.

Morgan meets my gaze. "So what? What could go wrong?"

"Um…Everything?"


*Everly*

Later that night, thoughts swirl around my head until I see myself standing in Central Park. I told Reese everything I wanted that day at the engagement photo session. I told him everything I wanted my wedding to be, and although it's not the actual wedding, he still made it happen.

That's when I notice a new email. My vows to Carter have been sent.

*He gave up.*

# Chapter Thirty-Four
## Speak Now or Forever Hold it

Everly

Clothes are everywhere. Suitcases are open. Bags are scattered across my bed and floor. I'm standing in the center of my apartment like I don't recognize it anymore.

My mom has flown back into the city for the wedding weekend, and now, one day before the rehearsal, I'm finally doing what I should have done days ago: packing.

Carter asked me if I planned to move in right after the wedding. This was the first fear I had the night of our engagement, and I guess I pushed it so far down the worry list that I haven't really considered the possibility since. But the truth is, I'm not ready to leave my apartment. It's my little oasis in this big city. It may not be as glamorous as his high-rise Manhattan condo with a doorman, gym, and full amenities, but it's comfortable, cozy, and all mine.

My mom moves around my apartment, folding, sorting, and packing. She has developed a system that makes packing look like a work of art.

"It's hard to pack for a wedding and a honeymoon at the same time," I say. I can't even imagine how it will feel to pack up this entire place for good.

"It's a lot, but we can do it," she says with a smile.

"It's just giving me anxiety. It feels like a lot," I say.

"Anxiety? Are you OK?" she asks.

"Yeah," I nod too quickly.

"Everly, you don't sound OK," she says as I plop down onto my couch in a defeated slump. "It's just… this apartment," I sigh. "It used to feel like the beginning of something."

"And now?" she takes a seat beside me.

I swallow. "Now it feels like abandonment—like I'm leaving something behind."

"Well, it depends on what you're leaving," she says, wrapping her arms around me. "When I met your father, I didn't feel like I was losing anything by gaining a life with him. And if he were here right now, he'd be telling you the exact same thing. Not to mention, he'd say the look on your face isn't that of someone about to get their happily ever after."

"Or my happily *Everly* after," I chuckle, remembering my father. "I'm just overwhelmed, I guess."

"How about I make us some tea?" She gets up from the couch and heads into the kitchen. After she boils a pot of water and takes out the tea bags, she reaches for a couple of mugs from the cupboard.

She grabs the one Reese gave me and reads it. "Well, would you look at that? I think I found your happily Everly after."

**It's the night of** the rehearsal dinner. We all arrive with our bags and dresses in tow. My bridal party settles into their rooms while I settle into mine. This will be the last time I sleep in a room by myself. Is it unbelievable that I wish I were spending it in my apartment instead?

I get into my rehearsal dress and do my makeup and hair. Morgan texts me to say she will meet me downstairs when I'm ready. But I wish I could stay up here longer. The peace and quiet feel soothing.

*Or is it the calm before the storm?*

## Morgan

"Phase one complete?" I whisper toward Kenny when I walk into the dining room.

"Phase one complete," he whispers back. "The tattooed heartbreaker is on his way."

"He bought it?" I ask.

"Hook, line, and emotional sinker."

*Everly*

The dining room glows with soft, romantic light. Champagne is everywhere, along with romantic sheets of poetry and paper flowers scattered throughout the room. Crystal vases of white peonies sit at the center of each table. I feel like I'm inside a classic romance novel. Everything looks perfect. A part of me lets out a sigh of relief.

I'm about to take a sip of my champagne when I notice Reese walking in from across the room. He shouldn't be here. He looks like he knows it. Yet he still is.

"Why is he here?" I ask Morgan when she walks up beside me.

"I think he has to help Kenny with something," she replies.

"Oh, is everything OK?"

"I don't know. *Is* it?" She looks at me. "You should talk to him," she encourages.

"You have got to be kidding me. I'm not talking to him—especially not after what happened that night. And I'm definitely not doing it the night before my wedding," I huff.

"Yeah, yeah," she dismisses me. "But you're going to," she says, taking my free hand and leading me out of the dining room.

*Reese*

*I really shouldn't be here.*
*I really shouldn't be here.*
*I really shouldn't be here.*
*I DON'T want to be here.*

I scan the dining room and spot Everly right away. She is standing next to Morgan, holding a glass of champagne and barely sipping it. The wedding party and immediate family members are scattered around the room, enjoying hors d'oeuvres before the rehearsal begins.

Kenny materializes by my side as if my anxious thoughts summoned him.

"Hey," he says. "I need your help."

"Is this why you dragged me here? It better be good," I say.

"Come this way," he says, barely acknowledging me as he leads me out of the dining room and into the parlor where I once spent an evening with Carter discussing his vows. Only this time, Everly is standing in the middle of the room when I arrive. As soon as we lock eyes, we bolt for the door, but Morgan and Kenny quickly shut us in.

"We love you!" they shout from behind the door just as my fist makes contact with the wood.

"You're not supposed to be here," Everly says to me as if I haven't already thought the same thing.

"Trust me, I'd like to leave," I snap.

"You're good at that, aren't you?" she snaps right back.

"Everly, I'm getting tired of you throwing that in my face. You were the one who made it very clear you didn't want anything more. What was I supposed to do? Be a jerk and hang around when you wanted me gone?" I say.

"I didn't want to get hurt, Reese! And you know what's funny? I still got hurt. That night, I did want more. I just thought after we talked, you would have figured it out," she says.

"I don't play games. If you wanted something more, you should have been honest about it. Trust me, it took everything in me not to stay," I confess.

"You wanted to stay?" she asks.

"Yes, and since we're going through round two on this, I've regretted it ever since. I even walked by your apartment from time to time, hoping to run into you, but never did. And the next time I see you? You're getting married, and I'm hired to write your vows. Talk about getting hurt."

"I'm getting married." Her breath shakes.

I nod. "I know. You don't need to keep reminding me."

"I'm not. I'm—"

"Reminding yourself?" I interrupt as her eyes well up. The last thing I want is to see her cry.

"You're asking me to ruin everything," she says.

"I'm not asking you to do anything of the sort. Don't put this on me." I step closer to her. Too close.

"I need to know," she says, then stops herself just as fast.

"Know what? What *this* is?" I ask.

"Do you think this is love? It was only one night…" she asks as I feel every part of me breaking into pieces, but instead of shattering onto the floor, they begin to rebuild into something unrecognizable.

"I left. He stayed. I'm obviously not the guy you build a life with, Everly. Carter is a good man. You'll have a good life with him," I say, because it's true.

"I'm scared," she says, tears spilling over in full force.

"Why are you scared?" I ask. "That I'd leave again if you chose me?"

"No. I'm not scared because there's a chance you might leave. You scare me because even though you did, you never left."


*Everly*

"So, is this love?" I ask again.

He bows his head. "It is," he says just as the door behind us swings open, and Carter stands on the other side. It's obvious by the look on his face that he's heard enough. Maybe not everything, but enough to make it look like he wants to punch Reese in the face. In all the time I've known Carter, he has never shown this side of himself. He's angry. Yet his voice remains calm and controlled.

"Am I interrupting something?" Carter asks.

Reese steps back from me as if the floor suddenly turned into lava.

Carter looks between Reese and me as if putting together pieces of a puzzle he never imagined he was meant to solve.

"You do write like a man in love," Carter begins, but is met with only silence.

Morgan and Kenny are standing by the door, wearing apologetic looks. I can tell they tried to stop Carter from coming in, but were unsuccessful.

Carter nods slowly. "I just didn't realize it was about my future wife." His words explode like a bomb.

No one is going to survive this.

The rehearsal space feels different now. Everything feels wrong. It's the right place, but the wrong time, feeling-wise. Everyone can feel it. It's palpable—even if they don't know why they're feeling it. I tried to get my mom alone to tell her, but the officiant, who clearly doesn't know how to read a room, claps excitedly to begin the rehearsal.

I stand at the top of the aisle as Carter waits for me at the altar. Reese and Kenny stand off to the side, trying not to draw attention to their argument. As for Morgan, I can't even look at her right now. I'm so pissed. What's even worse is that either Mrs. Jacobs senses something is off, or Carter has already told her what happened. If looks could kill, I'd be a dead woman walking.

"Can someone turn on the music?" someone announces as soon as I start walking. With each step toward Carter, my mind drifts further away. Nothing is as it should be. And that is the moment I freeze.

## Reese

Everly stops moving. I can't see her expression because her back is to me. I've seen many brides get cold feet like this—even during the rehearsal. But something tells me this isn't cold feet.

Carter's voice calls out softly. "Everly?"

Her head lifts as she looks at him, and then she turns and faces…

Me.

*Me.*

"I don't know if I can do this," her voice shakes as gasps ripple through the small crowd. Her mother stands and goes to her.

"Oh, no," Kenny whispers beside me as Carter makes his way toward Everly. He takes her into his arms. He whispers something in her ear, and she falls into him, crying. It takes everything within me not to run to her, but I step aside.

## Everly

We managed to get through the rehearsal on the second attempt. The guests all assumed it was cold feet or nerves, but those who know me best know better. However, the dinner afterward was terribly uncomfortable. Mrs. Jacobs whispered to her husband the entire time, glaring at me. I heard him tell her to let it go.

But that's the thing. She will never let it go. She will hold it over my head for the rest of our lives, accusing me of embarrassing her family. Again, this isn't her wedding. I wish she would just stop. As for me, I barely touched my food, but my mom saved me a slice of cake in case my appetite returns later.

After dinner, my mom and Morgan join me in my room. My mom brushes my hair, trying to soothe the parts of me no one can see—no one can touch. As for Morgan, she keeps apologizing profusely because she was only trying to do the right thing. She had my best interests at heart. I can't fault her for this. Had she not said anything in the first place, I might have ended up resenting her for keeping something from me. No matter how I look at it, she was put in an awful situation, and if the shoes were on the other foot, I would have done the same thing.

Morgan plays a movie on her laptop later that night after my mom goes to her room. She is watching *Friends with Benefits*. It instantly reminds me of the lie I told about the night I was supposed to go out with Carter.

"Why don't you get undressed?" Morgan says. "Get into something more comfortable."

I head over to my bag and start unpacking. I pull out shoes, leisurewear, a few other items, and a tie.

*A tie?*

The tie was dark and familiar. I stare at it in my hands. It's been so long since I last touched its fabric or even acknowledged its existence. After I gave up searching for Reese, I tucked it away in my closet, along with my feelings. Or so I thought.

"Morgan?" I hold up the tie.

She looks over. "Carter's?"

I shake my head. "No."

"Reese's? How?" she asks.

"It's the tie he left behind after that one night. I never got rid of it," I say.

"But why is it here? Why did you pack it?"

"I didn't. My mom packed this bag. She must have assumed it was Carter's," I say. "You don't think it's a sign, do you?"

She moves closer to me and takes the tie from my hand. "Sometimes, signs don't show up to throw a wrench in the plan; they show up to put the plan in place."

# Chapter Thirty-Five
## Vow or Never



It's 7:00 a.m, and there's a knock on my door. Morgan is sound asleep beside me, wearing her eye mask. Since I spent most of the night tossing and turning, I was already awake when I heard the knock. I grab my robe and make my way to the door. It's Carter.

"May we take a walk?" he asks.

"Sure," I say. "Let me throw on some clothes first." I quietly shut the door and throw on some sweats. I'm past caring about bad luck, so I'm not worried about seeing Carter on our wedding day. I can't possibly do any more damage than I've already done.

We walk through the gardens as the early-morning breeze sweeps past us. Like the first day we walked this path, it's as beautiful as ever. Yet what I saw then is not what I see now. Then again, did I ever see what I should have?

"Are you happy?" he asks as gently as the breeze. His tone isn't accusatory or angry. It's simply concerned, not for him, but for me.

I try to answer him, but I can't. All I can do is cry. "I thought I was," I tell him. "You are perfect and amazing in so many ways, and I love you very much."

A strand of my hair blows onto my face, and he carefully tucks it behind my ear. "I thought a lot last night and did a bit of soul searching. Do you want to know what I realized?" he asks me.

"What?"

"I never realized how differently you look at him. I guess I never thought much about it, but now that I know what I think I know, it makes sense. He wasn't memorizing you during our vows; he was mesmerized."

"Carter…"

"Everly, it's okay. I'm not mad. Like you, I want to be chosen—not just appreciated for who I am. Do you know what I mean?" he asks.

"I do." I know exactly what he means.

"Loving you means to love *all* of you. I can't fault you for following your heart," he says.

Everything we planned was perfect. The flowers. The cake. The menu. The aesthetic. However, it was all chosen for reasons I can no longer explain. We were planning for a wedding that would never be ours.

"Neither of us should enter into a marriage if our hearts belong elsewhere." He looks into my eyes. "Does your heart belong elsewhere?"

I say nothing, but my silence is louder than any answer I could give him.

"You don't deserve to settle for anything or anyone. I want you to feel fireworks, not just comfort," he says, breaking the silence.

It's in this moment that I finally tell Carter everything I should have said to him from the beginning.

"Reese is a good guy. I can't blame you," he says to me as we head back toward the estate.

"I want you to know I tried so hard to be the woman who could love you as you deserve to be loved," I say.

"That's funny," he chuckles. "I tried to do the same for you."

A small laugh escapes me through my tears. "That one night changed me, and it stuck with me. It only surfaced under strange circumstances. I want you to know that," I say.

"I can't say I'm not upset with how all of this turned out, but I want you to know I'm not mad at you. Love is unconditional, so if he makes you happy, all I can do is be happy for you, too," he says.

Even in this moment, Carter still showed up for me. He showed up for me when it didn't benefit him—when he had nothing to gain and everything to lose. And a part of me will always love him for that.

"Now, go find your happiness," he says, kissing me on the forehead before letting me go.


## Reese

"Kenny, why are you wearing sunglasses inside?" I ask him.

"I couldn't sleep. I have bags. I am so stressed," he says just as Genny storms through the front doors of the estate. She immediately grabs me by the ear and drags me into the parlor.

*Why does everyone drag me in here?*

"Speak now. What the hell happened?" She looks at me with a rage that I hope is more hormonal than genuine. But I don't dare ask. I'd rightfully be a dead man.

"If I may say something?" Kenny pipes up, but she quickly dismisses him, shooing him away like a fly. I swear I see a few tears slide down his cheeks behind his glasses.

"Genny, I'm sorry. I wasn't completely honest," I begin, but she holds up her hand to stop me.

"Why didn't you just tell me how you felt? I would never, as your sister, have put you through this." She looks at me as if she's no longer angry but filled with sadness and love.

"In all the years I've known your cynical ass, you've never believed in any of this." She gestures to everything around us, symbolizing weddings and the clichéd happily-ever-afters. "You've never put stock in marriage or vows, yet you always seem to get people to believe in them with their whole hearts. And now I've been told you poured your heart out to the groom…about his bride-to-be."

"What are you talking about?" I ask her.

"The vows you sent. After everything that happened last night, Carter read them with fresh eyes and realized they were meant for him. He told me everything," she says as Kenny begins to sob in the corner.

"Carter hates me. I ruined everything," I say, because I did. I am the bad guy.

"He doesn't hate you," she says. "In fact, and I quote, he said you were authentic, real, and passionate, and that you were deserving of all the happiness in the world."

"Are we fired?" Kenny asks, blowing his nose.

"Well, if it were up to Carter's mom, then...yes. But since it's up to me, I will give you both a warning," she says.

"What's the warning?" Kenny asks.

"For starters, you are not allowed to blow up any more weddings." She points to Kenny. "And you," she says, turning to me, "are never allowed to fall in love with another bride."

"Deal."

## Kenny

The entire estate is quiet, as if it's waiting to see what happens next. I'm finishing a few last-minute things when I spot Carter in the middle of the reception room. He is the most casually dressed I've ever seen him. He walks around, looking at everything as if this room were meant to hold his future, but now it's just a painful reminder of his past.

I lean in the doorway, watching him. "You know," I say. "The cake is still here."

Carter laughs. "That's good to know. I was excited about the cake."

I tell him to hold tight while I run to the kitchen to cut us a few slices.

When I hand him his plate, Carter holds up his fork like a microphone. "What does this cake say?"

I chuckle, even though his comment makes me want to tear up and pull him in for a hug. "It tastes like everything is going to be OK. You will ride off into the sunset and do great things."

"Thank you for that, Kenny," he says, taking a bite of his cake.

"If it's any consolation, I think you're a great guy, and it was a pleasure planning the wedding with you," I say.

"It was fun, wasn't it?" he smiles. "It's strange to think we spent months planning for something that never came to pass."

"Does anything ever go as planned?"

"Touché. But can I tell you something?" He looks at me. "I had this weird feeling the whole time—like I knew, deep down, that something was off. I just didn't know what it was."

"So, you're not surprised?" I asked, a little surprised myself.

Carter shakes his head. "Not totally."

"When did you—"

"The engagement party. I saw them together, and for a split second, I wondered if there was something more between them. And then I saw the way he looked at her, and"—he swallows—"the way she looked back."

"Are you mad at him?"

Carter looks as if he's contemplating my question. "No. How can I be? He didn't do anything wrong."

"Even if he's in love with your fiancée?"

"I'd be more concerned if he wasn't." He picks up his bag and walks closer to me. "If I ever find myself down this road again, you will be my first phone call. Take care, Kenny." He walks toward the doorway before turning back around. "The cake is all yours."

## *Reese*

I don't know why I'm still here. Everyone seems to have vacated the estate. Kenny, however, is around here somewhere, most likely trying to get his hands on whatever dessert is up for grabs.

I stand at the altar, wondering for just a moment what it would feel like to stand here for someone. I have written his moment for hundreds of grooms, but have never felt it firsthand. It's funny when you think about it. *Those who don't do, teach.*

So much of my adult life has been spent in meaningless relationships—ones I could walk away from easily. But with Everly, everything changed, and now I don't know if I can ever go back to the way things were. She was right. One night is history. It changed me in so many ways, and without it, I might not have become the man I am today. The man who now believes in happily ever afters.

But I never wanted to be the villain here. As much as I love Everly, I still respect Carter. He is a good man, and she would have had a good life with him. Had she chosen him, I would have respected that choice. But Everly never wanted crystal stemware or polished silver. She wanted mismatched coffee mugs and books stacked around her home.

As I'm about to step down from the altar, I see Everly walking down the aisle toward me. Of course, I must be imagining it. So many nights I've dreamed of this moment, and now my mind is playing cruel tricks on me.

When she stops a few feet from me, I know this isn't a dream.

"Tell me you're OK before you say anything else," I say to her.

"I'm OK," she says as music begins to play softly in the background.


## Everly

Reese is standing at the altar. I must be dreaming, because Reese never struck me as the kind of guy who would ever stand here. Oddly enough, he doesn't look lost. He looks like a man exactly where he wants to be.

He stops when he sees me, and for a second, everything else in the world disappears. It's only him and me.

As I make my way down the aisle, I feel as if my body is floating toward him. I can no longer feel my feet touching the ground.

"Tell me you're OK before you say anything else," he says to me.

"I'm OK," I say as soft music begins to play in the background.

Rain suddenly taps against the estate's windows, turning the grounds into blurred streaks of green and light. No one is around. It's only Reese and me.

I didn't want to be here. I wanted nothing more than to get back to my apartment and recalibrate. Yet now I'm standing here next to Reese, his sleeves rolled and his smile crooked. He looks like restraint wrapped in a dangerously attractive package.

Silence stretches between us. It's heavy, familiar, and full of possibilities.

"This is getting complicated, meeting like this," I tease.

"It's been complicated ever since I met you at the bar," he says as the sound of the rain grows louder.

"I have to ask, why did you leave?" I ask. The words slip out before I can stop them. "Was it really because of my rules?"

Eighteen months of unanswered questions hang in the air between us. I wonder whether we are brave enough to put them to rest once and for all.

"It hurt that you didn't say goodbye to me," I continue, my voice cracking despite my efforts to stay composed. "It made me feel like that night meant nothing to you—that I meant nothing to you."

## Reese

My jaw tightens as I watch her, saying nothing. It's time to tell her everything, and this time I refuse to hold back.

So, I slowly reach into my pocket and pull out my wallet. "It meant a lot to me," I say, pulling out the piece of paper, worn and creased so many times that the folds now look permanent. "I wrote this that morning at your kitchen table."

"You… what?" She looks at me.

"I woke up before you," I explain. "But you were still asleep, so I didn't want to wake you. You looked so peaceful. Trust me, I wanted to stay, but I was afraid of rejection. I was afraid you would have just told me to leave." My heart pounds louder with each word I confess.

"You said you wanted one night," I continue. "No last names, no phone numbers, and no expectations. Yet…"

"Yet?"

"Yet we still found each other."


*Everly*

My eyes start to burn.

"I thought when you left, it was over," I say when he hands me the piece of paper.

My hands tremble as I take it. I open the fold slowly and carefully. The handwriting is clearly Reese's, but it's messy and rushed with ink bleeding through the back as if emotion guided his pen more than his thoughts.

It reads:


*Last night felt like it was the beginning of something.*
*This is new for me.*
*But you made it seem like you didn't want a beginning.*
*And now, I'm forced to the ending.*
*-Reese*


My vision blurs. "You've kept this? All this time?" I whisper, disbelieving.

Reese nods. "I couldn't bring myself to throw it away. It was all I had left of you from that night."

A tear slips down my cheek before I realize I'm crying. "I waited for you," I confess. "That morning, I thought you'd gone out for coffee, and I foolishly waited around for you to come back."

"I just didn't think I was the guy you wanted to wake up to." He closes his eyes. His honesty slices through my already fragile heart.

I step closer and hold something out to him. Reese looks down and immediately recognizes it. It's his old tie.

"How do you have this?" he asks.

"You left it that morning. I never got rid of it," I say.

He exhales. "And *you* kept it all this time?"

All this time, we both walked away believing the other one didn't want more.

*Classic miscommunication trope.*

## Reese

Then she looks at me like she did that night, lying in bed. I wasn't just a flirt or some typical "bad boy." She looks at me like I was the man who carried a note in his wallet for a year and a half. The man who had chosen her long before she knew she was chosen.

Her voice breaks into static. "Why did you never say anything when we met again?"

"As I said, you were engaged, and I wanted you to be happy—even if it wasn't with me," I sa

"Funny, Carter told me something similar," she says.

"He's a good guy," I say as I step closer, just shy of touching her. "You know I tried really hard not to cross the line every time I was in the room with you. But pretending I had no feelings? Being truly neutral? That was the hardest thing I've ever had to do. And trust me, the dance lesson was a close call." I smirk as the small space between us shrinks.

"I'm scared," she says, looking back down at the note in her hand.

"I know. So am I," I say, looking down at the tie I'm holding. "But love isn't the safe choice; it's the brave one."

The air between us crackles with electricity. She looks at me as I offer her my hand.

"I think I knew from the beginning that you were the one. I just wasn't ready to turn the page," she says.

"And are you now?"

She nods as she brings her face closer to mine. "I am."

"Everly," I say as our lips are almost touching. "I just have one question for you first."

"What's that?" she breathes into my mouth, begging for a kiss.

"Are you ready to live happily Everly after?" I smile.

"You are so cheesy," she laughs as she presses her lips upon mine.

# Beyond
## THE VEIL

# Bonus Scene 1: When You Let Her Go



The reception room is quiet—too quiet, especially considering a wedding is supposed to happen soon. Half-packed florals. Chairs pushed aside. Boxes of champagne, decorations, and more are stacked in the corner, ready to be transported away. The room holds an echo of a wedding that never happened.

Carter stands near the altar, dressed in a shirt and jeans—clothes I never knew he owned. I hesitate before approaching. I'm unsure how he will react to seeing me.

Carter lets out a humorless laugh. "I should be mad at you.

"You should," I say. I deserve it.

Carter waits a beat before looking at me—_really_ looking at me. But he doesn't look at me like a man full of anger. He looks like a man full of acceptance.

"Did you know all along?" he asks.

"I had an idea," I say.

Carter exhales, jaw tightening. "Of course you did."

"I want you to know I didn't plan this," I add. "Not like this. I never wanted to hurt anyone, including you."

Carter turns, staring out into the garden terrace. "Do you love her?"

"Yes," I reply without any hesitation.

"She told me everything," he says. "I guess it's better late than never."

"Carter, I'm so—"

He puts his hand up to stop me. "You know, I think I always knew she wasn't all in with me." He lets out a quiet breath. "I just thought that if I gave her enough time, enough stability… she'd get there."

I lean back against the wall, still respecting the space. "She didn't need more time," I say carefully. "She needed… the right kind of chaos."

My words almost elicit a smile from Carter.

"Yeah," Carter mutters. "Sounds like her."

Silence settles between us, but it's different now. It's less sharp, with rounded edges.

Carter picks up what was supposed to be one of the centerpieces, then sets it back down. "I wasn't wrong for her," he says. "I just wasn't, well, *you*."

"Honestly, I thought you were the better man." I shake my head slightly. "I told her so."

"She told me," he smiles. "Remember that night I was talking about speaking fluently with the one you love?"

"You always spoke her language. I was just the guy trying to master it. I want you to know," he continues, "you're not the bad guy."

"I feel like I am." I let out a breath, tension easing from my shoulders as I watch him look around the room at a life that was supposed to start here.

"Take care of her, Reese." He looks back at me. He says this not as a threat or a warning, but with genuine care.

"I will," I say, my voice steady in a way it wasn't before.

Carter nods once, as if it's enough.

After a pause, he says, "For what it's worth, if she was going to choose someone else, I'm glad it was you."

I let out a breath. "Yeah?"

Carter shrugs. "I still think you're a phenomenal writer. If we cross paths again, promise me you won't love her, too." He smiles before heading toward the exit.

Each step he takes carries a finality. It's not as a man who lost, but as a man who let her go. And that might be the hardest thing of all.

Everly

The bridal suite feels smaller now. Claustrophobic. Or maybe it's just me. My dress still hangs in the corner. Layers of lace, chiffon, and expectation. I remember how it felt to wear that dress. Wearing it now would press against my ribs until I could no longer catch my breath.

I stare into the mirror. The mirror stares back. I imagine a different reflection: perfect hair, perfect makeup, a perfect almost-bride. Now all I see is messy hair, last night's makeup, and an ex-bride.

I reach over, fingers brushing the edge of my veil…then stop. Because suddenly, I can hear it. Not the silence in the room, but just the echo of everything that has happened.

I close my eyes, but all I can see is Carter's face. Calm, but not calm. Hurt, but refusing to show it.

And Reese?

Standing in that parlor yesterday with me, as if he'd burn down the entire world if it meant I didn't have to walk down the aisle.

My lungs constrict. "This is insanity," I whisper—because it is.

About fifteen minutes ago, Carter and I called off the wedding. As hard as it was, it was the right decision. For the first time since we got engaged, I feel like I can breathe. I can relax.

I think about Carter again. He was steady. Safe. Good. I did love him, and in some ways, I still do. But it was the kind of love that made sense on paper. It was not the kind that kept me up at night, replaying every word, every glance, every touch, every…*almost* because that was Reese—even when I didn't want it to be.

I walk over to my dress, and my fingers curl into the fabric. "I was really going to be a wife today," I murmur. The words should feel like regret, but they don't. Instead, they feel like a near miss, like standing on the edge of a life that would have been good, though it wouldn't have been mine.

My gaze drifts back to the mirror. This time, I no longer dwell on what could have happened. I think about what will.

A soft knock sounds at the door. For a split second, I wonder if it's Reese. But when I open it, Morgan stands there, eyes wide, voice gentle.

"Are you OK?"

I consider her question. I really consider it. Then, slowly, I smile. It's not fake. It's not forced. It's real. "Yeah," I say. "I think I am." Even though my life is a mess, it's mine again.

She nods in relief. "He's here."

"Who?"

Morgan smiles. "Reese. I think he's waiting."

"For me?" I ask.

"Well, to be honest, he's been waiting a long time," she smirks.

I throw on my shoes in a hurry because, for the first time, I'm not choosing what is safe. I'm choosing what is real. And I'm terrified.

But sometimes, when we fear something the most, it's because we have more to lose.

I open the door, knowing that everything is going to be OK because every love story deserves a second beginning.

## Everly

The estate has emptied. A few workers are carrying out flowers back into the florist's van.

First came the polite exits. Guests murmured sympathetic apologies, but I could tell many of them were lies—especially on Carter's side.

Then came the disgruntled guests. They lingered too long, as if they were sitting in the front row of some reality TV show. They wanted to see the aftermath.

What did they want to see? Half-melted candles? Wilted flowers? Broken glass? A broken heart?

I stood near the front doors after Carter, and I made our announcement, staring back into the estate where I almost lost my life.

That's when I heard the heels before I saw the person wearing them. They clacked sharply, deliberately, furiously.

"You!" she shouts across the foyer. "You are unbelievable!"

Mrs. Jacobs stops a few feet away, as if she can't imagine getting any closer to me. She is dressed for the wedding that never happened. If it weren't for the fire in her eyes, she would look ready to go.

"Do you have any idea what you've done?"

I look at her. Had this been a different time—even a week ago—I would have tolerated Carter's mom's attitude. I would have apologized and shrunk myself to meet her expectations. But now? I have no obligation to do anything of the sort.

"I think I have an idea, but why don't you tell me, Margaret?" I say. I use her first name, and I love the way it adds fuel to the fire.

"You have humiliated my son," her voice cracks through the room like glass. "Not to mention our family, friends, and business associates. People flew in for this wedding, Everly." She lets out a short, disbelieving laugh, as if someone might jump out and tell her this was all a joke. "So what? You could run off with some James Dean wannabe in a tailored suit?"

Guests still in the process of leaving stop suddenly as Mrs. Jacobs keeps yelling at me.

"My son gave you everything." She steps closer. "And this is how you repay him? What is this guy going to give you? Nothing."

Something hot rises in my chest. This woman, no matter the circumstances, would never have accepted me. She would always find something negative to bring up and hold over my head. But the only difference is that I no longer have to tolerate it.

"I did not humiliate Carter." I look her straight in the eye. "I did the right thing."

Mrs. Jacobs scoffs. "The right thing?"

"Yes, I spared him a marriage to someone who was trying to become the version he wanted me to be and for him to do the same with me."

Mrs. Jacobs opens her mouth to say something, but I don't let her.

"For so long, I have been judged by you. You always had something to say about me. Even at this wedding, you always had something to say, and you insulted me and my family without even an apology," I say.

"You are overreacting," she replies.

"No, I'm not. I see how you are with Carter's exes. You tolerated me, but you welcome them," I snap as her face flushes.

"You should be grateful we welcomed you at all," she snaps back.

And there it is: the truth. I almost laugh, but I catch myself.

"Thank you," I say.

"For what?"

"To make this decision even easier." I take a step forward, closing the gap between us.

"Margaret, leave the poor girl alone," Mr. Jacobs appears in the foyer, jacket folded over one arm, tie loosened, looking like a man who had aged five years and somehow come out kinder for it.

"Richard," Mrs. Jacobs looks at her husband. "This is between her and me."

He crosses the room, stops beside his wife, then looks at me. "I'm sorry," he says. Hearing him say this with such sincerity nearly undoes me more than all the shouting. "You should never have felt like you had to earn your place with us."

Mrs. Jacobs stares at him. "You cannot be serious."

"I'm entirely serious," he says as he turns to his wife, exhausted, as if he'd had this conversation in ten different forms for thirty years. "Yes, Carter is hurt, but he will heal. He will be OK."

"He was abandoned at the altar!"

"He was saved from committing to the wrong marriage," he replies.

Mrs. Jacobs recoils as if struck.

"Carter is a good man," he continues. "But good men are not entitled to love that isn't real."

My throat tightens as he gives me a small, sad smile.

"You did a painful thing, but it wasn't cruel." He places his hand on my shoulder as tears prick unexpectedly behind my eyes.

Mrs. Jacobs makes a sharp sound of disbelief and turns away on her heels, refusing to partake in this conversation a moment longer.

"For what it's worth, I always thought peonies were better." He winks as I feel a sudden rush of tears. He pats my shoulder once more, fatherly and brief. "Your father would be proud of you today.

When he walks away, I cry, alone, surrounded by almost 200 passing guests I really didn't know.

# Bonus Scene 4: You're a Messy Flower

Annie

The estate was in that in-between stage of setting up and cleaning up, happiness and catastrophe. Half of the guests who stayed back to pretend to help were really just listening for anything they felt would be worth repeating later, as if this were some spectacle and not about two people's lives.

At the center of it all, and to no surprise to me or anyone else, was Mrs. Jacobs. She was issuing orders as if the Titanic could still be saved if everyone just listened to her instructions.

"Let's just get this cleaned up. I don't want to be around *these* people anymore," Mrs. Jacob's voice cuts through the room like a champagne cork.

Heads turn instantly. I guess her playing nice has finally expired. She strides across the room in heels, clutching her purse like it contained expensive lipstick or a weapon.

She sees me boxing up a centerpiece. "What do you think you're doing? Those arrangements were custom-imported. I hope you don't think you're going to take them home." She points at me.

"I was just packing them up. I wasn't taking them," I say. To be honest, I'm quite offended. This lady sure has nerve.

We stare at each other.

"You must be very proud," she says to me. "Your daughter embarrassed my son in front of two hundred guests."

I nod because I am proud of my daughter. I'm proud that she stood up for what she wanted in life. Not many people do that. Many people settle.

"How dare you act so smug?" Her nostrils flare.

"Oh, I dare easily," I say back to her. This woman doesn't scare me. In fact, I'm two seconds away from telling her where to pack those centerpieces.

"You have spent months treating this wedding like some corporate merger and my daughter like some intern who should feel lucky enough to be included," I continue.

"That's absurd."

"Is it?" I ask. "Because I distinctly remember that for every decision she tried to make about her wedding, you had something to say. You even refused her favorite flower!"

"They are messy flowers. Anyone with taste would know it," she barks,

"You're a messy flower."

Kenny, who was directing a few staff members in the kitchen, laughs behind a pillar, but Mrs. Jacobs ignores him.

"My son offered her stability, success, and a beautiful life," she defends.

I snort. "Your son offered her a penthouse and a spreadsheet-planned life. Ultimately, that wasn't what she wanted. You should respect her decision and move on."

Her face hardens at my words.

"And you're OK with your daughter running off with some tattooed wedding employee?"

"No," I say, sharpening my tone like a pencil. "She ran toward someone who looks at her like she's the only person in the room."

"And my son didn't?"

"No. He didn't see her the way she needed to be seen, and that's not his fault. We all know that. It's no one's fault."

"You really think passion lasts? Chemistry fades, Annie. Excitement fades. Then what?" she asks me.

"It wasn't that way for me. You want to know why? Because there's respect underneath it," I say as Mrs. Jacobs blinks.

*Reese*

I came to help Kenny, and now I've stepped into a warzone.

Across the room, I freeze when Annie begins to raise her voice. Honestly, I didn't think the woman knew how to yell. "My daughter spent months making herself smaller so you could feel bigger. She apologized for things that she shouldn't have just to keep everyone happy."

Mrs. Jacobs opens her mouth, but Annie stops her. "No. You've had the microphone for too long. It's my turn."

"Shit, I should have grabbed some food for this," Kenny whispers to me.

"Carter is a great man. You raised a wonderful son. I will give you that," Annie says. "But Carter deserved honesty, and today he got it. And just so we are clear, you don't get to call my daughter selfish ever again. Do you hear me?" Her words land like a gavel. Case closed.

Mrs. Jacobs glances around the room, as if seeking someone to come to her aid, but no one does. She is alone in this battle. She straightens her pearls in embarrassment.

"She'll regret this," Mrs. Jacobs whispers to Annie, but loud enough for Kenny and me to hear.

"I promise you, she won't," Annie says as Mrs. Jacobs storms out of the room in a cloud of perfume and fury.

Then Kenny slowly starts clapping as if he's in one of those movie scenes where everyone joins in. Several guests clap awkwardly, but that's it.

"Your future mother-in-law is terrifying," Kenny whispers to me.

All I can do is smile.

Join Us for
the
Wedding of
Everly Hart
&
Reese Myers

Everly

The New York Public Library has always been a magical place to me. It's a place where stories start. It's a place where they all share shelf space. I'm just hoping my luck here is better than Carrie Bradshaw's.

Sunlight streams through the tall arched windows, turning the marble floors gold. The air is scented with the sweet scents of old paper, polished wood, and peonies. PEONIES.

Two guests. Not two hundred. Morgan is already crying in the front row. Kenny sits beside her, a handkerchief in hand. I can tell they are bickering, but it is cut short when soft music drifts through the room. Then everyone turns to face me.

I stand at the entrance, and for the first time since I set foot in an aisle, my feet feel warmer than they've ever felt.

## Reese

There have been millions of moments when I have thought Everly looked beautiful. But today, I am at a loss for words, which, as you know, is rare for me.

She is wearing ivory silk that skims her body like moonlight, pooling at her feet. A beaded belt is tied at her waist. A plunging neckline that teases. Nothing overly dramatic. It is simple, elegant. It's her.

In her hands is a bouquet of peonies—lush blooms gathered loosely and tied with a matching ivory ribbon. It's what she wanted all along.

Annie stands beside her. She whispers something to her as Everly smiles. Her eyes shine. They look at me.

I never thought I'd be the man given the chance to stand here, waiting for someone like Everly to spend the rest of my life with. For years, I never wanted to spend the rest of my nights and mornings with anyone, but now I couldn't imagine waking up without her. One night can change a person. It changed me. It changed my heart.

## Everly

Across the room, Reese stands at the altar, waiting between an arch of books and climbing white roses—something Kenny put together.

He wears a dark, tailored suit similar to the one he wore the night we first met. His tie is the same one he wore, however, and my "something old" is the letter he wrote, tucked safely in my bra.

His gaze locks on me as I start my way down the aisle.

There is no dramatic swell of strings, no grand ballroom chandelier, and no audience of strangers watching me.

When I reach him, I notice a small tear slide down his cheek as our officiant, a silver-haired woman with librarian glasses and the warm patience of someone who truly believes in love, smiles at us.

He never looks away from me. Not one.

"Dearly beloved, we are gathered here today in a place built on stories to celebrate two people who learned that the best ones rarely follow the first draft."

My throat tightens at her words.

"They found each other once by chance. They found each other again through courage. And today, they choose each other on purpose."

"Are you both ready to share your vows?"


*Everly*
*Reese,*

*Three years ago, I met a stranger in a bar (sorry, Mom).*
*You were supposed to be one night (again, sorry, Mom).*
*One fleeting, reckless mistake.*
*A story that I would laugh about later.*

370

But then I realized, as the night carried on, that you were none of those things.

That's why I said no last names. No phone numbers. No expectations. Because everything felt dangerous.

And so did...forgetting you.

So, I told myself it was just one night.

But that one night became months of me comparing every room to the one where I met you. Every laugh to yours. Every feeling I left behind for a man whose last name I never asked for.

I didn't know then that some people can enter your life for a few hours and then stay in your heart for years.

You found me twice when neither one of us was looking.

And once when I finally was.

I thought it was choosing the right person at the right time, checking the right boxes, and following the plan all the way to my happily ever after.

Then I met you.

And suddenly love became messy.

Unexpected.

Terrifying.

Chaotic.

You taught me that love isn't picture perfect.

It doesn't always arrive on schedule.

And that it rarely looks the way we planned.

Sometimes it looks like unfinished conversations.

Second chances and the courage to pursue the thing you fear most.

And sometimes it looks like the person you couldn't forget.

So, that night when I made those rules, I decided to give them a little update.

I vow to know your name, use it often, and love everything it's connected to. I should. It will be mine as well.

I vow to laugh with you, fight for you, grow old with you, and keep finding new reasons to fall in love with you.

I vow to stand beside you when life is easy and hold you tighter when it isn't.

I vow never to confuse safety with what is right.

Because loving you may not have been the easiest path, it was the best.

And if I had to live through every wrong turn, detour, and broken road again to find my way back to this moment, I would.

Most importantly, I vow to remember that the best things in life come with no expectations.

I love you, Reese Myers.

I loved you that night.

I loved you that morning.

And I will love you for all the future nights and mornings our life has to offer.

Forever.

## Reese

Everly,

No last names.

No phone numbers.

No expectations.

And somehow it still became the most unforgettable night of my life.

I used to be a man who believed love was about certainty. But loving you has taught me that it's not that simple. Love isn't predictable. It cannot be planned. It's the way you feel differently with the one you love. It's the way you see meaning in the ordinary things people overlook. It's in the way you chase stories even when you already know how they end.

And somehow, you have made me into the man who believes he deserves it all.

I'm not perfect. I can be stubborn. But even then, I will always promise to pay attention. I will notice the small things—the ones that matter more to you.

I vow to love you loudly, not quietly, in the same way your laughter fills the room, your presence is felt, and the way I feel you even when you're not touching me.

I vow to choose you from the mornings you're still asleep, the nights you lie in bed promising yourself one more chapter, and all the chaotic hours in between.

I vow to be your rock when life gets too loud.

I promise to be loud when the world tries to quiet us.

*Lastly, and I vow, with every breath, every heartbeat, every reckless, undeniable part of me that I will always stay.*

*So, here is my last name.*

*You are my number one.*

*And you have surpassed all my expectations and then some.*

*I love you.*

The room is silent. I never spoke my own vows before. I wonder if I did a good job. I wonder if it truly captures how much I love this woman standing in front of me.

But this silence wasn't the one that I have witnessed from guests when they are distracted by their phones, thinking about their drink or choice, or whether their meal option was the right one. This is the kind of silence when everyone is feeling the same thing.

I lower the paper in my hands, realizing how much my hands are trembling.

## Everly

I've never seen Reese so nervous. Usually, he exudes confidence. But not today. For a man who has succeeded in maintaining such a hard exterior, he looks one second away from falling apart. And if he does, I'm here to catch him. Just like I know he would do the same for me.

"In all my years of doing this," the officiant says, "I've learned that love sometimes arrives here based on planning. Sometimes by timing. Sometimes, even by luck." She pauses. "And sometimes it's because two people fight to get here."

"I think I know which one we are," Reese says, teary-eyed.

"Now, Reese, place the ring on Everly's finger," the officiant instructs.

I can feel his hands tremble and shake as he slides the band into place.

"It's OK," I whisper as I place the ring on his finger, and I notice how my pulse feels like a sledgehammer.

"Now, by the authority vested in me by the State of New York, I now pronounce you husband and wife."


*Reese*

I kiss Everly before the officiant finishes the rest.

My hands wrap around her waist, accidentally crushing the peonies between us.

The room erupts in cheers. Kenny shouts, "That's my best friend!"

And when I finally pull back, I rest my forehead against Everly's and whisper, "Mrs. Myers."

She wrinkles her nose as we walk down the aisle between all the shelves full of stories, knowing that we are about to write one fantastic story of our own.

## One Year Later...
## The Last Chapter

*Everly*

The Last Chapter looks different from how it did three years ago. This time, I have a permanent date, and he is my husband. *I still can't believe he's my husband. Reese Myers is my husband!*

Genevieve secured The Last Chapter for our reception. It was decorated with worn spines, pages of poetry, book pages in the shape of flowers, like Reese had planned the night of, well, you know. Our table, *Beauty and the Beast,* is waiting for us—the place where it all began. *We* began.

Candles flicker between stacks of classic romance novels, and Death Cab for Cutie plays in the background. Glasses of Java & Juliet catch the glow of string lights that Kenny had draped lazily across the wooden beams.

*It's everything I ever wanted*, I think as my fingers lace with Reese's. *He's everything I've ever wanted.*

Kenny leans causally at the bar, already holding a drink like it's in his job description as best man. No one is technically working this wedding. Everyone is a part of it.

"You good?" Reese whispers.

"I just married you, of course, I'm good," I say, because nothing matters more than the fact that I get to spend forever with this man.

The night is full of laughter. Love. And so much fun. No frills. It's everything I never knew I wanted. And now, I can't imagine living without.

When it's time for the toasts, Morgan goes first.

"Reese told me that the best speeches come from vulnerability. So I decided to try writing my own speech this time. Here goes nothing," she says as we all laugh softly.

"Everly is my best friend," she begins. "And in some ways, almost like a sister to me. I share everythign with her, and she does the same with me. And because we are so close, we share things we don't even know we are sharing, like how I know when she's not being honest with herself.

You see, I, too, thought it was nothing but a one-night stand. But the truth is, it never was. These two," she points to Everly and me, "almost missed each other. However, what really happened was that they simply met at the wrong time. They each went off and made mistakes. They took different twists and turns, and then they found each other again under the craziest of circumstances. And thank God they did, because if it weren't for team Morgan and Kenny—"

"Team Kenny and Morgan!" Kenny interjects.

"It's a working title," Morgan laughs. "Anyway, in my years of reading countless romance novels, I have learned that some love stories don't come with a neat happily ever after bow. Some kick the doors down. And this one did."

She raises her glass. "To Everly and Reese!"

## *Reese*

"Alright, alright," Kenny says, clinking his fork to his glass. "It's time for the best man to make his speech, and then, the moment we've all been waiting for… the cake!"

Everyone laughs as Everly leans into me. "*You* picked the cake?"

"You know exactly what I picked." I wink at her.

"I've been friends with Reese long before he knew we were friends," he laughs. "But here's the thing, he is the kind of guy who always thinks he's right."

"Think?" I ask as laughter breaks out again.

"Well, he's never been more wrong than he was before he met Everly. He shared with me how he felt. He trusted me enough to tell me he wished he had done things differently. And at first, I thought it was just a simple what-if, but I've never seen him look at anyone the way he looks at her. Like Everly isn't just part of the plan—she's the whole damn reason for it. And Everly, thank you for loving him. Challenging him. You have made him better, slightly more tolerable," he teases.

"Barely," I laugh.

"To Everly and Reese!"

"To Everly and Reese!" the room echoes, glasses clink.

My hand finds Everly's again, like it instinctively knows where it belongs.

And when I look at her, I don't see the woman who complicated everything.

I see the woman who made it all make sense.

This time with the same last names.

Memorized phone numbers.

And great expectations.

*One Year Later...*
*Leave a Note*

We decided to spend our wedding night in my apartment. We took a cab back to my place after way too many espresso martinis (on my end), bourbon (on him), and a few plot twist shots.

My apartment is quiet except for the sound of our breathing. I think about how we left The Last Chapter. The music faded into a dull thrum. Morgan is probably taking whatever decorations are left for her office. Kenny is most likely taking home whatever cake is left or flirting with the bartender. However, his gift to us made me cry. He somehow got the pictures of Reese and me from Central Park that day and had them framed. The guy really knows how to get the watery works going.

I kick off my heels the second the door closes behind us.

"Those shoes were painful," I say, wobbling into the room.

"You looked incredible in them. But I agree, they look better on the floor." Reese looks at me as he walks toward me, deliberate as ever.

I smile as he reaches me, his hands sliding to my waist, his thumb brushing the silk of my dress.

"Your vows were wonderful," I breathe.

"I'm good with words," he winks. "But I meant every word."

I slide my hands up his chest, undoing one button on his shirt because I can. He then reaches into his jacket pocket and pulls out a folded card.

"What's that?" I ask.

"My other vows," he says.

"What, like backup vows?" I look at him.

"No. I did the public version. But this is all for you."

"Read them to me," I say.

*Reese*

*Everly,*

*I vow to kiss you slowly when we have nowhere to go and absolutely when we do.*

*I vow to never walk past you without touching you.*

*Your waist.*

*Your hand.*

*The small of your back*

*Anywhere I can remind myself you're really mine.*

*I vow to make even ordinary places dangerous.*

*Kitchens, hallways, doorways. Any room, really.*

*I vow to learn every sound you make—especially the ones you make for me.*

*I want to kiss every inch of you with gratitude.*

*I vow to never let you forget how wanted you are.*

*And whenever you can't sleep...*

*I vow to give you better reasons to stay awake.*

She brushes her lips against mine. "Keep me awake."

My inhale is sharp.

I kiss her slowly, deeply, and with hunger.

"Coffee and muffins in the morning?" I ask as I sweep her off her feet and carry her into bed.

"Make sure you leave a note," she smiles.

# ONE-NIGHT STAND
## SPICY VODKA RIGATONI

## INGREDIENTS

- 1 lb rigatoni
- 2 tbsp olive oil
- ½ onion (chopped)
- 3 cloves garlic
- 2 tbsp tomato paste
- ½ tsp red pepper flakes
- ¼ cup vodka
- 1 cup heavy cream
- ½ cup parmesan
- Fresh basil

## INSTRUCTIONS:

Cook pasta (save pasta water)
Sauté onion + garlic
Add tomato paste (cook until rich)
Add red pepper flakes
Pour vodka → reduce
Add cream + parmesan
Toss with pasta

*"A bad decision you'd make twice."*

# EVERLY'S CINNAMON ROLL WEDDING CAKE

## CONCEPT

A SOFT CINNAMON-ROLL INSPIRED TIERED CAKE WITH:
SWIRLED CINNAMON LAYERS (LIKE A GIANT CINNAMON ROLL INSIDE)
BROWN SUGAR FILLING
CREAM CHEESE FROSTING (LIGHT + FLUFFY, NOT TOO HEAVY)
OPTIONAL CARAMEL DRIZZLE + EDIBLE GOLD ACCENTS FOR WEDDING ELEGANCE

## CAKE STRUCTURE (3-TIER WEDDING STYLE)

BOTTOM TIER: 10-INCH (3 LAYERS)
MIDDLE TIER: 8-INCH (3 LAYERS)
TOP TIER: 6-INCH (3 LAYERS)
EACH LAYER = CINNAMON SWIRL CAKE

## CINNAMON ROLL CAKE LAYERS

INGREDIENTS:
3 CUPS CAKE FLOUR
2 ½ TSP BAKING POWDER
½ TSP BAKING SODA
½ TSP SALT
1 CUP UNSALTED BUTTER (ROOM TEMP)
1 ¾ CUPS SUGAR
4 EGGS
1 TBSP VANILLA EXTRACT
1 CUP SOUR CREAM
¾ CUP WHOLE MILK
CINNAMON SWIRL FILLING (THE MOMENT):
1 CUP BROWN SUGAR
2 TBSP CINNAMON
½ CUP MELTED BUTTER
1 TBSP FLOUR (KEEPS SWIRL FROM SINKING)

*"Because some love stories deserve to be layered."*

# EVERLY'S CINNAMON ROLL WEDDING CAKE

## INSTRUCTIONS

PREHEAT OVEN TO 350°F
CREAM BUTTER + SUGAR UNTIL FLUFFY
ADD EGGS ONE AT A TIME
MIX IN VANILLA, SOUR CREAM, MILK
COMBINE DRY INGREDIENTS SEPARATELY, THEN ADD POUR
HALF BATTER INTO PANS
DRIZZLE CINNAMON MIXTURE
 ADD REMAINING BATTER
 LIGHTLY SWIRL WITH KNIFE (DON'T OVERMIX)
BAKE:
6" → ~25 MIN
8" → ~30 MIN
10" → ~35 MIN
COOL COMPLETELY

## BROWN SUGAR FILLING (BETWEEN LAYERS)

1 CUP BROWN SUGAR
½ CUP BUTTER
¼ CUP HEAVY CREAM
PINCH SALT
HEAT UNTIL SMOOTH + SLIGHTLY THICKENED
COOL UNTIL SPREADABLE

## WHIPPED CREAM CHEESE FROSTING

16 OZ CREAM CHEESE
1 CUP BUTTER
4 CUPS POWDERED SUGAR
1 TBSP VANILLA
2-3 TBSP HEAVY CREAM
WHIP UNTIL: SMOOTH, FLUFFY
SPREADABLE BUT NOT STIFF

## OPTIONAL: SALTED CARAMEL DRIP (HIGHLY RECOMMENDED)

1 CUP SUGAR
6 TBSP BUTTER
½ CUP HEAVY CREAM
PINCH SEA SALT
DRIZZLE BETWEEN TIERS OR
LIGHTLY OVER TOP

## ASSEMBLY

LEVEL CAKES
LAYER: CAKE → BROWN SUGAR
FILLING → CAKE
CRUMB COAT + CHILL
FROST WITH SMOOTH CREAM CHEESE
FINISH
STACK TIERS (USE DOWELS FOR
STABILITY)

*"Because some love stories deserve to be layered."*

# About the Author

Danielle is a born and raised Upstate, NY girl, living there with her two daughters and her Project Manager husband. She lives for '90s nostalgia and is currently collecting all things Clueless.

She never turns down Cinnabon or a hot Americano, and she will steal your French fries.

She writes heartfelt, messy, and occasionally glitter-covered romantic comedies about women who swear off love—then fall right into it again. When she's not writing, she can be found over-caffeinating, quoting 90s romcoms, and pretending she doesn't cry at Hallmark movies.

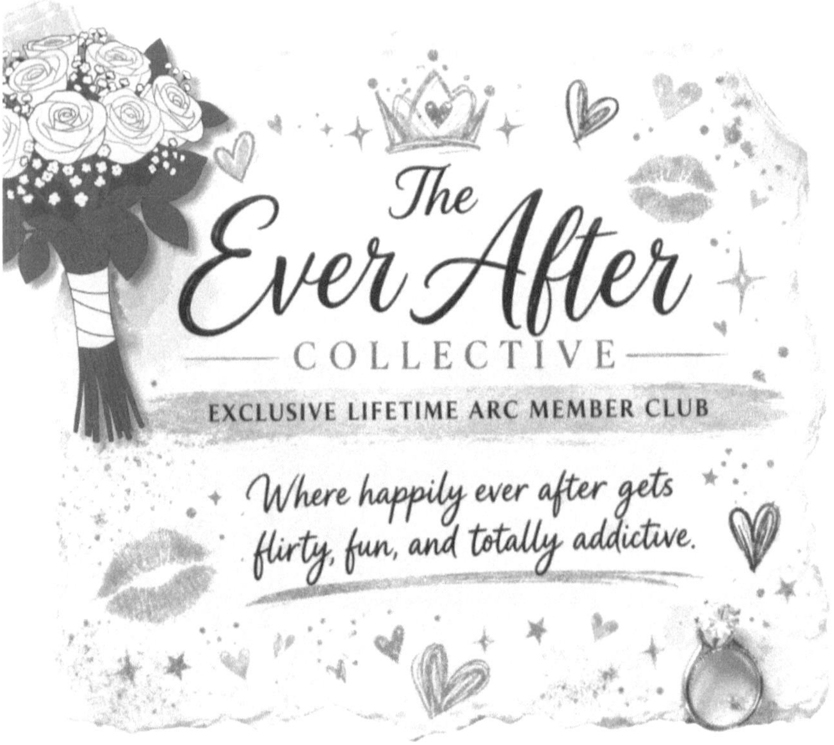

# The Ever After

## COLLECTIVE

### EXCLUSIVE LIFETIME ARC MEMBER CLUB

*Where happily ever after gets flirty, fun, and totally addictive.*

www.ingramcontent.com/pod-product-compliance
Lightning Source LLC
Chambersburg PA
CBHW051209130726
47988CB00001B/38